"Romance, passion, and thrilling adventure fill the pages of this unforgettable saga that sweeps the reader from England to the Old West. Jessy and Brady are truly lovers for the ages!"

—ROSEMARY ROGERS

"*Pieces of Sky* reminds us why New Mexico is called the land of enchantment. A truly original new voice in historical fiction."

—JODI THOMAS

"Generates enough heat to light the old New Mexico sky. A sharp, sweet love story of two opposites, a beautifully observed setting, and voilà—a romance you won't soon forget."

—SARA DONATI,
author of *Into the Wilderness*

"You're having fun with this, aren't you?"

"I admit I am." His mustache quirked up at the corners. "You make it so easy."

He reached into his shirt pocket. "And by the way . . ." He leaned forward, an odd glint in those aqua eyes. In his fingers he held a copper coin.

She tried to draw back, couldn't, and in mute helplessness watched him take her hand in his. With great care he placed the coin into her gloved palm. "I don't take money from women. No matter how grateful they are."

She forgot how to breathe. How to think, or move. He was so near she could smell sweat, horses, old smoke. And at that moment, as she stared into the bright intensity of those startling eyes, she realized how badly she had underestimated this man.

And to prove it he did the most extraordinary thing.

He smiled . . .

Pieces of Sky

KAKI WARNER

B

BERKLEY SENSATION, NEW YORK

THE BERKLEY PUBLISHING GROUP
Published by the Penguin Group
Penguin Group (USA) Inc.
375 Hudson Street, New York, New York 10014, USA
Penguin Group (Canada), 90 Eglinton Avenue East, Suite 700, Toronto, Ontario M4P 2Y3, Canada
(a division of Pearson Penguin Canada Inc.)
Penguin Books Ltd., 80 Strand, London WC2R 0RL, England
Penguin Group Ireland, 25 St. Stephen's Green, Dublin 2, Ireland (a division of Penguin Books Ltd.)
Penguin Group (Australia), 250 Camberwell Road, Camberwell, Victoria 3124, Australia
(a division of Pearson Australia Group Pty. Ltd.)
Penguin Books India Pvt. Ltd., 11 Community Centre, Panchsheel Park, New Delhi—110 017, India
Penguin Group (NZ), 67 Apollo Drive, Rosedale, North Shore 0632, New Zealand
(a division of Pearson New Zealand Ltd.)
Penguin Books (South Africa) (Pty.) Ltd., 24 Sturdee Avenue, Rosebank, Johannesburg 2196,
South Africa

Penguin Books Ltd., Registered Offices: 80 Strand, London WC2R 0RL, England

This book is an original publication of The Berkley Publishing Group.

PRINTING HISTORY
Berkley Sensation trade paperback edition / January 2010

Library of Congress Cataloging-in-Publication Data

Warner, Kaki.
    Pieces of sky / Kaki Warner.—Berkley Sensation trade paperback ed.
        p. cm.—(Blood rose trilogy ; bk. 1)
    ISBN 978-0-425-23214-9
    1. Single woman—Fiction. 2. Ranchers—Fiction. 3. English—United States—Fiction. I. Title.
PS3623.W37P54 2010
813'.6—dc22   2009033593

PRINTED IN THE UNITED STATES OF AMERICA

10 9 8 7 6 5 4 3 2 1

To Joe, Jason, and Sara, my patient and supportive family.
And to Lillie, the sister of my heart.

Acknowledgments

Many heartfelt thanks to:

Joe, my construction and railroad expert.

Jason, my gun expert.

Sara, who deftly managed the cheese meter.

Carlee, nurse extraordinaire and my medical expert.

Clara Garza, who knows way too many Spanish dirty words.

And my supportive critiquers, listeners, readers, and friends: Billee Escott, Frances Sonnabend, Cyndi Thomson, Bonnie Maltais, Janet Boyce, Carol Ranck, and of course, Jack Hoffman.

Bless ya'll.

One

New Mexico Territory, 1869

I'M A DEAD MAN.

Brady Wilkins dragged a hand over his face then wiped his bloody fingers on his shirt. Nine o'clock, and already he was wet with sweat. It soaked the headband of his hat, gathered in his eyebrows and mustache, stung like hell in the gash across his cheekbone. His left eye was swollen shut, his knee hurt like a sonofabitch, and if he was lucky, he might survive a day. *Hell.*

Despite the stupidity that had brought him to this sorry state, he didn't consider himself a stupid man. He knew in the high desert survival was a tenuous thing, challenged by flash floods, hostiles, rattlers, and sometimes, like today, something as commonplace as a low-lying, leg-grabbing sage branch. He also knew his chances of survival were slim—slimmer if he didn't start now.

But first he would have to shoot his horse.

Squinting through his right eye, he studied the rolling expanse of withered scrub that stretched behind him. He pivoted and checked the opposite direction. Through the heat shimmers dancing along the horizon, he barely made out the blunt-nosed shadow of Blue Mesa rising out of the flatlands thirty-five miles away. Five miles beyond it was the south boundary of RosaRoja and home. Forty miles on foot, in late spring, with a near-empty canteen and not even a tree to piss on. It might as well be a hundred.

With a sigh, he looked down at his horse.

Blood darkened the dirt beneath him, flowing from a pulpy mass of torn flesh, tendon, and bone just above the fetlock. With every breath out, he groaned.

"Damnit, Bob. Now look what you've done."

Mostly he was angry with himself. If he hadn't stayed up so late drinking and talking bulls with McPherson, he wouldn't have dozed off and he would have been more aware of where his horse was stepping. Now he would have to shoot one of the finest animals he'd ever owned.

"Hell, you probably killed us both."

As he approached the stricken animal, he noted that the saddlebags and his prized Winchester Model 1866 repeating rifle were pinned beneath Bob's twelve-hundred-pound weight. He couldn't leave them behind. Nor could he see a way to retrieve them without getting the animal back on its feet. Sickened by what he had to do, he unlashed the rope tied to the front of the saddle.

Mindful of thrashing legs and the injury, he slipped the rope around the broken leg above the knee, pulled it taut then looped it around the saddle horn. The trailing end he ran over his shoulder and across his back. Positioning himself out of kicking range behind the horse, he began to pull, hoping to use his strength and the rope sling to help Bob back onto his feet.

Bob fought him but Brady held on, plowing the dirt with the sloped heels of his boots. Air hissed through his teeth. His thighs shook. Muscles across his back burned where the rope cut in.

With a squeal of pain, Bob whipped his head back and thrust with his haunches, sending his body up and forward onto three legs. After finding his balance, he stood shuddering, his nose almost brushing the ground.

Breathing hard, Brady approached the trembling animal. "Easy, boy."

Bob snapped at him, eyes rolling, teeth clicking against the bit.

After stripping the horse, Brady drew his Colt from the holster on his hip. An unbidden image flashed in his mind of another day on the desert, another soul twisting in agony. He closed his eyes and tried to block it, telling himself this time would be easier; this time it was only a horse.

Bob's groan jerked him back from the past. Resolved, Brady checked the load, snapped the chamber closed, then raised the pistol. "I'll miss you, you clumsy bastard." Pointing the muzzle into Bob's ear, he squeezed the trigger and stepped clear.

The horse folded, slamming to earth in an explosion of dust quickly swept away on a hot gust of wind. Ears ringing, Brady reloaded and holstered the pistol, then lifted his head to study the endless maze of creosote and cactus fanning away on all sides. Overhead, not a single lint-ball cloud relieved the unrelenting blue, and in the distance the jagged silhouette of the Sacramento Mountains was as sharp as a Mexican blade.

Forty miles in this heat, wearing these boots, packing eighty pounds of gear. He'd never make it. Unless . . .

He looked east, plotting a map in his head, trying to gauge where the Overland came through on its way to Val Rosa. If he cut straight across, he had a chance. He might even get a horse at the stage stop. With renewed energy, he tied the bridle and canteen to the saddle, then tossed the saddlebags and rifle scabbard over one shoulder, the saddle over the other. He left the saddle blanket. With a final nod to a fine horse, he headed east, gaze fixed on distant landmarks hanging above the wavering horizon.

If he didn't lose his bearings and kept his pace up, and if his new custom-made pointy-toed riding boots didn't rub his toes to stubs, he might make it to the stopover before the westbound stage came through.

* * *

"You married?"

Startled from her worries, Jessica Thornton glanced across the aisle of the jouncing stagecoach to find Mr. Bodine staring at her breasts. Again. Ever since he'd boarded that morning, the man had engaged in the most astounding repertoire of activities to gain her attention— snoring, gawking, scratching, spitting, and now—wonder of wonders— actual words.

She ignored him. That was her plan. No conversation, no eye contact, no behavior that would draw notice; anonymity was her best protection. She just hoped it would be more effective against John Crawford than it apparently was on Bodine.

"I said, are you married?"

She glanced at the other passengers, fearful they had overheard. Stanley Ashford, the dapper railroad representative, dozed, his fair head bobbing against his chest. Across from him napped Maude Kinderly, slumped against the window frame, her coalscuttle bonnet mashed against her cheek, frizzy gray curls stuck to her brow. Her grown daughter, Melanie, was engrossed in another of her lurid dime novels. Jessica turned to Bodine.

"I am a widow." That was the story she had decided upon when she left England two months earlier, thinking it might provide respectability and protection from unwanted discourse.

"A widow." He grinned. "Wanna get married then?"

"I do not."

His smile faded. "It's not a bad offer, considerin'."

"Considering what?"

"Well, you're kinda tall and you got that devil hair and a funny way of talking, but I'm not picky." Somehow mistaking her stony silence for interest, he expounded on his offer. "I got diggin's over by Silver City," he told her breasts. "Not much yet, but promisin'. If you wanted, I could put up a soddy."

"I do not want, nor will I ever want, a soddy." Whatever that was.

"You'd rather a cabin, I guess."

"No. Never. Absolutely not." How many ways must she say it? She pressed a limp hanky to her brow, wondering what she could possibly have done to elicit such an offer—her third within a week and all from total strangers. Apparently women were so scarce in this wasteland, even twenty-six-year-old spinsters were preyed upon. She wondered if that would hold true should she open her traveling cape to reveal she was also five and a half months pregnant.

Merciful heavens, if Annie could see her now. All those years preaching decorum to her little sister, and now here she was fending off the advances of a strange man on a public conveyance. The irony of it was so ludicrous she didn't know whether to burst into peals of hysterical laughter or collapse with a wail of despair.

But then, ladies never wailed and rarely laughed aloud. As expressly stated in Pamphlet Five: "Public displays of emotion are to be avoided. Laughter must be subdued, and tears, if necessary, must flow in a discreet manner into a spotless linen held delicately to the mouth." Exactly as she had written it in her lovely office at Bickersham Hall in quiet, civilized Posten Cross, Northumberland, England.

Anguish clutched at her throat. Had Annie received her letter? Did her sister suspect why Jessica had run? Did she wonder what had become of her?

The coach lurched, throwing her against the door and driving her straw skimmer halfway down her forehead. Blinded by ribbons and plumes, she grappled for the safety strap and dug in her heels, barely keeping herself from toppling to the floor. With a hiss of irritation, she shoved the hat out of her eyes to find Mr. Bodine grinning at her bosom.

She was not unaccustomed to the attention of men. Perhaps it was because of her height. She was tall, but not freakishly so, despite what that dwarfish Frenchman said in New Orleans. Or perhaps it was her hair that drew notice. Some men liked red hair. She did not. In her case it came with unruly curls, a tendency to freckle, and a reputation for temper, which she felt was totally unfounded. She was neither voluptuous in figure nor flirtatious in manner, and although some might consider her passably attractive, no one had ever called her beautiful. Yet men looked at her, then they looked again. She found such assessments demeaning and intrusive. To armor herself against them, she had developed a directness of manner that most men found off-putting, which was precisely her intent. Obviously, Mr. Bodine did not.

He nudged her foot with the toe of his crusty boot. "You a man-hater?"

"I'm learning," she muttered. Men were betrayers and deceivers, violent faithless creatures, and there had never been a one in her life who had not let her down . . . a lesson learned by a father's abandonment and a brother-in-law's fist, and now reinforced by the inimitable Mr. Bodine, quite the nastiest of the lot.

"Maybe you're mail order. Lots of men send off for wives."

"Like ordering a farm implement? Lovely. But no." Realizing the man would persist unless she satisfied his curiosity, she added, "I am an authoress and a milliner."

"A miller? You make flour?"

"Hats." Were they even speaking the same language? "I also write pamphlets on deportment for persons of quality. Shall I quote a few pages?"

He studied her hat, once a lovely creation of straw and satin, now a drooping dusty tangle of tattered ribbon and wilted plumes. "Hats like that?"

"Precisely."

"So you're a whore then."

Her mouth fell open.

"Mrs. Thornton is a lady," a voice cut in before she could gather her wits.

Glancing over, she met Mr. Ashford's gaze and quickly looked away, heat rushing into her face. Stanley Ashford might not be as well turned out as a proper English gentleman, but he was clean, which set him apart from most of the Westerners she had met. That he had overheard and felt compelled to remark upon Bodine's vulgar comment was mortifying.

"I think you should apologize."

"But look what she's wearing," Bodine argued. "Good women wear poke bonnets. Only whores wear frilly hats like that."

Jessica waited for Mr. Ashford to leap to her defense, but he was suddenly engrossed in the sharpness of the crease in his trouser leg. Confidence waned. She eyed the hideous grosgrain bonnet mashed into the side of Maude's face. "That can't be true," she argued weakly. "Only a—a—" She faltered, unable to say the word.

Mr. Ashford continued grooming his trousers. Bodine stared at her chest.

Preposterous. Throughout Northumberland her hats were considered the epitome of style. "I have never heard of such a thing." Yet even as she spoke, memories rose in her mind—men leering from saloon doorways—calls and whistles as she walked by. All because of her hat?

"I shouldn't worry, ma'am," Ashford told her. "It's a very pretty hat."

"A downright doozy," Bodine seconded.

Possibly it was the condescension in Ashford's voice, or perhaps the smirk on Bodine's tobacco-stained mouth, or the lowering realization that her lovely hat had drawn more attention than she had, but something within Jessica snapped. She rounded on Bodine. "Are you implying the sole provocation for your unsolicited attentions is some backwoods misinterpretation of the latest European fashions?"

"Huh?"

"Did you approach me because of my hat?" *You leprous cretin.*

"Well, yeah. I thought—"

"Pray, think no more, Mr. Bodine!" And with a flourish that sent hatpins flying, Jessica snatched the offending hat from her head and sailed it out the open coach window.

Stunned silence.

Then Bodine slapped his knee and guffawed. Melanie Kinderly stopped reading to gawk at her, obviously finding Jessica's behavior

even more titillating than her book. Thankfully, Maude slept through
it all.

Mr. Ashford pursed his lips beneath his neat blond mustache. "This
climate can be quite harsh, ma'am. I hope you don't come to regret
such a rash action."

She already did. Heavens, what insane perversity had come over
her?

Bodine elbowed Ashford. "Think if I say her dress is flashy, she'll
toss it out, too?"

Battling an urge to drive the tip of her parasol through Mr. Bodine's chest, Jessica stared down at her clenched hands. She should have
stayed in England. She should have signed over the deed to Bickersham
Hall as Crawford demanded, or bowed to the mining consortium.

But would she have been safe even then? Once Crawford had the
land and coal royalties in hand, what need would he have for any of
them? And then there was the baby she carried. How could she explain
to Annie that the husband she adored had raped and impregnated her
sister?

Rage engulfed her. No, running was her only option. As long as
she held the deed and stayed out of his reach, Crawford wouldn't dare
harm any of them. *That rotter.* She sucked air past her clenched teeth,
so furious her body shook.

It wasn't fair. None of this was her fault. She had done nothing
wrong.

For one awful moment she wanted to dig her fingers into her own
body, claw through flesh and tendon and bone to tear out the life growing within. If only she had fought harder. If only she had stopped him
before he wrapped the silk—

"Are you all right, Mrs. Thornton?"

Jessica jerked up her head to find Melanie Kinderly staring at her.
She blinked, still trapped in the horror of the past, until slowly her
mind calmed. She took a deep breath, let it out, took another. "Y-Yes,
I am well, thank you."

"You're sure? You're very pale."

The worry in the younger woman's eyes almost made Jessica weep. It had been so long since she'd heard a kind word. "It's the heat. I fear I'm unaccustomed to it."

Melanie nodded in sympathy. Blessed with a sweet face, lovely blond hair, and a gentle aspect, she seemed a most pleasant young woman. To Jessica's mind, her only drawbacks were a bent toward romanticism and an overly biddable nature, of which her mother seemed to take full advantage with her constant demands. It was no surprise the poor woman took refuge in books. Glad of the distraction, Jessica motioned to the one Melanie held now, the cover of which boasted a rather florid drawing of a man on a rearing steed. "Is your book enjoyable?"

"Oh, yes. It's a true story, you know. Perhaps you've heard of him?" Sudden animation brightened Melanie's slightly protruding gray eyes. "Barnabas O'Shay, the Angel-Faced Killer of Buffalo Gap? He's from England, too, although over there he's better known as the Murderous Marquis of Cornwall. Do you know him?"

O'Shay? Marquis of Cornwall? Could Colonials truly be this ignorant?

"He doesn't exist." Seeing Melanie's confusion, Jessica explained. "O'Shay is Irish, not English. And there is no Marquis of Cornwall. Cornwall is a duchy held by Edward, Prince of Wales and heir to the throne of England."

"Oh." With an uncertain smile, Melanie turned back to her book.

Jessica mentally kicked herself. When had she become so snappish and rude? She seemed angry all the time and that was most unlike her. It was as if Crawford's attack had changed her, separated her forever from the person she had been, and now she couldn't seem to find her way back to herself. And at times like this, after doing something thoughtless or unkind, she realized how much that change had cost her, and how she no longer knew or particularly liked the woman she had become.

Forcing her mind from those vexing thoughts, she looked out the window, hoping to glimpse something of interest—a bird, a tree, anything green that didn't have thorns, spines, or a flicking tongue. She had never seen such a desolate landscape or choked down so much dust. It coated her skin, her eyeballs, left a gritty residue on her teeth.

Yet despite the discomfort, she found herself oddly drawn to the incredible vista beyond the window. In some unaccountable way, it reminded her of the bluffs above the North Sea. All that empty space. So much sky. The vastness of it uplifted her, challenging her with possibility and awakening her to hope.

A woman could lose herself out there. Or with a bit of help, a woman might find herself and begin anew beyond the taint of the past. A heady thought.

Heat built until it seemed to suck the very air from her lungs. Boredom ran rampant. Mr. Ashford carefully picked his jacket sleeves free of lint. Melanie continued reading while Maude slumped lower and lower against the door. Jessica tried to doze as well, but the smells emanating from Bodine reminded her of a refuse barge on the Thames and had her stomach bouncing even more than the coach. And with each bounce, the need to relieve herself grew. She doubted she could be less comfortable. Then Maude Kinderly awoke.

"Are we at the stopover yet?" Without waiting for a response, Maude unstuck the bonnet from the side of her face, and launched into another of her endless diatribes, fully refreshed from her nap. "Isn't this heat ghastly? I don't know how the wretched people in this area can bear it, although the Colonel says they deserve no better, foul degenerates that they are. Drunken Indians, Mexican banditos, Texicans—the list is endless. I could go on for hours."

Please don't, Jessica prayed, hoping to avoid yet another catalog of complaints.

"Daughter, is there any rosewater left? Look in my bag. Hurry, girl. My head is pounding. What I wouldn't give for a cool pitcher of water!"

Just hearing the word made Jessica squirm.

Melanie lifted a voluminous carpetbag from beneath Maude's feet, opened it, and peered inside. "I don't see it, Mama."

"Oh, honestly, can't you do anything but read those silly books?"

Maude grabbed the bag and began rummaging through it. "It's not here." She looked around as if seeking a target for her ire. She settled on Jessica. "Mrs. Thornton, wherever is your hat?"

"What hat?" Jessica asked, discomfort making her contrary.

Melanie gave her a startled look. "It blew out the window, Mama."

"Indeed? How careless. You foreigners." Maude dropped the bag to the floorboards. "I pray Santa Fe isn't this hot. Dreadful, dreadful country. Nothing like Baltimore. And Fort Union! Whoever heard of such a place? I just hope the Colonel knows what we've suffered to reach him. Are we slowing? I think we're slowing." She leaned out the window then drew back with a look of disgust. "A hovel. I daresay the food will be horrid. Be sure to leave on your gloves."

Jessica was beyond caring. She just wanted out. Now. Tapping a toe with impatience, she perched on the edge of the seat, reticule in one hand, parasol in the other, as the coach rolled to a stop. Without waiting for the driver to place the mounting step, she threw open the door, hopped out, and fled toward the cabin.

Bodine trailed after her like a slavering dog. "Hat Lady, wait up. I wanna talk to you."

"Please don't!" Half blinded by dust and the noonday glare, she darted up the steps and shoved open the door, just as a ham-sized fist clamped over her wrist.

With a shriek of outrage, she whirled, parasol swinging on her arm. She heard a grunt as the tip met flesh, then the hand released her arm so abruptly her momentum carried her backward into the cabin to topple over a saddle propped near the door. For a moment she lay stunned, heels still caught on the overturned saddle. Then a voice from the other side of the room sent her bolting upright.

"Woo-wee! Thank you, Lord!"

Parasol in hand, she scrambled to her feet to see a grizzled old man in a stained leather apron grinning at her through a face full of hair.

"What a tumble! Ass over elbows!" He waved a dripping spoon to illustrate, then cackled and turned back to stir a pot on a blackened cookstove. "Helluva treat."

Before she could make sense of that, movement drew her attention back to the doorway where her attacker bent, head drooping, hands braced on his thighs. Even though a dusty black hat hid his face, she could see by his size he wasn't Bodine. But why would a complete stranger attack her?

Brushing dust from her skirt, she lifted her chin and glared at her assailant. "I did not tumble. I was pushed."

Now that her eyes had adjusted to the dimness of the room and she was thinking more clearly, she wondered if she might have overreacted. Despite his hulking size, the man seemed harmless enough. Judging by his hunched posture, he was possibly elderly or weakened by illness. Scarcely threatening.

Then he lifted his head.

The walls of her throat seemed to constrict. For a moment she couldn't breathe, couldn't move. She felt pinned like a butterfly to a mat by the coldest stare she had ever experienced.

Definitely not old or ill. Furious.

She edged back as he slowly straightened to his full height, which was considerably more than hers. He looked like the loser of a tavern brawl—bloodstains on his dusty shirt, one eye swollen shut, and a nasty gash dripping more blood down the side of his dusty, beard-shadowed face.

"What'd you do that for?" he demanded in a raspy voice.

Cook's bark of laughter made her jump. "Cracked those *cojones* like eggs on a pan, didn't she, Brady? Won't be forkin' a saddle for a week, by damn."

Co-ho-nees? She frowned in confusion. Eyeing the man he'd called Brady, she noticed again the cut on his cheek. Had she done that with her parasol? The thought shocked her.

Without a word, Mr. Brady snatched up the saddle and limped out, almost mowing down the Kinderlys as they came up the steps.

"Oh, my," Melanie breathed as he stomped past. "Who was that?"

Maude shoved her through the door. "Never you mind, missy."

The cabin was small—a single room dominated by a table and

benches, with a stove against one wall, a rumpled cot against another. There was scarcely room to move without bumping a peg or shelf, and with the arrival of the passengers and driver, it became almost suffocatingly crowded. Stepping aside as the others entered, Jessica called out to Cook, "Could you please direct me to the convenience?"

He squinted at her. "The what?"

"The necessary."

"The necessary what?"

"She means the outhouse." Their driver, Mr. Phelps, hooked a thumb toward the rear of the cabin. "Out back. If you want to wash, there's a trough behind the shed. Watch for snakes."

"Snakes?" Maude clutched at Melanie.

Undaunted, Jessica ducked out the door. Heat engulfed her, so intense she could almost feel her skin shrivel. She'd have to get a proper bonnet soon or she'd be a prune by the time she reached Socorro. A prune with freckles. George would never recognize her—if her brother was still there and if he had even received her letter saying she was coming.

Moments later, gasping and half-nauseated, she fled the reeking facility and headed toward the shed and water trough. As she walked, she ran a hand over her abdomen, wondering if anything felt different since her fall. It would solve so many problems if she miscarried. A blessing really.

And yet . . .

At first she had denied even the possibility of a child. But after missing two courses, she knew for certain she carried her brother-in-law's baby. The horror of it had sent her to the edge of sanity. She shivered, remembering the day she had found herself crouched in the corner of her bedroom, weeping like a madwoman, the scissors clutched in her shaking hand. Had she intended to harm herself, or the baby? Even now, she didn't know. And that was the most horrifying thing of all. But lately, ever since she'd felt that first ripple of life, something had changed.

She slowed, flattened her palm against her body. If it was a girl, it wouldn't remind her so much of John Crawford, would it? It would simply be a baby. A daughter. Someone to love. Would that be so bad?

As if in response, something fluttered low in her abdomen. She jerked her hand away.

And what if it wasn't a daughter, but a son? What if she couldn't find George, or her brother turned her away? How long could she survive on the coins and few pieces of jewelry sewn into the hem of her underskirt?

For a moment she stood trembling, doubts weakening her resolve. Then slowly terror subsided. She would manage. She had done so after Papa abandoned her with a dying mother to tend and a little sister to raise, and again after George ran off to make his fortune in the gold fields of the West. She had survived rape. She had left the only home she had ever known and traveled halfway around the world. Surely she could raise a baby on her own.

Of course she could. Thrusting self-pity aside, she lifted her chin. "I am Jessica Abigail Rebecca Thornton and I am a woman to reckon with," she said in ringing tones as she rounded the shed and almost tripped over a stump beside the trough. Regaining her balance, she looked up, then froze when she saw she was not alone.

Mr. Brady bent beside the pump, water streaming from his mop of shaggy dark hair. Slowly he straightened, apparently unaware that his shirt was open and his upper person was exposed, or that he further exposed himself by lifting the tail of the shirt to mop his face. The man was built like a blacksmith. A very tall, very strong blacksmith. With a streak of dark hair running from his exposed parts straight down to . . . to his unexposed parts.

"You come to ogle or poke me again?"

"W-What? I—" Mortified to be caught staring, she whirled to present him her back. "No—yes—I mean, that is, if you have completed your ablutions, I—"

"Ab-whats?"

"Washing yourself." Had she truly said that? "Perhaps I should return later."

"It's all right. I'm done."

She hesitated, flustered and unsure what to do. He must have recovered from her earlier attack. His voice no longer sounded strained, although it retained a husky quality as if the dry climate had eroded the mellower tones, leaving him permanently hoarse. It was disconcerting. Like a whisper in the dark. She dared a glance.

Thankfully he had covered himself. Yet he still watched her, an odd twitch at one corner of his unruly black mustache. Her gaze slid to the trough. Despite the scum coating the inside walls—the only greenery she'd seen in days—the water looked so . . . wet. And she was so very hot.

She should leave. That would be the proper thing.

Oh, rot proper, she thought with sudden and uncharacteristic defiance. It was too hot to be proper. Besides, after that reeking facility, she was desperate for a wash. Refusing to be intimidated by Mr. Brady's looming presence, she set aside her reticule and parasol, stripped off her gloves and tucked them into her skirt pocket, then removed her traveling cape and placed it on the ground beside her other belongings. After carefully folding back the lace-edged cuffs on her gray bombazine, she dipped her fingers into the water. It felt heavenly against her parched skin.

Mr. Brady continued to stand there, gawking.

Ignoring him, she scrubbed the grit from her wrists and hands, then dampened a hanky, squeezed it out, and pressed it to her cheek. Bliss.

"I didn't push you."

She stiffened, taken aback by the denial and unsure how to respond.

Slowly she turned. He wasn't as old as she had originally thought, perhaps in his middle thirties. Like his voice, his face bore the mark of this harsh climate, his skin darkened by the sun, his features as harshly chiseled as the wind-carved bluffs. But his eyes were beautiful. A vibrant shocking blue that perfectly matched the turquoise gemstones so favored by indigenous Americans—pieces of sky, they called them. They were much too beautiful for that weathered face.

At least the unswollen one was. She turned back to the trough. "You did grab my arm."

"To warn you. About the saddle."

"Ah." She shot him a glance. "The one left in the middle of the floor? How thoughtful."

"I was coming back to get it."

"Indeed. Well then. I accept your apology. Please accept mine for striking you with my parasol. I certainly did not intend to injure you." Pulling a clean linen from her pocket, she wet it in the trough and held it out. "Perhaps this will help. Or if you would permit, I could tend it for you."

An odd look crossed his battered face. "Tend what? What the hell are you talking about?"

Since the man seemed somewhat agitated, although she couldn't fathom why insomuch as it was only a trifling injury, she allowed the profanity to pass unchallenged. "You are bleeding, sir."

"I am?" He glanced down at his belt buckle, then up at her. "Where?"

She motioned with the linen. "There. On your cheek."

"My cheek?" After a moment of confusion, realization dawned in those startling eyes. "Sonofabitch." With a long sigh, he sank onto the stump at the end of the trough. "I thought my luck was finally changing."

Jessica eyed him with disapproval. Granted, manners were more relaxed in the Colonies, but this was too much. After stuffing the wet hanky back into her reticule, she drew the strings closed with a snap. "Would you please refrain from using profanity in my presence, Mr. Brady? I find it most offensive."

"Do you?" He tugged off his right boot.

"I do." She quoted from Pamphlet Two: "'A gentleman should never use foul language in the presence of a lady. It is indicative of poor breeding and an affront to all within hearing.'"

He responded by removing the left boot.

She raised her voice a notch. "It is also written that profanity is the mark of a limited imagination and an untutored intellect." Abruptly she lost her thought when he pulled the stained sock off his huge foot. "What are you doing?"

"Blisters. Written where?"

"What? I . . ." Words deserted her as the second sock came off.

He gingerly lowered his feet into the trough. "You're not from around here, are you?"

She didn't—couldn't—respond.

"I'll take that as a no." Shading his eyes with one hand, he squinted up at her. "Since you're new, I'll make it as simple as I can. I didn't use profanity. 'Sonofabitch' isn't profanity. It's cussing. Profanity would be like 'goddamnit' or 'Christamighty' or—What's that in your hair?"

"My hair?" Caught off-balance by the abrupt change in subject, she started to lift her hands, then froze as visions of crawling things slithered through her mind. "What is it?"

"I'm not sure. It's just hanging there."

"Hanging there? In my hair?" She swatted at her head. Was it a bat? A spider? One of those tarantula things? "What is it?"

"Quit yelling. It's not alive."

A dead thing? In her hair? "Get it!" she cried, arms flailing. "Get it off!"

Snagging an arm to hold her still, he reached up, pulled something from her hair, then sat back. He stared at the object in his hand. "What the hell?"

Heart pounding, she inched closer to peer over his shoulder. Her hair form!

Almost dizzy with relief, she raised her hands to find her hair in disarray. Between the hat tossing and her fall, her twist had come loose, and now curls ran riot and pins poked out every which way. Irritated to be found in such a state, she snatched the form from his hand and stuffed it into her skirt pocket. "Thank you."

"You're keeping it? A wad of hair?"

"It is not a wad of hair," she said, striving for a semblance of dignity. "It is a hair form."

"Made of a wad of hair. Damnedest thing I've ever seen."

More cursing. Or was it profanity? She was so rattled, she scarcely knew.

In full retreat, she pulled her gloves from her skirt pocket, yanked them on with such vigor a thumb seam snapped, then snatched her belongings from the ground. She must have fallen into the fifth ring of hell, for undoubtedly, Mr. Brady was the gatekeeper.

"By the way . . ." He looked up, his narrowed eyes moving over her person in a wholly unacceptable manner. "It wasn't an apology. It was an explanation. There's a difference."

Awareness skittered along her nerves. She knew that look, and she would have none of it. Not again. And certainly not from this man. "I was unaware you were so discerning," she snapped. "But thank you for the clarification." A poor set-down, but the man had her so addled, it was the best she could do. Resisting the urge to bloody his other cheek with her parasol, she whirled and marched away. *Impertinent bounder.*

BRADY WAITED UNTIL THE ENGLISHWOMAN ROUNDED THE shed, then laughed so hard he almost fell off the stump. He hadn't been dressed down like that in years. Maybe never. Not even his brothers dared do that. Then he pictured her hopping around with that hair wad flopping like a dead rat and that set him off again.

Laughter faded. She seemed familiar and he wondered why. He would have remembered a woman with red hair and a funny accent. And tall. Being tall himself, he admired height in a woman. It made for a better fit all around.

After shaking the water off his feet, he dug two fairly clean socks out of his saddlebag and pulled them on. It hurt like a sonofabitch to cram his blistered feet into his boots, but he persisted. As he rose, he caught his reflection in the trough and realized how beat-up he looked.

It could have been worse, he supposed. It could have been him with a broken leg instead of Bob, or a hatchet instead of a ruffly umbrella. At least his cheek had quit bleeding and he could see out of his eye again.

He ran a palm over his bristly jaw, wondering if he should shave, then wondered why it would matter, and finally decided it didn't.

He was refilling his canteen when it came to him where he'd seen her. Not her, but a drawing of her, on a poster outside the sheriff's office in El Paso. He frowned, trying to remember. Something about a lost Englishwoman with red hair. And a reward for information. A big reward.

Lost? Or on the run? Either way, somebody wanted her back real bad. He wondered why. The woman was stark crazy. As he walked toward the cabin, he pictured her holding out that lacy doo-dad, offering to tend his injury. Damned if he shouldn't have unbuckled and let her have at it. That would have been a fine way to apologize.

The idea of it made him laugh out loud.

Two

"OGLE. AS IF," JESSICA MUTTERED AS SHE STOMPED ANGRILY toward the cabin. First Bodine and now Mr. Brady—the arrogance of men was astounding.

It didn't improve her mood to hear Maude's contentious voice even before she reached the porch steps. The woman had lungs a London rag merchant would envy, and from what Jessica could hear, the cook was no less gifted. With a feeling of weary resignation, she pushed open the door and stepped into the fray.

"How could they set a man like that free?" Maude demanded of Cook.

"Needed prison space for all them Rebel renegades they been rounding up, that's how."

Bodine snorted. "Better a Reb with a gun than a Mex with a knife, I always say."

When her eyes adjusted to the dimness of the cabin interior, Jessica noted the only unoccupied benches were at either end of the table.

Moving to the one farthest from Bodine, she dusted it with her hanky then sat. As the words grew more heated, she studied the others.

Maude's high color hinted at encroaching hysteria. Cook and Bodine seemed bent on pushing her to that end by gleefully recounting grisly details of recent violence, despite Coachman Phelps's repeated attempts to restrain them. Melanie watched with wide-eyed enthusiasm, and Mr. Ashford attended to his meal without comment.

Her companions on the westbound to Bedlam.

"Heard he jumped a guard in prison," Bodine mumbled through a mouthful of God-knows-what. "Heard they had to bust a knee to get him off."

Cook slapped a plate in front of her. "Shoulda aimed higher. Right, missy?"

She looked in dismay at her meal. Chili. Again. She had a rather low opinion of Southwestern cuisine. What was recognizable was unpalatable and the rest was so spicy she doubted even a Frenchman would eat it. Disheartened, she settled for water and a biscuit, hoping that would sustain her until they reached their final stop of the day in Val Rosa. Wincing as Maude's voice rose in a rambling denouncement of frontier justice and territorial prisons, she turned to Melanie, seated on her right. "Of whom are they speaking?"

"Oh, a horrible, dreadful man. He burned his own parents to death." The young woman gave a dramatic shiver. "Did you notice the man who was here earlier, the big handsome one with the odd-colored eyes and shoulders so wide they—"

"Mr. Brady?"

"You know him?"

Heat flooded Jessica's cheeks. "Only in passing. Is he the murderer to whom you're referring?" Crude and ill mannered . . . but a murderer? Surely not.

"Oh no, that's Sancho Ramirez. Cook says he and Mr. Brady have been fighting for years over an old Spanish land grant. A blood feud. Can you imagine? And now after ten years in prison, Ramirez is back, thirsting for revenge against the hapless Mr. Brady and what family he has left. Isn't it tragic?"

Hapless? It was absurd, and about as plausible as a plot in one of Melanie's frivolous novels. Jessica doubted that real people, even Colonials, behaved that way.

Mr. Ashford must have shared her view even though he couldn't have overheard their whispered conversation. "Perhaps we're overreacting here," he said in an attempt to calm Maude. "Over time such things often become exaggerated."

"Exaggerated?" Cook thunked his tray onto the table so hard two biscuits bounced off onto the floor. "Tell Brady that. Tell it to them folks on the eastbound. Them that survived, that is."

"Survived?" Maude asked in a quavering voice.

Phelps sent Cook a warning look.

The old man ignored it. "Last week out of Palovar. Ramirez locked six folks in the coach and burned 'em like cordwood."

Melanie's eyes almost popped out. Maude paled. Phelps cursed under his breath.

Bodine laughed. "The man does like a fire." Pushing back his plate, he rose. "Potent chili," he told Cook, offering as proof a sputter of intestinal wind before hurriedly exiting the cabin, leaving in his wake a foul stench as pertinacious as a wet coastal fog.

Jessica watched a fly drone listless circles above the table and waited for it to fall dead into the lard. When it didn't, she allowed herself to breathe again.

"But we'll never find space for a man his size," Maude said in protest to something Phelps had said. "We're crowded as it is."

"It's a six-passenger coach, ma'am. And he's only going as far as Val Rosa."

Maude's chins quivered in outrage. "First you tell us a madman is lurking out there"—she waved toward the flyspecked window—"now you say we must make room for the very man he's—"

The door swung open. Maude froze as the man himself ducked inside.

In hushed silence, six pairs of eyes tracked Mr. Brady to the bench at the opposite end of the table from Jessica, where he plopped down with a sigh. Seemingly impervious to their stares, he dropped his dusty hat onto the floor beside his foot and looked around, his gaze pausing on Jessica before moving on. "Afternoon," he said, shattering the awkward silence.

Maude closed her mouth. Melanie sighed. Jessica brushed biscuit crumbs from her skirt and wondered how a man could so completely dominate a room full of people without saying or doing a single threatening thing.

"This here's Wilkins," Phelps said.

Her head snapped up. *Wilkins?*

"I thought his name was Brady," Melanie said.

"It is. Brady Wilkins."

Jessica's lips went numb. The dolt could have corrected her rather than allow the gross impropriety of her using his given name. She glared at him.

He stared back, that silly mustache twitching, those vibrant eyes alight with laughter.

Resisting the urge to throw her biscuit in his face, she forced herself to resume eating.

No one spoke. The clatter of spoons on tin plates seemed unnaturally loud in the hushed room. Phelps pulled out a timepiece, checked the hour, then slipped it back into his pocket. Cook set a filled plate before Wilkins then bent to retrieve the two biscuits that had fallen to the floor. After dusting them on his sleeve, he returned them to the tray, taking care to arrange them just so.

Jessica sensed he had something to say but hoped he would refrain from doing so.

Alas, not. "You gonna tell him or not?" he demanded of Phelps.

"Don't you ever shut your mouth?"

"I can talk if I want. It's my house. Besides, he's got a right to know, don't he?"

"Know what?" Wilkins asked, chewing something brown.

"Aw, hell." Phelps sighed and wiped his palms on his thighs. He took a deep breath, let it out, then said, "Ramirez is out."

The chewing stopped. Other than a slight widening of his eyes, Brady Wilkins went utterly still. Then, in a voice so low it wouldn't have been heard had the room not been so silent, he said, "What did you say?"

"He's out, that's what!" Cook shouted. "Him and Alvarez. Can you believe that?"

Wilkins set down his fork and splayed his big hands on either side of his plate. "Explain."

Phelps sent Cook another warning look. "I thought Sheriff Rikker might have been out to the ranch to tell you, but Cook said you been in El Paso scouting bulls."

"Maybe he told your brothers," Cook offered hopefully.

"Maybe." Wilkins pushed aside his plate. Wrapping both hands around his tin mug, he lifted it to his lips, took a sip, then gently set it back down—each move executed with the careful precision of a man struggling to stay calm.

But he was far from calm. Jessica could see it in his breathing, in the way his grip tightened on the mug, and the way his eyes had changed to an even brighter, colder blue. Fear fluttered in her chest. She knew about rage, knew the damage a man's hands could do. And Brady Wilkins had very large hands. She glanced at the others, wondering if they sensed the danger, too.

By their expressions, they did. The Kinderlys sat in wide-eyed silence. Ashford looked wary, his gaze as watchful as a card player waiting for the hand to play out. Cook fidgeted. Phelps looked ill. But perhaps that was the chili.

"The law may have him by now," Phelps said, ending the tense silence.

"Like hell," Cook muttered. "That man's slippery as a heifer's butt."

"Well, I won't have it!" Leaping to her feet, Maude rounded on Phelps. "As our driver, you are sworn to protect us, and we shan't go another step until that man is apprehended."

"You sure as hell ain't staying here."

Phelps's palm slapped against the tabletop. "Open your mouth one more time, old man, and I'll put a bullet in it, swear to God."

"It's my house."

Beneath her cape, Jessica began to perspire.

Wilkins continued to stare into the mug he gripped so tightly.

"Gentlemen, please." Ashford graced Maude with an indulgent smile. "I'm sure there's no danger, ma'am. Remember, you'll have four men riding with you."

Small comfort, Jessica thought, since one of them was Bodine and another was every bit as menacing as the madman they hoped to avoid.

Sniffing into her hanky, Maude allowed Ashford to assist her from the table. "I told the Colonel we shouldn't have left Baltimore. Now we're all going to die."

"I think it's a grand adventure," Melanie said, following them through the door. "Just like in *The Cannibal Diaries*."

Anxious to make her own escape, Jessica rose and gathered her belongings, wishing Phelps would take the hint and stand so she could slip past him without crowding the stove.

Finally, with the stiff movements of a man who had traveled too many bumpy roads, the driver rose. He hesitated, then turned to the silent man at the end of the table. "Ramirez might not go to the ranch, Brady."

Wilkins stared into his mug.

Jessica watched the rim slowly bend.

Phelps didn't seem to notice. "Why would he? The feud's long over."

"Is it?" Wilkins lifted his head. Light slanted across his face, and for a moment Jessica glimpsed such a profound fury, his eyes seemed to glow like blue fire.

Finally taking note, Phelps edged back, almost bumping into Jessica. He raised both palms in a conciliatory gesture. "All I'm saying is, things have changed. We got a Federal Marshal now."

Wilkins's hand jerked. Coffee sloshed over the bent rim. Jessica watched it drip across his knuckles and thought he had the most powerful hands she'd ever seen. Broad and long-fingered, roughened by dark hair and marred by calluses and scars. Capable, hardworking hands. Hands that could cause a great deal of pain.

"Hell, Brady, your father's been dead more'n eight years. It's over."

Control shattered. Wilkins exploded off the bench, the mug flying through the air. "I'll kill him! This time I'll kill the sonofabitch!"

Cook lunged for the door. Jessica ducked behind Phelps. The mug bounced off the wall, spattering coffee in all directions. Then silence.

Parasol at the ready, she peered around Phelps.

Wilkins stood staring at the wall, his big hands clenching and unclenching at his sides. His rage was so consuming it seemed to suck all the air from the room. He took a deep shuddering breath, exhaled, took another. Bending, he snatched his hat from the floor. He studied it for a moment, turning it slowly in his hands. Then in a voice so taut with fury his lips scarcely moved, he said, "This *feud* has cost me most of my family and a lot of good men." As he spoke, he settled the hat on his head, tipping it front to back, a final tug on the brim. "I've got two brothers left."

His head swung toward Phelps. His expression held such deadly intent it lifted the hairs on Jessica's nape. "I won't bury another brother, Oran. This time I'll kill the bastard and I don't care who gets in my way. Tell that to your Marshal."

CHRIST! HOW COULD THEY LET THE BASTARD OUT?

Brady charged toward the corrals, driven by emotions he hadn't felt in a decade—fear that he'd be burying Hank or Jack next—rage that everything he'd worked for could still be lost—guilt that he hadn't ended this ten years ago when he'd had the chance. But mostly, churning inside hot and bitter as bile, there was hate, not just for Ramirez but also for the man who had set all these events in motion over two decades ago—his own father, Jacob.

Are you satisfied? Is this what you wanted, you bastard?

A kaleidoscope of images spun through his mind. The cabin, fire, his father silhouetted by flames, his head thrown back in a howl of despair.

Was she worth it?

Fury swirled through him, aimless and impotent, leaving Brady shaking and wet with sweat. Breathing hard, he gripped the top rail of the corral and waited for reason to return.

He'd end this damn feud and this time he wouldn't let the truth get in his way. He'd kill Sancho Ramirez and end it once and for all.

JESSICA STEPPED FROM THE CABIN INTO A BREEZE THAT FELT like a gasp from hell. Squinting against sunlight so stark it robbed the world of color, she looked around.

The other passengers stood at the open door of the coach, arguing with Bodine, who sat inside. Cook was leading two horses from the corrals. No sign of Wilkins.

Relieved, she descended the steps and went in search of Phelps. She found him at the front of the coach, hitching the new teams. "Might I ask a favor, sir?"

He threaded the reins through the harness rings then checked the girth buckle. "Such as?" As he straightened, his gaze moved past her to a point beyond her shoulder.

Sensing a looming presence, she whirled. For one insane moment she expected to see John Crawford leering down at her, which was absurd, since he was half a world away and had no idea where she was.

Instead, it was Wilkins behind her, a saddle in one hand, a rope-strung bundle in the other.

She lurched back. "W-What are you doing?" she almost shrieked.

Perhaps she shrieked it after all, judging by his startled expression. He stepped back, as if to distance himself before she did something even more shocking, like speaking in tongues or bolting giggling through the cactus. Clearly he thought her deranged. Perhaps she was.

"You shouldn't sneak up on a person," she accused in a shaky voice.

"I don't sneak."

Of course he didn't. A man his size couldn't sneak up on a fence post, especially carrying all that paraphernalia. She was definitely deranged.

While the two men discussed where to stow Wilkins's gear, she struggled to calm her breathing, infuriated that she had allowed emotion to overcome reason. Again. Why, after three months and thousands of miles, was Crawford still in her head, ready to pounce? Would she never be rid of him?

By the time Phelps had climbed topside to load Wilkins's belongings, she had regained a measure of control. Stepping around Brady Wilkins, she moved along the off side of the coach. "While you're up there, Mr. Phelps, would you please retrieve my bandbox?" Rising on tiptoe, she tapped a half-buried hatbox with the tip of her parasol. "That one, please." Stepping back, she hooked the parasol over her forearm and straightened her cape. "I would be most grateful."

"Aw, hell," Phelps muttered. "Can't it wait?"

"I regret it cannot."

"It'll take me an hour to unpack and repack."

"Surely not."

"Aw, hell."

With Wilkins's help, it took less than five minutes. Gratified to have the ordeal over and anxious to get out of the sun, she pulled two Indian head coppers from her reticule. She handed one to the driver. "Thank you for your help, Mr. Phelps."

He stared blankly at the coin in his palm. "What's this?"

"A token of my appreciation." Steeling herself, she turned to Wilkins. "And thank you for your help as well." She extended the second coin.

His big hands started up.

She almost flinched but caught herself. She even managed to keep her hand steady.

But instead of accepting the coin, he folded his arms across his chest. "No."

"You won't accept my offering?"

"No."

She had no response to such blatant rudeness. Nor was she inclined to stand bareheaded in this lung-searing heat and allow herself to be drawn into some tiresome game of insistence-and-refusal. Irritation overcoming fear, she grabbed Wilkins's hand and slapped the coin onto his callused palm. "Accept it with my gratitude. I insist."

His magnificent eyes narrowed.

But before he could voice objections, she snatched up the hatbox and marched around to the door of the coach. *Men. Rot them all.*

The other passengers had already taken their seats—except for Bodine, who stomped angrily toward the front of the coach. Apparently his digestive indiscretions had resulted in his banishment to the driver's box. Relieved, she climbed aboard.

Even with Bodine gone, the air was ghastly. Breathing through her mouth, she removed from the bandbox a simple straw bonnet with lilac rosettes and a white silk scarf. After securing it with a fluffy bow, she set the empty box on the floor as a brace for her feet, then sat back, hoping they would get under way soon and force fresh air into the stifling coach.

That prickle again, like fingertips brushing along her neck. She looked over to see Brady Wilkins in the doorway, frowning at the hatbox. "What the hell is that doing there?"

"I put it there." Mindful of the other passengers, she leaned forward and spoke in a low voice. "Can you possibly speak three sentences without cursing?"

"Where am I supposed to put my feet?"

"In a stable, perhaps?" She sat back, and meeting his glare with a gracious smile, she added, "However, if the hatbox is such a bother, I am sure the others will be delighted to wait in this stultifying heat while you and Mr. Phelps—"

"What's in it?"

"At the moment, nothing, but—"

He yanked the box from beneath her feet and threw it out the door. Then before she could muster a thought, the coach rocked as he climbed aboard.

"Watch where you step." Maude jerked her skirts aside as he rooted around, knees and elbows wreaking havoc in the confined space. Finally he plopped down beside Ashford and across from Jessica, his spread knees imprisoning her skirts, his big feet taking up most of the floor space. With a deep sigh, he tipped his head back, his hat forward, and closed his eyes. By the time the coach hit its rhythm, he was snoring. It was quite a bit longer before Jessica could relax enough to unclasp her hands and take a full breath.

Brady Wilkins was nothing like Mr. Bodine. He was much, much worse.

As her nerves settled, exhaustion set in. She tried to doze, but the swaying of the coach and the movements of the baby upset her stomach, so she gave up.

The baby. She. *Victoria.* It fit.

Smiling, Jessica closed her eyes and traced her fingertips over her abdomen. Was it larger than yesterday? Flattening her palms against her body, she shaped the roundness. Definitely bigger. Firmer. Despite the concealing cape and being long in the waist, she wouldn't be able to hide it much longer.

"You still don't have it right."

Her eyes flew open.

Brady Wilkins watched her from beneath the brim of his hat. His gaze dropped to the fingers splayed across her abdomen.

She yanked her hands away, heat rushing into her face. Had he guessed her condition? Judging by his speculative look, he had.

"I didn't curse. This time I used profanity."

The words were slow to penetrate. When they did, she stiffened. Hoping to discourage further conversation, she looked away, wondering why she had ever said anything in the first place.

"Cursing would be like 'sonofabi—' "

"Don't." She whipped her head around. "Not another word."

"Just figured before you go correcting people, you ought to get it right."

She narrowed her eyes at him.

He raised his brows.

She gave up. Sometimes maintaining proper decorum was simply too difficult. With a weary sigh, she sank against the backrest. "You're having fun with this, aren't you?"

"I admit I am." His mustache quirked up at the corners. "You make it so easy."

She pressed her lips together to keep from smiling, fearing that would only encourage him. How tedious she had become—spouting quotes from her pamphlets, dressing down strangers—she could scarcely stand her own company; no wonder he found her so ridiculous. "I'm delighted to be able to entertain you," she said dryly.

"I'm delighted to be entertained." He reached into his shirt pocket. "And by the way . . ." He leaned forward, an odd glint in those aqua eyes. In his fingers he held a copper coin.

She tried to draw back, couldn't, and in mute helplessness watched him take her hand in his and gently pry open her clenched fist. With great care he placed the coin into her gloved palm. "I don't take money from women. No matter how grateful they are."

She forgot how to breathe. How to think, or move. He was so near she could smell sweat, horses, old smoke. She could see gray sprinkles in the dark stubble of his beard, a pale scar running through one dark eyebrow, a bruise forming under the new cut on his cheek. And at that moment, as she stared into the bright intensity of those startling eyes, she realized how badly she had underestimated this man.

And to prove it, he did the most extraordinary thing.

He smiled.

Just that.

Yet it changed his entire face. The whiteness of such lovely teeth against his black mustache and sun-browned skin was contrast enough, but the transformation from scowl to rakish grin was astonishing. Boggling.

Oh my. Dimples, too.

Releasing her hand, he sat back, pulled his hat over his forehead, and closed his eyes.

She let out air in a rush, only then realizing she had been holding it. Blasphemy with a dimpled smile—threats spoken in a velvet voice—eyes that changed color with his mood. Was anything about Brady Wilkins what it seemed?

She repressed a shiver of . . . something. Thank heavens he was riding only as far as Val Rosa. In a few more hours, she would be rid of him altogether.

As the afternoon wore on, heat built. Even with the shade down, dust kicked up by the horses sifted through every crack to settle in the damp creases of Jessica's neck and wrists, turning perspiration into mud. Her throat was so dry her tongue stuck to the roof of her mouth.

The road grew steeper, tilting the coach and pinning her against the backrest. Wilkins, riding backward against the slant, slouched lower and lower as he napped, his long legs flopping against her skirts with every bump, those oversized feet taking up most of the narrow aisle. She wondered what he would do if she stomped one but lacked the courage to find out.

The coach slowed to a crawl. Above the rattle of wheels, she heard Phelps urging the horses on. Lifting the shade, she saw that the ground beyond her window dropped sharply away in a long, rock-strewn slope that ended in a treeless canyon far below.

"Will you be stopping in Val Rosa, Mrs. Thornton?"

Letting the shade drop, she turned to Mr. Ashford. As she did, she saw that although he hadn't moved, Wilkins was awake and watching her. "No, I shall be continuing on to Socorro."

"Perhaps that's where I've seen you," Ashford continued. "Although I'm sure we've never met, you seem familiar. Have you been there before?"

Before she could answer, Maude leaned forward to peer past Melanie. "Socorro is Indian country. Dreadful place. Is that where your
husband is, Mrs. Thornton?"

Jessica looked down at her hands. "No. My brother. My husband is
dead."

"A pity. How did he die, if you don't mind my asking?"

She did mind, but knew if she didn't answer, it would only invite
vulgar speculation. "A hunting accident." That seemed the simplest.
Less complicated than disease or drowning, and certainly less dramatic
than murder. Or being bitten by a rattlesnake, or one of those giant
Gila monster lizards. Or being scalped by natives, or burned to death
in a stagecoach. The West offered so many options.

"He was shot? Oh, how tragic." Leave it to Melanie to dramatize
the simple.

Jessica smoothed a pleat on her skirt. "Not shot . . . precisely. He
was on his way home and fell." It sounded weak, even to her own ear.
She was such a wretched liar.

Ashford joined the interrogation. "Fell, how?"

She cleared her throat. "Actually, it was his horse that fell. Slipped.
On ice. It was snowing, you see, and when he jumped a hedgerow, he
fell and hit his head. My husband, not the horse. Although the horse
fell, too, of course." She knew she was babbling but couldn't seem to
stop herself. She hated lying, hated the reason for the lie, hated the way
they were all staring at her. Even Wilkins. Especially Wilkins, with his
knowing little smirk.

"What was he hunting?" Ashford asked.

Mercy's sake, what difference does it make? "Grouse, I think."

"In winter?" Maude frowned. "Surely he wasn't poaching?"

"Certainly not. My husband would never do anything unlawful."
Now she was defending a man who never existed; her perversity knew
no bounds. "It was August, I think. Perhaps September. I try not to
think about it."

"Odd time to snow," Maude muttered as she sat back.

Too late Jessica realized her mistake. If her husband had died eight months ago, she should be much further along in her confinement. Unless the baby wasn't her husband's. *Blast*. If she was to continue this fabrication, she really must perfect her lying. Luckily no one knew she was pregnant or that her timing was off.

No one except Wilkins. She recognized that speculative look in those hard blue eyes. Apparently the dolt could count. No doubt he thought her wanton. Or a liar. Or both. Not that she cared. To prove it, she hiked her chin and returned his smirk, refusing to let him see her shame.

His mustache twitched. For a moment she feared he might say something, then thankfully, Mr. Ashford drew his attention. "Didn't I hear Cook mention you had a ranch in this area?" he asked him. "Rose-something?"

With one long big-knuckled finger, Wilkins pushed back his hat and turned to study the man beside him. "RosaRoja," he finally said in that husky voice.

"Ah yes. The Red Rose Ranch, named for the roses planted by the previous owners, the Ramirez family, I think it was." Ashford brushed dust from his sleeve. "I hear it's quite a spread. Part of an old grant sold for back taxes after the Mexican war. Pennies on the dollar, I heard."

Wilkins didn't respond. But that coiled energy was back.

Ashford seemed oblivious. "I do advance work for the Texas and Pacific," he explained. "Banking, labor—"

"Right-of-ways?"

"That, too." He didn't appear to notice the chill in Wilkins's voice. "Hard country," he went on, nodding toward the window and the rocky slope rising on his side of the coach. "Frostbite in winter, heatstroke in summer. Unless you have water, of course. Good water is worth its weight in gold out here. Especially to a railroad."

"Or a cattleman." Wilkins's unblinking gaze never wavered.

"Or a cattleman," Ashford agreed. "Ever think of selling out?"

Before Wilkins could answer, something under their feet snapped with a crack as loud as a gunshot. The coach lurched to the left. Ashford fell into Melanie. Maude screamed. Above the shriek of metal on stone, Phelps shouted in panic. "Jump clear! Jump clear!"

The coach tipped up, then started over.

Jessica crashed against the door. Cursing, Wilkins threw out an arm to keep from falling on top of her, then yanked her clear as the coach slammed onto its side. The door exploded in splintered wood. Dust billowed in. Screams rose above the squeal of horses and the crack of breaking wood as the coach started to roll.

Jessica felt herself falling. Rough hands caught her. A flash of bright aqua eyes, then the next instant she was windmilling through sunlight and empty air.

The coach thundered past.

She hit hard on her side and began to slide down the slope on loose rock. She grabbed at a passing bush, felt her glove rip as branches tore through her fingers. Stones pelted her back. Dust filled her nose. In a roar of cascading rock, she slipped faster and faster.

A hand grabbed her arm, stopping her downward slide with a yank that sent a shock of pain through her shoulder. She clung to it, fighting for air as stones clattered past. The grip shifted and suddenly a hard arm clamped so tightly around her ribcage she couldn't draw in air.

Time spiraled backward and fear exploded.

"Don't!" She bucked, legs kicking. "John, no!"

His grip tightened as they teetered. "Don't fight me or we'll both go down!" he shouted in a voice that wasn't his.

In mindless terror she clawed at his arm, ripping through cloth, digging deep with her nails. "John, stop! Let me go!"

A rock slammed into her head.

A burst of light and pain.

Then blackness sucked her down.

Three

PAIN CAME AT HER FROM ALL SIDES—HER BACK, HER SHOULder. A pulse hammered inside her head. Sharp rocks dug into her back, and the ground beneath her was so hot it burned into her skin.

Then she felt hands moving across her body.

With a strangled cry, she tried to roll away, but the hands pushed her back down.

"Hold still. You're safe. You're all right."

Squinting against the sun, she saw a dark, blurry shape looming over her. Wilkins. What was he doing? Why was he touching her? She felt his fingers move through her hair and flinched when they touched a tender spot beside her left ear.

"Just a bump. Move your arms and legs."

She did, but it hurt. Bruised and battered but nothing broken. She struggled up on one elbow, then hung there as tiny suns collided behind her eyes.

"Do you remember what happened?" he asked.

Pain knifed through her shoulder as she lifted her head. Fifty feet away was a dark mound. Beyond it, the coach lay on its side like a giant wounded beast, spilling clothing and luggage across the ground like entrails. She remembered the coach falling. Someone grabbing her. She looked down, saw blood on her dress, and air rushed from her lungs. "No . . . oh no . . ."

"It's mine. You're all right."

Befuddled, she looked over, saw a bloodstained rag tied around his forearm, and sagged in relief. Not the baby. Not Victoria.

Wilkins rose. "Can you stand?"

"I—I'll try."

He bent toward her, his broad hand reaching out to offer help.

She shrank back. "No. I can do it." She knew it was rude, but at the moment she couldn't bear to be touched. "Just—just give me a moment."

He straightened. "Don't take too long. I need help."

As she watched him limp toward the coach, she realized the dark mound beside it was a dead horse. Behind it lay another. What of the passengers? With painful slowness, she turned to study the long slope behind her. Halfway down were two more horses, one motionless, the other frantically fighting the traces. A man—Phelps?—worked at the leathers to cut it free. Below them, luggage and clothing littered the slope in bright splashes of color, and near the bottom, thrown across the rocks like a discarded rag doll, lay the single twisted form of a man.

Swallowing hard, she looked away.

"Over here," Wilkins called, bent over another still form beside the coach.

Untangling her legs from her tattered skirts, she struggled to her feet. Dizziness swept over her. Without warning, bile surged up her throat. She bent, heaves wracking her body.

When the nausea passed, she straightened, spots dancing behind her eyes. She took a shaky step and almost tripped on the tattered hem of her cape. Loosening the ties, she let it fall. Her hat was gone. Her gloves were shredded, but habit and principle wouldn't allow her to discard them, so she tucked them into her skirt pocket. On legs as weak as warm pudding, she worked her way toward Wilkins.

As she passed the first horse, it stared blindly up at her, flat-edged teeth bared in a frozen grimace. A fly darted in and out of its nostril. The second horse was also dead, its forehead caved in, brains matting the dark fur like clabbered milk. The stench of blood made her stomach reel. Pressing a hand to her mouth, she forced herself to keep moving. When she finally slumped to the ground beside Wilkins, she was so dizzy she could scarce hold up her head.

"I need cloth," he said.

She looked over and gasped when she saw the two-inch-wide sliver of wood stuck in Mr. Ashford's side and the huge bruise darkening the left side of his face. Dear God, was he dead? Wilkins said something, but she could make no sense of it. Everything was suddenly off-kilter as if the world were slowly tilting.

"Hell." Wilkins's hand closed over the back of her neck and shoved her head down until her forehead almost touched her knees. "Breathe."

She sucked in air. After a moment, the spinning slowed. As her mind steadied, she realized his hand was still there, a hot, heavy weight against her skin, his fingers so long they almost encircled her neck. She shrugged him away and slowly straightened.

"No more fainting," he said gruffly.

"I do n-not faint." Her tongue tripped over the words. "I have never done so, and I—" Her throat constricted when Wilkins ripped open Ashford's vest. Blood was everywhere, soaking into Ashford's shirt, caking in the creases of Wilkins's hands. It smelled worse than the horses and left a sweet, metallic taste in the back of her throat. How could a man lose so much blood and live?

"Get something for a bandage," Wilkins ordered.

What if he died? What if they all died?

"Do it. Now!"

She pushed herself to her feet. "Wh-What kind of cloth?"

"Anything clean. And check the driver's box for whiskey and a canteen."

Careful not to look at the dead horses, she retraced her steps to the front of the coach. In the driver's box, more blood. Flies. Under the seat she found a canteen and a tin flask. As she climbed back to the ground, she chided herself for being such a coward. She had seen injuries before, even death. She had to pull herself together or she would be of little use to Wilkins and the others.

"Mrs. Thornton, is that you?"

Turning, Jessica saw Melanie limping toward her. She looked wretched, her skirts torn, blood from a dozen abrasions showing through a coating of dust. Absurdly, her prim bonnet was still pinned to a knot of hair halfway down her back. But at least she was alive and whole. "Are you injured?" Jessica asked.

"I'm all right, but I'm worried about Mama. Her ankle's swollen. It's not bleeding, but she's in terrible pain and I don't know what to do."

Jessica blinked at her, feeling trapped in a slow-moving nightmare that seemed to go on without end. "Ashford is hurt," she said in a hollow voice. "Wilkins will come when he can."

"Please," Melanie begged, reaching for her arm.

Jessica stepped back. "I can't. He needs me." She frowned, trying to think, then remembered. "I have to find cloth for a bandage," she said and turned away.

Melanie called after her, but Jessica shut her out and concentrated on the simple task of finding cloth for a bandage. She knew it was cowardly, but she didn't want to think about the Kinderlys or Mr. Ashford or that crumpled body on the slope. She simply needed time. Soon she would feel stronger and be able to do more. Until then, she would do as she was told and let Wilkins take care of everything.

When she returned with a shirt, two petticoats, and several men's kerchiefs, she saw the piece of wood still protruded obscenely from Ashford's body. Averting her eyes, she knelt beside Wilkins. "Will he live?"

Wilkins shrugged, his mouth a grim line beneath his dark mustache. "Whiskey?"

She held out the flask. He took it in fingers that glistened wet and red. "What about Mr. Phelps?" she asked.

He worked the cork loose with his teeth and spit it aside. "He's managing."

That meant the body on the slope was Bodine's. She should have felt sad. Or relieved. Or something other than this terrible emptiness.

Wilkins thrust the flask toward her. "Hold this."

She did. The metal was sticky with blood. Numbly, she watched Wilkins tear a petticoat into thin strips. "When I tell you," he instructed as he tied the ends together to form one long band of cloth, "pour half the whiskey over his side, then the rest on a kerchief. Understand?"

She nodded, her stomach quivering.

"When I pull the stick out, there'll be blood. As long as it's not spurting, wait a few seconds, then pour. Ready?"

The flask started to jump in her hand. She took a deep breath, then another, and another. Yet the harder she tried, the less air she seemed to draw into her lungs.

"Stop that. You'll pass out."

Why couldn't she breathe?

"Hell." He jerked the flask from her grip, picked up one of the kerchiefs, and without warning, clamped the cloth over her mouth, cutting off her air. Frantic, she fought him, but he held her fast with his other arm around her shoulders, pinning her firmly back against his chest. "Breathe," he ordered, cupping the cloth over her nose and mouth.

She gasped, drew in the warmth of her own breath. Within moments her vision cleared and the whirling in her head slowed. When reason returned and she realized he was still holding her, she shoved his hand away and straightened.

Setting the kerchief aside, he sat back on his heels, watching her. "Better?"

She pressed a palm over her thundering heart and nodded, not yet trusting her voice. She wasn't sure which terrified her more, being unable to breathe or having Wilkins grab her like that.

"Then pick up the flask." Turning back to Ashford, he gripped the stick. "Ready?" And before Jessica could respond, he yanked. A terrible sucking noise, then blood gushed in thick, dark rivulets down Ashford's side and into the dirt. The smell was ghastly. "Pour."

She tried, but her hand shook so badly she wasn't sure if any whiskey got into the wound. Apparently some did. Even unconscious, Ashford's body jerked like a puppet on a string.

"Now the rest over the cloth."

Again, she poured.

"Press it against the hole. Hold it there while I wrap him."

She did. The cloth grew hot and wet against her palm. Feeling her stomach roll, she tried to send her mind to a kinder place where pain never intruded and death—

"Let go."

She blinked at him.

"Move your hand."

Snatching her hand back, she wiped it on her skirt. The red wouldn't come off. Battling panic, she searched for her gloves. "Do you see them? My gloves? I know they're here." She felt hysteria build, then found the gloves in her skirt pocket. As soon as she pulled them on, she felt calmer, more in control.

Wilkins tied off the wrappings, then wiped his hands on his shirt, leaving dark streaks on the dusty cloth. He sat for a moment, studying her. He must have sensed her alarm because his expression softened— just a slight crinkling at the corners of his eyes, but enough to ease her fear. "You did all right, Your Ladyship."

"I am not a Lady," she muttered, smoothing the tattered glove over her fingers. "I mean I am not entitled—that is—I am a lady, of course, but not with a capital 'L'—oh, never mind." She clasped her hands in her lap, squeezing hard, trying to force strength into her wobbly arms. "Miss Thornton will do."

"Miss?"

"Mrs. I meant Mrs., of course." She stared down at her hands, feeling miserable and foolish and so disheartened in spirit she almost burst into tears.

"Look at me."

She couldn't. Wouldn't. She would start crying and she couldn't bear that.

From the corner of her eye, she saw Wilkins reach out, then those same fingers that had bent a cup and tended a wound gently tilted her head up, forcing her eyes to meet his. "Do what I tell you and I'll get you through this. Understand?"

Currents jumped between them, moving from his fingertips to the tender skin beneath her jaw. For a moment she forgot to be afraid, to be wary of his touch, to armor herself against the pull of those intensely vibrant eyes.

"I'll keep you safe. That's a promise."

She wanted so badly to believe him. But she had been lied to before.

He must have read her doubt. With a look of impatience, he let his hand drop away and rose. "I've got to check on the old lady and her daughter."

As she watched him limp away, sunlight reflecting off the quartz-rich earth blinded her, inflaming the pulse beat in her temple. She closed her eyes. A sense of detachment stole over her, a drifting sensation so seductive she almost gave in to it. What would it matter if she drifted away forever? Who would care?

Victoria.

With a sigh, she opened her eyes. Wilkins said he would keep them safe. For now, she would believe him. But if he was lying . . .

BY LATE AFTERNOON, WHEN THE HEAT RISING OFF THE SUN-baked earth was at its worst and the sky was beginning to take on an orange cast, Brady realized Oran Phelps was dying. Something was busted inside him, and with each passing hour the pain grew.

To his credit, Oran never said a word, but struggled diligently to stay on his feet and do what he could for the passengers in his care. He insisted on helping Brady stack rocks over Bodine's body, then because the water barrel strapped to the coach had broken in the crash, he gathered what water they had, which consisted of Brady's full canteen and Oran's half-empty one. He even helped tend the old woman's ankle, which was only sprained and not broken, although to hear her wailing, it was a fatal injury. But with the day starting to fade, Brady could see Phelps was wearing down. And he wasn't the only one.

He glanced over to where the Englishwoman struggled to prop that ball-busting umbrella over the railroader to keep the sun off his face. So far she'd handled herself well and he admired her for it. But studying her now, he could see she was lagging and he knew she was hurting. Not a crier or a complainer, which in his experience was an unusual thing in a woman, especially a woman like her. He just hoped she held true to that when he told her he was leaving.

"The horse is pretty sore." Oran's voice was raspy with pain. "But he should get you to Jamison's. Leave the saddle. Less weight."

Brady knelt beside him. He noted the tremor in the older man's hands as he mashed mescal leaves on a rock with his gun butt.

"I know with Ramirez out there, you got worries of your own."

Brady didn't need reminders. Nor did he want Phelps worrying away what strength he had left. "I'll tend this first, Oran. My word on it."

Phelps nodded. The gun slipped from his fingers. With a groan, he slumped back onto the ground. "Think I'll rest a minute."

Brady drew his long knife from his boot and scraped up the mescal paste. After pulling a packet of jerky and a tin cup from his saddlebag, he picked up the fuller of the two canteens and walked toward the Englishwoman. He wondered how to impress on her the direness of their situation without scaring her. Five people—three injured—with no food and hardly any water, stranded in a canyon next to a dry arroyo. If it rained, they'd be caught in a flash flood. If it didn't, they'd likely die from too little water and too much sun. Unless Sancho found them first.

Brady forced that thought aside. But as soon as he did, another took its place. Unless Sancho went to the ranch instead. *Sonofabitch.*

"What's wrong?"

Startled, he looked down to find himself standing over the English-woman. She was staring up at him with that skittish look she seemed to favor whenever he was near. Adopting a bland expression, he squat-ted on his heels so they were at eye level, hoping that would put her at ease. He knew his size and manner could be intimidating, but he'd never used his strength against a woman, and it irritated him that she so clearly thought he would.

Handing her the knife, he told her to spread some of the paste on a clean kerchief while he unwrapped Ashford's bandage. He was relieved to note the wound wasn't stinking and showed no sign of infection yet, but it was early. After he'd changed the bandage and retied the wrappings, she offered to put the rest of the paste on his arm. It wasn't necessary—despite the blood, the scratches weren't that deep.

He let her do it anyway. He knew she didn't like touching him and figured if she saw she could do it without coming to harm, she might lose some of her distrust. Plus, he liked watching her. Even sunburned and dirty, with that lumpy bruise on her temple and her face half hid-den by a tangled mess of curls, she was easy on the eyes. She reminded him of one of those fancy Arabian horses—all pride and not much sense, but a heart that wouldn't quit.

She studied the cuts. "Did I do this?" When he didn't answer, she looked up, her eyes showing confusion and concern. "If so, I am sorry. I was not myself."

Brady forced himself to look away before he drowned in those whis-key brown eyes. "It's all right." Apparently he hadn't been himself ei-ther, but some bastard named John.

She applied the paste in careful little dabs as if fearful she might hurt him, which was laughable, since she'd already damn near gelded him. But her kindness moved him, and as he watched her slim fingers slide over the dark roughness of his arm, he couldn't help but react. And it wasn't just gratitude he was feeling.

When she'd finished basting and trussing his arm like a Christmas goose, he pulled a strip of jerky from the linen-wrapped packet and held it out. "This is dried meat. Chew it slow."

She held it between her thumb and forefinger, like it might come alive and bite her. "What kind of meat?"

He picked the most likely. "Beef, I think."

"You think?"

"I'm sure. Eat it."

She ate. When she swallowed the last of it, he gave her a quarter cup of water and told her to go slow. She didn't, and a minute later puked it back up on a sage bush.

He offered to help, but she waved him away, which was fine with him. Once the heaves stopped, she sank onto the ground beside him, her face so pale her freckles stood out like flecks of faded rust. "How humiliating. And how crass of you to watch."

Hell, with her pear-shaped butt up in the air that way, hiking her skirts to expose trim ankles and a gratifying portion of those long legs, how could he not look? Biting back a smile, he held out another strip of jerky.

She hesitated, then shook her head. "It wouldn't be fair to the others."

"It would if there were two of you."

That took the pinch out of her mouth. He almost laughed. Did she think he couldn't tell when a woman was breeding? He was a cattleman. He dealt with pregnant females all the time. "Take it." He pushed it into her hand. "I doubt the railroader or Phelps will want their share."

While she took tiny bites and tiny sips, he explained that he would be leaving for the stage stop and she'd be on her own until he got back, which would hopefully be by morning. He warned her that once the sun set, it would get cold, and she would need to find extra clothes to keep everybody warm. He told her how to build a fire ring, and that mesquite wood burned hottest, and how important it was to keep the fire going to ward off scavengers coming in for the horses after dark.

He added that he would leave her his repeater and some cartridges, but unless a big cat showed up, he doubted she'd have need of it.

At some point she quit chewing to stare at him, and even though her face lost some of its color, she didn't interrupt, which he took as a good sign.

So he continued, explaining that since snakes sought warmth at night, before she went to sleep, she should wrap her skirts tight around her legs and cover her feet well. And finally, in an effort to soften the bleakness of their situation with a little humor, he cautioned her to sleep with her mouth closed lest she wake up chewing on something other than jerky, such as a scorpion or a lizard or even a hairy tarantula. He grinned to let her know he was joking and thought she seemed to be handling it all pretty well, when she suddenly jumped to her feet and started hitting him in the face.

"You're leaving?" she shrieked, going at him with both fists. "You blighter! You bloody bastard!"

Brady was so astounded he took a couple of roundhouses before he managed to get to his feet, grab hold of her wrists, and shove her to arm's length. He waited until she played herself out, which didn't take long, then eased her to the ground. He stepped back.

Christamighty. He wiped blood from a cut on his lip, so rattled he didn't know whether to hog-tie her or shoot her. What the hell was wrong with her?

Yet as he watched her glaring up at him, teeth bared, that fiery temper a match to the riot of red curls haloing her face, he thought she was by far the damnedest, most confounding, excitable and exciting woman he'd ever come across.

"I should have known not to trust you," she snapped, rubbing at her wrists.

He put some space between them, then hunkered on his heels so their heads were on the same level. "Why?" he asked calmly.

"You said you would take care of us."

"I'm trying to."

"By deserting us?"

It bothered him the way she kept rubbing at her wrists, as if he had grabbed her too hard and hurt her, which he knew he hadn't. When she caught the direction of his gaze, she fisted her hands in her lap.

"I'm not deserting you."

"Deserting, leaving, abandoning. It's all the same." She shot him a look that could fray wire. "And something at which all men excel."

At that moment, as if a window into her mind had opened to him, Brady gained insight into the reason for her distrust. Some man—her father, husband, that bastard, John—had left her, and now she colored every man with the stain of that betrayal. Well, he wouldn't allow it. He wouldn't carry the blame for another man's mistake. He had enough of his own. "Look at me."

Her head snapped up, eyes crackling with fury.

Leaning closer, he pinned her with his gaze and the force of his will, compelling her to see past her anger and fear to the truth. "I am not deserting you," he said with quiet emphasis. "I'm going for help. There's a difference." He waited, forcing her to look away first.

"Fine!" She pressed trembling fingers against her forehead. "Go then."

Of course, when she said it like that, there was no way he could. So as calmly and simply as he could, he tried to explain. "We need a wagon. And the only way to get one into this canyon is down twenty miles of bad road. But first they have to realize we're missing. Then they have to find us. Then they have to round up that wagon and get it in here, all of which could take two and a half, maybe three days." He waited for that to sink in. When he saw her weakening, he finished her off. "Three days with no food, almost no water, and two tons of rotting horseflesh—"

"Enough!" She held up a palm to stop him. "You made your point."

Brady reined in his temper. He wasn't accustomed to explaining himself or having his judgment questioned. "The point, Your Ladyship, is I can get to the stopover and back by morning with enough supplies to hold us until help comes."

"Why can't Mr. Phelps—"

"Phelps is dying."

For a second he thought she might cry, which rattled him. It also surprised him and said a lot about her character that she would weep for a man she didn't know, but not shed a tear for herself. The woman was a paradox.

"I am not deserting you," he told her for the third and final time.

"You promise?" She said it with a wobbly smile, as if the answer he gave wasn't the most important thing she would hear this day.

He didn't smile back. "I give you my word." She didn't look particularly reassured, but he'd done all he could. "I'll check on the Kinderly women before I go, then move Phelps over here so you won't have to build two fires."

When she didn't respond, he rose and started away, then stopped. He scratched his chin and thought for a moment before retracing his steps. He stopped beside her. "By the way," he said to her bent head. "You being English and an expert besides, maybe you could tell me." He paused, waiting for her to look up. When she did, he gave her the full force of the legendary Wilkins smile. "Would 'bloody' be cussing, or profanity?"

She didn't disappoint, God bless her, and gratified by the look of shock and indignation on that dirty, sunburned face, Brady tipped his hat and walked away.

In his experience, a little anger could go a long way on a cold, lonely night.

TWENTY-TWO MILES NORTHEAST, SANCHO RAMIREZ LED FOUR HORSE-men up a dusty trail along the south face of Blue Mesa. It was a hard climb over sharp rocks and through prickly scrub, and so steep in places, the men had to lean forward, gripping the manes of their horses to keep from tipping backward. By the fourth switchback, the horses were dripping foam, their sides heaving as they fought for air.

At the top, Ramirez cut between two granite boulders. Motioning the others to stay, he waved the drag rider forward, then rode out onto a wide, flat shelf that ended in a sheer drop. Dismounting, he let the reins drop and walked to the edge.

The drag rider, Paco Alvarez, a stocky man with quick, darting eyes, dismounted and ducked into the shade of a sandstone overhang to roll a smoke. He didn't like heights. And he didn't like being so near the rancho. What if someone saw them up here? What would happen to all of Sancho's plans then?

Through a veil of tobacco smoke, he watched Sancho walk back and forth along the ledge, muttering to himself, his long, gray hair whipping around his face like thin wisps of smoke. Paco noted he was limping, coming down hard on his bad knee as if he wanted the pain, needed it to keep his mind focused. Paco wondered if he was drifting again.

It happened a lot lately. Sancho would forget things, like what day it was, or the names of the men they had hired, or the fact that his mother, Maria, and her lover, Jacob Wilkins, had both died years ago. It was as if the present was slipping away and his mind was sliding back into the horrors of the past. Paco didn't like that either. In prison, Sancho had promised him half of the rancho if he would help him destroy the Wilkins family. It was the only thing that had kept Paco alive during ten years of hell. He wouldn't let Sancho's craziness ruin it now.

Out on the ledge, Ramirez threw back his head and laughed.

"*Cállate*," Paco hissed, knowing how sound carried on the rocky slopes.

Sancho turned, a look of surprise on his gaunt face as if he'd forgotten Paco was there. He grinned, showing gaps where teeth used to be, and waved Paco closer. "*Ven, Paco. Mira.*"

Reluctantly Paco moved to the edge and peered down. The valley opened below him—rolling grasslands, the silver ribbon of the creek, piñon canyons sloping inward like spokes on a wheel, and at the hub, perched on a bend of the creek by the mesquite tree, the rambling hacienda where he had been born. Paco felt something tighten in his chest. Even at this distance, he could see the slash of red at the base of the adobe walls, blooms from the hundred rosebushes Maria Ramirez had planted thirty years earlier to commemorate the birth of her son.

The favored son. The true son. The son that would kill her.

"See, Paco? *Es lo mismo. Nada* is changed."

Feeling dizzy, Paco stepped back. "He added a porch."

Sancho tipped his head back, eyes closed, nostrils flaring as he sniffed the wind. "Do you smell them? Her roses?" A half smile softened the sharp angles of his face. "She knows I am back."

Disgusted, Paco flicked the butt of his cigarillo at a passing beetle. "She knows nothing, Sancho. She's dead. *Muerta.*"

"No. Listen." Sancho cocked his head as the wind whispered through the overhang with a sound as mournful as a woman's sigh. "She calls to me."

Paco lost patience. Grabbing the other man's arm, he jerked him around to face him, trying to break the hold of the past. "Forget her, Sancho. What about the rancho? What about Wilkins?"

It was a foolish move. Despite his haggard appearance and damaged leg, Sancho was neither weak nor slow to react. His shoulders were solid, his arms knotted from years of being worked like a mule, his hands still so fast Paco never knew the knife was there until he felt the blade against his throat.

"*¿Qué dice, Paco?* Forget her?"

Paco didn't move, didn't breathe. Sancho was an artist with a knife. Paco had seen him cut a man to ribbons and still keep him alive for hours, and he knew the only way to survive was not to fight back. "*Hermano,*" he choked out, staring into glittering black eyes that were so like their father's it made his stomach clench. "It is me. Paco. Your brother."

Sancho thrust him away. "Half brother, *pendejo.* Do not forget." He sheathed his knife, then turned, his attention caught by activity at the rancho.

A woman came out the door in the courtyard wall. Paco couldn't see her face, but he recognized the lurching gait.

Sancho must have seen it, too. "*Puta,*" he spat out. "This time I kill her."

At a sound, both men turned to see a lanky, bearded man watching them from the boulders. "We gonna jaw all day or find someplace to hole up?"

There was a moment of confusion, as if Sancho didn't recognize Haskins, the mean-eyed Texan they'd recruited in a San Pedro cantina. Then his face cleared. "*Vámonos*," he said, shoving Paco ahead of him toward the waiting horses.

"Where we going?" Haskins asked as Sancho swung into the saddle.

Sancho gave a cackling laugh that made the skin between Paco's shoulder blades quiver. "To a place where even *el diablo* cannot find us."

Four

Moonlight filtering through tall pines lit the trail as Brady's weary horse clattered through a dry wash in front of Jamison's cabin. Because he approached from upwind, Brady wasn't prepared for what he found, and when the smell hit him, it triggered such an onslaught of images he went spinning backward in time.

Flames. The cabin. Inside, two bodies entwined like lovers, matching bullet holes in their foreheads. Outside, Jacob's voice rising into the fiery night sky. "Jesus God, what have I done?"

The horse shied, snapping the hold of the past. By the time Brady brought him under control, he realized the smoldering cabin wasn't the line shack at the ranch, and the bodies on the porch weren't those of Don Ramon and Maria Ramirez, but Lemuel Jamison and his wife.

Shaken, he leaned over to spit the stench of burnt flesh from his mouth, then reined the limping horse toward the trough. It had been riddled with bullets, and except for a scant inch of murky water, it was empty. The pump handle had been shot off, so Brady couldn't pump more. After scooping what he could with his hands, he let the horse suck up what was left as he looked around.

The timbers in the house were almost burned through, which meant the Jamisons had died at least a day before the stage was due. So whoever did this wasn't after the stage or its passengers, but something Jamison had, such as food or whiskey, horses, guns and ammunition.

Brady hunkered to study the ground. With the full moon almost directly overhead, he could see tracks in the damp earth around the trough—shod horses, shod men, the pinched-out butt of a Mexican cigarillo. Not Indians. White men or Mexicans.

Sancho. And this time he and Paco weren't alone. With a sense of urgency, Brady remounted and headed northeast.

The vegetation was sparse. The soil, comprised mostly of decomposed limestone and pale caliche, reflected back the bright moonlight, so it was like riding across a thin blanket of snow at dusk. He should make good time. If the horse got him as far as Blue Mesa, he'd find a way to make the last climbs on foot. He could be on his way back with a wagon by afternoon.

The horse gave out three hours later and well short of Blue Mesa. After slipping off the bridle, Brady left the crippled animal munching withered grass and started walking toward the notch that marked the south pass into the home valley.

The day warmed. The sun burning into his back and the heat rising off the ground made him feel like a chicken on a spit. By midmorning he knew he was in trouble; his feet felt like half-cooked meat and he wasn't sweating enough. Breaking off a prickly pear leaf, he cleared it of spines then settled in the shade of a scraggly mesquite to chew the moisture from the pulpy leaf.

He tried wiggling his toes. They didn't move, so swollen the creases in his new boots were stretched smooth. A mixed blessing. At least now the fit was snug enough to keep him from sliding around on the ooze from his popping blisters. After chewing the cactus dry, he spit out the pulp, then rose and started moving again.

Three miles. Five. Dirt caked in the dampness spreading along the sides of his boots. Every step sent pain shooting up his legs. The sun peaked, began the slow downward slide into the hottest time of the day.

He staggered on, his head pounding, his tongue thick as a brick. The cramps in his calves moved up into his thighs and it became a struggle to keep his mind on track. Landmarks seemed no nearer, as if he had been wandering in circles, and the thought came—at first no more than a whisper in the back of his mind, but growing more insistent with each lurching step—what if he had miscalculated? What if he didn't make it?

By the time he started the last climb, he'd lost feeling in his feet, his thighs were a mass of knotted, cramping muscles, and his vision was starting to waver. Squinting against sunlight ricocheting off a caliche outcrop, he studied the faint trail zigzagging up the steep slope. It seemed so far and he was so damned tired. Swaying with weariness, he closed his eyes against the glare. But the image of the trail remained imprinted in his mind, showing him what his sluggish brain had been slow to accept. Freshly turned earth, broken sage branches, flattened tufts of bunch grass. The trail had been used recently and by more than one rider.

Sancho.

His eyes flew open, and before reason could assert itself, he was charging up the slope. A hundred yards and the false strength gave out. He tripped, went down on his knees, then hung there, hands splayed against the hot ground, his head sagging between his trembling arms. After he caught his breath, he tried to push himself upright but couldn't balance. His legs gave out and he fell hard, driving the air from his lungs.

Maybe he slept. Maybe he passed out. At first all he knew was blackness. Then shapes appeared in the shadows of his mind, backlit against a fiery sky. The smell of fear and scorched flesh burned in his throat as a voice called his name.

With a gasp, he sat up, eyes wide, heart thudding.

A red-tailed hawk blinked back at him from a boulder thirty feet away. With a high-pitched "skree," it lifted off and the images faded, leaving behind a bitter taste like hot copper on the back of his tongue.

With a groan, he forced himself to his feet and started up the trail. At the top, late-afternoon sunlight hit him full in the face, almost blinding him. Chest heaving, terrified of what he might find, he staggered out onto the ledge and looked down.

RosaRoja spread below him. Safe. Whole.

Relief buckled his knees. He tilted. The last thing he saw as the ground rushed toward him was the pinched-out butt of a Mexican cigarillo.

IT WAS JUST AS PACO REMEMBERED IT—THE MEADOW DOT-ted with wildflowers, the clearwater creek, the ring of tall timber crowding the bluff. And above it, half-hidden behind a pile of boulders, the entrance to the cave.

Dread settled over him like a heavy cloak.

Telling the other three men to make camp, Sancho dismounted and motioned Paco to follow. The steep trail up to the cave was al-most gone, buried beneath a tangle of brush and grass and blocked in places where rocks had tumbled down over the years. It didn't slow Sancho. He tore at the overgrowth, kicked rocks aside, scrambled for new footholds. By the time he neared the top, he was almost running on all fours.

But Paco's feet dragged like they were weighted. A knot in his stom-ach grew tighter with every step. As he climbed higher, the sandstone arch became a mocking grin—the boulders, huge jagged teeth.

Sancho reached the top and turned. He shouted something and waved Paco on, then disappeared between the gaping jaws. Wishing he had the courage to run and leave this madman behind forever, Paco forced himself forward. At the entrance he paused, winded and sweat-ing. Somewhere in the darkness, water dripped. His heart responded to it, speeding up as if compelled to match the stronger rhythm.

Warily, he stepped inside. Blackness closed around him, bringing with it a smell—musty, rank—the smell of madness. Ten years, yet it seemed only yesterday that he had watched Sancho stumble through this same arch, his clothes singed, his hands blistered, and a look in his eyes that would make the devil cringe.

A cramp knifed through Paco's gut. He doubled over, one hand braced against the damp wall of the cave. *Madre de Dios.* He hated this place. He hated the smell of it, the thought of it. He hated Sancho for making him come back.

"*Mira, Paco.*"

Paco straightened as Sancho emerged from the darkness, holding a lantern high. "It still works." The play of light across his face gave his brows an upward slant and made his eyes look like they were lit from within. Paco shivered, wishing he hadn't given his mother's crucifix to that *puta* in Ruidoso.

"*Ven.*" Sancho turned back into the darkness of the cave.

On dragging feet, Paco followed.

The cave narrowed as they went deeper. Walls slanted in. Out of the darkness loomed the darker shadow of the tunnel entrance. Sancho ducked inside, taking the light with him. The sudden blackness sent Paco rushing after him. They had to bend almost double to clear the tunnel's low ceiling. Water dripped onto Paco's back. His boots slipped on mossy rocks. The air grew thick with the stink of fear and sweat and decay. Thirty more feet, a dogleg right, then the tunnel opened into an inner cavern twice as tall as it was wide. Deafened by the pounding of his heart, Paco straightened and looked around.

Maybe it would be all right. Maybe this time it would be different.

"I am back!"

Sancho's voice bounced off the rocky walls with such force Paco cringed, hands clamped over his ears. As he watched his half brother spin a circle, laughing, his arms wide, the lantern bobbing in his grip, hate churned in Paco's gut. He wanted to kill Sancho, tear out his throat so he would never have to listen to that laugh again.

So why didn't he?

Paco let his hands drop. An idea formed in his mind, familiar yet elusive, and gaining strength with every heartbeat. He took ahold of it, studying it from all angles, shaping it until it fit comfortably in his head.

Why didn't he?

Sancho's plan to raid the rancho would never work. Everyone in the territory knew of the bad blood between the Ramirez and Wilkins families. They would know it was Sancho. But if they did kill the Wilkins brothers, what would happen to the rancho then? Would it revert back to the old grant? Back to the Ramirez family? And if there was no one left from that family either, would it then fall to the closest blood kin—to Paco, the illegitimate son of Don Ramon Ramirez?

Paco chewed the corner of his mustache as he thought it out. They would have to make it look like an accident—say, in a fire or a landslide. And then Paco would have to kill Sancho and Elena. He could do that. Sancho had trained him well. It might even be fun.

Don Francisco. Don Francisco Ramirez, patrón de RosaRoja Rancho.

Paco smiled. He liked the sound of that.

BRADY BOLTED UPRIGHT, FULLY AWAKE AND MAD AS HELL BE-cause someone was pounding on the soles of his feet and someone else was licking his face.

Faces stared back at him—Jack, his usual grin turned upside down into a scowl—Consuelo, teary-eyed, clutching her medicine basket—Hank, looking fierce despite the worry in his dark brown eyes—and Bullshot, his mouth open in a toothy grin, his tail wagging more than his body did.

"What's wrong?" Thoughts of Sancho bounced through his mind.

"You're fried, that's what." Hank shoved a pitcher into his hands. "If Bullshot hadn't found you, you'd be jerky by now."

Brady tried to go slow but the water tasted too good, and by the time Hank wrestled the pitcher from his grip, he felt queasy. He didn't resist when his brother planted a beefy hand on his chest and shoved him back down. It was then Brady realized he was in his own bed and

Jack was cutting off his new boots. He started to protest, then the first boot came off and the sudden release of pressure sent blood pounding through his foot in such an agonizing rush, for a moment he couldn't even breathe. By the time they'd peeled away his socks and lathered the soles of his feet with Consuelo's slippery elm salve, he'd recovered enough to ask for more water.

"Let the other settle," Hank advised.

"It's settled. Give me the pitcher."

"You'll get sick if you take too much."

"Christ, man! I'm so dry my balls are rattling. Give me the damn pitcher."

Hank gave him the pitcher. Jack and Consuelo finished wrapping his feet, then Consuelo left, dragging Bullshot with her. Propping his feet on a folded blanket to ease the throbbing, Brady looked at his brothers. "Sancho's out."

They didn't seem surprised. "Sheriff Rikker told us," Jack said.

"Where's your horse?"

Leave it to Hank to worry more about the livestock than his older brother. Trapped in age between Brady and Jack, he was close to neither, preferring the predictability of a column of numbers or the quiet companionship of animals to the constant bickering of his brothers.

Brady told them about Bob, and his hike to the stopover, and how the stage broke an axle and ended up in the canyon below French Pass. He didn't go into any detail about the passengers except to say five people were waiting for him to bring help and three of them were injured.

Consuelo returned with tortillas, a big bowl of frijoles, and another pitcher of water. Between mouthfuls, Brady related what he found at Jamison's.

His brothers came to the same conclusion he had. Sancho.

Hank sighed. "So now it starts again."

Jack stared out the window. "Sometimes I hate this damn place."

No surprise there. But Brady didn't have time to get into it with

Jack. He could see the light was fading and knew he would have to leave soon. Her Ladyship expected him back over twelve hours ago.

"Rikker thought Sancho might head for Mexico instead of coming up this way," Hank said.

"He's already here." Brady set aside the bowl of beans, his stomach suddenly queasy. He told them about the tracks on the south slope and the pinched-out smoke he'd found on the ledge. "We need to be ready."

"We are." Jack listed their preparations. All hands were to ride in twos. In addition to the bunkhouse cook, Sandoval, two men would be at the house at all times. To protect against fire, water barrels and gunnysacks had been set throughout the house and brush had been cleared from around all the buildings. Extra ammunition, canteens, and a two-day ration kit had been issued to each rider.

"Good." Brady was relieved he didn't have to worry about preparing the ranch in case Sancho showed up. He needed to get the stage passengers situated first.

"Good? You approve?" Jack put on a show of surprise. "Hear that, Hank? He approves."

Ignoring him, Brady turned to Hank. "What about the Army herd?" Ever since snowmelt they'd been gathering cattle to meet the Indian Reservation beef contract the Army put out for bids every fall.

"We're bringing those in the tally closer in. Don't worry, they're under guard."

"Hell, he likes to worry," Jack muttered. "That and nag."

This time Brady let his irritation show. "I'm not nagging. I'm asking. There's a difference. Has anybody told Elena about Sancho?"

Jack swung back to the window.

Hank glanced from one brother to the other then shrugged. "She knows, but she won't leave her cabin."

"She has to," Brady said. "Tell her she won't be safe out there alone."

Jack turned with a smile that didn't reach his gunmetal blue eyes. "Why don't you tell her, Big Brother? I'm sure she'll come running when she hears you're hurt."

"Damnit, Jack—"

"We don't have time for this," Hank cut in with that edgy tone he used whenever Brady and Jack butted heads. On the rare occasions he allowed himself to be drawn into their arguments, he usually responded with a ferocious burst of impatience that left someone other than himself bruised, or bleeding, or both.

Jack the hothead, Brady the hardhead, and Hank the reluctant peacekeeper caught between. It was a long-standing family joke, but Brady had stopped laughing years ago. "Somebody needs to tell her."

When Jack didn't volunteer, Hank muttered something, then sighed. "I'll tell her."

"She'll take it hard, so be nice," Brady warned.

"I'm always nice, damnit."

Brady allowed that most of the time he was. Hank wasn't mean-hearted; he just preferred being around creatures that didn't feel the need to muddy a fine day with a lot of words or emotion.

With a yawn, Brady slumped back. Fatigue hummed along his nerves. Hot bursts of pain jumped across his shoulders and into the back of his head. Maybe if he rested just a few minutes . . .

But as soon as he closed his eyes, a face appeared—whiskey colored eyes, cinnamon freckles, wild chestnut hair. *Christ.*

"I have to go. They're waiting." He started up.

Hank pushed him back down. "We'll take care of it. Tell us what you need."

Brady told him to load the hay wagon with a water barrel, blankets, food, lanterns, and Consuelo's medicine basket. "And Hank," he called as his brother started for the door. "I want Buck on shotgun and at least two, maybe three, riders with us. Whoever you can spare."

Hank nodded and left, his heavy footfalls sending vibrations through the plank floor.

"You're going back there tonight?" Jack asked, turning from the window.

"They won't make it another day." Muscles twitched and jerked as Brady pressed the heels of his hands against his stinging eyes. "Besides, I gave her my word."

Damn. Realizing his mistake, he lowered his hands to find Jack watching him. Hoping to avoid more questions, he quickly added, "Send a rider for Doc and Rikker and tell the Overland office what happened."

"You're bringing the passengers back here?"

Brady yawned. His lids felt heavy as stone. "Val Rosa's too far." He felt like he was sinking under water. "Wake me . . . later."

HE AWOKE TO FULL DARK AND A GENTLE TOUCH ON HIS BROW. He started up, then the pain hit, and he flopped back with a curse.

"Shh," a soft voice said. "Rest."

Cracking open one eye, he saw the familiar face that was so stunningly beautiful it never failed to take his breath away. "Elena." She had her rosary out. Did that mean he was dying?

Her smile told him no. "What have you done to yourself this time, *pobrecito*?"

Before he could answer, footsteps sounded in the hall.

Jack came through the doorway. When he saw Elena, he stopped. "Hope I'm not interrupting," he said in a cold voice.

Elena's smile faded. She rose. With a hand braced on the back of her chair for balance, she turned toward the doorway. "I will go."

"Stay," Brady ordered, bringing her to a halt. He glared at his brother, but said nothing, knowing it would only upset Elena if he did. Despite his self-professed reputation as a backdoor Romeo and an expert on women, Jack could be dumber than cordwood sometimes. "Get me a fresh shirt," he told his brother.

Grabbing a shirt off a peg beside the door, he tossed it toward the bed. "Wagon's loaded. Putnam's gone for Doc and Sheriff Rikker. Everybody's ready but you."

Biting back a groan, Brady pulled himself upright. Joints popped in protest. The rank aftertaste of frijoles bubbled in his throat. But when his feet touched the floor, any lingering numbness left his mind. "Jesus!" He stared down at his throbbing feet. Consuelo must have wrapped them in a dozen yards of cotton sacking. All that showed were the tips of his blistered toes, and they looked like venison sausages. It would be a month before he got boots on again.

Moving gingerly, he removed one shirt and pulled on the other. "Elena, I want you to move into the house for a while," he said as he buttoned. "And not just because of Sancho. I'm bringing the passengers back here. There's a woman—three women." As he tossed the dirty shirt into the corner beside his bloodstained boots, he saw Jack frowning at him. "They might feel better having another female around."

"I will be glad to help." Elena limped toward the door, then hesitated. "Be careful," she said, glancing at Jack, then quickly away. "Both of you."

A FEW MINUTES LATER THE WAGON LUMBERED OUT THE gate, Brady resting against the side rails in back, Buck and Jack sitting up front. Three other men rode with them—Rufus on point, Abe on drag, and Rodriquez on the east ridge—all armed to the teeth. Luckily it was another cloudless night and the moon was up early. By Brady's calculation, they should reach the canyon just before dawn.

Hoping to get some rest, he stretched out and closed his eyes, but Jack started in before they cleared the first rise. "So who's the woman?"

Brady kept his eyes closed, pretending sleep.

"What woman?" Ru asked, reining his sorrel beside the wagon.

"The one my brother won't talk about."

"Boss has a woman? The hell you say!"

Brady wondered why he sounded so surprised. Just because he didn't chase after everything in skirts didn't mean he didn't like women. He liked them fine. More than fine. But unlike these pudknockers, he had responsibilities and a ranch to run. He couldn't afford to let his cock do his thinking for him.

"Brady says three of the passengers are women," One-Track-Jack said.

"Three! The hell you say!"

With a silent curse, Brady opened his eyes and sat up. Realizing where Jack was headed, he tried to head him off. "In El Paso I met a man from Australia. Sydney, I think it was."

Jack went for it like a bull trout after a mayfly. "Australia? Did he say anything about the Blue Mountains? I read they're so misty it's like riding through clouds."

Buck wasn't as easy to fool. He turned and gave Brady a thoughtful look, although he didn't say anything. He rarely did. His wife, Iantha, said the man was so tight-mouthed it was a wonder he didn't starve to death. Mostly he let his eyes do the talking, and right now they were asking Brady why he would bring up such a sore subject when it was well known the two brothers couldn't talk about Australia without squaring off. But Brady ignored Buck and let Jack ramble on about kookaburras, wallabies, and koalas—whatever the hell they were. He knew no matter how much Jack wanted to emigrate, he wouldn't leave until this thing with Sancho was finished. So for now, he just let him talk.

Buck faced forward again. Jack moved on to tales of sheep stations a hundred miles across, wild dingoes, and an animal named Joey that could perch on its tail and box like a man with its back feet. The kid would believe anything.

Relieved to be out of his little brother's sights for a while, Brady settled back again.

Somewhere on the ridge a coyote yipped, was answered by another, then another. Brady hoped Her Ladyship had enough firewood for tonight and wished he'd shown her how to use his repeater. He didn't want another death on his conscience. He had one too many as it was.

He thought about all the lives that depended on him. Dozens of good people—a family. Ru, who'd been orphaned at the age of ten and had been with them ever since. Abe, who fancied himself a gunfighter until he saw up close the damage a bullet could do. Red, one of the many displaced children from the war. And Buck. Especially Buck.

His gaze drifted toward the man who had been his mainstay ever since his father died. He noted the frailness of bony shoulder blades where muscle used to be, the kinky whiteness of hair that had once been coal black, and he wondered what he would do when Buck was gone, too. The thought awakened those same feelings of panic he'd felt a decade ago when he'd first taken up the reins of RosaRoja and realized how heavy that burden would be.

Buck had been there through it all, ever since he and Iantha had fled the South. Rather than be sold apart, they had run west until they hooked up with Jacob in late '48 and Buck started scouting for the Missouri Volunteers during the war with Mexico. He was there when Jacob found RosaRoja and paid the back taxes to get it—there when Jacob almost lost it over another man's wife—and there when Jacob died. Through all those hard years, Buck had never faltered in his loyalty to Jacob.

"A man don' turn agin' his own, nawsuh," he would say, trying to get Brady to make his peace with his father before it was too late. "If he do, he only hurt hisself."

But Brady had been too overwhelmed by the responsibility of RosaRoja and his brothers to pay heed. He had been too angry, too afraid of what he might find if he dug too deep. Then Sam died. And when he laid his youngest brother's body to rest, Brady buried with him any hope of reconciling with his father. There were some things a man could never forgive.

It had been ten years since the night of the fire when Don Ramon and Maria died and Jacob suffered a fit that had left him mute and paralyzed. Ten years since Sancho went to prison. Ten years of wondering what really happened. Brady never spoke of that night, never told his brothers what he suspected their father had done—why burden them with that poisonous knowledge? And when he buried Jacob beside Sam and his mother and baby sister, he thought he was shutting that door forever.

But now it was opening again.

Who would he bury next?

A voice broke through his dark thoughts and he looked over to see Ru grinning at him over the side rail. "Tell me about the women. I ain't had my turnip tweaked in a month."

Brady sighed. "Just an old lady and her daughter, and a widow-lady."

"How old's the daughter?"

"You wouldn't like her. She reads."

"What about the widow-lady?"

Jack smirked at him from the driver's box. "Yeah, Brady. Tell us about the widow-lady."

"I suspect she reads, too." Where else would she learn to use so many words to say so little?

Pulling his penknife from his pocket, Brady worked at a broken cactus spine in his thumb.

"What else?" Abe asked, moving up alongside Ru.

Brady felt cornered. "She's got a lot of rules." None of which made much sense. "And I think she might have weak lungs."

"You mean little tits?"

The blade jerked, nicking his cuticle. Carefully he folded the knife and slipped it back into his pocket, then wiped the blood on his pants. "No, I mean weak lungs. Like asthma."

"So her tits are all right?" Abe persisted.

Brady swung toward him. "Aren't you supposed to be riding drag?"

"Yessir."

Brady looked at him.

Abe dropped back.

Ru took his place. "Maybe she's snaggle-toothed."

"And aren't you supposed to ride point?"

"Rodriquez is."

"Hope she's not wall-eyed," Jack mused. "A wall-eyed woman's hard to lie to."

"You would know," Brady muttered, wondering why he'd ever allowed this conversation to start in the first place.

"What color's her hair?" Ru asked.

Oiled red oak, threaded with gold. "Red, I think."

"That's trouble." Ru straightened and shook his head. "Next to a whistler, a redheaded woman is the worse kind."

"I heard women with gold teeth were," Jack argued.

"You're thinking of tattoos. They're the worse worst."

Peckerheads. Brady closed his eyes and drifted to sleep.

Five

It was almost dawn when they rolled down the rut-
ted track into the canyon. Brady noticed the stench of rotten meat first,
then the absence of firelight. As they neared the half-eaten carcasses,
low-slung shadows scattered through the brush and wide-winged birds
took to the air. The teams sidestepped and snorted, forcing Jack to
jump down and lead them past the overturned coach.

The Kinderly girl ran to meet them, waving a sage branch like a
sword until she spotted Brady in the back of the wagon. Then she burst
into tears and ran back around the coach where they could hear her
yelling to her mother.

No sign of Her Ladyship.

Brady lit a lantern. Ignoring the burning pain in his feet, he slid
from the rear of the wagon and limped toward the two figures stretched
on the ground beside the ashes of a cold campfire. As he drew closer,
he could see it was three figures, not two, and none was moving. Cursing under his breath, he knelt. Reaching past Oran, he checked the

Englishwoman's neck for a pulse. Weak but steady. Her skin felt hot. Oran's was cold.

The railroader didn't rouse when Brady checked his wound. Infected, but no red streaks. After smearing Consuelo's salve on a fresh handkerchief, he rebandaged then had Jack and Ru carry the unconscious man to the wagon. Then he turned to Her Ladyship.

She didn't move or open her eyes, even when he dribbled water on her cracked lips or picked her up and carried her to the wagon. The extra weight on his raw feet hurt like a sonofabitch, but he preferred doing it himself rather than allow anyone else to handle her. He wasn't sure why.

After the passengers were settled in the back of the wagon, Jack and Buck loaded luggage while Ru and Abe laid Oran beside Bodine, covering him with rocks to keep scavengers at bay until Overland took both bodies to Val Rosa for proper burials. Just after dawn, with the rising sun backlighting the ridges like a distant fire, they turned toward home.

It was a quiet trip. The old lady and her daughter huddled in one corner while Ashford tossed and muttered in the other. Her Ladyship slept straight through. With barely enough room to stretch out his legs and prop up his feet, Brady rode sandwiched between valises and Her Ladyship, who was radiating so much heat it was like lying next to a slow fire. In some ways, it reminded him of when he was a kid and a howling Missouri snowstorm would drive his little brothers into his bed—Jack, sharp knees and icy feet on one side, Hank, hot as banked coals on the other.

But in other ways, it made him damned uncomfortable.

He didn't like feeling responsible for her, or worrying about her, or wondering who she was running from and why. He didn't want all the complications she brought.

But he did like the way she made him laugh.

He looked down at her, amazed that such a small head could grow so much hair. It was everywhere, an undisciplined tangle of curls so silky-fine they caught on anything in reach—the straw, the blanket, the stubble of his beard. He wondered what it would feel like running through his fingers.

He'd never known a woman like her. She was a puzzle he couldn't fit in his mind—too many contradictions, too many unanswered questions. And sometimes, when she was afraid or in pain and trying hard not to show it, when she looked at him with those whiskey brown eyes, it was Sam all over again. And for one shocking and desperate moment Brady had to fight the urge to grab hold of her and promise this time he would find a way to fix it and make everything right again.

But she wasn't Sam. And some things could never be fixed.

The afternoon sun had leached the color from the sky by the time they crossed under the wrought iron arch a quarter mile from the house. Bullshot ran to meet them, making the team hop as he darted between their legs. Two horses stood at the hitching rail in the yard— Doc's calf-kneed gelding and a big buckskin Brady didn't know. As they stopped before the house, Hank came onto the porch followed by Consuelo and several ranch hands.

"Any trouble?" Brady called.

"Not a sign." Hank's gaze swept the passengers then backtracked when he saw the Kinderly girl gawking at him. He looked away, a flush rising above his beard.

Brady directed two hands to take the Kinderly women to one of the two upstairs bedrooms. "Where's Doc?" he asked as Hank tromped down the steps.

"Coming. Sheriff Rikker's here, too. Wants to talk to you."

"Later." Relieved to see Doc's round form emerge from the house, Brady rose on his knees and gently nudged Her Ladyship. "We're here."

She didn't respond.

Doc lifted the railroader's bandage. "Sweet Mary." After sending Consuelo to boil needles and a tube of horsehair ligatures, he directed Abe and Ru to carry the unconscious man to the other upstairs bedroom. Then he peered through the side rails at Her Ladyship. "What do you have there, lad?"

Hank crowded in, his head and half his chest visible above Doc's sparse white hair.

"A knot on her head and hardly any food or water for two days." As he spoke, Brady motioned for Hank to come to the back of the wagon. "Carry her inside. And be careful." The warning wasn't necessary. Although Hank was the biggest in the family—hell, the biggest for a hundred miles—he was also the gentlest, especially with anything helpless. But cross him, or lie to him, or get his temper up, and he became unstoppable. Both Brady and Jack had the scars to prove it.

Hank carefully lifted her from the back of the wagon. She hung like a rag doll in his arms, her long chestnut hair fanning across Hank's muscular thighs as he carried her toward the house.

"Put her in my room," Brady called after him.

"Won't that be cozy," Jack muttered, jumping down from the driver's box.

Brady ignored him and tossed valises out of the back of the wagon to men waiting to carry them inside.

Doc studied the wrappings on Brady's feet. "What about you, boyo?"

"I'll keep. Tend the woman. And Doc." Brady stopped tossing and motioned the old man closer so Jack wouldn't hear. "You probably should know she's breeding."

Doc reared back. "Breeding? Faith, are you saying the lass is pregnant?"

Brady winced. It was obvious from the way Jack stared at them that he'd heard Doc's announcement. Hell, anyone within fifty yards heard it.

"Jasus!" Doc hurried up the steps. "Sure, and leave it to a woman to complicate things."

Brady tossed out the last of the luggage, then let his legs dangle off the end of the wagon while he mustered the courage to put his weight on his bandaged feet. The numbing effect of Consuelo's salve had long worn off.

Jack leaned against the rear wheel and studied him. "Two days and already breeding. No wonder you want her in your room."

"Don't start." Teeth clenched, Brady eased to the ground. As soon as his feet touched dirt, pain exploded up his legs.

"I'm surprised, though," Jack went on as Brady struggled to catch his breath. "Didn't think you had it in you, Big Brother. Or in her either."

Fueled by pain, Brady's anger ignited. Without thinking, he swung out, catching Jack on the side of the head with a backhand that knocked his hat askew and sent him staggering for balance. "Watch your mouth," he snarled. "This isn't one of your cantina whores and I won't let you drag her through the dirt to get at me. Understand?"

Jack gaped, a hand cupped to his ear. Then fury twisted his face. "You moralistic bastard! I'm not the one treating women like whores, stashing them all over the house!"

Brady frowned, confused.

Jack reared back. "You forgot about Elena, didn't you? Or did you plan to jump from one to the other, you sonofabitch!" His fists came up, and he would have started swinging if Elena hadn't come out of the house.

"No!"

Jack froze, arm cocked. He glared at the woman on the porch.

"*Por favor*, Jackson. Do not do this. He is your brother."

Brady watched the battle his brother waged. He recognized it, understood it, but couldn't say the words that would ease Jack's mind.

Jack let his arm drop. "Go to hell. Both of you." His back stiff with anger, he whirled and stalked toward the barn.

Brady hobbled onto the porch, every step burning as if he walked on hot nails. Elena hovered beside him, wanting to help but mostly getting in the way. By the time he'd settled into the oversized rocker his mother had carted all the way from Missouri, his stomach was cramping from pain. Elena helped him prop his feet up on the railing and almost immediately the throbbing eased.

"You need to tell him, Elena," he said after he caught his breath.

"Soon." She gave him a sad, wistful smile. "But I am not yet ready to leave, *comprendes*?"

"You don't have to leave. This is as much your home as ours."

She spread her hands in a helpless gesture. "But how could I stay if he did not want me?" When he started to argue, she shook her head. "No, *querido*. We have said it all many times before. I will speak soon. But now, I must help Consuelo."

As Brady watched her limp into the house, all the regrets and guilt and love he felt for this beautiful, damaged woman settled like a stone in his chest. One more thing he couldn't fix. With a weary sigh, he tipped back his head and closed his eyes and tried not to think of how empty the place would be if Jack emigrated and Elena left and Hank struck out on his own. Why was it, the harder he fought to hold his family together, the faster it threatened to split apart?

He must have dozed. When he opened his eyes again, Sheriff Rikker was leaning against the porch post, thumbs hooked in his gun belt, watching him.

"You look like hell, son." Rikker was slightly more talkative than Buck—a quiet seeker, as patient as a faro dealer and as persistent as a bad tooth. Brady knew him to be a fair man not given to rash impulses or hasty decisions, a man whose single-minded dedication to the law had brought him great respect but few close friends. Except for Jacob.

Rikker eyed Brady's bandaged feet. "Been dancing with my wife?"

"You don't have a wife."

"No? Then I guess we're both lucky." The older man pulled the makings from his vest pocket and worked at rolling a smoke. It was a task. With his gnarly hands and sideways fingers, he spilled more than he rolled. After sealing the paper with a lick, he lit it, drew deep, then exhaled on a long sigh. "So what happened?" he asked through a cloud of smoke.

Brady told him about the coach crashing, and how when he went for help, he found Jamison and his wife dead in their cabin but no sign of their son.

"What were you doing so far from the ranch?"

"Heading home from El Paso. I was scouting those white-faced crossbreeds McPherson is so proud of. Twenty percent higher yield, he says. Thinks they'll be in high demand once the railroads come in, since they'll travel better than longhorns." He realized he was rambling and was grateful for the distraction when Bullshot bounded onto the porch and tried to climb into his lap. He wrestled the hound off, and under his stroking hand the dog finally settled against his knee, tongue lolling, mouth open in a sloppy grin.

Rikker thumbed a head of ash off his smoke. "The Jamison boy stumbled into Val Rosa last night. Scared to hell. Said there were five of them, led by a Mex with a bad knee."

"Sancho."

"Maybe. Figured I'd ride by after I leave here. Anything you want to tell me before I go?"

Brady felt like he was slipping back in time into the same conversation they'd had ten years earlier. Every word, every gesture, seemed the same—him in the rocker, Rikker smoking at the rail, and the smell of roses and charred meat hanging all around them in the still air. "I've told you all there is to tell." Which were the same words he'd said that morning when he'd ridden in with Sancho and Paco in tow.

He hadn't exactly lied to Rikker back then, but he hadn't told him the whole of it either—not about what Jacob had said before he fell unconscious in front of the burning cabin, or his own doubts about his father's part in the deaths of Don Ramon and Maria. After his fit, Jacob had been as good as dead anyway, and Sancho already had so many marks against him, one more hadn't mattered. So Brady had kept his silence, hoping to save himself the lie. Like Buck said, a man didn't turn against his own.

In the end, Rikker had drawn his own conclusions; Sancho had gone to one prison, while Jacob rotted in his own, with none but Brady the wiser. Yet even after ten years, the uncertainty of what really happened that night still stuck like a burr in Brady's throat. Did Jacob kill Don Ramon and Maria, or did Sancho? Would he ever know?

Rikker watched a small dust devil spiral across the yard, then sighed and pinched out his smoke. "Should have killed that bastard ten years ago." He flicked the butt into the roses, then turned to study Brady. "But neither of us could have done that, could we, son?"

Brady gave Bullshot's ear a scratch then looked up, careful to keep his eyes steady, his face without expression. He could feel the older man stalking him with his mind, and wondered if the sheriff guessed his doubts.

Rikker looked away first. He rubbed a knuckle across the gray stubble under his chin then sighed like a man who had searched so long and hard to find answers, he had forgotten what the questions were. "Reckon it's a hard thing, killing a man in cold blood, no matter how much he deserves it. Sometimes it's easier to just let the cards ride. Ain't that so, son?"

"We playing poker here, Sheriff?"

Rikker showed tobacco-yellowed teeth in a crooked grin. "Hell no, boy. Your daddy taught me years ago not to bet against a Wilkins."

"I'm glad to hear that." Brady pinned the older man with a look that said their little game was over. "Because this time when I find Ramirez, I'll kill him. Just so you know."

Rikker studied him a moment, then gave a rueful smile. "Sometimes, Brady, you're so like your daddy you scare me. He was hard to read, too. Guess that's what made him a good poker player." Something in Brady's expression caused his smile to fade. A sad look came into his eyes. "That was a compliment, son. Your daddy was a good man. He might have made mistakes, but he always tried to do the right thing."

At one time Brady had thought so, too.

Rikker pushed away from the post. "I'll let Overland know you've got the passengers. They'll probably want you to keep them here until they're well enough to travel. They'll pay for their keep." He clumped down the steps toward the buckskin hitched to the rail. "I'll be sending trackers after Sancho. See you don't get caught in the crossfire."

Not long after Rikker left, Doc came onto the porch. He looked worried, his bushy white eyebrows drawn in a scowl above his red-veined pickle of a nose.

"Well?" Brady asked.

Doc let his medical satchel drop to the plank floor with a thud, then looked around for a chair. The only one with all its parts was loaded down with seed catalogs. He tipped it forward to clear the seat, then sat. "Well, the lad with the hole in his side lost a lot of blood, but I'm thinking he'll make it. You did a good job there, boyo. The old lady has a simple sprain, and her daughter has naught but scratches and bruises. The redhead is sunburned, dehydrated, and bruised to hell." Leaning over, he opened his satchel and rummaged inside. "She's also running a fever and holding water. Could be uremia." He sat back with a grin and a flask.

"What's that mean? She's not dying, is she?" Brady pictured her doing battle with that hair wad, then later doing battle with him. The woman had too much spirit to die.

"I'm not knowing that, lad," Doc said as he worked the stopper loose. "But if we can get her fever down, get some fluids into her, and keep her quiet and off her feet for a while, I'm thinking she'll make it." He held the flask high. "Here's to Mick Flanagan, may he rest in peace, the manky bastard." Tipping his head back, he took a long swallow.

"And her baby?"

Doc shuddered and dragged his sleeve across his watery eyes. "If she doesn't start her labors too soon, they should be fine." He offered the flask.

Brady ignored it. "They?"

"Unless she's got a heart murmur, boyo, I'm thinking the lass is carrying twins." Doc recorked then dropped the flask back into his satchel. "But don't say anything for now. I'll have to read up on it to be sure. I must have a book about it somewhere."

Twins? Brady knew double births were good for cattle and bad for horses, but he wasn't sure about humans. "Is that a good thing? Twins?"

Doc shrugged. "Never delivered twins myself. But since she won't be going anywhere for the next three months, I'll have plenty of time to study on it."

Brady reared back. "Three months?"

"She sure as hell can't travel, boyo." Doc must have read Brady's shock and dismay. "Would it be so bad having a pretty face to rest your eyes on?"

"It's not that, it's . . . well, she's . . ." In his agitation, Brady couldn't find words to express all the conflicting thoughts in his mind. "Have you *talked* to her?" Five minutes in the woman's company was enough to give any right-thinking man hives. How was he to manage three months?

"She's unconscious," Doc reminded him.

Three months. "She's not going to like it."

"She won't have a choice."

"She'll like that even less." Brady pictured her propped in his bed like the Queen of England, wearing some frilly night thing, expecting everyone to wait on her, while he . . .

Hmm . . .

Her Ladyship. In his bed. In his house, living under his rules and his watchful eye. Just thinking about all the possibilities made him smile. He would have to hide her umbrella.

It wasn't until Doc went inside to find something to eat that Brady realized he hadn't asked Rikker if he'd seen any posters about a lost Englishwoman with red hair.

He wondered if he should.

Then decided he wouldn't.

Like the sheriff said, sometimes it's easier to just let the cards ride.

Six

THIRST AWOKE HER.

Like a voice shrieking inside her head, it overrode everything, pulled her away from the safe cocoon of numbness into the chaos of light and sound and pain.

Her head hurt. Her throat burned. Every nerve and cell in her body screamed for water.

With a groan, she opened her eyes.

Shadows and soft golden light. She blinked, but still everything seemed fuzzy and indistinct. Was she drugged? After a moment her vision cleared enough that she saw it was night and the room was lit by a kerosene lamp on a table beside the bed. Whose room? Whose bed?

It should have mattered, but it didn't.

And that should have distressed her, but it didn't.

All she could think of was the baby.

Lifting a trembling hand, she pressed it to her abdomen. Round and hard. Movement beneath her palm. Still there. Still alive. Relief stole her strength. She sank into the pillows as jumbled images flashed in her mind, so distorted and disturbing she couldn't distinguish what was real from what was not.

She heard a soft, muffled sound. A snore.

With painful slowness she lifted her head to see feet at the end of her bed—not hers but a man's—crossed at the ankles and resting atop the counterpane. Huge feet, unshod and wrapped in dusty bandages so only the tips of red swollen toes showed. Her gaze moved slowly up long legs clad in worn denim to equally huge hands clasped loosely across a lean waist. His shoulders outspanned the width of the chair in which he slouched. He slept, his head tipped back, his jaw slack beneath the thick black mustache.

He needed tending. His dark hair was overlong and it looked as if he hadn't shaved in days. A disreputable, formidable-looking man. One who should have frightened her, but didn't.

She frowned, realizing she knew that face, those work-worn hands. But how? And why was he in her room? She studied him, this stranger who was not a stranger, while half-formed memories drifted through her sluggish mind. When no answers came, she scanned the room, trying to fit the pieces of the puzzle together.

It was a man's room, unadorned and filled with masculine clutter— a fleece-lined jacket hooked over one bedpost, a dusty black hat on the other. Leather leggings hung from a peg behind the door. Propped in one corner stood a well-oiled rifle, and on the floor beside it sat a pair of stained boots that had been cut open along the inside seam. On the dark, heavily carved bureau stood a half-empty bottle of amber liquid—whisky, no doubt—and a china bowl bearing an inch-wide chip on the rim. A straight razor and shaving mug rested beside it, and on the wall above it hung a tarnished mirror in an ornate, equally tarnished silver frame. The walls were bare adobe with intricate tile work at the floor and crown. The deep-set window boasted neither drape nor shutter.

His room. It might not have been designed by the man dozing at the foot of her bed, but she was certain this was where he slept. Alone.

No woman resided here. If one ever had, it had been so long ago or of such short duration, she had left no feminine mark behind.

Then why did the scent of roses hang so thick and sweet in the still air?

She glanced back to the man at her feet. "Who are you?" she asked, her throat so dry her voice was little more than a whisper.

He jerked. His head came up, gaze wide and searching. The instant those turquoise eyes met hers, storm gates opened and memories flooded her mind. "It's you."

He pulled himself upright, wincing as he lowered his feet to the floor. "Thirsty?" he asked, rising to retrieve a dented metal pitcher and tin cup from a chest at the end of the bed.

At the thought of water, her throat constricted. "Please."

He poured, then shuffled toward her. But rather than give her the filled cup when she reached for it, he leaned over and slid one thick arm under her shoulders to support her in a half-sitting position. Even that small movement sent waves of dizziness surging through her head.

As he pressed the rim of the cup against her lips, she caught the scent of smoke and leather and cotton cloth dried in the sun. "Go slow," he said.

Placing her hands over his, she gulped greedily until he pulled the cup away. After he lowered her back to the pillows, he set the cup on the table beside the pitcher, then returned to the chair. He sat back, watching her. His stillness was complete, yet the air around him seemed to hum with an energy she couldn't define. He made her uneasy in a wholly unfamiliar way.

And yet here she was in his room, in his bed, as if it were the most natural thing in the world.

"You came back," she said, feeling so faint she could scarce keep open her eyes.

"I said I would."

She smiled sleepily. A man who actually kept his word. She should write to the archbishop. "It took you long enough."

"I had problems."

She tried to smirk. It made her lips sting. When she touched them with her tongue, she felt cracked skin and greasy ointment. "I thought I was dying." Just the memory of it made her heart pound. Blinking hard, she watched lacy cobwebs flutter along the overhead beams and tried not to think about that long hideous night when the smell of death was so thick it coated her throat, and she lay in shivering terror, listening to the crunch and growl of feasting scavengers and wondering when they would brave the dying fire and come for her. "Mr. Phelps died."

"I know."

"The others?"

"Recovering."

That jolt of relief again. They were alive. She was alive. Victoria was alive. They'd survived because of this man. Battling tears again, she turned her head toward him. "Thank you."

He nodded, his face betraying nothing. But those eyes . . .

Suddenly it was too much. Her mind couldn't take it all in. Weariness pulled her down toward the smothering darkness where snarling shadows and snapping jaws waited. *No . . . I don't want to go.* Terrified, she reached out, straining for the light.

A hand closed over hers. "You're all right. You're okay." The palm was broad and warm and rough with calluses. Solid. Safe. Her talisman against the dark.

Desperate for the contact, she clutched it with both hands, tucking it close to her heart.

Safely anchored, she surrendered to the dark.

FOR A LONG TIME BRADY DIDN'T MOVE, SO RATTLED BY WHAT she'd done and where his hand was, he wasn't sure what to do. He tried not to notice the warmth, the softness against his fingers. Instead he studied her face, marveling again at the delicate features that hid such surprising strength.

She was a conundrum, this woman who plagued his thoughts. Like a swan in the desert, or a rose in a burned-out draw, she was unexpected and unexplainable and so disconcertingly beautiful it made him forget how to think. With his free hand, he gently loosened a long strand of red-gold hair stuck to her cheek. At least she had been beautiful before the sun left crusty blisters across her nose and lips, and Consuelo's salve left greasy clumps matted in her hair.

"She is better?"

He turned to see Elena in the doorway. "Somewhat." Pulling his hand from Her Ladyship's grip, he wiped his palm down his thigh and sat back. "The fever broke just before dawn. She woke up long enough to take some water."

"*Gracias a Dios*." Elena limped to the bed, her rosary twined through her fingers. "She looks better. I prayed she would recover." She slanted a look at him. "You were here all night?"

"A few hours." He bent to adjust the wrappings around his foot, avoiding Elena's sharp gaze. "Consuelo looked ready to drop, so I sent her to bed." He straightened. "Besides, with these feet, I can't do anything but sit around."

"Have you told her about *los gemelos*?"

Brady shook his head. "Doc wants to wait. Just to be sure."

"Two babies." A wistful look crossed Elena's face. "*Una mujer afortunada*."

She didn't *look* lucky, Brady thought, studying the exhausted woman in his bed. But she was alive, and her babies were alive, and luck probably played as big a part in that as his worrying or Elena's praying had.

"Shall I bring Consuelo?" she asked.

Brady shook his head. "Let her sleep. But there is something you could do." He gave her his biggest grin, even though he knew it didn't work on Elena like it seemed to on the Englishwoman. "You could get me something to eat."

Elena rolled her eyes. But she went for food, so maybe the Wilkins smile worked on her after all.

He stretched the kinks in his back, rubbed a hand over his gritty eyes, then leaned over and blew out the lamp. The rosy glow of dawn filled the window. He sat listening to the ranch awaken—cattle bawling as they headed to the river, the nicker of horses anxious to be fed, the chatter of birdsong and chickens, the low voices of his men as they moved to the cookhouse and the day's first bitter cup of coffee. Familiar, reassuring sounds that were so much a part of his life he couldn't imagine a day without them. This was what he knew, what he understood and was comfortable with.

His gaze swung back to the woman in his bed.

This woman didn't fit that. She didn't belong here any more than he belonged at an English tea party, and it was a waste of time and energy to think different.

He had three months to convince himself of that.

WHEN JESSICA OPENED HER EYES, THE ROOM WAS BRIGHT with sunlight and she was perspiring beneath a thin quilt.

He was still sitting there, hunched over his bent leg, trying to peek under the bandages on his foot. He must have felt her gaze because he abruptly looked up. Seeing she was awake, he lowered his foot and grinned. "About time. Thirsty?"

She blinked, stunned all over again by the remarkable change in his face when he smiled. He should do that more often. Or perhaps not. She was dizzy enough as it was. "Yes, please."

The earlier ritual repeated itself. Once she'd taken her fill and he'd eased her gently back onto the pillows, the cobwebs in her mind had thinned. "What happened to your feet?" she asked, her voice sounding scratchy and hoarse in her own ear.

"Rubbed to a nub going for help. You hungry?"

She shook her head. Her stomach was still trying to settle the water. "Where am I?" *And why are you in my room and how did I get into my nightclothes?*

"The ranch. Consuelo might have some soup. I could ask."

"Consuelo?"

"She tends house and cooks for me and my brothers. She'll probably tend you from now on."

"Who's tending me now?" *And why do I need tending?*

"Lots of people." He bent to scratch under his bandage.

"*Lots* of people? What people?" Instinctively her hand went to her abdomen. "What's wrong with me?"

She must have shouted it because his head flew up, his aqua eyes wide and alarmed. "Calm down. You're all right. You've been sick for a while, that's all."

"Sick with what? For how long?"

"Fever. Three days." When she started to speak again, he held up a hand to stop her. "Doc's coming this afternoon. Save it for him." He started to rise. "I'll see if Consuelo—"

"Wait." There were still too many questions, too many fears. She wasn't ready to face them alone—even though she was growing desperate for a chamber pot and some privacy.

He sank back down, but his expression was that of a man poised to bolt.

"Are the other passengers here as well?"

"Yes." He didn't seem pleased by that.

"Mr. Ashford is recovering?"

"For now."

"Maude Kinderly?"

This time she had no doubt of his irritation. "Still alive, but I'm thinking of shooting her if her daughter doesn't get around to it."

At her shocked reaction, he sighed. "That's a joke. Anything else?"

She cast about for a way to delay his departure, unsure why keeping him near was so important. Perhaps because he was a familiar face. Or because his solid presence was a barrier against the terrors that threatened. Or because she had lost good sense altogether. "Are your brothers here, too?" If so, it must be a large house to accommodate so many people. Which made her wonder where Mr. Wilkins slept if she now resided in his room, and why she was in his room and not a clinic if she was so ill she needed tending. Feeling a headache build, she pressed fingertips to her temple. Dare she ask if they had indoor plumbing?

"They won't bother you if you don't show fear. Or dangle raw meat at them."

Lowering her hand, she stared at him.

"That's another joke. Don't they have jokes in England?" He rose, reminding her again of his great height. "If that's all . . ." He started toward the door.

Realizing he was about to escape, she blurted out the first thing that came to mind. "I'm sorry."

He stopped, then swung back. "For what?"

"Your feet. For imposing on you. For Mr. Phelps. I know he was your friend."

"Yeah. Well." He shifted, a flush darkening his sun-browned cheeks. "I don't know how it is in England, but in hard country like this, we look out for each other."

"I see. Of course. Well then, thank you."

"Thinking to pay me again, are you? I told you I don't take money from women."

Was he teasing her? No one ever teased the redoubtable, most proper Spinster Thornton. She rather liked it. "I would, but I don't know where my reticule is," she said, fighting a smile.

Unbelievably his grin stretched wider, showing at least two dozen of the whitest teeth she'd ever seen. "Too bad. This time I think I earned it." He started again toward the door.

"You never answered my question," she called once she'd regained her senses. "Who has been tending me?"

He stopped in the doorway.

She noticed his sturdy frame nearly filled the opening, and he had to duck to clear the top. Such prodigious size almost made her feel petite.

He glanced back over one broad shoulder. "Who do you think?" Then he slipped away, leaving a soft echo of low laughter drifting from the hall.

That cad.

She scowled at the empty doorway, her vivid imagination filling in all the gaps he had purposely left. She pictured herself lying helpless and insensate, babbling in a fevered delirium while he hovered over her, listening and staring and doing—well, God knows what. Just the thought of it made her stomach cramp.

Or perhaps it was the water. Or hunger pains. Or the need to relieve herself.

By the time she had gotten herself in hand, he was back with a tray of food, which he set on the bureau, and a portly, middle-aged Mexican woman, who he introduced as Consuelo.

The woman smiled, her round face dominated by dark eyes as kind and welcoming as any Jessica had seen in a long time. With a promise to bring the others by later—what others?—Brady Wilkins shuffled out again, trailing loose wrappings from his injured right foot.

Consuelo spoke only broken English, and with such a strong accent, Jessica understood little of her continual chatter. However, the woman's innate kindness communicated itself well enough that Jessica soon began to relax. After an awkward interlude with the chamber pot, followed by a quick wash and another layer of ointment on her face, luncheon was served.

It consisted of a bowl of chicken broth that Consuelo spooned into her—which added to Jessica's sense of helplessness—accompanied by flat round corn cakes dripping cinnamon-spiced honey. Despite her irritation at her own weakness, Jessica was grateful for the help. She felt as wobbly as a new kitten and doubted she could have managed the meal on her own without making a mess of it. She was trembling with exhaustion by the time Consuelo set the tray aside and began putting the room to rights, chatting away the entire time.

Jessica tried to listen but weariness claimed her, and after a few minutes, she slowly sank back into the velvety blackness.

SHE AWOKE TO THE TERRIFYING SENSATION OF HANDS PUSH-ing against her midsection, trying to hurt her baby. Lurching upright, she flailed at her assailant, a scream tearing through her throat.

Hands gripped her wrists, pinned them against the pillows. "Ja-sus, woman, *ara be whist!* Faith, but it's loopers, ye are!"

Jessica froze. Watery, bloodshot eyes stared down from a round, rosy face topped by a halo of white, bushy hair. His nose and breath named him a drinker, which sent renewed strength through her trembling limbs. With a snarl, she yanked her wrists free just as the door crashed open.

Brady Wilkins loomed in the doorway, shirttail loose, sleeves rolled up, hair mussed as if he'd been roused from a nap. He looked around as if he expected to find someone lurking in the corner, then his gaze swung back to Jessica and her assailant. His expression of alarm became one of confusion. "I heard screams. What's going on, Doc?"

"Doc?" Jessica frowned at her attacker. "Are you a physician?"

The old man's eyebrows lifted like startled white caterpillars. "Saints preserve us! You're English!"

"You're Irish!" Jessica shot back with equal disdain.

"And it's proud of it I am!" Drawing himself up to his full five feet, the little Celt puffed out his chest. "Bartholomew Patrick O'Grady, blessed son of the land of Erin and Medical Officer of the First Regiment of the Irish Brigade, at your service."

Jessica rolled her eyes. An Irish physician. *Saints preserve us all.*

"I can see ye're near fainting for joy, colleen." He gave her shoulder a reassuring pat. "Sure, and don't be awed by the loftiness of my own self. For all that you're English and a woman besides, I'll hold to my oath as a healer."

Impertinent Druid.

Brady Wilkins still hovered in the doorway. "Is everything all right, Doc?"

"It will be if she minds her temper and stays abed for the next three months."

Jessica couldn't believe they were discussing her private female issues as if she weren't even in the room, as if—suddenly his words blasted through her head.

"Three months!" She must have shrieked it, judging by their expressions. "You expect me to just lie here for three months!" The idea was so absurd, so beyond reason, Jessica couldn't get her mind around it. "Why? What is wrong with me? Is it because of the baby?"

The scurvy bone-cutter threw up his hands. "It is, but don't be listening to me, Miss Laudy Daw. Faith, I'm only the physician, don't you know."

"No, I do not know!" Fear and distrust put her on the defensive. "You were a military physician. What do you know about babies?"

"Well and enough to know you're acting like one!"

"Shut up! Both of you! Christ!" Wilkins stomped into the room. "Doc, give us a minute."

After the muttering Irishman left, Wilkins closed the door, then turned to Jessica.

Ashamed of her outburst, she clasped her hands tightly atop the coverlet. "When I woke up, he was . . . touching me. I didn't know who he was."

"Now you do. He's a good doctor."

"A good doctor? Or the only doctor?"

"Both. You wouldn't be alive if not for him. Do what he says and everything will be fine."

She didn't see how she could. Idleness was abhorrent to her. "I will go insane," she said flatly. "I won't last a week in this bed, much less three months." In her zeal to convince him the whole notion was wrong—it had to be—she wasn't truly in danger of losing her baby, was she?—words came tumbling out in a frantic rush. "I simply need to get to Socorro. Once I find my brother, I will see a real doctor and do whatever—"

"Find him? You don't know for sure he's there?"

"Of course he's there. His last letter—"

"Christ."

"Besides," she ground out, ignoring his reprehensible language and determined to find a way past this impossible restriction. "It would be an imposition to stay here." She waved a hand at the boots, leathers, male paraphernalia decorating the cluttered room. "Unchaperoned, an object of charity for months on end. It simply would not be proper."

"Proper!" Brady Wilkins came across the room in two long, limping strides. She shrank against the headboard as he bent over the bed, leveling his face inches from her own. "Hell, woman! You've poked me, clawed my arm bloody, damned near loosened a tooth, and I may have permanently crippled myself going for help on your behalf! You're already a damn imposition!"

She gaped up at him, saw his righteous indignation, and resistance died. Strength left her. Defeated and overwhelmed, she did what she swore no man would ever make her do again—she dropped her head into her hands and wept.

"Aw, hell."

Dimly she heard movement, voices, a door opening and closing. Then the bed sagged as someone sat beside her. She hoped it was the doctor. If she was going to shame herself with this maudlin behavior, she would prefer that he, rather than Brady Wilkins, be witness to it. Yet she wasn't surprised when she peeked through her fingers to find that very man studying her.

"Go away," she mumbled, humiliated by her own weakness. She, who never cried, lay sprawled in some strange man's bed, sniveling like a puling babe. It was disgusting.

"Then quit crying. Here." He stuffed a wad of cloth into her hand.

His utter lack of sympathy actually helped. After she mopped up with what appeared to be a faded man's neckerchief, she fluffed the pillow, carefully arranged the counterpane so that it covered her from toe to chin, then leaned back against the headboard and waited for him to leave.

Which, of course, he didn't.

Uneasy under his intense gaze, and unable to find a plausible excuse for her mawkish display, she ignored it altogether. "Will you truly be crippled?"

One corner of his mustache quirked up. "A slight exaggeration." He waved a big hand in a vague gesture that seemed to encompass herself, the damp kerchief in her hand, the world in general. "Are you done now?"

Condescending dolt. "If you are referring to my regrettable bout of self-pity, then yes, I am quite done." She dabbed one last time at her puffy eyes then, with utmost care, folded the cloth and placed it on the bedside table. "Thank you so much for asking."

He missed her sarcasm or chose to ignore it. "Will you do what Doc says?"

Three months. Heaven help her. She would be an eggplant ripe for the vegetable bin after a single week. But if the doctor felt that would keep her baby safe, she would manage. Without Victoria, she would have little reason to go on. What would be the meaning of it? "Of course."

"Good." Wilkins rose. He hitched up trousers dangerously close to slipping off his lean hips, then with the smug look of a man convinced he had efficiently handled yet another crisis involving an unbalanced female, he said, "We'll think of something to keep you busy. Maybe mending. How does that sound?"

"Titillating. You will wash the items first?" She gave his rumpled attire a pointed look.

He ignored that, too, and opening the door, yelled for Doc.

Dr. O'Grady had one simple rule: She was not allowed on her feet for any reason whatsoever for at least two weeks. Other than a daily sponging, she was forbidden to bathe and must take all her meals in bed. When he returned in a fortnight to check on her, *if* she showed improvement, she *might* be allowed to sit in a chair for short periods of time. She absolutely would not be traveling by carriage, coach, horse, or foot to Socorro until after her confinement. In fact, she couldn't even walk as far as the indoor water closet. In other words, for the next three months she was a virtual prisoner in Mr. Wilkins's home—in his room, in fact.

Meanwhile, Consuelo would handle the nursing chores and see to Jessica's needs. Doc thought they would get along just dandy.

The absolute fifth ring of hell.

Seven

For the next few days Jessica slept, rousing only to eat, swallow copious amounts of water, and use the chamber pot. Thankfully only Consuelo was witness to her complete helplessness. The woman's giving spirit made the intolerable tolerable, but since she spoke such limited English, she did little to ease the feeling of isolation that seemed to build with each day.

By midweek, Jessica felt rested enough to count the blisters that had crusted across her nose and forehead from overexposure to the sun. Such had never been a problem at home, where the sun only occasionally came out of the mist, and when it did, ladies always wore hats. But who would confuse her with a lady? With her tangled hair, spotty complexion, and swollen temple, she looked as if she might be quite at home swinging with Esmeralda from the bell tower ropes of Notre Dame de Paris.

"You up?" Brady Wilkins stuck his head in the door.

"No."

He entered anyway. Under his arm was a parcel. "The stage office found this at the wreck. Is it yours?" Removing the burlap wrapping, he held it out.

Jessica bolted upright. "You found it!" Taking it reverently from his hands, she opened the latch with trembling fingers, fearing what she might find.

Nestled in a bed of straw were two saucers and two fluted china cups, each decorated with tiny rosebuds and twining ivy. Not a single crack or chip. Even the seal on the caddy of India tea was unbroken.

Tears burned in her eyes. "Great-Grandmother's china. I thought it was lost."

"You're not going to cry, are you?"

Blinking hard, she gave him a weak smile. "I might."

"Then I'm leaving."

As he disappeared out the door, she called after him. "Would you ask Consuelo to bring hot water when she has a moment?"

He muttered something she didn't catch.

Great-Grandmother's china. Smiling and crying at the same time, she ran her palms over the worn wooden box. This was her link to home. To the women who had gone before her, and to all she had left behind. It was like having a part of her soul back.

"Thank you," she yelled, finally remembering her manners. Then she laughed out loud when she realized how ludicrous that was. What manners? Yelling from room to room, receiving men in her bedroom while she lay abed in a state of undress—Annie would faint to see her now.

During one of her many naps, someone—doubtless Consuelo— removed Brady Wilkins's belongings and replaced them with her own. It was a comfort to see her own brush on the bureau, her small tintype of Annie and the children on her night table, and her own clothing on the peg behind the door.

It was a busy household, echoing with the sounds of Consuelo's musical chatter, deep masculine voices, heavy footfalls, and frequently, a distant tinkling bell. She knew that outside her window was a porch. And a very vocal dog. Consuelo pinned a blanket drape over the window opening, which gave some privacy but didn't muffle sound.

Jessica soon realized the porch was a gathering place. She often heard men's voices out there and every now and then a woman's soft laugh—not Consuelo's. And sometimes, long after the house had settled for the night, she heard a slow rhythmic creak as if someone rocked in a swing or a rocking chair not far from her window. It was a comforting sound and reminded her of evenings at home when Mama sat in her rocker by the fire, working on a bit of mending or reading aloud from one of the few letters Papa sent during his long absences.

Intuition told her it was Brady Wilkins out there. She could feel his presence, that faint but unmistakable change in the air whenever he was near. It mystified and intrigued her, and when she awoke sweating and terrified from dreams of John Crawford, it comforted her.

As her strength returned, her sense of isolation increased. Other than a brief trip to dump an armful of mending on her bed, Brady Wilkins kept his distance. Luckily Melanie managed to escape her mother's demands and made frequent visits and even brought some of her dime novels for Jessica to read. The girl was in a dither of excitement. Not only was she living out one of her True West Adventures, complete with lurking desperadoes, lusty ranch hands, and a damsel—namely herself—in distress, but she had also developed *entendres* for all three Wilkins brothers. At the moment, the middle brother, Hank, held a slight lead in her affections.

"Today I am having a bath," Jessica announced on the twelfth day of her confinement when Consuelo brought in hot water for her morning tea.

Apparently Consuelo understood English better than she spoke it, because she deduced immediately what Jessica wanted and launched into a garbled explanation of why she couldn't have it. From what Jessica could discern, there was no hipbath on the lower floor and all the washtubs were currently being used to dip calves infested with ticks and lice. But surely she'd heard wrong.

She finally had to settle for a bed bath and an oatmeal dusting for her hair. Not much, but some improvement, and just in time, for that afternoon the Wilkins brothers descended.

She had just finished plaiting her hair into a thick braid when she heard an ominous tromping in the hall. A loud warning knock, then the door swung open to reveal three huge figures crowding the hallway. Forefront was Brady Wilkins. He leaned in, gave her a quick once-over, then motioned the others forward. "She's dressed."

"Damn," a voice muttered just loud enough for her to hear.

She snatched the covers to her chin as Brady Wilkins stepped inside followed by the other two men. "These are my brothers." He nodded toward a young, sandy-haired man nearly as tall as himself but leaner, and another who was one of the largest men Jessica had ever seen, and possibly the hairiest, his features nearly hidden beneath a mop of dark brown hair and an untrimmed beard.

She forced a smile. "Pleased to meet you, I'm sure."

The younger brother stepped forward, whipped off his hat, and bowed with a flourish. "Andrew Jackson Wilkins, the pick of the litter, ma'am, and pleased to meet you, too." He elbowed the giant in the stomach. "This here's Patrick Henry Wilkins—Hank. I'd ask him to make his bows, but with all that hair I'm not sure which way he's facing, and I wouldn't want him to do something unmannerly or improper. Brady said you had a keen interest in such things. He also said you'd been having a hard time of it, but it's clear he was lying and hoping to keep you all to himself, because if I may say so, ma'am, you're looking as pretty as a speckled pup. By the way, you can call me Jack. And as often as you'd like." He gave her a wink.

Brady Wilkins rolled his eyes.

Hank Wilkins muttered something and left the room.

Jack Wilkins watched him go, then turned back to Jessica with a grin that was almost as arresting as that of his older brother. "He means well, our Hank. Not much of a talker, though. At least to humans." He started toward the chair.

Brady yanked him back. "She needs her rest."

With a see-what-I-mean look to Jessica, Jack headed out the door. As he passed his older brother, she heard him mutter, "You're right. She does talk funny. Nice pair, though."

She wasn't sure what he meant, but judging by the flush inching up Brady Wilkins's neck, it was obviously something untoward. Dimples *and* blushes. Amazing.

He stepped into the hall, stopped, and swung back. "Do you want me to have Sheriff Rikker contact the sheriff in Socorro? See if he knows anything about your brother?"

"Would you?"

"What's his name?

"George. George Adrian Thornton."

He looked puzzled. "I thought he was your brother."

Too late Jessica realized her mistake. If she was a widow and George was her brother, how could they carry the same surname? "My brother-*in-law*." Even worse. She couldn't live with a man who wasn't blood kin. She was hopeless at lying.

Apparently he came to the same realization. His eyes grew as cold as two chips of ice. "That dog won't hunt. Let's try again, and this time the truth. Who's in Socorro?"

She looked away. "I told you. My brother." At least that part was true.

"And who's John?"

Her gaze flew to his. How did he know about John Crawford? What had she said? And when? Her throat ached with the need to blurt out the truth. But the truth was such an ugly thing—too ugly to expose to the judgments of others—too ugly even to share with her sister.

Leaning one shoulder against the open doorjamb, Brady Wilkins crossed his arms over his chest. "There was never any husband, was there?"

"Well . . . no."

She could tell by the subtle shift in his expression that he was drawing conclusions, unwelcome conclusions, the same conclusions most people would draw—that she was wanton, had a lover or perhaps several lovers. The idea sickened her. But before she could even attempt to explain, a voice drifted down the hallway.

"*Querido.*"

A soft, musical voice with a Spanish accent. The woman from the porch.

Wilkins turned. The change in his expression was immediate. Reaching out, he looped an arm around the woman's shoulders and pulled her into the doorway. "Your Ladyship, this is Elena," he said, smiling down at the woman.

Jessica could only stare. Black up-tilted eyes, a flawless heart-shaped face, a smile that rivaled that of Brady Wilkins. She was easily the most beautiful woman Jessica had ever seen. No wonder he looked at her that way. Ignoring an odd twist in her chest, she smiled back—and somehow managed to keep her surprise from showing when the woman moved into the room. She was terribly crippled, and it was apparent in every halting step that she walked with pain.

"Brady teases, yes? You are called 'Your Ladyship'?"

Jessica recovered enough to glare at the dolt hovering in the doorway. "Of course not." She held out her hand. "I'm Jessica. Jessica Thornton."

The woman took her hand in hers. "I am so happy to meet you, Jessica. And how nice it will be to have another woman at the rancho."

Her smile was so welcoming, her beautiful eyes so kind, Jessica felt an immediate liking for this lovely woman. "You live here, too?" she asked, delighted at the prospect of having someone new to talk to who might help ease the boredom that chaffed more each day.

"*¿Aquí en el rancho?* *Sí.* All my life. But not at the main house." Elena released Jessica's hand and sank down onto the foot of the bed. She aimed a scolding look at Brady Wilkins. "But for now, Brady insists. He is very bossy. He thinks to manage everyone. You agree?"

"I definitely agree."

The man under discussion smirked.

Elena motioned Wilkins toward the rope-strung chair in the corner. "Sit, *querido*. With your poor feet, you have nothing better to do, yes?"

He seemed reluctant until Elena gave him a look of such familiarity, Jessica felt like an intruder. It was obvious they shared something special, something intimate and rare.

As he positioned the chair so he could prop his injured feet on the windowsill, Elena leaned toward Jessica. In a whisper loud enough for Wilkins to hear, she said, "Make him stay for a long visit. He is much underfoot, and with the *vieja* upstairs making her demands, Consuelo and I are too busy to entertain him."

Wilkins snorted.

"And you, *querido*," she said, turning her attention to him, "be nice to your guest." She added something in rapid Spanish that Jessica didn't understand.

Apparently Wilkins did, because he blushed. Again. Another miracle for the archbishop.

"And now I must help Consuelo." With one hand on the footboard, Elena awkwardly pushed to her feet. "I will come tomorrow, *sí*?" she said to Jessica.

"I would like that very much."

After Elena left, Jessica glanced at Wilkins. He was staring out the window, his elbow propped on the armrest of the chair, his fist braced at his jaw. He seemed miles away.

"She's very beautiful."

He sighed and let his arm drop to extend past the end of the armrest. "Yes, she is. The image of her mother, the fabled Rose of Rosa-Roja." It didn't sound like a compliment.

His sleeve was rolled at his elbow, and when she saw the half-healed gouges on his forearm, she suddenly remembered how he'd gotten them. It embarrassed her that she had been so out of control, that she had felt so afraid whenever he was near. Yet now, when she was more helpless than she'd ever been, she wasn't frightened at all.

Then his words clicked in her mind. "Are you saying Elena is related to the family that lived here before? To that murderer, Sancho Ramirez?"

"His sister."

"I don't understand. If his sister is able to put the feud aside, why can't he?"

"He's crazy, that's why. Always has been."

"Is he a threat to her?"

Wilkins took so long to answer, she thought he intended to ignore the question. Finally, he said, "Elena was six years old the first time I saw her." He continued to stare out the window as he spoke, his gaze distant, his voice flat. "She was running across the courtyard, crying. Sancho was chasing after her. He had a braided rawhide whip in his hand and was swinging it at her legs. Every time he drew blood, he laughed." Wilkins turned toward her then, and Jessica saw that same fury in his face she had glimpsed at the stage stop. "So yes, he's a threat to her."

"Was there no one to protect her?"

"Maria tried, but Sancho threatened her, too. Her father did nothing. I took the whip away."

Jessica clenched her hands on the counterpane. "How could her father allow such a thing?"

"Allow it? Hell, he fostered it." Wilkins turned his gaze back to the window, his expression grim. "The Don collected song birds. Little bright-colored birds the *mestizos* brought up from Mexico. He thought they sang better without distractions, so he blinded them. I think he enjoyed doing it. He did the same with Indio and Apache slaves who tried to run . . . before he turned them over to Sancho to work on. He made Elena and her mother watch. A reminder, I think, of what would happen if they thought to escape."

Jessica was so shocked she couldn't find words to express it.

"Like father, like son, they say."

Horrified, she stared down at her abdomen, wondering if that was true. If her baby was a son, would he be like Crawford? Would she see her rapist in the face of her child?

That thought haunted her as the days passed and her body expanded. She tried to keep it at bay by staying as busy as her condition allowed, sewing until her fingers felt raw and her brain was numb, letting out seams to accommodate her ballooning girth and cutting down her oldest petticoats to make napkins and night sacks for Victoria. Thank goodness Elena often came by to ply her needle and keep her company.

The friendship between the women grew rapidly. Hearing of Elena's abuse had struck a chord within Jessica, and although they carefully avoided mention of either Jessica's "lost" husband or Elena's murderous brother, an invisible bond grew between them.

Melanie helped with the sewing as well. She had a decided flair for design and was able to make Jessica's altered dresses look quite fashionable. As they stitched, she kept them entertained with dramatic retellings of the dime novels she so fancied. Their chatter and laughter helped pass the hours away and ease the worries that never strayed far from Jessica's mind.

She had missed female companionship. Until John Crawford had come into their lives, she and Annie had been as close as sisters could be. Afterward, too . . . for a while. When Jessica insisted they live with her at Bickersham Hall after their marriage—it was much too large for one person, after all—Crawford had been so quick to agree she had wondered if such had been his intent all along. If so, she hadn't minded; she'd just been grateful to have her sister beside her.

But after the children came, things changed. At first Jessica thought Annie was simply preoccupied with her growing family, but gradually she became aware of the growing tension between her sister and Crawford. Always given to sulks, he grew impatient and overbearing, complaining bitterly of the lack of funds and tedium of country life. Annie tried desperately to placate him, but by the time their second child was born, he had all but moved to London.

Jessica had been grateful for the respite from the unrelenting tension. But without Crawford, Annie had seemed to fade into a shadow of herself. He never asked her or the children to accompany him to Town, and as his visits home had grown more volatile and less frequent, Annie's natural shyness had become fumbling uncertainty under his critical eye.

And the debts had mounted.

And that critical eye had turned to Jessica.

And then the real brutality had begun.

But that was behind her now, and Jessica refused to dwell on it or allow her worries to overshadow the joy in having new friends. She strove for a measure of serenity and calmness, hoping in some way that might communicate itself to the child growing within her and override the evil of the man who fathered it.

She didn't know how she would have managed without their visits.

Surprisingly, at different times both of the younger Wilkins brothers stopped by—although Jessica wondered if they came to see her or the ladies visiting her.

Hank Wilkins rarely spoke, and when he did, even if he addressed Jessica, his attention never wavered from Melanie. It was a bit unnerving. He was so quiet and so well masked by his full beard and shaggy hair, it was difficult to guess what he was thinking. He was certainly intelligent enough to carry on a conversation. The few times Jessica had found his gaze aimed at her, she had almost felt dissected by those dark, assessing eyes. Yet she never felt in danger. She sensed curiosity behind his fierce concentration. And loneliness. It was difficult not to respond to that hint of vulnerability in such a physically powerful man. Melanie must have felt it as well, because she flew to the rafters whenever he was near. Jessica liked him, too. Despite his size and shuttered demeanor, Hank Wilkins made one feel safe and protected, rather than threatened. He calmed her.

Not so with the youngest brother. Jack Wilkins was outrageous, charming, so full of energy he was like a whirlwind through her mind. He and Elena didn't converse, yet Jessica sensed strong currents between the two. Antipathy or attraction? She couldn't decide. In many ways he was the opposite of Brady Wilkins. Although they were both tall, Jack was leaner. He was blond, while his brother was dark—volatile and undisciplined, while Brady was tautly controlled. There was no question who held the reins of the family, and no question who chaffed under that restraint. But they both shared that disarming smile, although

Brady's was rarer and for that reason more precious. Jessica wondered if they knew the effect it had on impressionable females. And pregnant spinsters.

Brady, Hank, and Jack. It was too confusing to call them all "Mr. Wilkins," and after a while, she gave up the pretense. She had fallen so far beyond the bounds of propriety—she was receiving visitors in her bedclothes, for heaven's sake—what did it matter what she called them? Besides, the brothers seemed oblivious to proper decorum, or perhaps they didn't remember her name; even the younger two followed Brady's lead and simply called her "Your Ladyship." It was disrespectful, improper, and familiar in the extreme.

How refreshing.

Three months. A terribly long time to have to rely on charity from this boisterous and outlandish family. But oddly, Jessica found she wasn't that anxious to leave.

"Try these."

Brady looked up from a battered copy of *The Cattleman's Gazette* to see Hank coming across the porch with a pair of worn boots in his hand.

"You'll have to double up on socks." Dropping the boots beside Brady's chair, he reached down to give Bullshot a scratch.

Brady studied the broken-down leathers. "What'd you do? Drag them behind your horse?"

Hank picked up the boots and started back the way he'd come.

"Okay, okay." Reaching out, Brady snagged the boots before Hank got out of reach. "I'll take them. Christ."

With Hank and Bullshot watching, Brady gingerly worked his sore feet into the oversized boots. Because of the swelling, it was a tight fit, but he managed. After two weeks of sitting in his rocker, scanning the slopes with his eyeglass while Bullshot twitched in dreams and passed wind by his side, Brady had reached the limit of his patience. It was time he went after Sancho. He knew his brothers wouldn't approve of him tearing off with no plan in mind and no idea where to find the bastard, but he was tired of sitting and doing nothing. So he wouldn't tell them.

He stood and took a few steps. It still hurt to walk but at least now he could ride. If he didn't trip and fall on his face first. "Jesus, you got big feet," he muttered.

"Comes with the territory."

Brady limped down the porch and back, the hound trailing his heels.

"Why you getting dressed up?" his brother asked when Brady plopped back down into the rocker and the hound settled once again at his feet.

"I'm not getting dressed up."

Bending, Hank picked up a broken chair part. He studied it a moment, then reached into his trouser pocket and pulled out his penknife.

"Just because I put on your beat-up old boots doesn't mean I'm dressing up. Why would you think I'm dressing up?"

After cutting off a sliver, Hank held up the stick and examined it, turning it this way and that. Apparently satisfied, he started another slice. "You shaved twice this week."

"So?" Brady eyed his brother's bushy beard. "You want, I'll teach you how."

Hank gave it some thought, then shook his head. "Wouldn't be fair."

Brady frowned up at him.

"You know how the ladies get when I clean up." He flashed that astonishing grin that had women panting like race horses whenever he allowed them to see it. "I wouldn't want to interfere with your courting."

Courting? "Who said I was courting?"

Using short strokes, Hank shaped the end of the stick into a sharp point.

The hound stretched and yawned.

Brady contemplated the sunset. It wasn't as bright as it would be

later in the season when the dust haze brought out the reds and oranges, and purple-tinted thunderheads crowded the peaks, but it was
still a wondrous sight. "I'm not courting."

"Then all this fixing up is for Sancho?"

Damn. "I didn't say anything about Sancho. Did I say anything
about Sancho?"

Having put a point on one end of the stick, Hank flipped it and
started on the other.

The sun continued its downward slide. Reds faded to gold, and
wispy clouds darkened to deep blue. "I know what you're thinking,"
Brady said after a while. "You're thinking he's out there waiting, and if
I go after him, I'll be playing into his hands."

Hank looked at him.

"You think I should stay put so he'll have to come to me, don't you?"
Hank was right, of course. Brady knew it would be foolish to force an
issue when patience might yield a better result. But the waiting was
killing him. "Hell." He sighed. "All right. One week, but that's all."

Hank tossed the stick into the roses, then folded the penknife and
slipped it into his pocket. "I'll leave you to your courting then." Turning, he clomped down the steps and into the yard.

"Damn that Hank," Brady muttered to Bullshot as his brother disappeared into the barn. "He plays me like a lute every time." With a
sigh, he reached down to scratch Bullshot's ear. "We're a worthless
pair, aren't we?"

"I'll say."

Startled, he looked up to see Jack mounting the porch steps. Other
than when he had introduced his brothers to Her Ladyship, Jack had
been scarce since their run-in. Brady felt the distance between them
grow wider every day and that saddened him. Jack had always been a
hard dog to keep under the porch, and Brady knew one day he'd slip
the leash and take off. But he regretted that it might happen when there
were still hard feelings between them.

"Bullshot's been asking after you," he said. "He's missed you
sorely."

Jack bent down to rub the hound's belly. "Said that, did he?"

"I think so. He coughed up something that sounded like 'Jack,' but it could have been a chicken feather." He nodded toward the house. "Get the jug and sit a spell."

Jack retrieved the whiskey jug from the larder then returned to sit in the chair by Brady's rocker. Ru and Tobias and Red came by. Brady asked how the tally was going and they told him it was going well, and unless something happened between now and fall, they should have a fine showing. They understood how important it was to have the best stock ready for the Army bid in the fall. If they won it, there would be bonuses and money for some of the improvements Brady had planned. If they didn't, it would be another tough year. They'd have to cull the herds, drive what they could east to join the big cattle drives heading up the Chisholm Trail to Abilene, Kansas. But if they could hang on a few more years until the railroads came through, they'd be sending Wilkins beef all the way to Kansas City or Chicago. And once that happened, Brady knew he could start the horse and cattle breeding programs he'd dreamed about.

But that was a long way off with a mountain of "ifs" in between.

"How long these stage people staying, Boss?" Rufus elbowed the man beside him. "Toby here has his eye on the young one."

"Too long," Brady muttered. He thought of the railroader recuperating upstairs. He didn't trust him and hoped Doc would send him on his way soon. "The man from Overland said the Army was sending a Dougherty wagon and escort for her and her mother. Should be here in a few days." Hopefully the railroader would be well enough to go with them.

"Then how about the redhead?"

Jack looked over, but Brady didn't meet his gaze. "She's breeding. Stay away from her."

He had avoided Her Ladyship for the last few days. Seeing her in his bed put ideas in his head that shouldn't be there. He was a cattleman born and bred to run this ranch. He needed it like he needed food and water, needed the challenge of managing an eighty-eight-thousand-acre spread and keeping it safe while building something that would last long after he was gone. She didn't fit into any of that.

Yet sometimes, after the ranch bedded down for the night, and he was sitting on the porch in the still of the evening, with just the hound and the crickets and the "what-ifs" for company, thoughts of her would slide quietly across his mind like a gentle drift of smoke. He would picture her in his bed a few feet away, or remember something she said, or the way her mouth pinched when she was amused and trying not to show it, and the sharp reminder of all that was missing from his life and all he would never have would cut as deep as a well-honed blade.

The three cowboys wandered off.

Jack and Brady shared the jug and a companionable silence as the waning moon drifted across the night sky, leaving in its wake a trail of stars. Feeling mellow and relaxed and enjoying Jack's company in a way he hadn't in a long time, Brady said, "So what do you think of her?"

"Who?"

"The Pope's second wife. Who do you think?"

"Her Ladyship? I like her fine. Why you asking?"

Wondering the same thing, Brady tried to make a joke of it. "I'm thinking of selling her to the Muscaleros and was trying to set a price."

"Not much. Indians don't like uppity women."

"She is that." Brady smiled. "She makes me laugh."

"I noticed." A pause, then, "Are you drunk?"

Brady ignored that and reached for the jug. "It's tough, though. Not knowing who he is—if he's out there somewhere—if she still has feelings for him. It's got me tied in knots."

Another pause. "He who? I thought she was a widow."

"Hell, I thought so, too."

Jack started to laugh.

"What's so funny?"

"You and Her Ladyship. Be like teaming a fancy carriage horse with a rented mule."

Brady didn't like that analogy. A Shire warhorse maybe. Or a Friesen stallion. Definitely not a mule. Mules were impotent.

"She and Elena seem to get along," Jack said.

Brady's comfortable mood faded.

"Doesn't that bother you?"

Brady looked over to meet his brother's frown. All Jack had to do was open his eyes. The truth was right in front of him. But Jack had always been incapable of seeing past the obvious. As irritating as that could be sometimes, Brady often envied his brother's ability to view life in such simple terms. Careful to keep his voice neutral, he asked, "Why should that bother me?"

Jack looked away. "Sometimes I don't understand you, Brady."

"Well, you are pretty dumb."

"How can you do this to Elena? Nothing against Her Ladyship, but hell, Brady, all these years you and Elena—"

"Jack, look at me."

When he did, Brady saw the confusion and hurt in his brother's eyes. He was weary of it. "There is no me and Elena," he said with quiet emphasis. "There never was and never will be. Haven't you figured that out yet?"

"What's that mean exactly? Why would she still be here if not because of you?"

Brady lifted his brows but said nothing. He watched Jack wrestle with it, hoping his brother could put aside his resentments and summon up the intellect to look beyond the surface and piece it all together. When it was clear he couldn't, he sat back with a sigh. "Get off my porch. You're too stupid to talk to."

Jack started to argue, but Brady waved him away. "You want answers, go to her. I'm done talking." And signaling an end to it, he tipped his head back and pulled his hat over his eyes.

Eight

"Is something wrong?" Jessica asked.

Dr. O'Grady had finally returned to check on her, and she fully expected him to lift the impossible restrictions he had placed upon her. She felt fully recovered. In fact, she felt so robust, she was itching to tackle a thorough cleaning of this somewhat neglected room and any others in a similar condition. So why was he hesitating?

O'Grady removed the stethoscope and folded it into his medicine satchel. He studied her with sharp interest. "Ever had heart problems?"

"No."

"A high fever when you were still a lass?"

"Nothing unusual. Why?"

"Maybe a heart murmur?"

"No. And why are you asking about my heart?"

The doctor scratched thoughtfully at the stubble under his chin.

"Sure, and it could be an echo. Or maybe . . ." Suddenly he grinned. "It could be twins."

O'Grady said more, but Jessica couldn't hear him over the buzzing in her head.

Twins? Two babies? How could that be? Dizziness assailed her. Her chest felt odd. She couldn't seem to catch her breath, and the harder she worked at it, the worse it became.

Suddenly a noxious odor exploded in her nose. "Easy, lass. Breathe easy."

Jessica shoved the bottle of smelling salts away. But once she brought her breathing under control, her mind started racing in all directions. "You could be wrong," she argued. "If you were a military surgeon, you probably don't know. How many babies were born on the battlefield?"

"You're doing it again."

"It could be something I ate or—"

"Is it a sniff of the bottle you're wanting?"

Jessica raised a hand. "No!"

O'Grady recapped the vial and returned it to his satchel. "It's not the end of the world, lass. Two wee babes—it's a blessing, is what it is. How can you be thinking otherwise?"

A blessing for anyone but her. Jessica felt the betraying sting of tears. She pressed a trembling hand to her chest to calm her racing heart. "How can I take care of two babies?" One was challenge enough. But two? "And why didn't you tell me when you examined me before?"

"I wasn't sure then. I had to check my books."

Dear God. Was the man a complete incompetent? "You have delivered a baby before, haven't you?" If he turned out to be a horse doctor, she would kill Brady Wilkins.

"We'll do fine, colleen. We've gotten this far, haven't we?" The doctor patted her shoulder, a useless platitude to an unmarried woman with no home and no means of support, who had just been given the blessed and terrifying news that she would give birth to not one, but two babies. And in less than three months.

"In fact, you're doing well enough to get out of bed. Short periods at first, then if all goes well, a little longer each day. How does that sound, lass?"

It sounded like she had better find her brother George, and quickly.

DR. O'GRADY SEEMED TO HAVE LITTLE REGARD FOR THE PRI-vacy of his patients. Within minutes of his leaving, women descended like a flock of chattering birds—Elena, Consuelo, Melanie, and an older Negro woman Elena introduced as Buck's wife, Iantha. Apparently twins were rare enough to cause a great deal of excitement.

As the ladies prattled on about babies and what they needed and how they could get it all together, the mother-to-be stared numbly into the tarnished mirror above the bureau as she brushed out her hair, and tried to hide her terror behind a vacuous smile.

Twins. What would she do if she couldn't find George?

"Will you eat, Jessica?" Elena set a plate of food on the bureau.

Jessica looked at the thinly sliced chicken, early peas, and buttery mashed potatoes, and almost cast up her accounts. "Perhaps later."

"Do not worry, *mi amiga*." Elena patted her shoulder. "God sent you to us, and we will do all that we can to help you. But you must eat and make those babies strong."

Jessica smiled weakly. What choice did she have but to put herself and her babies in the care of these generous people and Dr. O'Grady? After months of flight, she was finally run to ground. All she could do now was trust in God and the kindness of strangers. A humbling thought, one that reinforced what she had learned during that ordeal on the desert—the margin between survival and death was narrow indeed.

The next afternoon Melanie bustled in with one of Jessica's newly altered dresses and news of a fiesta to be held in the courtyard that evening. "Because of some battle back in May of '62 when the Mexicans beat the French. They'll have food and music and dancing, and everybody will be there. Isn't that grand? I haven't been to a party in so long.

Do you think this will do?" She shook out the gown, one of Jessica's favorites, a pale yellow silk with a green underskirt and sash and low-scooped neckline. "I altered it for you."

"Thank you, but the doctor—"

"Oh, he says it's fine. As long as you don't dance, of course." Melanie held the dress to Jessica's shoulders. "The color is lovely on you. Do you think the Wilkins brothers dance? Oh, I hope so. Do try it on. I took a piece out of the underskirt to make a fichu so it would be less dressy and provide more coverage for your, ah . . ."

"Ballooning bust line?" Jessica stared down in dismay at her suddenly voluptuous bosom. At least it was keeping pace with her ever-growing waist. But Melanie was right—with the addition of lace across the shoulders and neckline, the dress was more appropriate for a woman in her condition. Or, say, the Cheviot Hills back home. The girl truly had a gift.

Melanie continued her chattering monologue, babbling on about Hank and Jack and the news that the escort was on its way and how she didn't want to go and wasn't Jessica simply thrilled to be having twins?

When she was permitted to, Jessica made the appropriate responses. Melanie insisted Jessica allow her to dress her hair, which she deftly fashioned into an elaborate bun with wispy curls dangling at her temples and nape. Jessica thought it attractive but impractical, and the high topknot made her impossibly tall. But Melanie was so pleased with her efforts, Jessica said nothing other than to compliment the results. And the results were amazing.

She scarcely recognized herself in the cheval mirror Consuelo had moved into her room. The blisters had healed, leaving behind a sprinkle of freckles and a rosy glow that wasn't wholly unattractive, and the sun had softened the bold red of her hair with golden streaks and highlights. Pleased, Jessica smiled at her reflection. Despite her mammoth proportions, she looked quite the thing. Confidence renewed, she pushed her worries aside and, hiking her chin, followed Melanie down the hall and into the courtyard, ready to face the world again.

The world, even within the narrow confines of the Wilkins ranch, was larger than she had expected. The ladies, all three Wilkins brothers, and Dr. O'Grady were present in the courtyard, along with several other women Jessica didn't know and twenty or more men who apparently worked on the ranch. Even Maude was there, ensconced in a carved throne-like chair, her foot propped on a worn damask footstool. Mr. Ashford attended also, as impeccable as she remembered, despite the sling and fading bruises on his face. Sadly, neither seemed to be enjoying themselves, judging by their unsociable expressions.

Three tables stood in the center of the courtyard. Two sagged under the weight of dozens of platters of food—both Colonial and Mexican, as well as something Iantha called "down-home vittles." But the third table made Jessica's mouth drop in astonishment.

It was covered with baby items, some new, some used, all handmade. Baby quilts in gay designs, lovingly stitched and softened by many washings. Lacy gowns and satin caps so tiny they could have fit the finest china dolls. Stacks of napkins and cuddly stuffed dolls with embroidered faces and yarn hair. There was even a cradle, so beautifully made the finished wood was as smooth as satin.

Jessica was speechless. That these kind people, many of whom she hadn't met until tonight, would be so giving to a stranger astonished her. For a moment she simply stood there, emotion clogging her throat as she trailed her fingertips from one gift to another and struggled to find words eloquent enough to express her gratitude. When she finally regained her composure and looked up, the first face she saw was that of Brady Wilkins. He slouched against the far wall, arms folded across his chest, his head a half-foot higher than the men around him, watching her with such fierce concentration it seemed to draw all the air from her lungs.

Because of him, she was alive. Because of him, her babies had a chance at survival. Because of his generosity, she was here this day, sharing this moment with his family and friends.

Blinking against the sting of tears, she smiled directly at him. "Thank you," she said in a voice loud enough for all to hear but meant especially for him.

He didn't move, didn't smile. Yet she felt a bond so powerful it was as if he had reached across the crowded courtyard and brushed his fingertips against her face.

Frightened but not sure why, she tore her gaze from his. Gripping a quilt to hide the tremble in her hands, she smiled at the ladies gathered around her. "It is a comfort to know my babies will be wrapped in such love. Your generosity overwhelms me."

They smiled back. She forced herself to relax, thinking the worst was over. Then they commenced parading her around the courtyard like a prized heifer. A big, awkward heifer.

Every lady had her own predictions about the babies—gender or genders, hair color, eye color, size, arrival date. She admitted the only thing she knew for certain was that one was a girl and her name was Victoria. It pleased her to be able to openly acknowledge her daughter at last. Just saying her name aloud made Victoria seem real to her in a way she never had before.

But the men made her uncomfortable. Especially Brady. She could feel his gaze tracking her progress around the courtyard, and the weight of his attention was like a breath against her back.

Uneasy among so many strangers and rattled—by what? Blue eyes? A smile? A look she couldn't define?—she muddled through the introductions and congratulations as graciously as she could, until finally she was able to escape behind a table of food.

Female hysterics, she decided as she loaded a plate with fried okra and smoked beans and spicy sausage. Emotional aberrations brought on by her condition. Nothing more.

"Worked up quite an appetite, have you?"

Looking up from her overflowing plate, she found Brady Wilkins grinning down at her. She almost choked. Setting the plate aside, she dabbed bean juice from her chin and tried not to dither.

Seeing him up close, she realized again how shockingly handsome he was in his blue chambray shirt, new denims, and turquoise-studded belt. He'd even shaved and slicked down his unruly black hair, although it was already sliding over his forehead. Without his hat, he looked younger, almost comical with that band of paler skin stretching from brow to hairline that his hat usually covered. If possible, he seemed taller, too. But perhaps that was the boots.

She took a deep breath to clear her head, then immediately exhaled when she saw how the action drew his attention to her bosom. "I see you found your razor," she said inanely.

"I did." His gaze moved up to her face, then to the top of her head. He frowned. "What'd you do to your hair?"

"What's wrong with my hair?"

"I like it better when it's down. Can't understand why a woman with hair as pretty as yours would wad it up like a cow pie."

He thought her hair was pretty?

No, wait. She narrowed her eyes. "Did you say cow pie?"

He flicked a curl dangling by her cheek. "The curls are nice. But it's prettiest when it's hanging loose and the wind sends it flying so it catches the light like a fiery halo."

She blinked, so addled she couldn't marshal a single coherent thought.

"Well." He gave her that dazzling smile, dimples and all. "Eat up. If we run out, I'll have the boys butcher another calf for you. And by the way"—he motioned to the punchbowl at her elbow—"don't drink that. The one for the ladies is on the other table."

Nonplussed, she watched him walk away, wondering why she always felt so uncertain and confused whenever he was near. Maggots in the brain, no doubt. Or demonic possession.

He thought her hair was pretty, did he?

Once the meal had ended, men pushed the tables back against the walls of the courtyard and Dr. O'Grady unwrapped his fiddle. One of the ranch hands stepped forward with a mouth harp and another held a guitar. Iantha's husband, Buck, tapped an intricate rhythm with two hollow sticks while Iantha kept a jingling beat on a beautiful hide-wrapped tambourine. It was lovely, the fiddle music lively and exhilarating as only a true Irishman could make it, and soon dancers filled the center of the courtyard while watchers clapped in rhythm.

Weary from the excitement and being on her feet for so long, she glanced around for a place to sit. When she saw poor Melanie unhappily positioned at her mother's side, Jessica took pity.

"How are you feeling, Mrs. Kinderly?" she asked, stopping before Maude. "Melanie, would you mind surrendering your chair for a moment so I can visit with your mother?"

"Of course." Before her mother could protest, Melanie was off like a runaway carriage.

Seeking a new target, Maude turned her disapproving glance to Jessica as she settled in the chair beside her. "I wasn't aware you were in a family way, Mrs. Thornton. When did you say your husband died?"

Jessica was saved from answering by Mr. Ashford's approach.

"Ladies, may I join you?"

Jessica nodded, grateful for the interruption.

Whipping out a handkerchief, he positioned a chair beside hers then sat, carefully straightening his trousers as he crossed his legs at the knee. "So. Do twins run in your family, Mrs. Thornton?"

"They do. My grandmother was a twin." Jessica watched his elegant, almost feminine fingers pluck a tiny puff of lint from his cuff. Oddly, the fastidiousness that had once impressed her now put her off. He must spend hours trimming his skinny mustache into such a precise line. And where did he put all that lint he collected? And had he always been so short?

"I must thank you, Mrs. Thornton." Ashford gave her a rueful look. "I understand Wilkins burdened you with my care while he went to his ranch. I'm shocked he would ask that of a woman in your condition. One wonders how we would have fared had he not returned."

"I daresay we would have perished." Jessica leveled her gaze at him. "So I am sure you must be as grateful as I that he did return."

He pressed his lips in a tight smile, then directed his attention to Maude. "I hear Colonel Kinderly is sending an escort to see you and Miss Melanie on to Santa Fe?"

"Yes, with an ambulance wagon. Perhaps you might care to travel with us. Dougherty wagons are quite roomy, you know."

"I might take you up on that." Smiling, he glanced at Jessica. "And you, Mrs. Thornton?"

"The doctor was most specific that I not travel."

Maude clucked. "Of course. You poor dear." Then recovering from her burst of sympathy with amazing speed, she turned back to Ashford. "When will you be able to travel?"

"Not a moment too soon, ma'am."

Jessica was surprised by the disgust in his tone. "Have you been ill treated here?"

"Not at all," he said dryly. "Unless one would consider the doubtful ministrations of a lame Mexican woman, the wretched food, and these less than clean conditions ill-treatment."

Jessica was astounded. But before she could call him to accounts, Maude cut in. "I quite agree. I am most anxious to be shut of this place." She then launched into a litany of complaints encompassing not only Indians, Mexicans, Southerners, and Texicans, but also all three Wilkins brothers, the condition of their home, and anyone hapless enough to be in their employ.

Astonishment turned to fury. Admittedly, from the little Jessica had seen when Melanie ushered her to the courtyard, the house was a bit unorthodox—the dining room serving as an armory, the front parlor a cluttered office, the back parlor a storage place for everything from tack to catalogs to unused furniture. But that might be expected in a household run by men. What she found incomprehensible was Maude Kinderly and this officious little railroader presuming to criticize the very people who had saved their lives and seen to their care for almost three weeks. It was too much by half. "I am sure our hosts are as anxious for you to depart as you are," she snapped. "In fact, we shall all breathe a sigh of relief to see you safely on your way." She rounded on Ashford. "And if you found a *lame* woman's untiring efforts on your behalf so distressing, you might consider the discomfort *she* must have suffered traipsing up and down the stairs, pandering to your every whim. I daresay it was considerable." Barely able to hide her disdain, she rose. "Now if you will excuse me, I feel the need of fresh air."

Either those two had gotten worse or she had grown smarter. Probably both. *Despicable ingrates.*

After circling the courtyard, she found another chair half hidden behind a lanky shrub with tiny yellow flowers. From there she happily watched the dancing grow rowdier and more high-spirited as the men's trips to their designated punchbowl grew more frequent. Colonials certainly knew how to enjoy themselves.

As the sun set, the mountain air cooled, and workers lit warming fires in footed braziers along the walls. Lanterns strung on ropes overhead gave the courtyard a festive air and cast flickering light over the whirling dancers. The open sky, the smell of food, and the sound of music and laughter brought up memories of country fairs back home.

Should she write Annie again to let her know she was safe? A hollow ache filled her chest. Did Neddy still have nightmares? Had Rebecca outgrown her lisp? Did they even remember her?

"Why are you hiding in the bushes?"

She looked up to find Brady hovering over her.

"Should I get Doc? I'll get Doc."

"I'm fine." She smiled to reassure him, wondering how he'd found her and if he'd been watching her every move all night. An unsettling thought . . . but rather nice, too. "I'm not hiding."

"Then what's wrong? Did Jack do something? I told him to leave you alone."

She was a bit taken aback by the ferocity of his concern. She'd never been fond of helpless women and certainly didn't consider herself one. "Do stop hovering," she chided. She pointed to where Jack leaned against the far wall watching Elena chat with some of the wives. "He's over there by Elena."

Jessica watched his eyes narrow on Jack and wondered if the rivalry she sensed between the two brothers encompassed Elena as well. For Jack's sake, she hoped not. How could he hope to win out over Brady? He and Elena were a beautiful couple and they obviously shared deep feelings for each other. Another unsettling thought. *Jessica, you're such a ninny.*

She sighed. "It's been a lovely party, but I think I shall retire." As she gathered herself to rise, he reached down to help her, and before she could stop herself, she shrank back.

His hand dropped to his side.

She tried to cover her embarrassment by brushing imaginary dust from her skirt.

"I won't hurt you, you know."

That unruly forelock had fallen over his forehead again, softening the rugged angles of his face and giving him a boyish look. It disarmed her. Charmed her. How could she fear a man who couldn't even make his hair behave? "I know."

At least, her heart knew. But her mind had heard those words before and look what it had gotten her. "Good night, Brady."

She felt him watching her as she crossed the courtyard. But once she'd stepped into the house, the thought of going back to the room that had been her prison for a fortnight sent her wandering the dim hallways. It was a sad house, a monument to a way of life long passed, and like the men who resided here, it needed tending. She passed her room and continued on until she found a doorway onto the porch that ran beyond her window. The tang of fresh-cut wood mingled with the sweet scent of roses growing against the foundation. There were only two usable chairs—an oversized rocker and a straight chair with a much-used saddle pad on the seat. All the others were either missing an arm or a leg or loaded down with a variety of horse paraphernalia, seed packets, catalogs, and discarded apparel. Jessica chose the rocker and settled back with a sigh.

The sinking crescent moon hung low, and pinpricks of starlight dotted the black dome of the eastern sky. The breeze was soft and cool, bearing the chirp of crickets and the lonely calls of night birds. It was a lovely evening. As she rocked, a feeling of contentment came over her. "We'll be all right, Victoria," she said as she gently stroked her rounded belly. "We can do this." She would find George. She would have two beautiful babies to love and then she would feel whole again.

At a sound, she looked over to see Brady crossing the yard toward the porch. His head was down and he was talking to himself. It must have been something amusing because he laughed. He didn't look frightening to her then. Just a man. A strong, honest man who liked to tease, who talked to himself when he thought no one was looking, who made promises he actually kept. Elena never need fear anything with him at her side. Except perhaps the wrath of God for his reprehensible language. She watched him draw nearer, wondering when he would see her, and was almost run over before he did.

"Whoa," he said, jerking to a halt. "What're you doing out here?"

"Rocking." When he just stood there, she said, "Would you care to join me?"

"Sure." His gaze flicked from her to the other usable chair and back. He didn't move.

"Let me guess," she said with a sigh. "This is your chair."

"Well. Yeah. I'd break the other one."

"So you want me to get up, even though I shouldn't be on my feet more than necessary, and move to the chair with that nasty saddle pad, even though I'm wearing my best—"

With an economy of motion, Brady kicked off the saddle pad, lifted her out of the rocker, and gently deposited her in the straight chair. "There. Now we're both happy." Then with a long sigh, he settled into the rocker beside her. "You like my porch?"

Still disoriented and somewhat shocked that he would—or was even able to—hoist her about like a sack of feed, she glanced over at him.

He was looking up at the oversized logs that served as rafters, his profile a dark silhouette against the starlit sky. She noted the angles of his jaw, the way his Adam's apple stood out in sharp relief, the cords of muscle in his neck as it dipped down to form a hollow at the base of his throat.

She had a theory about a man's neck. If it was too thin, he looked weak. Too long, and he might be indecisive. If it was too thick or too closely attached to his shoulders, he lacked imagination and possibly good sense. But if it were the perfect blend of strength and masculine grace, it would look exactly like Brady Wilkins's.

"It is very nice," she finally answered. "And big."

He looked over at her. "Too big? Jack thinks it's too big."

Jessica studied the uprights that were almost too stout to reach around, the floor made of slabs of wood rather than planks, the railing that would stand long after the house collapsed. It was a reflection of the man who built it—big, sturdy, beautiful in its simplicity. "It's perfect," she said.

He studied her for a moment, then said, "Yeah. Perfect."

But it didn't sound like he meant the porch. Ignoring a flutter in her chest, she looked away.

For a long while they sat without speaking, facing the valley and the stars hovering on the fingertips of the mountains. For Jessica, it wasn't a comfortable silence, sitting in the dark with a man she scarcely knew. But she sensed her discomfort stemmed more from the lack of propriety than the presence of the man beside her.

"I'll have Buck build you a rocker," he said, ending the long silence. "You'll need one for when the baby—babies—come."

She was touched. "That's not necessary, but thank you." She would have to remember to add "generous" to her list for the archbishop.

"I'm not giving up mine."

Or perhaps not. "I'm not asking you to."

"Yeah, but you're thinking about it."

"You have no idea what I'm thinking."

His head turned toward her, and even though his expression was lost in the shadows, she sensed his grin. "Don't I?"

The audacity. For one shocked and irrational moment, she wondered if he had read her thoughts then realized that was impossible. "If you truly knew what I was thinking, you would be begging my forgiveness."

"For what?"

"The list is endless."

He grunted and faced the railing again. "I'll have Buck make you a rocker anyway."

How deflating to try to trade barbs with someone who wouldn't play. Silence again. This time it was she who ended it. "I wanted to thank you for—"

"You already did." He sounded almost irritated.

"Yes, well. It was a lovely party and I—"

"You already said that, too."

"Nonetheless, you and Elena outdid—"

"I didn't have anything to do with it. It was all her and the other women."

"Are you trying to be disagreeable?"

"Am I being disagreeable?" He looked over. "I thought it was you."

The man was an unrepentant tease. "I don't know how Elena can bear it," she muttered.

"Bear what?"

"You."

"Me?"

She waggled a finger at him. "You don't deserve her and that's the truth of it."

"Elena is like a sister. Why is that so hard for everybody to understand?"

Jessica blinked at him. "You mean . . . you're not . . . she's not . . . ?"

"I mean there is no me and Elena. Christ! Do I have to carve a sign?"

Startled by his outburst, Jessica pressed back against the slats of the chair.

He saw it and gave a mocking laugh. "So now you're afraid of me again?" In the dim light she could see white teeth beneath the black shadow of his mustache. A smile or a sneer? "Did you think you were safer with Elena between us? Did you think that would protect you?"

Protect her? From what? Was he threatening her?

He stopped rocking. He leaned closer. "I have news for you, Your Ladyship. If a man wants something bad enough, he won't let anything stand in his way."

Alarmed by his sudden change of mood, she started to rise. "Yes. Well—"

"Your brother's not in Socorro." He started rocking again.

She plopped back into the chair. "He's not?"

"Left last year, headed up the northwest coast. Probably in Alaska chasing gold."

Alaska? How would she ever find him in Alaska? She wasn't even sure where Alaska was.

He must have sensed her agitation. "It's not as bad as you think. You've got three months to find him, right? Meanwhile you can stay here, where the ladies can take care of you, then you'll have your babies and everything will—"

"Oh, be quiet!" she snapped. "You have no idea. None. And don't you dare patronize me!" She felt him staring at her but was too distraught to care. She had to think, come up with a solution to this latest catastrophe. A plan. She needed a plan.

Two babies. No brother. No place to go. How could she plan for that?

"Maybe there's someone else I could try to reach?"

She pressed her fingertips hard against her temple. She felt herself sinking, her mind sliding back into that dark place where fear and anger reigned. She could scarcely breathe, could scarcely think. How could she take care of Victoria with no home, no money? They would starve.

"Maybe someone in England?"

His voice sliced through her terror like a blade, severing the last frayed thread of her control. The next instant all her pent-up fear spewed out in a rush of angry words. "Who? My sister? She doesn't even know where I am. My husband? I don't have one. Or a lover. Or anyone who could help me." Fury churned in her chest, rose in her throat like bile. "There is no one who would even care except the filthy beast who drove me from my home, my family—God."

Tears she'd held back for too long spilled down her cheeks in a hot rush. That wounded part of her wanted to rise up and scream at the outrage, the unfairness of having her life, her soul, so violated. "It wasn't my fault. I did nothing wrong." Unable to stop herself, she pressed her clenched fists over her eyes and gave in to wracking sobs.

Brady sat stunned, not only by what she had revealed but also by the suddenness and rawness of her pain. Had he triggered this? Said something? He stared at her, this woman who was suddenly a stranger to him. Her anguish was a tangible thing, so powerful it held him pinned to the chair. If he knew what was wrong, he'd fix it. But what could he do? Reasoning wouldn't work, and he was afraid if he touched her or said the wrong thing again, she might shatter into a thousand jagged pieces.

As if in great pain, she bent forward in the chair, shoulders shaking, hands over her face. Other than great gasping breaths, she made no sound.

Jesus. He had to stop this. Now. "Come here." A calm touch soothed fractious horses. Maybe it would work on her.

She began to keen.

"Okay. I'll come to you." He scooted the rocker over until it butted up against her chair. "Give me your hand."

She didn't, so he gently pried it from her face. It was wet from her tears. Twining his fingers through hers, he bound them together from palm to elbow along the arm of the rocker.

Then he sat back and waited.

Christ. He hated this. Crying women made his stomach knot. His mother had cried a lot that summer Sam died, and Brady had been helpless to cope with his own misery much less hers. So he had blocked it, armoring himself against her grief and his own guilt and despair, until eventually when she slowly drifted away, he had felt nothing but a distant and regretful relief. It was a cowardly and unworthy act and it shamed him still.

He wouldn't make the same mistake now.

Steeling himself to patience, he let her cry herself out, wondering if she would permit him to comfort her and, if she did, would he even know how. He didn't have much practice in such things, but for her sake, he was willing to try.

It took a while, but in inches and degrees she gave in to him, first allowing herself to lean against him, then resting her forehead against his shoulder, and finally pressing her face into his arm as she wept. A small thing, but a victory nonetheless.

It scared the hell out of him. Not only because in breaking through her barriers he had formed a deeper connection to a woman he didn't understand, but also because it revealed to him how deeply it mattered to have gained even a small measure of her trust.

You stupid bastard.

"Tell me," he said once the crying slowed and she got herself in hand. He knew the cost of silence, and how unspoken words could grow into an unswallowable mass lodged in your throat.

"No." With the back of her hand she blotted tears from her cheeks, a purely feminine gesture that made something clench deep inside his chest. "I just want to forget."

"You'll never forget. Tell me."

At first he thought she wouldn't. Then in a voice devoid of the firestorm of emotion that had burned through her earlier, she spoke. "His name is John Crawford. He's my sister's husband. She doesn't know and I—I couldn't tell her. She thinks he's perfect, you see. A diamond of the first water. Perhaps he is and it's only around me that—"

"It's not your fault," he cut in, furious that she would think it was.

With two fingers she plucked at a pleat in her skirt. She cleared her throat. "Thank you for saying that. But there's no denying I brought it on myself. I chose wrong, you see."

He waited.

"As the firstborn daughter, I inherited Bickersham Hall. He wanted to mortgage it to pay his creditors. I could either sign over the deed or suffer the consequences. I wouldn't sign."

He said nothing, just listened, chewing silently on his rage while she told him in short, faltering sentences absent of detail or emotion, how John Crawford, her brother-in-law, a man she had trusted, a man who was part of her family and who should have been her protector, had become her rapist instead.

Brady didn't know what to say. What any man could say. It shamed them all.

"After—after it was over, he righted his clothing and asked if I had enjoyed 'our little interlude.' That's what he called it. An interlude." She made a strangled sound that could have been a laugh or a sob, he wasn't sure which.

"I told him I would never give him the deed. He became very angry and he—he put his hands on me again—and hurt me. When that didn't work, he used his fists, but only where it wouldn't show."

Brady worked to keep his breathing even.

"He said he would come back the next day . . . and the next . . . and the next until I signed over the deed. Instead, I ran." By the time she had finished, she was shaking again.

Stroking his fingertips over the hand that held his in a stranglehold, Brady tried to focus on her pain rather than his rage. "You're safe now. I won't let him get at you here." He thought about that poster outside the sheriff's office in El Paso, and wondered if it would be wrong to lure the bastard to the ranch. A word here or there, just enough to bring the sonofabitch—

"Rescuing me again, are you?" She gave him a wobbly smile.

He forced himself to smile back. "If you'll lend me your umbrella." It was a good thing she wasn't a crier because she didn't do a pretty job of it. Her eyes were swollen, her hair was a mess of tangles, and her nose was running. Yet unaccountably, he had an almost overwhelming urge to wrap her in his arms.

When he felt her start to rise, he tightened his grip on her hand, not ready to relinquish it before he made some response to all that she'd told him. But what could he say? Words wouldn't change anything, wouldn't make her pain or his rage go away.

So he gave her what he could. "You want me to kill him for you?" He wasn't altogether sure how sincere the offer was, especially if he had to go all the way to England to carry it out, but it sounded good when he said it, and if a little bloodletting was what was needed to make her feel better, he would surely consider it.

She either laughed or hiccupped, Brady couldn't tell which. Then she patted his arm with her free hand, a friendly gesture that told him she would be all right now. He wondered if he would.

"You're daft. But you do say the sweetest things."

"Just tell me where he is." Now that she'd refused the offer, he felt it wouldn't matter if he embellished it a bit.

This time she did laugh, and a welcome sound it was. "You. In England. I think not."

"I could send Jack. He wants to go to Australia and that's almost the same."

She reared back. "It most assuredly is not. Australia is full of convicts."

"And kookaburras."

"Kooka-whats?"

Taking advantage of her distraction, he reached across with his free hand to tuck a drooping curl behind her ear. It pleased him she didn't flinch from his touch. "Jessica," he chided softly, using her name for the first time. "How could you ever think it was your fault?"

She looked down at the fist she clenched in her lap. "I should have stopped him. Fought harder. Done something."

"You did exactly what you were supposed to do. You survived." He pressed the tips of his fingers under her forceful little chin. "Look at me."

When she lifted her head, he could see the hint of shame in her eyes and it awakened his fury all over again. "Someday you'll face him."

She stiffened. "No."

"Yes. And you'll take back all he stole from you. And you'll never be afraid again."

"No. I couldn't." It was a whisper, almost a plea.

"You could and you will. Because you're Jessica Rebecca Thornton and you're a woman to reckon with."

Her mouth opened, closed, opened again. He could almost see her mind searching through memories and he knew the exact moment she found the right one.

"You heard," she accused. "That day by the water trough when I found you dipping your nasty feet into the water."

Brady lowered his hand to the armrest. "They weren't nasty. They were hurt. There's a difference."

"At any rate, you have it wrong. It's Jessica *Abigail* Rebecca Thornton."

Brady knew that, but pretended he didn't. He remembered everything about that day, and her most of all. "It's late," he said, making a dismissive motion with one big, suddenly clumsy hand. "If you're through trying to guilt me out of my rocker . . ." He let the sentence hang.

"You're dismissing me?"

"I'm sending you to bed before you goad me into doing something foolish. So yeah, I'm dismissing you."

She bounded to her feet.

He let her get to the door before he spoke again. "And by the way . . ."

She froze, her back straight and stiff.

"You looked real pretty tonight."

She hesitated in the doorway as if trying to find something objectionable in his words. Then finally she replied, "Thank you."

He let her take another step. "No. Thank *you*."

This time she turned to glance back at him over her shoulder.

Light from the sinking moon angled under the porch eaves to highlight her high cheekbones and make her eyes glitter like living stars. She looked so beautiful standing there, her hair in silvery disarray, her body round and ripe with life, for a moment he could hardly breathe.

"I like it," he finally said in a strained voice. He waved a shaky index finger at that impressive, ever-growing chest barely hidden by a green scarf-thing. "It's a wonderment." He listened for her gasp, then added, "And one helluva fine-looking dress."

A worthwhile sacrifice, he thought, listening to her angry footsteps stomp down the hall. She might be peeved, but at least she'd go to sleep thinking of him rather than that sonofabitch, John Crawford.

Nine

"WHAT DID YOU DO TO HER?" ELENA AMBUSHED HIM IN THE kitchen before Brady could even pour his first cup of coffee.

He yawned, still groggy from the worst night's sleep he could remember. Bad enough that with all these people in the house he had to share a room with Hank, who worked sums in his sleep, but he couldn't stop thinking about what Jessica had told him, and all the fun things he wanted to do to that sonofabitch, Crawford. "To who?"

"Jessica. I saw you on the porch. She was crying. What did you do?"

"Sí. ¿Qué pasa?" Consuelo joined the attack, positioning herself at Elena's elbow and armed with a wooden spoon.

A formidable duo. "Nothing." He rubbed a palm over his bristly jaw, trying to wake himself up enough to figure out what they were talking about.

"Then why was she crying?"

Brady shrugged. "She was upset."

"*¿Por qué?*"

"Ask her. She was the one crying."

Apparently that wasn't the answer they wanted. Consuelo whacked him with her spoon. Elena's black eyes snapped with anger. "Brady! What did you do?"

"You think I hurt her?"

Elena crossed her arms, her mouth as pinched as a tailor's stitch. Consuelo gave him the evil eye.

That finally woke him up. "Listen to me. Both of you." He leaned down until the three of them were eye to eye to eye. "I did not hurt her. She was upset. If she wants you to know why, she'll tell you. But it wasn't because of me." He glared at Elena. "You understand?"

She nodded.

He turned to Consuelo. "*¿Comprendes?*"

"*Sí, jefe.*"

He straightened. "Then get me my damn coffee."

They did, and he went out onto the porch, where he enjoyed at least thirty seconds of blessed quiet before Elena came out, looking sheepish and wanting to talk. He didn't, but bless her heart, she didn't let that stop her.

Women, he'd found, needed to talk. And listening, or pretending to, was the price a man had to pay to maintain peace. It did little good to try and make sense of what they said. Like a puzzle with all the wrong pieces or a map drawn with false trails and missing landmarks, a woman's mind was an unsolvable mystery . . . or at worst, an emotional quagmire that could suck a man down before he even knew he'd stepped off high ground. So while Elena talked, he kept his mouth shut and pretended to listen.

Until his mind registered two words in the same sentence: "Jessica" and "Ashford."

He straightened in the rocker. "What about Jessica and Ashford?"

"Ah. Now he listens." She gave him that smug superior smirk that women did so well. "I ask if you saw the way he watched her last night?"

"He was watching her?" *That sonofabitch.*

"I watched also. But I watched you."

Why would he be watching her? Absently Brady tugged on the corner of his mustache with his thumb and index finger, trying to remember if he'd even seen them together last night. He would have noticed. He'd noticed everything else—how much she ate, how her toe tapped time to the music, how pretty she looked in that fine yellow dress. It seemed he'd been so busy noticing her, he hadn't noticed if anyone else was noticing her, too.

"When you are with her, you look different. *Contento.* Happy."

That sonofabitch would be dust on the horizon by the end of the day.

"I think you care for her."

"What?" He glanced over. "What're you talking about?"

"It is good," she went on, as if he hadn't spoken. "You have how many years now? Thirty-three? It is time you took a woman."

Hell, he'd taken lots of women, but that wasn't something he would ever discuss with Elena.

"And I think she cares for you, too," Elena added.

That shocked him. He tried to think of something clever to say, something offhand and humorous that would show he regarded her comment of so little consequence he didn't take it seriously. "She does?" he said instead, dumb bastard that he was.

Elena pounced like a cat on a June bug. "So you do care for her." A statement, not a question. That smug look again.

"She makes me laugh." That explanation had satisfied Jack. Maybe it would work with her.

Apparently not. "In what way?"

That was another thing about a woman. The simple answer was never good enough. In fact, it often triggered more questions. "It's complicated. She's complicated."

"She is alone, Brady. And afraid."

"I told her she could stay here as long as she wanted." He hadn't actually said the words but he'd implied it, which was almost the same.

Apparently he was wrong about that, too. "A woman needs more, *querido*." A wistful longing clouded eyes so black Brady couldn't tell iris from pupil. "She needs a hero. Jessica needs you, Brady."

She's got me, he thought, remembering how he felt when she leaned into him last night. *And I don't know what to do about it.*

But he wouldn't discuss it with Elena. Pretending he didn't understand what she meant, he said, "Well, she needs something, that's for damn sure. The woman's beset. If the obvious problems weren't enough, she's got this . . . this thing . . ."

"Thing?"

He gestured to his throat. "With her breathing." Adopting a look of grave concern, Brady elaborated. "One minute she's breathing too much, then the next she's not breathing at all. It's disturbing. I have to remind her all the time—" At a choking sound he looked over to see Elena laughing. "What?"

"Oh, Brady." Shaking her head, she patted his cheek as she might some dearly loved but woefully dumb little kid. "I think you take her breath away."

"Really? I thought it was the asthma." *Dumb, hell.* With a grin, he slumped back, feeling pleased with himself and enjoying his own wit, until Red rode into the yard, his horse lathered and his hat askew, yelling "FIRE!"

Jessica awoke to chaos—the barking of the hound, horses thundering past, men calling out, and beneath it all, Brady's deep voice shouting orders.

She rolled out of bed and rushed to the window, but dust kicked up by the horses was so thick she could scarcely see beyond the porch posts. Quickly she threw on one of her recently altered dresses and, without bothering with her hair, raced down the hall toward the sound of Brady's voice.

She almost planted her face in his chest as she bolted onto the porch.

"Whoa, there," he said, catching her before she fell down the steps. He gave that heart-stuttering grin. "You're that glad to see me, are you?"

Realizing his hands still gripped her shoulders, she shrugged them away. "What's wrong? I heard shouts. Are we under attack?"

"Maybe." He looked her over. His eyes took on that studied look, darkening to a sharper, deeper blue. "I like your hair like that, all fiery and wild, like you just woke up from a long satisfying night."

What was this fixation with her hair? "I did just wake up, you big dolt! Tell me what's happening?"

Jack's face appeared at Brady's shoulder. "What's the shouting about?"

"I told her I liked her hair."

"That upset her?"

"Seems so."

She felt like shoving the both of them back down the porch steps. Luckily Elena and Consuelo came to intervene.

Elena passed out two linen-wrapped parcels while Consuelo gave each brother a leather bag still dripping water. "Take other canteens also," Elena instructed. "And cloth to wet and throw over your heads. And spare bullets."

"Yes, Ma."

"Brady, do not make jokes!" She said something in rapid, angry Spanish.

The only word Jessica understood was "Sancho." She looked anxiously at the men in the yard methodically loading saddlebags, filling canteens, checking guns. They seemed intent but not overly worried. In fact several, like these two nitwits, were actually laughing. She didn't know what to think.

"Look at me," Brady said.

She realized the others had left and she and Brady were alone on the porch. He was no longer smiling and the seriousness of his expression put her on guard. When he put his hands on her shoulders, she didn't shrug them off. She waited, staring up at him, so close she could see silver whiskers in with the black stubble on his chin, smell coffee on his breath, feel the hot heavy weight of his palms through the thin fabric of her dress. It created within her a sense of urgency she didn't understand.

"There's a fire in one of the canyons," he said. "If it rains, we should have it out pretty quick. Otherwise it might take a day or two."

Jessica gazed past him to the dark clouds hanging above the jagged tips of the mountains. If they were in a canyon and it rained, there could be one of those flash floods she'd heard about. They could all be drowned.

"A couple of men will be guarding the house while we're gone," he said, drawing her attention again. "You'll be safe here, so I don't want you worrying."

"Is it Sancho?"

"Maybe. Keep an eye on Elena for me. She'll be scared and worried."

And I won't be? She nodded but didn't speak, afraid her voice might betray her panic. What if the fire was a ploy to lure them out into the open away from the house? What if Sancho came here while they were gone?

"Pay attention. This is important."

Her gaze flew back to his.

"Take a deep breath."

She did. But before she could exhale, he bent down and pressed his lips to hers.

Just like that. No warning. While her mouth was still open.

Jessica was so shocked, she froze. Mesmerized. Shaken. Enthralled.

Her first real kiss.

It wasn't his best, Brady thought, feeling awkward and clumsy as a green kid. Yet it awakened within him a fire that sent heat rushing through his body. So he kissed her again. And because she just stood there and let him, he did it again. And suddenly he was so lost in the wonder of her, he couldn't think at all, and might have kept at it all day, if he hadn't felt her hands on his chest. He reared back.

They stared at each other.

He felt like he'd been running uphill. She wasn't breathing at all. Yet in the midst of his confusion, Brady realized an important thing—the hands on his chest weren't pushing him away.

Confidence restored, he gave her his biggest grin. "That wasn't so bad, was it?"

She gaped up at him, lips swollen, eyes so wide he could see white all around the amber-brown irises. Taking her silence as a good sign, Brady gave her another kiss for luck then bounded down the porch steps to vault into the saddle of the horse waiting in the yard. With a quick wave, he galloped after the other men riding through the gate.

By the time Jessica's befuddled brain reminded her to wave back, he had already disappeared behind the hill. She pressed fingertips to her mouth, not sure whether to laugh or cry. Her lips tingled. Her stomach felt tight as a drum. Her heart was in chaos. And all she could think was that his mustache wasn't nearly as prickly as she had imagined it would be.

Bad? It was wonderful.

To Paco, it sounded more like water than fire. Like the roar of a river at snowmelt or a waterfall or a hard, driving rain. A tree crowned in the canyon below, sending a spike of flames a hundred feet into the air. The heat of it forced him back from the edge of the bluff as twisting black clouds boiled out of the canyon. The sun turned brown in the orange sky.

Sancho was right. It was a beautiful fire.

"Here they come!"

Paco looked back to see Rawlins on the ridge behind him, a dark silhouette against the rolling sky. "*¿Cuántos?*"

"Fifteen or twenty. Moving fast."

"Wait until they come into the canyon. Tell the others."

Rawlins nodded and worked his way along the narrow trail that rimmed the box canyon. Paco walked to where Sancho hunkered on the ledge, staring down into the inferno. He rocked back and forth, laughing and muttering to himself. *Happy as a pig in shit*, Paco thought in disgust.

"*Vamos*, Sancho. It is time."

Sancho stopped rocking and looked around. His eyes gleamed wet and red, irritated by the smoke. When he smiled, his mouth looked like an open wound in his sooty face.

"I have him now, Paco."

"*¡ESTÚPIDOS!*" ELENA SNAPPED OPEN A PEAPOD WITH SUCH vigor peas shot across the porch floor to bounce past Melanie and Iantha as they sat on the top step, pulling stems from beet greens. "Did you see? They want to go. *Idiotas*."

Jessica tried to attend to what Elena was saying. She was still so astonished that Brady had kissed her she could scarcely gather her thoughts. Why would he do such a thing? And why had she allowed it? It was grossly familiar and entirely beyond the bounds of proper behavior.

It was also the first time she had ever been kissed on the lips by a man.

She didn't count that sordid little episode with the groom's son— Griffith or Gunter or Gerald, whatever. Not particularly memorable. A mere peck and rather wet, but to an eleven-year-old, heady stuff, indeed.

Admittedly over the years there had been other attempts by avid young men anxious to call Bickersham Hall home, but she had been too busy tending Mama and Annie, trying to keep kith and kin together, to become involved in such foolishness. Or in kissing. Until now.

And now . . . well.

The irony of it didn't escape her. Pregnant six months and never truly kissed. Until now, she had never thought it would happen. And since her attack she hadn't wanted it to.

But now . . . well.

How pathetic she was to be so undone by a mere kiss.

"They do not care that we wait and worry," Elena said, cutting into her thoughts.

Jessica reached over to pat her worried friend's arm. "They will be fine."

Elena was too distraught to be comforted. "Always he laughs. As if he cannot be hurt or killed. He does not see the danger. *¡Estúpido!*"

"I am sure he'll be careful. Brady isn't foolish." Only outrageous. Unpredictable. Confounding. It was insanity. A scary, shivery, breathless sort of insanity that almost made her giggle. *Giggle.* Clearly, she had lost her mind.

"Brady, *sí*." Elena looked up, her eyes distant and unfocused. "But the other?" She shook her head again. "He makes jokes. He does not know."

The other? Jessica studied Elena, wondering if she meant Jack. Had she been correct in surmising there were feelings between the two?

"Well, I'm glad Hank stayed behind." Melanie idly fanned herself with a limp beet frond. "I feel much safer with him around. He's so strong." She winced as distant thunder rumbled over the mountains. "Let's hope it's just a fire and not that bloodthirsty madman running around loose."

Jessica frowned at Melanie's insensitivity. Apparently she'd forgotten the bloodthirsty madman was Elena's brother.

"It is Sancho," Elena said with conviction. "I know this. I feel it here." She pressed a palm against her crippled hip. "It aches when he is close."

"Is he the reason you're lame?" Melanie asked, curiosity overtaking good manners. She must have caught Jessica's glare because she quickly added, "I'm sorry. I didn't mean to pry."

Elena made a dismissive gesture. "It was long ago. And, *sí*, it was Sancho."

"What happened?"

"It is a long story." Elena set the bowl of peas on the floor beside her chair and laced her hands tightly together in her lap. "But to understand Sancho, I must first tell you of the feud and how it began."

Across the valley, thunderheads rolled over the mountains, mumbling angrily as they snagged on jagged peaks. A sudden gust spiraled across the yard, peppering them with grit and sending chickens in squawking disarray. The air was cool and thick with the scent of roses.

Jessica thought of flash floods and didn't know whether to wish for rain or not.

Elena took a deep breath and let it out, her posture stiff, as if bracing herself. "My father was like a king," she began, her voice soft and distant, as if that might insulate her from the pain behind the words. "And RosaRoja his kingdom. He answered to no one. After Mexico lost the war with the United States in 1848, all the old land grants had to be registered with the new government in Santa Fe. My father would not do that. He was Spanish, not Mexican, *comprendes*? It was not his war. So RosaRoja was opened for resettlement.

"Jacob Wilkins bought it. He was a generous man. Because we had nowhere else to go, he allowed us to live in one of the line cabins. Sancho had only ten years when we lost the rancho, but even then he was cruel and full of anger. The loss of his home made him worse . . . *un diablo*. He killed cattle and set fires and did other more terrible things. No one was safe."

In her mind, Jessica saw a frightened little girl with bloody legs, and suddenly she didn't want to hear more. Reaching out, she took Elena's hand in her own. "You don't have to do this."

Elena shook her head. "*Sí*. I must. It is important that you understand. For Brady."

Jessica didn't know what that meant, or how to respond, so she said nothing as she stared out at the empty road. Before it crossed under a high arched metal gate, it curved gently to the left around the base of a small hill. A footpath wound up to the top, where a single drooping tree shaded a small fenced graveyard of overgrown weeds and tilted tombstones.

I've buried most of my family and a lot of good men.

Elena's voice grew strained. "For two years, Sancho brutalized everyone, even his own family. No one was safe. Then something happened that sent him beyond reason. Our mother, Maria, fell in love with Jacob Wilkins."

"Oh, my," Melanie breathed. "What did your father do?"

"He had many more years than my mother. I think he did not love her, so much as he prized her, as he did his horses. He did not like anything or anyone slipping beyond his control. She became his prisoner in our tiny cabin. We both did. It was a difficult time."

Elena turned to Jessica, her gaze earnest. "Jacob was an honorable man. He tried to be a good husband and father. But his wife . . . she had already lost two babies at birth, and that summer she carried another." Elena sighed and shook her head. "The strength was gone from her. This place, this life . . . it was too much. *¿Entiendes?*" Tears filled her eyes. "Then Sam died."

"Sam?" Melanie cut in.

"The youngest brother." Elena's voice broke. She swiped tears from her cheeks and took a deep, shaky breath before continuing. "One day he rode out to find Brady. Instead, he found Sancho and Paco. They beat him. Then Sancho dragged him behind his horse. The ground was rocky and full of cactus. And it was very, very hot."

Jessica closed her eyes, tried to block the images forming in her mind.

"It was Brady who found him. I do not know what happened on the desert that day. Brady will not speak of it even to his brothers. But it changed him. Now he holds his brothers close, not in love, but in fear that he will fail them, too."

Jessica's eyes snapped open. *Fail them?* "How was any of this Brady's fault? It was his own father who started this feud and Sancho who killed his brother. Whom did he fail?"

Elena shrugged. "Perhaps himself. I know he blames his father for starting the feud, but for some reason I do not understand, he blames himself for Sam."

And he still does, Jessica thought, remembering that haunted look on his face at the stage stop. *I won't bury another brother.*

"Later that summer, Jacob's wife bore the daughter she had prayed for. But it was too late. Her spirit had died with Sam. Jacob tried to help them, but the babe was small and her mother weak. He buried them beside Sam. Two months later he began to meet with my mother."

"Did Brady know?" Jessica asked. A man as honorable as Brady would disapprove of that.

Elena nodded. "It made him very angry. But for Sancho, it was the last insult. First his home, then his mother . . . it was too much. It became a summer of blood."

On the hilltop, the wind whipped the drooping branches into a frenzy and sent weeds slapping furiously against tilted tombstones.

"One day, I heard Sancho and Paco making plans," Elena continued. "They would kill all the brothers, from the youngest to the oldest, then set fire to the Rancho. And after they had taken everything from him but his life, they would burn Jacob alive."

"My word," Melanie said. "And Sam was the first."

"Which meant Jack was next," Jessica added.

Elena nodded, her lips pressed in a tight, grim line.

"What did you do?"

"There was little I could do. I rode to the Rancho to warn them, but Sancho caught me." In a flat voice, Elena told how her brother pulled her from her horse and kicked her again and again until she fainted from the pain.

"As with Sam, he left me in the desert to die. *Un vaquero*—a cowboy—found me and took me to Jacob. When he saw what Sancho had done, he went to bring my mother to safety as well.

"I am not sure what happened that night. When Brady went after his father, he found my parents dead and Jacob unconscious outside the burning cabin. He had had a seizure of some sort, and because he never spoke or walked again, he could never tell us what happened.

"Brady went after Sancho, determined to end it. He found him and Paco wandering in a canyon not far from the burned cabin." A bitter note edged Elena's voice. "I know it is wrong and I ask God's forgiveness, but I wish he had killed them then. I ask him why he did not, but he will not speak of that night. Not with me. Not even with his brothers. And now the killing begins again."

Jessica was so numbed by Elena's horrible revelations she simply sat there, unable to fathom the heartache these two families had inflicted upon one another.

She thought again of Brady's words at the stage stop. She hadn't understood then but she did now. This time he would die before he'd bury another brother.

Oh, Brady, she thought sadly. *You work so hard to watch over everyone else—but who watches over you?*

Ten

THE MEN SLUMPED IN THEIR SADDLES, HOLLOW-EYED AND spent. Paco didn't wonder that they'd soured—Rawlins dead, Haskins with a bullet through his leg, and Crocker nursing a twisted ankle. Sancho was there in body only. Luckily the rain had washed out their tracks. Paco had made them backtrack a couple of times just to be safe, but if he hadn't found that back trail over the ridge, they might all be roasting with Rawlins right now.

Not that Sancho cared. He seemed oblivious to the looks sent in his direction and the way the men muttered behind his back. Paco didn't blame them. He had doubts of his own.

When they reached the canyon, Paco left Crocker to tend Haskins and followed Sancho up the slope to the cave. Once inside the entrance, he collected twigs and brush for a fire while Sancho sat against the wall, watching in silence. It made Paco uneasy. He knew Sancho was stewing because the rain had doused the forest fire. He just didn't know what his half brother would do about it. Set more fires? Slaughter cattle? Go on a killing rampage like he had ten years ago?

His unpredictability was more frightening than the man himself.

After building a small fire behind the boulders where it couldn't be seen, Paco got out the tin of coffee. Once it boiled, he filled a cup, topped it off with whiskey, then passed it to Sancho.

They drank in silence. Mist beaded on the rocky walls, trickled down to form puddles on the sandstone floor. The chill dampness settled into Paco's bones, but Sancho seemed unaffected and continued staring out at the rain, absently working at his mustache with his bottom teeth. When the fire was down to steaming coals, he finally spoke. "That man in the canyon. It is his son?"

Paco pulled his poncho up to cover the back of his neck. "The oldest. Brady."

"I remember. The one with Jacob's eyes. I will enjoy killing him."

Sancho seemed calm. Hoping the worst was over, Paco tossed more twigs on the fire. With a hiss they caught, sending a coil of smoke up into the shadows overhead.

"Do you hear her, *hermano*?" Sancho whispered.

Paco looked over. The flickering firelight distorted Sancho's face in a way that reminded Paco of things that crawled through his nightmares. Shivering, he looked away. "Hear who?"

"She haunts me, Paco. No matter how many times I kill her, she is still here." He tapped his forehead. "*En la cabeza. ¿Por qué?*"

Paco clenched his teeth in anger. Always Maria. That was all Sancho thought about. *What about me?* he wanted to shout. *What about our plans to regain the rancho?* Then as suddenly as it came, anger faded. He could not fight her—not in life—not in death. Maria would always win.

"It was not I who shamed our family, Paco. You saw. You were there."

"I saw." Wearily, Paco leaned back against the wall, wondering if Haskins and Crocker would stay, or if come morning, it would be just him and Sancho.

"I only do what I must, Paco. What she forces me to do. When she sees him burn, she will know and then she will let me rest."

Unease crawled up Paco's neck. "Know what? What are you talking about?"

Sancho smiled. A sudden gust sent sparks flying upward in a spiraling dance. As it swept through the tunnel, it moaned like a woman's cry.

"Soon, Paco."

THE STORM BROKE IN A SUDDEN DELUGE OF HAILSTONES THAT quickly gave way to a hard, driving rain. Jessica loved thunderstorms, loved the smell of spent lightning, the sweet scent of wet grass, that crackle of energy that filled the air. But this was a bit much. Shivering with the abrupt drop in temperature, she retrieved her wool shawl from her room then returned to the porch. Settling into Brady's rocker, her heels tapping a drumbeat against the plank floor, she rocked and watched the storm and waited for the men to return home.

The escort came first. A half dozen mounted troopers and an ambulance wagon splashed into the yard just as the sky went twilight dark. Hank came out of the barn and spoke to the lead rider, then the man dismounted and began barking orders barely heard over the stomp of horses and jangle of harness. With practiced efficiency, the troopers tied their horses to the corral rails and lashed oilskins over their saddles before ducking into the barn. The lead soldier, boasting two yellow bars sewn across the shoulder of his uniform, detached himself from the others and came to the porch. Snapping to attention and shaking water off his hat, he introduced himself to Jessica as Lieutenant Jarvey, here to escort Mrs. Kinderly and her daughter to Santa Fe.

Jessica directed him to the Kinderlys' room. As he disappeared into the house, she turned to see more riders coming through the gate.

They rode slowly, heads tucked against the rain, hats pulled low. She studied them as they filed past. Two wore red-stained bandages.

Another rode facedown across his saddle. Suddenly wobble-legged, she gripped the porch rail so tightly the rough wood bit into her palms.

A horse carrying two riders stopped at the barn. Hank came out to meet them. They spoke for a moment, then the man in the rear slid down and motioned a soldier forward. The rain drowned out his words, but not his voice.

Despite the tired slump of his shoulders and his sooty face, she recognized Brady's distinctive drawl. Just hearing it triggered such a swell of emotion, she sank into the rocker, too weak to stand. The depth of her relief shocked her, made her realize how frightened she had been, and how involved her emotions had become.

Dimly she heard all three Wilkins brothers arguing with the trooper. The beleaguered soldier shrugged and pointed toward the house just as the lieutenant came back out the door, staggering under the weight of three bulging valises. As he dumped them by the steps, Brady came forward.

"I need your men," he said as he came up the stairs. "Two days. Maybe less." He explained about the fire, and how four men led by Sancho Ramirez had tried to ambush them in the canyon. "We got one of them, but they got two of ours. We need to stop him before someone else dies."

The lieutenant was reluctant. "If he's not Indian or Army, we can't interfere."

"He tried to burn us out, including the colonel's wife and daughter."

"Yes, but—"

"They're military, aren't they?"

"Yes, but—"

"Christ, if you can't make the decision, wire Kinderly. Get his okay."

Jessica refrained from patting the young officer's shoulder in sympathy. She knew how intimidating Brady could be—especially with two scowling brothers behind him.

Red-faced and defeated, the officer finally left to wire Colonel

Kinderly. Brady told Jack to have Consuelo bring her medicine basket to the bunkhouse, then asked Hank to carry the dead man into the dining room and send someone for Doc and Rikker. Then he turned to Jessica.

Sadness swept her. Beneath a rain-streaked coating of soot and ash, he looked drawn and worn. She sensed a weariness that went deeper than flesh—a weariness of spirit.

"Keeping my rocker dry for me, are you?"

She couldn't see any sign of injury, but she needed to ask. "Are you hurt?"

"No."

That heady relief again. She tamped it down. "The others . . . the wounded . . . can I—"

"No."

She blinked, put off by his abrupt refusal. "I can help, Brady. I want to."

"It doesn't concern you." Perhaps he realized how brusque he sounded, or he read the hurt she wasn't able to hide. Pulling off his hat, he dragged a hand across his forehead, leaving dark streaks across the paler skin. In a gentler tone he said, "I don't want you pulled into this, Jessica. I don't want blood on your hands, too."

"Then what can I do?"

"Keep my rocker warm." He turned toward the house, then stopped, eyeing the pile of luggage by the door. "Any of this yours?"

"No. It belongs to the Kinderlys."

"Good." Opening the door, he went inside.

As the rain continued, the thick adobe walls that had kept the heat out now held the chill dampness in. Water seeped under doorways, puddled under windows. As men trooped in and out, the floors grew slippery with mud.

Jessica bustled through the rooms wiping and mopping until Elena insisted she get off her feet. Determined to help, she sat at the kitchen table and assisted Iantha with supper preparations, while Consuelo and Elena tended the wounded in the bunkhouse.

Apparently Iantha was as unimpressed with beans and tortillas as Jessica. Together they cooked up a hearty meal of roasted beef with potatoes and carrots, fresh beets and greens from the hail-battered garden, a mountain of green beans, several loaves of freshly baked bread, and pudding for dessert. Just the smell of it cooking made Jessica's stomach rumble. It clearly had a similar effect on the Wilkins brothers. By the time the meal was ready, they crowded the doorway, washed and combed, all but smacking their lips in anticipation.

They ate like men on the brink of starvation. But what they lacked in table manners and polite dinner conversation, they made up for in noisome enthusiasm, and Jessica took comfort in that. While they busily gorged themselves, Iantha loaded a tray for Buck and left. Jessica was debating fixing a tray for the Kinderlys when Melanie swept in, looking for the lieutenant.

"Val Rosa," Brady mumbled through a mouthful of food.

"When will he return? Mama wants to know when we'll be leaving."

Brady reached for another slice of bread. "Two days. Maybe three."

"Two days?" Melanie stared from one brother to the other as if seeking a different answer. When none came, she started twisting her hands. "But Mama—"

Brady waved her off. "If she's got questions, send her to me."

Hank gave her a sympathetic look. Melanie met it with a shy smile, then quickly filled two plates and left.

A few minutes later Elena came in, looking tired and worried. As she filled a plate, Jessica noted one of her sleeves showed spatters of blood. Brady asked her something in Spanish. She answered and shook her head. Assuming they were talking about the injured men, Jessica asked Brady how they were.

"Red will be fine. Sanchez is lung shot."

Jack reached for the platter of roast beef. "Too bad. He was a good hand. Darnell, too. Is there more coffee?"

"I'll make some." Jessica rose and went to the stove. Trying to remember how Iantha had made it, she dumped what she hoped was the correct amount of ground beans into the blackened pot, filled it with water, and set it to boil. Satisfied, she returned to the table.

They ate in silence. After finishing her meal, Elena loaded a tray for Consuelo and carried it back to the bunkhouse. Hank spooned more beets and greens onto his plate, Jack took second helpings of everything, and Brady finished what must have been a pound of green beans. Although it gladdened her to see how much they enjoyed the meal, she was astounded at the amount of food these men had already consumed and wondered if there would be enough.

"It's fortunate you raise your own food," she murmured as Brady loaded his plate again.

"It's tasty." Jack nudged Hank. "I think we ought to keep her, don't you?"

She narrowed her eyes at him. "Keep me?"

"Well, you know what they say." Jack popped a slab of bread into his mouth. "The quickest way to a man's heart is through his stomach."

"Indeed?" She smiled sweetly. "I thought it was through a hole in his chest."

Jack choked. Hank gave her that assessing look. Brady threw back his head and laughed.

Rain beat a gentle tattoo against the shutters, but in the kitchen the air was warm and cozy, redolent with the smell of cooking, wood smoke, damp men. Despite the dead man resting in the next room, a comfortable, homey feeling crept over her and she sighed, filled with a calm joy.

Brady shot her a curious look.

She met it with a smile, amused at the way his cheeks bunched when he chewed, the way his Adam's apple bobbed when he swallowed.

She wanted to tell him how grateful she was to be here, safe and alive. To tell him how worried she had been today, and how glad she was that he had come back unharmed. She wanted to say how sorry she was about Sam, and find out how he had gotten that scar across his eyebrow, and ask him why had he kissed her.

As if he read her thoughts, a slow, crooked smile tipped up one corner of his mustache, and she felt it again, that oddly intimate bond that had gripped her last night when she'd looked at him across the crowded courtyard.

From upstairs came the tinkle of a bell. His smile faded.

The bell rang again, louder, longer. A look passed between the brothers.

Since Melanie had already taken a tray to Maude, Jessica surmised the insistent bell ringer was Stanley Ashford. She glanced around, wondering if she should answer it. No one else seemed inclined to.

Brady's eyes bored into her almost in challenge, as if waiting to see what she did, as if this were some sort of test. But why would he care if she answered Ashford's summons?

Unless . . .

Ridiculous.

Yet warmth rushed up her neck. Abruptly she rose and went to the stove. Her hands were so clumsy she almost dropped the cup when she pulled it from the shelf. He couldn't be jealous, could he? Of Stanley Ashford? Why?

She glanced over. He was watching her, his brows drawn in a scowling ridge above his nose. She looked away, her heart bouncing in her chest. Brady jealous? It was ludicrous, beyond belief, ridiculous in the sublime.

She rather liked the notion.

Acutely aware of his gaze, she tarried at the stove. By the time she'd checked the coals, peeked into every pot, and filled the coffee cup, she'd regained her composure enough to see the absurdity of it. Whatever animosity existed between the two men, she wouldn't allow herself to be drawn into the middle of it. She would simply show Brady how foolish he was acting by turning the game back on himself. Under his watchful eye, she walked back to the table and set the filled cup beside his plate.

"Sugar?" she asked sweetly.

He looked down at the cup, then up again. "Ah . . . no."

"I'll take some."

"Shut up, Jack," Hank ordered, his gaze moving from Brady, then back to Jessica.

Ignoring the gawking younger brothers, she lifted the small pitcher. "Milk?"

Brady shook his head.

"More potatoes? Meat? Dessert, perhaps?"

His mustache twitched. "Dessert would be nice."

"Of course." She went to the stove, loaded a saucer with warm bread pudding, then came back and set it before him. "Anything else?"

He sat back, his gaze traveling up slowly—too slowly across her bosom—until it met hers. That slow dimpled smile. "Maybe later."

Wicked man.

Jack snickered. Hank elbowed him in the ribs. Jessica fled to the stove.

"There she goes, another one over the fence. You do have a knack, Brady."

"Shut up, Jack."

By the time she got herself back in hand, the bell ringing had stopped and the brothers were gobbling food as if nothing had happened. Perhaps nothing had. Perhaps she had imagined it all. Perhaps she had lost all reason.

A few minutes later Stanley Ashford came in. With a terse greeting that only Jessica acknowledged—earning another sour look from Brady—he settled in the chair Elena had vacated.

Jessica set a fresh plate before him and returned to her chair at the table.

If conversation had been slow before, his presence stopped it alto-

gether. With a halfhearted attempt to muffle a belch, Jack tipped back
his chair to pull the coffeepot from the stove. He started pouring, then
stopped and frowned into the cup. "What's this?"

"Coffee," she answered, surprised.

He sniffed the pot. "What'd you put in it?"

"Coffee."

"I can see bottom."

At a nod from Brady, Hank rose and took the pot back to the
stove. After dumping in another full cup of ground beans, he waited
for it to boil, then to Jessica's amazement, added a handful of broken
eggshells.

Brady pushed back his plate. "They finished with Darnell?"

Jack nodded. "On the dining room table, Sunday duds and all. Tobias found an address for his folks. I left it on your desk. The boys will
be in soon to say their good-byes."

Brady rose, went into the larder, and came back out with two
earthen jugs. His brothers each grabbed an armful of cups from the
hutch shelf then filed out after him, leaving Jessica alone in the kitchen
with Stanley Ashford.

She studied him from beneath her lashes. He ate with small precise bites, scooping with his fork rather than impaling his food. Unlike
their hosts, he knew the difference between his shirtsleeve and a table
napkin and used the latter often.

For some reason that irritated her. He irritated her. Although
he was the same handsome, well-mannered man she remembered,
when compared to the Wilkins brothers, Stanley Ashford seemed a
bit too . . . civilized? Prissy? Short? Being alone with him made her
vaguely uneasy.

Hoping to forestall conversation, she rose to clear the table. As she
reached for his empty plate, his hand closed over hers. She managed
not to flinch.

"I'm leaving with the escort. I think you should come, too."

"Indeed?" She stared down at his elegant fingers with their buffed
nails and pale unblemished skin. His hand felt small and smooth and

slightly clammy. Pulling from his grip, she wiped her palm down her apron. "As I explained before, Dr. O'Grady forbids me to travel."

"It's an ambulance wagon with reclining benches. You'd be safe enough."

"Would I? You're quite sure? Sure enough to risk the lives of my babies?"

"I see I've upset you."

"Not at all." How had she ever thought this insufferable man attractive? "However, although it was neither warranted nor solicited, I thank you for your concern. May I serve you coffee?" *You twit.*

"I'm sorry if I've offended you, Mrs. Thornton. I'm simply worried about leaving you stranded out here with no one to care for you."

"No one? You mean, no one other than Consuelo, the woman who nursed you so ably? Or Elena, who has watched over me like a mother hen? Or Iantha, who has force-fed me five times a day? What other care would I possibly need?"

Ashford smiled thinly. "A couple of Mexican women and an ex-slave?"

That was the last straw. Planting her hands on her hips lest she give in to the urge to strike the pasty-faced ninny, she bent down until her face was level with his. "Those women are my friends," she said through clenched teeth.

He blinked at her, clearly taken aback by the vehemence of her defense.

"And you will not denigrate them in my presence. Do you understand?"

At a sound, they both looked over to see Brady Wilkins watching from the doorway, his expressive eyes alight with fiendish delight. "Problems?"

Jessica straightened and glared down her nose at the preening popinjay she had once admired. "Not now. He was just leaving." Then before she forgot good manners altogether, she went to the washbasin, snatched a dishrag from a peg, and attacked the stack of dirty dishes.

How dare he? Consuelo and Elena had run themselves ragged on his behalf.

She heard the scrape of Ashford's chair. But only one set of footsteps faded down the hall.

She tensed, knowing Brady was still there. She could feel him somewhere behind her, his presence as palpable as a touch. A shiver of anticipation shot through her, heightening her senses to the point that she almost gasped when the familiar weight of his strong hands settled on her shoulders.

"You don't have to do that," he said, his breath fanning the top of her head.

She couldn't think, couldn't even look around. But she sensed him looming behind her, so close, she could feel the heat of his body down the length of her back. "Yes, I do," she said in a fluttery voice. "They're my friends."

His arm reached around her to gently pull the dishrag from her clenched fingers. He tossed it onto the stack of dishes. "I mean you don't have to wash the dishes."

"Oh." Feeling foolish, she stared down at her empty hands, waiting for him to move away so she could breathe again. Instead she felt his fingers brush across her cheek and down the side of her neck to where her collar brushed her nape. It made her heart tremble in her chest.

"You please me, Jessica," he whispered against her ear. Then his hands fell away, and cool air whispered down her spine.

Unable to stop herself, she looked around, but he was already gone.

Eleven

B RADY GOT HIS TROOPERS, BUT FIRST THE ESCORT HAD TO DE-
liver the Kinderlys to an Army post on the north bank of the Rio
Hondo. They would leave the next morning and return within two
days. Meanwhile, Brady would send for help from the outlying ranches
as well as Val Rosa, so that when the soldiers returned, there would be
enough men to do a thorough sweep of the whole area.

Despite the dead man resting in the dining room, a sense of
anticipation permeated the house and excitement ran high. The
night before, in preparation for the influx of men answering Brady's
call, Sandoval, the bunkhouse cook, buried the dressed carcass of a
steer in a coal-lined pit, covered it with an oiled canvas to protect
it against the rain, and left it to roast undisturbed for the next two
days.

During the night the rain stopped, and by morning the creeks had
receded, assuring the Kinderlys of a sunny, if muddy, trip. Jessica stood
at the porch rail, watching the endless preparations and wondering if

the Dougherty wagon would sink to its hubs under the weight of the passengers and all their luggage.

She had mixed feelings about their going. Together they had suffered a terrible ordeal and their survival had forged a bond among them that would never be forgotten. The moment the coach crashed down that rocky slope, everything in Jessica's life had changed. *She* had changed. These people were the last link in the chain that bound her to what she had been, and the life she had known before. In their eyes, she was still Mrs. Jessica Thornton, grieving widow, author of pamphlets of deportment, and maker of overblown hats—a woman worthy of their respect. But now? Now she didn't know where she fit anymore. She was a kite without a string.

It promised to be an awkward leave-taking. Throughout the bustle and confusion of packing and making sure that there was ample water, that the benches were properly cushioned, that everything humanly possible had been done to ensure Maude's comfort, neither Maude nor Ashford had afforded Jessica a single glance. An insubstantial loss as far as Jessica was concerned, but she would dearly miss Melanie.

The poor girl was in near hysterics. Apparently her attachment to Hank went deeper than mere infatuation. Hank must have shared those feelings, for although he had made himself scarce throughout the morning, Jessica had seen him in the doorway of the barn, watching the preparations and glowering behind his beard. She noticed he was there now, staring at Melanie with that same intensity Jessica had seen in his older brother's eyes, although to her mind it was much more affecting when those eyes were sky blue rather than dark brown.

"Oh, Jessica, what if I never see him again? I'll die. Surely I will."

"I doubt it." Jessica tucked a loose strand of blond hair beneath the brim of Melanie's bonnet. "But why tell me?" Taking the girl by the shoulders, she turned her toward the barn and gave her a gentle push. "Tell him."

When Melanie saw Hank watching from the doorway, she let out a squeak and charged across the muddy yard. Luckily Maude was too busy supervising her escort to notice.

An hour later, the wagon stood ready to depart. Jessica said good-bye to Maude and gave hugs to a surprisingly recovered Melanie.

"Hopefully I'll see you again soon," the girl whispered with a sly wink before skipping down the porch steps.

Stanley Ashford hesitated beside her. "You can still change your mind, you know. There's ample room."

"There's more room here," a deep voice cut in.

Jessica pursed her lips, wondering why Brady felt the need to insinuate himself whenever she and Ashford were together. "Good-bye, Mr. Ashford. I wish you a safe journey."

A few minutes later, the wagon rolled forward, leaving deep ruts in the soft ground. Hank watched until it cleared the arched gate then went back into the barn.

"I do believe our Hank's smitten," Brady observed, sounding somewhat surprised.

"As is Melanie."

That didn't seem to surprise him at all. "Well, he is a looker. Couldn't seem to hold the girls off until he grew all that hair. It's a family curse, I guess."

"Growing hair?" she asked innocently.

He glanced over, gave her the full benefit of that dazzling, dimpled grin, and she realized what a naïve ninny she had been. He knew exactly the effect of that smile and employed it without conscience to further his own aims. The man was a shameless bounder and an utter cad.

Whatever boost in spirits the departure of the Kinderlys and Ashford brought, it quickly faded when word came that the other wounded ranch hand, Sanchez, had died from his chest wound. Now there were two men awaiting burial in the morning. A pall fell over the house. Jessica had never seen Brady look so grim, and even Laughing Jack lost his cheerful smile. After a somber lunch, the brothers retired to Brady's office, where they spent the hours poring over maps and making plans.

With the help of several ranch wives, Elena and Consuelo readied the spare rooms for more guests while Buck put clean hay on the barn floor so the latecomers wouldn't have to sleep on damp ground. By late afternoon, riders from other ranches began to arrive, as well as Dr. O'Grady and a group of men from Val Rosa led by Sheriff Rikker. Soon the rumble of men's voices echoed through the house.

Jessica avoided them by staying in the kitchen, helping Iantha prepare mountains of potatoes, the usual pinto beans, tortillas, roasted peppers, cornbread with honey, and what greens they could salvage from the depleted garden. By the time long plank tables had been set up in the courtyard, Sandoval had unearthed the steer, and the clang of the dinner bell rang through the house.

Uncomfortable around so many strangers, especially in her condition, Jessica didn't join the guests in the courtyard, but carried a plate to her room instead. She was just finishing her meal when footsteps sounded in the hall. A moment later her door swung open.

"What're you doing?" Brady asked in his usual curt manner.

Did the man ever knock? She swiveled in the chair to give him a pointed look, then turned back to her plate. "Eating. What are you doing?" She could feel him watching as she took a final bite of potatoes and pushed her plate aside.

"You're hiding. Why?"

The man knew her too well. "I am not hiding."

"Then why are you in here all by yourself? Did something happen?"

"Nothing happened. I am simply a bit tired." Hoping to forestall further interrogation, she gave him a reassuring smile. "I have been helping Iantha in the kitchen all afternoon and I—"

He spun on his heel and left.

Before Jessica could recover from her shock at his rudeness, he returned with the doctor in tow. Shoving O'Grady into the room, he said, "She's tired."

The doctor scratched his head, clearly confused.

"Well, see to her," Brady ordered. "She's working too hard. We tell her to stop, but she won't listen. You tell her."

O'Grady turned to Jessica. "Stop working so hard."

"Of course, Doctor."

He turned to Brady. "Now can I finish my supper?"

Brady's scowl sent him back a step. "Sure, and she's looking fine, boyo. But if it will ease your mind, I'll check on her later . . . and without your lofty self there to frighten the wee thing. Will that settle your worries?"

Wee? Jessica almost laughed aloud.

"I'm not worried. I'm concerned. There's a difference."

She hid her amusement behind a gracious smile. "Then thank you for your concern, Brady, but I am well. Truly."

"You're sure?"

"Absolutely. Attend your guests. I'm for bed."

Brady hesitated. He tugged at the corner of his mustache. "Well, that's the thing, see."

She narrowed her eyes. "What thing?"

"The boys want to do Darnell and Sanchez proper, and it may get, um, a bit rowdy."

"Rowdy?"

O'Grady rubbed his palms together. "What he means is there may be a wee bit of drinking involved. Come on, lad."

"D-Drinking?" Jessica knew what demons men became when they drank, and the thought of dozens of drunkards reeling through the halls made her tense with fear. An image burst into her mind—John Crawford reaching out, his fingers curled like talons, his mouth wet and reeking of whiskey. She felt herself sway.

"Jasus. Best get my satchel."

"I'll take care of it, Doc. Go."

More words, but she lost them in the thundering in her ears. The door opened and closed, then Brady dropped onto his heels beside her chair. "Look at me."

She tried, but everything was spinning so furiously she could scarcely focus.

He took her hand in his, prying open her clenched fingers to gently lace them through his. "Nothing's going to happen. Just breathe. Slow and easy."

Strengthened by his calm assurance, she struggled to bring her breathing under control. The tightness in her throat eased. Her racing heartbeat slowed. As the panic ebbed, she realized she still held his hand, gripping it so tightly her nails dug into his skin. He allowed her to loosen her hold, but wouldn't allow her to pull away.

"You're safe here. No one will hurt you. Do you believe me?"

The force of those eyes was more powerful than a touch, robbing her of thought, vanquishing the fear. She nodded, feeling foolish and exposed and so grateful he was there, she couldn't say a word.

"I told you about the wake because it may get a little noisy and I didn't want you to be scared. These are good men. They would never hurt a woman. Especially not my—not in my house. Understand?"

She took a deep breath, slowly released it. "Yes."

He rose and went to the dresser. A moment later he returned. "Use this if it'll help."

He put a heavy brass key into her palm. It was still warm from his touch. "Thank you." But she didn't put much faith in it. A locked door hadn't stopped John Crawford. She attempted a weak smile. "I'm sorry. I'm not usually such a fearful person."

"I know." Still, he didn't move away. "I have another key, so don't think you can hide out in here forever."

"I am not hiding out." It was a relief to be irritated with him again. Anything other than that paralyzing fear. It was also a bit unnerving to realize she couldn't lock him out even if she felt the need to. Not that she felt the need to. She trusted him. As much as she was able.

He scratched thoughtfully at his whiskered jaw. "Or I guess I could drag you out and parade you around for a while. Once they saw you were pregnant, they'd never come near."

"Mercy. As appealing as it would be to have my *un*appealing person *paraded around* to ensure that your drunken friends left me alone, I fear I must decline. Hopefully a locked door will suffice. As would my parasol. Or a loaded scattergun if you have one to spare. Check the dining room. I believe that's where dead people and guns are kept."

Was he laughing at her? Before she could ask, he braced his hands on the arms of her chair and lowered his face to within inches of her own. "I never said you were unappealing. You're very appealing. Too appealing. But if they saw you were with me, they'd never think of coming near. Now do you understand?"

She pulled back, acutely aware of the masculine power that radiated from every cell in his big body. "No—yes—perhaps. Stop looming." He thought her appealing? *Too* appealing?

He didn't move.

She thought of the other day when he kissed her, and yesterday when his fingers trailed across her neck, and something moved within her, something low and liquid that wasn't the babies.

He leaned closer.

She didn't pull back.

"Maybe if I do this often enough"—his lips brushed the right corner of her mouth—"and this well enough"—another brush on the left—"someday you will." A final lingering kiss square in the middle, then he pulled back just far enough for her to feel the full impact of those aqua eyes.

"Will w-what?"

"Understand."

"Understand what?"

With a sigh, he straightened. "You know, this might work better if you closed your eyes. We'll practice on it."

Jessica gaped up at him, her mind in such disarray she couldn't form a single coherent thought. If his first kiss had been shocking, this one was amazing. Tantalizing. Addictive. She licked her lips, still tasting him, still feeling the heat of him, wondering if he would do it again.

"Don't look at me like that."

"Like what?" She was gratified to see he wasn't breathing so calmly either.

"Maybe I should give you both keys," he muttered and left the room.

THEY BURIED DARNELL AND SANCHEZ THE NEXT MORNING.

Brady told Jessica to stay at the house, which naturally she argued about. But when he explained that it would mostly be men at the gravesite, she handed him two ribbon-tied bouquets of roses and sent him on his way.

In a way, Brady would have liked having her there to bring a touch of gentility to an ungentle circumstance. But he also wanted her as far away from this mess as possible. She was like a clear, calm pool in his mind, a place that was clean of the taint of this feud, a place where goodness existed and hope still flowed. He needed to keep it that way.

As they headed back down the hill after the burial, the escort rode through the gates.

Brady had a late breakfast set up in the courtyard. After everyone had eaten his fill, he herded the ranch owners, Rikker, and Lieutenant Jarvey into his office, where he laid out the maps he and his brothers had been working on.

"This is where we are now." He thumped a cluster of squares marked on the map. "And these"—he pointed out a dozen other marks—"are all the places where Sancho's been seen. If you draw a line between them, it would be a circle, more or less. And this"—he pointed at Blue Mesa— "would be the center."

Lieutenant Jarvey looked doubtful. "That's got to be two hundred square miles. You expect thirty men to cover all that in two days?"

"Thirty-eight men. Between us, we cover about that every year at roundup."

Sheriff Rikker leaned closer to study the marks. "Isn't that where you found him and Alvarez the night he killed his folks?"

"And on foot," Jack added.

"You figure he was holed up close by?"

Brady nodded. "We've checked it time and again but it's hard to track on rock. There's a lot of places to hide and he knows them all."

"So what's the plan?"

It was a simple pie-shaped grid: twelve wedges of three men each, starting eight miles out and working inward to the center point at Blue Mesa.

After a brief discussion, Rikker deputized the whole group to keep things legal, explained some of the finer points of the law, which no one heeded, then gave up and went outside for a smoke. As the others filed out after him, Doc came in.

He looked worried. And thirsty. Knowing he'd been to see Jessica, Brady sent his brothers on with instructions to saddle his horse, then poured a "wee dram" for Doc and himself. Sitting back, he propped his boots on the desk and waited.

It was a natural curiosity. Since she was under his protection, he had a right to know how she was progressing. If there were problems ahead, he needed to prepare for them, to see that Consuelo was always on hand and Doc was nearby. That was his job, to organize, to see that everything ran smoothly, to take care of issues before they became problems. He didn't like surprises. And he damned sure didn't want those babies coming when there was no one around to deal with it but him. He was a rancher, not a midwife.

Which was probably why he got so upset when Doc mentioned the possibility that those babies might come early, and if so, there might be complications, and sadly, they might be adding more graves up on the hill before it was over.

Brady's boots hit the floor with a thud. "You mean she could die?" He thought of his mother and baby sister, and something twisted in his chest. "You never said she could die."

"Saints preserve us, lad, calm yourself!" With a look of alarm, Doc waved him back into his chair. "Faith, I never said she was dying. I said there might be complications—but for the babies, not for her. Jasus."

Brady let out an explosive breath. He realized he was standing and sank into the chair. The force of his reaction shocked him as much as it seemed to have shocked Doc. It also revealed more than he was willing to admit, although he shouldn't have been surprised after the way he felt last night when he kissed her, randy bastard that he was.

Disgusted, he pushed his whiskey aside. There must be something profoundly wrong with him to be lusting after a pregnant woman this way. "So you're saying her babies might die."

"What I'm saying, boyo, is more times than not, twins come early. And when they do, they don't always survive. But for all that she's English and has a tongue that could clip a hedge, Your Ladyship is healthy as a spring shoat. Give your fears a rest on that score."

He tried.

Then in a tone that instantly undercut his progress, Doc said, "There's something else I'm needing to talk to you about, lad."

Christ, now what? He didn't have time for this. He had men waiting. With a sigh, Brady tipped back his head and stared at the fine cobwebs swinging between the exposed rafters overhead. It was times like this, when worries plagued him like a cloud of biting flies, that he wondered if he had the strength or the will to carry the weight of all he was expected to carry. Sancho and Elena, two brothers, dozens of other lives, thousands of cattle, tens of thousands of acres, and now a pregnant woman and her babies. It was enough to drive a man to his knees.

"Elena's asking about her hip. Wants to know if I can fix it, or know a doctor who can."

Frowning, he looked over at Doc. "I thought it was permanent."

"Likely is. But they learned a lot during the war. Trial by fire, it was. And there was a poor sod named Mike Sheedy who learned more than most, it's sad I am to say." Doc refilled his mug. "Did I ever tell you about Fredericksburg, lad?"

Before Brady could tell him he had, many times, Doc drifted into the past.

"Twelve hundred strong we were that morning, all foine and true sons of Erin." He took a deep swallow, then dragged his sleeve over his mouth. "When the smoke cleared and the cannon stilled, only two hundred and sixty-three brave lads still stood on that bloody field. Over nine hundred proud Irish souls lost." Doc swiped at his watery eyes. "Faith, and it was a dark day for the Irish Brigade. God bless us all."

Before Doc drifted too far, Brady reined him in. "You think this doctor could help Elena?"

With obvious effort, and another dose of whiskey, Doc pulled himself back to the present. "Might could. But she'd have to go to San Francisco, where Sheedy does his surgery. I thought I'd put it to you before I wrote to him."

"Hell, yes, write to him. Do whatever you can." Brady would give anything to have Elena whole again. He'd tried to send her to doctors in the past, but she wouldn't go. As he rose and loaded cartridges for his Sharps .50 into his pocket, he wondered what had motivated her to do it now. Or was this just a way to leave, as she'd always threatened to do?

"It'll be costly, I'm thinking."

"I don't care." He'd find a way. This was the most hopeful news he'd had in a long time, although he didn't like the idea of Elena heading off to San Francisco. But if she did, it might just be the prod he'd been looking for to get his skirt-chasing little brother off his butt and on the right track. "Write to him today."

THE SWEEP MET WITH ONLY MARGINAL SUCCESS.

Late the first day, a soldier brought news that a man's charred carcass had been found in the canyon Sancho had set afire several days earlier. Since he wasn't one of Brady's men, he must have been with Sancho. Which meant that unless Sancho had recruited more men, his group of five was down to four.

Then Doc sent word that a man with a festering bullet wound and a gangrenous leg had wandered into Val Rosa, delirious with fever and babbling about Sancho. Doc tried to save him, but the infection had spread too far. So now there were three.

The second day, Brady and his men came across a small band of Mimbreno Apaches, mostly women and children and a few old men,

remnants of Mangas Colorado's copper mine tribe. It was ranch custom, dating back to when Mangas supplied Jacob's regiment with
horses and mules during the Mexican war, to allow friendly hostiles
free trespass across RosaRoja as they migrated to and from the Sierra
Madres in Mexico. After Mangas died in '63, Geronimo had continued
the truce. Consequently, RosaRoja hadn't lost a single man to Indians
in almost twenty years. Such a policy might cost a few steers every
spring and autumn, but if it spared RosaRoja the carnage other ranches
suffered, Brady considered it a small price to pay.

He held parley with a couple of the old men. Although they hadn't
noticed riders the last few days, right after the rain, they'd seen fresh
tracks in the mud at Cedar Creek. A single rider, shod horse, heading
south toward Mexico. One of Sancho's men cutting out on his own?
If so, the band was down to two—Sancho and Paco. Good odds for a
gunfight. Not so good for tracking; five men left a sloppier trail than
two. After gifting them a steer, Brady accepted a beaded pouch in return, then continued the sweep.

Nothing. Two days and over two hundred square miles covered,
and still no sign of Sancho. They were either looking in the wrong
place, or the bastard had slipped past them.

On the third morning, Jarvey and Rikker called their men off the
search. With promises to stay alerted, the other ranchers left, too.
RosaRoja was on its own. So frustrated he could bite through whang
leather, Brady led his men home.

All he could do now was wait for the bastard to hit again.

Twelve

THE DAYS GREW HOTTER, THE NIGHTS SHORTER. AFTER A week with no sign of Sancho, an uneasy peace settled over the ranch.

Jessica's life fell into a comfortable but busy routine. Rising before dawn, she fed the chickens and gathered eggs, then helped Consuelo and Elena put together a huge breakfast for the brothers—beef steaks, game sausage, eggs, grits, potatoes with sausage gravy, flapjacks with honey, stewed dried fruit, biscuits, tortillas, a half loaf of Iantha's sourdough bread, accompanied by some of the bitterest, strongest coffee Consuelo could make. They took on food the way a locomotive took on coal—by the shovel full and as quickly as possible.

On bread days, she helped Iantha bake the dozen loaves the household would need throughout the week. Then she would help Elena and Consuelo plan and gather whatever would be necessary for the evening meal. The brothers rarely came in for luncheon, but in case they did, Consuelo always had a big pot of chili warming on the stove.

Then if there was any time left before the day grew too hot, Jessica worked in the garden as best she could with her expanding girth. Elena recognized her predicament and, through Brady, arranged for several of the ranch children to help her with the weeding and bending and carrying. While they worked, Jessica taught them English words and they taught her Spanish. The children found these lessons most entertaining and often dissolved in helpless giggles at her efforts at pronunciation.

She was astounded by the vastness of RosaRoja, both in space and operation. The ranch was like a living entity, never sleeping, driven by the pulse beat of thousands of lives. Over eighty-eight thousand acres. It was almost beyond imagining. Yet Elena assured her it was a small holding compared to the huge ranches in Texas and the enormous herds John Chisum held at Bosque Grande, south of Fort Sumner.

"It is not Brady's dream to have the biggest rancho," Elena told her one morning as they lingered over a late breakfast. "But to have the best. He wants RosaRoja beef to be the finest in the West."

Jessica had no doubt Brady would make it into a reality. "Why did he never marry?" she asked. "I would think it important to a man like Brady to have sons follow in his footsteps."

Elena shrugged. "For many years Jacob spoke of Brady taking the oldest daughter of Tom Logan to wife. It would have been a joining of two ranches as well as old friends. But after Jacob died, Brady was so busy holding his family and the rancho together, there was no time for courting. Several years ago Sara Logan married Tom Burkett, another rancher, and moved to Taos."

"Did that upset Brady?"

Again Elena shrugged. "He gives so much of himself to RosaRoja there is little left to give a wife. I am sad for him. He has seen more heartbreak than joy between a man and a woman, and I think that has turned his mind against marriage. But the land"—she made a grand gesture with one hand, even as her voice took on a wry note—"the land will never let him down, will it?"

Jessica studied the tea leaves in the bottom of her cup. "Perhaps he sees a wife and children as simply another burden."

"Or perhaps he thinks all women are *débil*—fragile—like his mother. Or faint of heart—like mine. He has known few strong women."

Jessica looked up with a smile, thinking again what a beautiful couple Elena and Brady would have made. "He has known you."

"And now you," Elena added slyly.

Jessica looked away, uncomfortable under those knowing black eyes.

But Elena was relentless. "You care for him, yes?"

"I am very grateful, of course."

"And you need a strong man to protect you and your babies, *sí*?"

What she needed was to stop any ill-conceived matchmaking efforts. "I will never marry, Elena," she said with quiet conviction.

"You loved your husband so much?"

Hearing the concern in Elena's voice, she realized she didn't want to deceive this woman who had been such a good friend to her. She didn't want walls or unspoken lies to come between them. "There was no husband, Elena."

"No *esposo*?"

"My sister's husband . . . forced me." The words didn't come as hard this time and, with this telling, brought more anger than fear.

"*Lo siento mucho, pobrecita*." Tears flooding her eyes, Elena reached over to grip Jessica's hand. "I am so sorry."

Jessica waited for the shame to come, but it didn't, and when she looked into Elena's eyes, she saw only sympathy and sadness. That acceptance bought up such a well of gratitude, she had to look away.

After a moment Elena released her hand. Rising, she retrieved the pot of hot water from the stove. "Your sister knows of this?" she asked, refilling Jessica's cup.

"I never told her. She loves him. Besides, what could she have done?"

Elena returned the pot of hot water, brought the one containing coffee to the table, and refilled her cup. "Will you tell her of *los bebés*?"

"Someday I shall have to." That familiar sense of shame sent heat into her face. "You think me cowardly for running away and leaving her with that man."

Elena set the coffeepot back on the stove and returned to her seat. "No, *mi amiga*. I think you are very brave. You chose to protect your babies, did you not? You could not have done that had you stayed."

If only she were that selfless. But terror strips away everything—hope, reason, even love. Ultimately, all that's left is the need to escape. If she had been protecting anyone, it had been herself. How brave was that? "I am shamed to say that at the time I thought only of myself. I was so very afraid."

"And you still are."

This was too hard, too uncomfortable. Just thinking about it awakened that suffocating feeling of panic.

"That is why you fear men, *sí*?"

"Some men." But a little less every day.

"*Yo comprendo*. Because of what this man did, it makes you feel less than you were."

Jessica swirled her cup, watched the leaves slowly settle. "In many ways, yes." How could a woman suffer such a thing and not lose part of her soul?

She felt Elena watching her and wondered how she could gracefully change the subject. Her friend was too astute, her questions too pointed. Jessica was starting to feel raw from all the probing. But before she could steer the conversation in a more comfortable direction, Elena sighed and patted her hand. "You are ashamed, even though in your mind you know it was not your fault. I know this because I feel the same."

"You do?" Jessica looked at the other woman with surprise. "Because of what Sancho did? That's absurd, Elena."

"I know that here." Elena tapped her temple with one long graceful finger. "But in my heart I am not so sure. I look at my damaged body and feel unworthy. *¿Tú también?*"

Unworthy? The word shocked her. Then Jessica realized it was true. She had been marked by a man's violence. Because she saw herself in those terms—*identified* herself in those terms—she expected everyone else to see her that way, too. But what if she were wrong? What if she truly were as blameless as Brady and Elena seemed to think?

With a wistful smile, Elena set her empty cup aside. "No woman wants to go to a man she loves crippled in spirit or body. In the eyes of our lovers we wish to be perfect. To be less makes us feel unworthy." Wiping her palms down her aproned thighs, she awkwardly rose, putting as little weight as possible on her injured hip. "But you, *mi amiga*, will someday heal. And perhaps soon . . . I will also."

Jessica gave her a sharp look. "What are you talking about? Your hip? Did Dr. O'Grady say something about your hip?" Elena's sly expression told her she was on the mark. Bolting to her feet, she gripped Elena's shoulders. "Can he fix it?"

Elena laughed. "*Quizás*—maybe. He writes to a doctor in the Californias."

"Oh, Elena, what if he could? Does Brady know?"

Elena nodded, then raised a cautionary finger. "But no one else. *¿Comprendes?* For now no one must know but you and Brady and the doctor."

Not Jack? Was Elena worried about raising his hopes . . . or her own? "Oh, Elena, how wonderful it would be if he could fix it!"

"*Sí*. So many possibilities. For both of us."

"I FEEL LIKE A CUP OF TEA," JESSICA SAID SEVERAL DAYS LATER as she rose from the table. "Will you join me?"

Elena gave a tentative smile. "I have never had tea."

"No? Then you must."

It had become a cherished morning ritual—a late breakfast with Elena after they completed their early chores. Jessica had shared a similar time with her sister at Bickersham Hall. Tea on the terrace on sunny days, or in the morning room when the weather turned. Lovely times. She missed them dearly.

An idea came. Smiling, she motioned to Elena to remain seated, and swept from the room. After retrieving the small wooden crate from her bedroom, she returned to the kitchen. "We shall have a proper tea," she announced, setting the box in the center of the table. "With proper cups, and India tea, just like a proper garden tea and—oh wait!"

Dashing back to her room, she plucked two of her more elaborate hats from their bandboxes and returned to the kitchen. "And what garden tea would be complete without the proper attire?"

Laughing, she held out the hats. "Which would you prefer? The green or blue?" Before Elena could answer, Jessica settled one of the hats on Elena's dark hair, then took it off and replaced it with the other. "Definitely the blue. It so brings out the roses in your cheeks, my dear," she added with a haughty aristocratic accent. "La, you look quite the thing,"

Elena lifted her hand to her mouth, but couldn't stifle her laugh. "*Estás loca, mi amiga.*"

After setting her green hat, with its wide brim and pleated satin underlining, at a jaunty angle on her head, Jessica tended Elena's chapeau, tying the long organza scarf into a fluffy bow by her ear and leaving the trailing ends to drape across her shoulders. "Perfect. Now if you will set out the cups, I shall boil a pot for the tea."

"These cups are very beautiful," Elena said, running her fingertip along the fluted edge. "They come from your home, yes?"

"They belonged to my great-grandmother. Henrietta Louise, *Lady* Bottomsley of Bickersham Hall." Jessica made a grand flourish, then dipped in a curtsy that would have made any debutante proud. "A woman of great consequence, I assure you. Despite the fact that she was only a baronet's wife, Grandmother Henrietta Louise could out-snob the most arrogant aristocrat. I loved her dearly. Annie and I had the grandest time dressing up in her fripperies when we were children. I daresay she was the inspiration for the most flamboyant of my hats." Lifting the pot from the stove, she swept toward Elena. "Tea is served, my dear," she said as she filled the dainty cups.

Elena took a tiny sip, then cleared her throat and set her cup carefully on the tabletop. "You miss your home?"

Jessica smiled. "I do. Very much."

"Tell me what you miss," Elena urged. "I know nothing of England."

Jessica thought for a moment. "The pace," she finally said. "The traditions, the sense of history. The safety."

Elena blinked at her in surprise. "You do not feel safe at the rancho?"

Jessica laughed. "Of course . . . except for the poisonous snakes and deadly insects, mountain lions, giant bears, wild pigs, wolves, plants with sharp spines, a sun that will burn you by day, and a wind that will freeze you at night. How can I not feel safe?"

Elena rocked back in laughter. "You forgot Mexican banditos and Indians on the warpath."

"And landslides and flash floods and stage crashes," Jessica added, joining in her laughter.

"And scorpions." Elena shivered. "I hate scorpions."

Footsteps sounded in the hall. A moment later, Brady came through the doorway. He stopped abruptly when he saw them. "Good God."

Jessica laughed at his look of surprise.

"What the hell are you doing?"

Jessica and Elena exchanged haughty looks. "Why, my dear man," Elena said, trying to mimic Jessica's accent and failing miserably. "We are having a proper tea party."

"Tea party."

"Quite so." Jessica struggled to keep from breaking into giggles. Brady was at a loss for words. Amazing. "Would you care to join us? I can give you a hat, if you like."

His gaze flew to her hat, then quickly away. "Ah . . . no." He backed toward the door. "Well. You ladies enjoy yourselves."

"Oh we are," Jessica sang gaily.

"Indeed, we are," Elena mimicked as she tossed the trailing end of her fluffy bow over her shoulder. "Except for the tea, it is positively marvelous."

Jessica looked at her in surprise.

Elena shrugged apologetically.

Both women burst into laughter.

THAT NEXT WEEK SUMMER ROUNDUP BEGAN.

It was one of the busiest times of the year for RosaRoja, and there weren't enough hours in the day to do all that needed to be done. Every man, woman, and child above the age of ten contributed. After gathering all the cattle in huge milling throngs, the new calves were branded, young male animals castrated, culls set aside to be sold, and late springers— cows that were late giving birth—separated so they could be monitored until their calves were old enough to send into the mountains. It was difficult, dirty work, and when Brady and his brothers staggered in for their evening meal, they hardly spoke other than to report on each day's progress. As soon as they finished eating, they left again.

Even so, and despite the grueling pace, long hours, and exhausting work, there was a feeling of excitement in the air, because these men loved what they did. It was a life totally different from any Jessica had known. At home the landed gentry lived off the labors of their tenants but rarely worked alongside them, and distinctions of class were so well marked, a landowner might never know the names of the people who toiled on his behalf. Here owners and ranch hands worked side by side with a shared purpose and deep commitment. And no one worked harder on this ranch than Brady Wilkins. If RosaRoja was a living entity, Brady was its beating heart.

Pamphlets on deportment and fancy hats seemed rather banal in comparison.

As Jessica watched the cycles of RosaRoja unfold around her, the precariousness of her own situation plagued her. She couldn't stay here forever, and the possibility of finding George dwindled with each passing day. She would have to find a way to sustain herself and support her babies without relying on the charity of others. There seemed scant opportunity here, but if Elena went to California to see the doctor about her hip, perhaps Jessica could go with her. She had heard there was a flourishing and fashionable society in San Francisco, one that might become a market for her hats. She had supported herself on her millinery talents before. Perhaps she could do so again.

It was more of a hope than a plan, but simply having one did wonders for her spirits. She would see what Elena decided about the doctor in California, then make her own decisions.

She stayed as busy as her pregnancy and the weather allowed. Even though the days grew longer and hotter, as soon as the sun slipped behind the mountains, the temperature cooled. After the dinner meal and the men returned to their chores, she often took her sewing basket to the porch to enjoy the evening breeze. In addition to the endless mending on the brothers' clothing, she had begun samplers for the ladies who had been so generous to her babies.

Evening was her favorite time of day—bands of color exploding across the western sky, cattle lowing in the distance, crickets chirping their evening song to the thump and creak of the rocker. It was a kaleidoscope of color, spinning to the music of RosaRoja and perfumed by the heady scent of summer roses.

The sunsets were magnificent—blood-streaked reds, fiery oranges, tattered purple clouds shot with ribbons of gold. Each evening the colors seemed brighter and lasted longer, peaking toward the middle of the month when an early full moon rose. For a moment, it perched on the fingertips of the mountains like a giant glowing orange ball, then the riotous color faded into a milky glow, and one by one, awakening stars dusted the indigo sky.

It was too beautiful to be believed.

"Quite a show, isn't it?"

Jessica looked over to see Brady in the doorway of his office. He leaned against the jamb, arms folded over his chest, one ankle crossed over the other, watching her. She had missed him at supper, had hardly spoken to him in days, and hadn't been alone with him at all since that night in her room when he'd kissed her. Seeing him now, posed as he was with that lazy self-assurance evident in every line of his long form, she felt bewitched all over again.

"I heard you creaking around out here," he said with his lopsided smile.

"It was your rocker creaking, not I."

Pushing away from the jamb, he walked toward her.

She loved the way he walked. Graceful and fluid but utterly masculine, with the loose-hipped rolling gait of a horseman—weight coming down authoritatively on his heels, the swinging motion of his long legs balanced by the sway of broad shoulders. A swagger, almost.

"Got something for you." Stopping behind the rocker, he bent down until his lips almost brushed her ear. "Something you've been wanting for a long time."

She stared down at her clasped hands, reminding herself to breathe, to ignore the way his breath rustled in her ear.

With a chuckle, he straightened. "I've missed your blushes, woman." He walked to the other end of the porch and leaned over the railing. Hooking two fingers in his mouth, he gave a high shrill whistle toward the bunkhouse. A minute later, one of the workers ran up. Brady spoke to him, then the man left and Brady walked back toward her. This time she didn't watch him, although she was acutely aware when he stopped at the railing beside her chair.

"It's because of the dust," he said, bracing his hands on the railing as he stared out at the twilight sky. "That's what gives the sunset its color."

She looked up, realized he was grinning over his shoulder at her instead of watching the sunset, and quickly looked away. "Yes. Amazing. I, ah, have never seen anything quite like it."

"I'm gratified to hear it."

She folded the shirt she had been hemming and dropped it back into the basket at her feet. "Because of dust, you say?"

He straightened. Propping his shoulder against the porch post, he slid his long fingers into the front pockets of his denim trousers.

Jessica tried not to watch, but her eyes wouldn't behave. *Licentious ninny.*

Luckily, he didn't seem to notice her noticing. "The dirtier the air, the prettier the colors," he explained, his eyes drifting over her. "During a brush fire the sky can turn deep red or fiery orange or even a golden brown. All the colors in your hair."

The man could say the most astounding things.

The worker came around the side of the house. He carried a smaller version of Brady's rocker, with a gingham cushion and gently curved arms. She watched in openmouthed delight as he carried it up the steps, then left. "Is that for me?"

"If it still fits," Brady said doubtfully, positioning the new chair beside his.

"What is that supposed to mean?" She tried to sound severe but couldn't stop smiling as she pushed herself out of Brady's rocker.

"When Buck started on it, you were a skinny little thing, but now . . . you're not."

She waved him out of the way so she could sit. "I was never a little thing."

"Compared to me you were. How's it feel?"

"Lovely." She ran her palms over the satiny finish of the arms, tested the smoothness of the rocking motion, leaned into the gentle curve of the slatted back. "I must thank Buck."

When she started to rise, he waved her back down. "Tomorrow. He's in the cutting pen."

With a deep sigh, he lowered himself into his own rocker. "It's nice to have my chair back," he said as he settled into a steady but overly vigorous rhythm.

"I never had your chair. Is this a race? Slow down."

"You've got rules about rocking, too?" But he nonetheless adjusted his rhythm until they rocked in a perfectly matched tempo.

She smiled, enjoying the gentle motion of her new rocker, the beautiful evening, the company of the man beside her. *I could be happy here.*

"Give me your hand."

She looked over to see Brady holding out his hand, palm up. "Why?"

"So I can hold it."

"Why do you want to hold it?"

"Because the sun's down and I'm afraid of the dark. Or because you've been ogling me like a buyer at a cattle auction and I figured I'd give you a treat. Or because I like doing it. Just give me your damn hand."

She gave him her hand. His palm was warm and rough against hers, his fingers long enough to encircle hers in a sturdy grip. It made her feel secure and safe and petite. "I was not ogling," she said after they had rocked for a while.

"You were."

"I was noticing. There is a difference."

He leaned closer until his shoulder rubbed against hers as they rocked. "And what did you notice?"

"You need a haircut and a shave, and you have very large feet." Confident that she had taken him down a peg, she gave him a wide smile.

For a moment he blinked at her, clearly surprised. Then a chuckle rumbled through his chest, followed by another and another until he was in full laughter. "Aren't you just full of surprises."

She tried to snatch her hand away, but he wouldn't let her go. "I have no idea what you find so amusing. Release my hand."

Instead he lifted it to his mouth and kissed her knuckles. "You know what they say about the size of a man's feet, don't you?"

To her horror she remembered something George once said. Big hands, big feet, big . . . hearts? Or parts? *Good heavens.* Why was she forever tumbling into these pits of her own making? No wonder he laughed at her. It was so absurd she was hard-pressed not to do the same.

He nipped the tip of her middle finger.

She tried to pull away.

He tightened his grip.

"This conversation is over," she said firmly, trying to ignore the tickle of his mustache against the back of her hand.

"Maybe someday I'll show you just how big my—"

"Hush!"

"—feet really are."

"I have seen your feet and I was not impressed."

"Ouch."

This time the laughter burst out before she could quell it. Was there ever a more ridiculous pair than the two of them in their rockers, trading jabs and innuendoes like sparring lovers or old friends? But they were neither, were they? She sighed. *I shall miss this*, she thought with sharp and sudden clarity. *I shall miss the companionship, the banter, the teasing. And him.* With that thought came the alarming realization that she had permitted herself to care for Brady Wilkins more than she should.

Foolish, foolish woman.

He must have sensed her change of mood. He gave her a questioning look she couldn't answer. The rocking slowed. With his free hand, he reached across to brush his fingertips down the side of her face. "Stop worrying, Jessica. Everything will work out."

"Will it?" she whispered, wanting so badly to believe.

He leaned forward, pressed his lips gently against hers, then sat back. "I give you my word."

Such a simple thing, a kiss. But the sweet promise of it brought an ache to her heart. *You will be the ruination of me*, she thought, staring out into the night. *But I fear I'm too lost to care.*

As the days passed, Jessica spent more and more evenings on the porch with Brady, holding hands while they rocked in tempo. Sometimes they sat without speaking, simply enjoying the sunset in companionable silence. Other times Elena or the brothers joined them, or several of the ranch hands stopped by. At first, unwilling to invite speculation, she had tried to slip her hand from his. But he simply tightened his grip, leaving her no choice but to brazen it out, and pretend it was not unusual to be swollen with one man's twin babies, while she held the hand of another. After a while she almost believed it herself.

But the best evenings were when they talked. She told him about Bickersham Hall and Mama's long illness and how difficult it had been after Papa died and George left. He told her about screwworm and gotch ear, and how a Brahma could handle ticks but not cold. When she spoke of grouse hunts and riding to the hounds on a misty fall morning, he described snake hunts and riding for his life ahead of a Kiowa war party. It was less a meeting of minds than a collision of cultures. And a fascinating glimpse into a world she'd never imagined.

For the most part she found the differences between them intriguing, sometimes shocking, often amusing. At other times they saddened her because they reminded her of the futility of allowing herself to care so deeply for this man. He was not for her. Brady's first and deepest love was RosaRoja, and it was against her nature to settle for second best. An untenable situation, and she knew the longer she allowed it to go on, the more heartbreak it would eventually bring her. Yet she couldn't seem to stay away from the porch—or him—or the companionship he offered.

"Do you have regrets, Brady?" she asked one particularly lovely evening, several weeks after roundup was over and the ranch had settled back into a less hectic routine. "You've given up so much for RosaRoja. Are you ever sorry?"

"Sometimes." He looked over, studying her with an intensity that left her breathless. "But not today. Today everything I want is right in my hand."

She had no response to that. And couldn't have spoken it aloud if she had.

Another part of the evening ritual was the goodnight kiss. He never forced it on her, and because the rocker arms stood between them, rarely touched her other than on the lips, so she never felt overwhelmed or suffocated. If she made a halfhearted and admittedly insincere attempt to turn away, he gently steered her back with no more than the brush of his fingertips along the side of her face. It was the tenderest of assaults and, by its very sweetness, impossible to resist.

She didn't understand why she allowed it, and didn't know where it would lead her. But she was unable to tell him to stop.

Then one evening the kiss lasted longer, and led to another, then another, until her pulse hammered and she could scarce catch her breath. "Why are you doing this?" she gasped when he finally paused long enough for her to breathe.

"Kissing you?" His head came down again. "It's fun."

By the time he came up for air again, she could scarce remember how to think at all. "No. Pursuing me."

She felt his smile against her lips. "Am I pursuing you?"

"Aren't you?" When he didn't answer, she pulled back to study his face. It pleased her to see he was as affected as she.

With an explosive exhale, he sat back and dragged his free hand over his face, then through his hair, then over his face again. "I guess I am."

"Why?"

"Hell if I know."

His answer sent her defenses up. "Well, stop."

"I don't think I can." His gaze never leaving hers, he pinned the back of her hand against his chest, letting her feel the fast drumbeat of his heart so she would know the effect she had on him. "I don't think I can," he said again.

Anger seeped away, leaving her feeling shaken, yet oddly buoyant. "Why, Brady?" She pulled her hand free of his and sat back in her rocker. "Look at me, for mercy's sake. I am as graceless as a duck in dancing pumps. I look like I'm wearing a bustle backward, my ankles are as big as tree trunks, and my hair has turned to straw. Are you blind?"

He shrugged. "You're pregnant."

"Exactly. So why are you pursuing me?"

"I can't pursue you when you're pregnant?"

"Why would you even want to?"

He studied her for a long time. "Maybe I think you're pretty," he finally said. "Or maybe I like springers. Or maybe I'm thinking that someday you won't be pregnant, so I'd better make my moves now, while I've got you in hand, so to speak."

Not something the infamous Lord Byron would have said, but touching nonetheless. "But we're so different."

"Hell. Women." With a labored sigh, he tipped his rocker back and hooked his heels over the porch railing. "You're going to work this to death, aren't you?" His crooked grin took some of the sting out of his words.

"I am simply trying to understand."

"It's not complicated. When I look at you, I don't see differences. I see possibilities."

"Of what?"

"Of everything. Anything. A better life. A better me." He spread his big hands in a palms-up gesture. "I don't know how else to say it."

How else indeed? She almost went dewy eyed. In less than a dozen words he had captured her heart and put prissy Lord Byron to shame. If she had not been graced with good sense and strong morals, she might have flung herself on his neck. As it was, it was a near thing.

But typical of Brady, with the next breath he sucked all the sweetness out of a beautiful sentiment. "So I'd be grateful if you'd have those babies so we can get on with it. I'm tripping on my tongue here." His grin showed both dimples and spoke of sin.

Choking back laughter, she dropped her head into her hands. One minute he had her on the verge of violence, then tears, and now laughter. The man would surely drive her insane.

Thirteen

"COMPANY," RUFUS SAID.

Brady straightened to see riders coming through the gate. He and Ru had been working in the cutting pen for most of the day and he was glad of the distraction. Castrating was filthy, backbreaking work, and between the stench, and the flies, and the bawling of the calves, his nerves were stretched thin. Wiping sweat from his eyes with the sleeve of his shirt, he squinted into the late afternoon sun at the two men riding toward them.

He recognized Langley, one of his top hands, but didn't know the other man nor did he recognize his horse, an underfed bay Langley ponied on a short lead.

"That rider looks hurt," Ru observed.

Frowning, Brady pulled off his blood-soaked gloves and dropped them and his cutting knife in a bucket, then unbuckled his leather *chaparreras* and tossed them over the fence. As he swung over the top rail, Langley reined in.

The other rider sagged, head drooping, and might have toppled from the saddle but for the rope that lashed his hands to the horn. The dark head told Brady it wasn't Sancho, but it wasn't until Langley grabbed a handful of black hair to yank the man's head up that he saw it was Paco Alvarez, Sancho's sidekick and half brother.

A surge of emotion shot through him. "Where'd you find him?"

"Boot Creek. Two got away. I sent Red and Tobias after them."

"Take him to the barn. I'll get Hank and Jack."

When Brady and his brothers entered the barn, they saw that Langley and Rufus had tied Alvarez to the center pole. The man needed the support. By the condition of his battered face, it seemed he'd been reluctant to accompany Langley back to the ranch. And by the look in his eyes, he still had some fight left.

Good. Brady didn't want this to be easy.

Enough light came through the open loft door for them to see, so Brady closed the big double doors. After his eyes adjusted to the gloom, he walked to within an arm's length of the bound man and stopped.

He felt the fury build, growing with every heartbeat until he could taste it, feel it, hear it humming through his veins. He waited until Paco lifted his head, then said in a calm, quiet voice, "Where is he?"

Alvarez responded with a barrage of curses in both English and Spanish.

Brady backhanded him. The bound man's head snapped back against the post with a thud. A new cut opened at the corner of his mount.

"Look at me, Paco."

Alvarez glared up at him, showing his defiance in bared, bloody teeth.

"You're not leaving this barn alive. Nothing you do or say will change that. Understand?"

Alvarez didn't respond, but his struggles stopped.

"Good. Now what you *can* control is how many trips we'll make when we carry you out. It can be one man-sized trip, or a lot of bucket-sized trips. Your choice. Do you understand that?"

Alvarez's swarthy skin took on a gray hue. He watched Brady with the unblinking wariness of an animal in a trap.

"Good. Now I'll ask you questions. If you answer right, this'll be over pretty quick. If not, it'll get messy." Even in the dim light, Brady could see the sweat beading on Paco's forehead. It made him smile. "Now once again. Where is he?"

Alvarez repeated his earlier answer, but this time his curses carried less conviction and his voice began to wobble.

Brady waited for him to finish, then waited longer, until the rasp of Paco's breathing sounded loud in the hushed barn. As he watched the terror build in those round, black eyes, something dark and cruel pulsed through him, rousing the savage inside.

He nodded to Jack. "Get the axe. And a bucket."

Before his brother had taken two steps, Alvarez was fighting the ropes. Two more steps and he was screaming. "*¡Espérate!* Stop! *Yo te digo todo,*" he finally choked out, his head drooping in defeat. "I will tell you."

"Good." Brady's relief was so great he curled his hands into fists to hide their shaking. He didn't know if he could have followed through with his threats. He liked to think he was better than the man before him, but with the hate so strong inside him, he was glad he didn't have to put it to the test. "For the last time, Alvarez. Where he is?"

"*Una cueva.*"

"A cave? Where?"

"Blue Mesa. On the north slope there is a canyon. *La entrada*—the entrance—is hidden by a landslide. The cave is a mile in. Up high. You would not see it unless you knew where to look."

Brady was shocked. He'd ridden this land for almost twenty years, but had never known such a place existed. No wonder they hadn't found Ramirez.

"Describe it." He wanted no surprises when they went in after Sancho.

Clearly Alvarez held no loyalty to his half brother, and in fact, seemed to relish the idea of leading Brady to him. He described the slope up to the cave, the tunnel, and the inner cavern. He told them about the three men they'd lost—the one in the burned canyon, the one who died in Val Rosa, and the one who ran off after the fire ambush failed. He said Sancho had sent him to Mexico to get more men, and that he and the two new recruits had been on their way back to the cave when Langley and his men caught them. So now it was just Sancho.

"You will never find him," Alvarez said in a weak attempt at bravado. "He is more animal than human now. He does not sleep, does not eat. But he is out there even now, watching and waiting." He grinned, blood from his cut lip smearing across crooked teeth. "He knows every move you make, *cabrón*. You will not see him until his knife is in you."

Brady told Jack to hitch the buckboard, then motioned Hank and the other two men to leave.

Jack nodded and headed for the door, Langley and Rufus trailing after him. Hank didn't move. "What're you planning?" he asked, frowning.

"Nothing. Just go." Brady tore his gaze from the prisoner and met his brother's troubled eyes. Hank, the reasonable one, the family conscience when he thought his brothers treaded dangerous ground. But this wasn't about Hank or him or Paco Alvarez. It was about Sam. Striving for a calm tone, Brady said, "Go on, Hank. It's all right. I'm just going to talk to him."

Hank searched his face, then reluctantly left. After the door closed behind him and Brady's eyes adjusted to the dimness once again, he pulled his long knife from the scabbard in his boot.

Paco's gaze fastened on the blade as Brady moved toward him. He started to whimper. A wet stain spread down the front of his trousers and the stink of urine overrode the smell of horse manure and alfalfa in the closed barn. He shrank back, eyes wild, breath coming in quick bursts as Brady slid the tip of the blade into the knot. A quick twisting motion and the knot loosened. When Brady pulled the rope free, Alvarez sank to the straw, shaking with fear and relief.

Slipping the knife back in his boot, Brady hunkered in front of Paco.

He wasn't a man who enjoyed inflicting pain or watching someone suffer. But what he felt when he looked at Paco Alvarez pushed him as close to brutality as he'd ever been. It was a struggle to hold himself in check.

"Tell me about Sam."

"W-Who?"

"My brother."

Paco stared at him through greasy strands of black hair. Then he laughed.

And something snapped. Suddenly Brady was swinging the rope like a whip, again and again across that sneering face, until his arm wearied and Alvarez's cries finally penetrated the red fog in his brain.

Chest heaving, he lurched to his feet, the rope still clutched in his shaking hand. He sensed a cold and dangerous blackness hovering just beyond his vision, a terrible place that would swallow him forever if he didn't bring the fury in check. With monumental effort, he took a step back. Then another. Slowly the noise in his head dimmed.

Outside, a horse nickered. He heard cattle bawling and Bullshot's throaty bark. Familiar, everyday sounds a world apart from the shadowy confines of the barn, where the air was filled with the rasp of their breathing and the stench of sweat and rage and fear.

"Do you believe in God, Paco?" he asked, once his breathing had settled. "I do. The proof is that you're here, now, in my hands. The devil is here, too, and he's tempting me to do some really bad things. For the sake of both of our souls, we should avoid that, don't you think?"

Paco didn't answer. But that look was back in his eyes.

"I'll take that as a yes." Needing to keep his hands busy, Brady slipped the rope through his fingers, working it into even, precise loops as he spoke. "I know it was you and Sancho. Elena told me some of it. You tell me the rest."

Paco let out a long, shaky breath. "It was Sancho's idea to drag him. Not mine."

"But you helped, didn't you, Paco? Everything. From the beginning."

"We watched the rancho," Paco began in a defeated voice. "We saw you leave and waited for you to come back. It was you we wanted. Instead, we got the kid."

"His name was Sam," Brady managed, fighting a sudden pressure in his chest. "Go on."

"He must have thought we were from the rancho. When he saw us, he pulled up to wait." Paco sneered. "You should have taught him better, *cabrón*."

Brady worked the rope and concentrated on his breathing. "Then what?"

"We stripped him and beat him."

In his mind, Sam screamed. *Help me, Bray. Make it stop.*

"And then Sancho got out his knife."

Brady forced himself to listen, neither moving nor speaking throughout the grisly recital. It was important that he hear this, that each horrific detail be imprinted on his mind, so that after Sancho and Paco answered for what they'd done, there would still be someone left on this earth who knew what Sam had suffered.

But every word was a whiplash across his soul, and listening was the hardest thing he had ever done.

By the time Alvarez had finished, the rough rope was almost embedded in his palms.

Alvarez's bruised lips curled in a smile. "If you had come back sooner, your little brother would still be alive. Do you think about that, gringo?"

Every day. "Get up."

Paco struggled upright, his body tense, his gaze scanning the barn.

Brady wished he would try something, anything, that would give him a reason to get his hands around the sonofabitch's throat.

Alvarez's shoulders sagged in defeat. Bracing one hand against the post, he spit blood then straightened. "So now you kill me?"

"Now you choose. The bucket, or this." He tossed the rope at Paco's feet.

Don't do this, a voice whispered through his mind. But Brady blocked it. "You know how to tie a noose, don't you?"

Paco's face paled. His lips moved in silent prayer.

Brady knew Alvarez was Catholic and believed suicide was an unforgivable sin. He knew Paco would try to buy his way into purgatory, to make his deal with God. But not today. Not ever. Suicide was the fast road to hell, and Brady was determined that Paco Alvarez make the trip. He wanted this man to die without hope of salvation, to burn forever at Satan's side. Just like him.

"Do it, Paco. Or I'll take the next two days and a rusty axe to convince you."

Paco made a choking sound. His mouth fell open. "*Por Dios.*"

"Pick up the rope."

Brady watched, detached, thinking it an odd thing to see a man die while he was still alive. It began in the eyes—a faint dimming, like a lantern slowly going out. Then the body seemed to shrink into itself, as if the spirit had already flown. And finally all that was left was a trembling shell with the resigned, numb look of a steer in the slaughter line. Seeing it happen to Paco Alvarez filled Brady with a cold and bitter satisfaction.

Are you watching, Sam?

Weeping openly, Alvarez picked up the rope.

Brady stayed through to the end. After the last twitch and gurgle, he leaned over, vomited into the straw, and left the barn. He told the men waiting outside to cut Paco down and load him in the buckboard, then he walked to the house. He felt like he was moving in a dream, his body going through the motions, but his mind left somewhere behind.

You'll pay for this, that voice warned.

But Brady knew he was already doomed. He had moved beyond redemption that morning on the desert with Sam over a decade ago, and even though his actions, both then and now, damned him for all time, he knew he would do it again.

As he mounted the porch steps, Jessica came out the door. She saw Alvarez's body being loaded into the wagon, then stared in such horror at the bloody stains on Brady's shirt, he felt compelled to explain it was from castrating—the calves, not Alvarez—although he was sorry he hadn't considered it—for Alvarez, not the calves. That sent her scurrying.

After grabbing clean clothes, he went to the creek. He scoured with river sand until his palms stung, but still couldn't wash away all of the taint of death. Finally he dressed and headed back for the jug.

Jack met him by the corrals. "When are we going after Sancho?"

Brady hadn't thought that far, hadn't thought beyond anything except what Alvarez had told him in the barn. Dragging a hand through his damp hair, he tried to focus. "First light. We'll take enough men to cover the ridge above the cave, as well as the canyon below. That sonofabitch isn't getting past us this time." He continued toward the house.

Jack fell in beside him. "You did what you had to."

That startled Brady. Then he realized Jack was talking about Alvarez, not Sam. It wedged a space between them, that withheld knowledge, and it made him feel tenfold the burden that came with it. "It was his doing." To forestall more questions, he added, "Have Alvarez dumped at the boundary line. Send someone to tell Rikker he can take him to Val Rosa or let him rot. I'll burn the bastard before I let him rest in Wilkins land. Does Elena know?"

"I'll have Hank—"

"You tell her."

"But—"

Brady rounded on him. "Christ, can't you for once do what I ask?"

He regretted the outburst as soon as he heard his words. He felt flayed and ragged, and for one brief moment his resentment was so strong he wanted to get on his horse and ride away and never look back. But he couldn't do that. This was the work he was required to do. And he'd do it because that was the way it was.

"Jack, I can't deal with this right now," he said by way of apology. "She'll take it better from you."

Some of the anger faded from Jack's eyes. "I'll tell her."

Dinner came and went while he slumped in the rocker, trying to drink the rage away. Unfortunately the whiskey only made the fires inside burn hotter. Elena came out and tried to get him to eat, but he waved her away. After a while she gave up and went inside.

The sun set and the moon rose, a fat crescent with a dusty reddish cast. He drifted from disheartened, to morose, to downright savage. Even Bullshot stayed away. Hearing what Sam had suffered had sent his mind in a downward spiral. He couldn't think past it, and as hard as he tried, he couldn't seem to drink past it either. Even after all these years, his little brother's death was still a bleeding wound in his mind.

Red and Tobias returned to report the riders that were with Paco got away, cutting a fast trail toward Mexico. After they left, Jack came to say the men would be ready to ride at dawn. He said Elena had taken the news about Paco well, although she seemed more concerned about Brady than Alvarez. He stood for a minute as if expecting something— a comment, a reply, an invitation to share the jug—but Brady was too foul tempered to rouse himself. Eventually, he left.

Brady had almost reached a comfortable level of numbness when Her Ladyship came out again, this time armed with a look of deter-mination and a plate of food. He ignored one and declined the other, perhaps more forcefully than he should have, because she slapped the plate onto the floor beside his chair with enough force to send peas bouncing into the roses. Then she yanked the jug out of his hand and sailed it after the peas.

Brady swiveled in the rocker to blink up at her, so astonished he couldn't find words to express it.

"Are you inebriated?" she demanded.

She made it sound like being drunk was the lowest a man could go. But he knew better. "Hell, no," he said in indignation.

"Then talk to me." She stood ready to do battle, feet planted, her round belly almost nudging his shoulder. She was so close he could see the little bump of her navel pushing against the thin fabric of her dress. It weakened him, seeing that bump, and knowing that behind it, life grew, untouched and untainted. He lifted a hand, wanting to lay his palm against it and draw some of that purity from her body into his, and maybe wash away all the ugliness and rage and despair.

But before he could touch her, she moved past to gracelessly lower herself into the rocker beside his. He watched her, feeling the differences between them more keenly than ever, and resenting that they mattered so much. He dropped his hand back to the arm of the rocker. "Go back into the house, Jessica."

"Not until you talk to me."

"I don't want to talk. Go inside."

"Tell me what happened in the barn."

Jesus. He belched, saw her look of distaste, and belched again. "I gave him a choice. He chose the rope. Good night."

"You hanged him?"

Gingerly he pressed his fingertips against his throbbing temples to slow the spinning. "I supplied the rope. He did the rest. Please. For chrissakes. Go."

He realized she had been holding her breath when she let it out in a rush. "Thank goodness. I told Elena you couldn't do it. I told her you were incapable of killing a man in cold blood."

Brady lifted his head to stare at her. That she would make such a judgment without knowing anything about it infuriated him. "You don't know what the hell you're talking about." His voice rose with every word. "You've got no idea what I'm capable of, so shut the hell up!"

Maybe he was drunk after all. He saw her hurt and confusion, and tried to bring himself in check. *Christ.* He felt smothered—by the past, by her, by the weight of his own guilt. In desperation, he reached for the jug, then muttered a curse when he remembered it was gone.

"Stop yelling and tell me."

"No."

"It may help."

"Sonofabitch!" He threw up his hands so abruptly he almost toppled out of the rocker. "Will you just get in the goddamn house?"

"*You* get in the goddamn house!"

He reared back, wondering if he'd heard right. He must have, judging by her owly look. But she stood her ground, damn her, offering no apologies or excuses. "Is this about your brother? About Sam?"

"Aw, Jesus." The woman could wear down stone.

"Elena told me what happened. That Sancho and her half brother killed him."

"They didn't kill him." As soon as he heard the words, he wanted them back. But it was too late. They were out there for all time, and he could never call them back.

"If they didn't kill him, who did?"

Oh shit. Suddenly, he felt like he was losing his balance, being pulled in two directions at once, and he wasn't sure which way to fall. If he spoke now, what would he accomplish? If he didn't and continued to lie and deny and pretend everything was okay, no one would ever know.

Whiskey churned in his throat as he leaned forward, elbows braced on his knees. Threading his fingers through his hair, he pressed the heels of his hands against his blurry eyes. *I can't do this anymore. I can't live like this anymore.*

"Brady?"

He felt her watching, felt the press of all her questions, her needs and expectations. And at that moment, more than anything in the world, he wanted to be the man she thought he was—to be sure and honest and worthy.

But how could he, with the past hanging over him like a bloody knife?

He owed them the truth. He owed it to Sam, and in some twisted way he didn't fully understand, he owed it to himself. But mostly, if he was ever to become the man this woman needed and wanted and expected him to be, he owed it to her.

He let his hands drop. Unable to look at her, he stared down at the planks between his feet. "I did. I killed him."

He waited for her to get up, walk away, run screaming into the house.

When she didn't, he straightened and looked over at her to see the effect of his words. Her head was down so he couldn't see her face, but he sensed her withdrawal. It opened a hole in his chest. *You stupid bastard. You've lost it all now.*

Wearily he sat back, telling himself it was for the best. They didn't fit and never would. But he would miss their evenings on the porch, and holding her hand, and stealing kisses in the dark. He would miss the laughter. And her. Tipping his head against the back of the rocker, he closed his eyes and waited for her to leave.

Instead he felt a touch against his wrist. He looked down, realized she was trying to take his hand in hers, but he was gripping the arm of the rocker so tight she couldn't loosen his fingers. He let go and turned his wrist so her palm fitted against his. He tried not to grip her too hard. He knew his hand shook, knew she felt it, but it was so good to touch her again, and he was so grateful she was still there so he could, he didn't care.

"Tell me," she said.

"You don't want to hear it."

"Tell me anyway. What happened when you found him?"

"Let it go, Jessica. Please."

"I can't."

In her ferocious need to know, she peeled him like an onion, layer by layer, until all that remained was the hard bitter core of the truth. Somehow he found the words but he used them sparingly. He didn't want to put images in her mind that would haunt her as surely as they haunted him. So he didn't tell her how broken Sam was, or the terrible things Sancho had done, or how he couldn't even touch his little brother without making him scream.

Sam's cries echoed in his head. *Help me, Bray. Make it stop.*

Swallowing hard, Brady tried to keep his voice steady. "He kept drifting in and out. When he was awake, he screamed. When he wasn't, I did what I could. It wasn't much. He was dying, and it would be a long, ugly death."

Brady closed his eyes, but still couldn't get away from it—the pleading, the reek of blood, the rasp of his brother's breath. And the flies—God, the flies.

Beside him, Jessica wept, her sobs muffled by her free hand.

Desperate to distance himself from the pictures in his mind, he focused on the dark silhouette of a nighthawk looping through the darkening sky. "So I did what he wanted. What he asked me to do." He glanced over to gauge the impact of his words.

Her eyes glistened silver in the starlight but she didn't look away. That gave him the strength to tell her all of it, to make her understand why he did what he did.

"He was just a little kid, Jessica. He was hurting so bad. And he kept begging and begging, and the flies—I didn't know what else to do."

Help me, Bray. Make it stop. That's all Sam wanted. All Brady could give him.

"I thought about shooting him, but I couldn't. A bullet is . . . so . . . impersonal. But I had to do something. I couldn't let him suffer any more."

The nighthawk dipped down then up, a moth trapped in its beak. "So I waited until he passed out. Then I picked him up and put my hand over his mouth and held him tight against my chest. As tight as I could." He didn't realize he was acting out the motions until he felt his palm pressing with such force against his chest he couldn't breathe. He jerked it away and dragged air into his lungs.

Jessica's head pressed against his arm. He heard her crying, felt the hot wetness of her tears. She squeezed his hand so hard he felt tremors in her wrist.

"It didn't take long. Or maybe it did. I don't remember anything but sitting there, rocking him, telling him everything would be all right. It seemed forever."

Somewhere in the roses, a cricket chirped. From under the porch came Bullshot's snore. The nighthawk dipped and soared. Life went on. Uncaring. Unchanged.

Sam. I'm sorry.

His vision clouded. He knew his voice shook, but he couldn't seem to steady it. "He didn't struggle. He just . . . left. I'm not sure when. One minute he was there, then he wasn't."

Suddenly the horror of it sent him to his feet. He made it no farther than the porch rail before words tumbled out. "Why didn't I know, Jessica? How can someone die in your arms and you not even know? Jesus—"

Breathing hard, he braced one hand high on an upright post and stared blindly out into the night. "He was my brother. I should have known." He took a deep breath. The air was so thick with the stink of dying roses it made his stomach roll.

He waited for her to speak, but she didn't. After a while her silence wore him down.

"It changes things, doesn't it?" he asked, without turning. "Knowing about Sam. Knowing what I did."

She didn't answer.

And still he waited, choking on hope and unspoken words, silently demanding that she stay, that she answer him, that she not walk away.

Then he heard her move up behind, and felt her arms snake around his waist.

"I'm so sorry, Brady," she whispered against his shoulder, her body pressed so tightly against his, he could feel the vibration of her heartbeat against her back. "I'm so sorry."

He looked down, saw the pale hands gently stroking his chest, and strength left him.

Jesus.

He didn't want this.

He didn't deserve it.

Damn her.

Dropping his forehead against his upraised arm, he closed his eyes. It was just a touch—but coming now—from this woman—it nearly broke him.

Fourteen

SANCHO CROUCHED IN THE SHADOW OF A CREOSOTE BUSH AND watched the two men in the road. He had seen their wagon leave the rancho earlier and had followed them to this boundary gate. Now the wagon had stopped and the men were walking toward the rear.

He thought about killing them. There were only two of them. He could sneak up, tie them, then set them on fire. He smiled, picturing it in his mind.

Another picture intruded and his smile faded.

The smoke might alert Wilkins. Sancho had seen the patrols. He knew they hunted him, and he did not want Wilkins to know he was still in the area until Paco came back with more men. A sudden memory sparked in his cloudy mind. Frowning, he looked around.

¿Dónde está Paco? He should be back from Mexico by now.

Movement drew his attention back to the men on the road.

They dragged a long canvas bundle from the bed of the wagon. Staggering under the weight of it, they carried it to the side of the road. As they dumped it on the ground, the canvas unrolled to reveal a man's body.

After tossing the canvas into the wagon, they climbed back into the driver's box and reined the horses in a wide arc through the brush, circling back the way they had come.

As soon as they disappeared down the road, Sancho crept forward.

It was Paco. For a moment Sancho was so stunned he just stood there, staring into the bloated face of his half brother. Then rage exploded.

¡Pendejo! How could Paco do this to him? What about the men he was to bring back? The injustice of it rocked him, sent his mind spinning. Cursing and shrieking, he kicked Paco again and again until his half brother's face was a pulpy mass and Sancho's bad knee ached. When pain overrode fury, he lurched back, panting from his exertions.

The coward had probably told them everything. Even now Wilkins and his men could be on their way to the cave . . . unless he was out there now . . . watching him. The idea sent Sancho lurching in a circle as he scanned the brush. He could almost feel those icy eyes boring into him. In the fading light, shadows seemed bigger, closer, almost alive. Fear sent him into a blind panic.

Racing back through the brush, he threw himself into the saddle and kicked his horse into a gallop. After riding hard for several miles with no sign of pursuit, he pulled his winded horse back to a trot. He needed to think, to make a plan. A better plan.

He could do it without Paco. He had planned to kill him anyway for daring to call himself brother. Wilkins had saved him the trouble—and the enjoyment—of doing it himself. Another debt that *cabrón* would pay. But for now, because of Paco, Sancho had to start again. He would go to Mexico and gather his own men, promising gold, land, anything to gain their help. It would take time to find the right men, but when he did, he would come back and then . . .

He frowned, trying to remember the plan he and Paco had devised. The details kept slipping from his grasp, but the end was as certain as death.

Fire. Bright dancing flames roaring straight up to God. Just picturing it in his mind made Sancho laugh out loud.

JUST BEFORE DAWN, BRADY LED HIS BROTHERS AND A DOZEN ranch hands out the gate toward Blue Mesa. He set a fast pace, so driven to find Sancho and end the feud, it wasn't until Hank dropped back that Brady realized he was pushing the men and the horses too hard. He slowed and tried to curb his impatience, but his mind raced on.

It had been a shocking thing last night on the porch with Jessica, telling her about Sam and what he'd done. He'd wrestled with it most of the night and still couldn't believe he'd blurted out the whole sorry tale. It spoke of a loss of control that was at odds with his usual way of doing things. He should have been relieved to have finally gotten it off his chest. Instead he felt ragged and unsure, like the man who carried a heavy load for so long, when he finally got to set it down, he didn't know what to do with his empty hands. His mind didn't know how to deal with the unburdening of that terrible secret. Or her.

It must have been the whiskey. He normally didn't drink that much. Still, he shouldn't have unloaded all that misery on her. He could hardly face it himself—how could he expect her to deal with it?

He'd expected her to bolt. Instead she'd put her arms around him.

A voice jarred him from his muddled thoughts. He looked over to see a rider angling toward them. Recognizing the sheriff's big buckskin, he motioned for the others to rein in so the horses could blow while they waited for the sheriff to reach them.

"Found Alvarez," Rikker said once his buckskin had settled. "Someone stomped his face in. I'm thinking it wasn't you."

"It wasn't."

Rikker reached into his vest pocket for the makings and built a smoke.

It tested Brady's patience, but he didn't push it. He could see the older man had something on his mind, and the sooner they got through it, the sooner he could go after Sancho.

Once the sheriff had the smoke drawing well, he flicked the ash into his cupped hand, shook it to cool it, then tossed it away. "Appears he was hanged."

"His choice."

Rikker's bushy brows rose. "He hanged himself?"

"More or less. He told us where Sancho is. You're welcome to ride along."

Rikker pinched out his smoke. After rolling the butt between his thumb and forefinger to make sure no spark remained, he dropped it to the ground. "Figure Sancho will hang himself, too?" he asked, nudging the buckskin into step beside Brady's bay.

Brady smiled grimly. "Sancho's a knife man. He'll probably slit his throat."

Sancho did neither, because he wasn't at the cave. And even after Brady's men did a thorough search of the whole canyon and the ridge above, there was no sign of him. Brady was so mad he couldn't even speak for most of the ride back to the ranch.

JESSICA HAD SPENT A RESTIVE NIGHT. WHEN SHE HAD FINALLY dozed off, she slept so hard she hadn't heard the men ride out and didn't realize Brady had gone after Sancho until Elena told her over their morning cup of tea.

"They will be fine." Elena held up her rosary beads. "I pray for them. This time it will be Sancho who will die."

Jessica didn't know what to pray for. She just wanted this terrible feud to end.

It was the waiting, she decided later as she wandered through the house. As the end of her confinement approached, she was often plagued with restlessness, but today, there was a feeling of presentiment as well, a sense that something awful was about to happen and she could do nothing to stop it. No doubt it had something to do with the terrible things Brady had told her about Sam.

Her heart ached for him.

It had taken her most of the night to come to terms with it. She understood why he'd done what he did. She even admired his courage in facing such a terrible decision. But it wasn't until the wee hours of the morning that she fully realized the extent of his sacrifice. To ease his brother's agony, he had put his own soul at risk.

It was astounding. Blasphemous.

Yet could there be greater love than that?

She knew of no one who would willingly put those he loved above his own salvation—not her father, not George, not herself. But Brady Wilkins had done it without hesitation. What a gift it would be to be loved by a man like that.

As the day wore on, her unease translated into a nagging headache and an inability to sit still. She had little appetite, no interest in gardening, and no inclination to sit and sew. She decided to walk. Because thoughts of Sam had haunted her all day, the path she chose led up to the graveyard on the hill.

The tree beckoned, limbs drooping toward her, luring her into eyelet shade.

It was a dusty windswept place—two new graves and two-dozen older ones enclosed within a rusty fence. A sad place, eerily quiet except for the squeal of the hinges as she pushed open the gate and stepped through.

Like most everything at RosaRoja, this little graveyard needed tending. Cactus tangled with the iron bars of the fence, weeds crowded the headstones. Several of the tilted stone markers were so worn by time and wind, the words were barely legible. The oldest bore long Spanish names and dated back into the last century. Those added later had heavily carved borders of twining roses with back-to-back *R*'s chiseled across the top. The two most recent graves carried temporary wooden crosses and were so new the earth was still slightly damp. As she wandered the rows of this forlorn and lonely graveyard, Jessica realized it was as much a history of the feud as a resting place for those it had claimed.

She found Sam in a shady corner beside the other Wilkins family graves. Three were clustered together and carried the same year, 1859: Samuel Adams Wilkins, Katherine Brady Wilkins, and Rachel Charlotte Wilkins. Off to the side stood a gravestone dated two years later: Jacob Nathaniel Wilkins.

She hadn't realized so many were lost in so short a time. Brady had buried two-thirds of his family and taken responsibility for his younger brothers and this vast ranch, all within the span of two years.

Bending awkwardly, she set a small bouquet of roses beside Sam's marker, then straightened. Elena said Brady never spoke about what happened when Sam died. Yet he told her. She had never spoken about her rape. Yet she told him. It made no sense.

The wind whispered through the leaves and rattled the long mesquite pods, but brought no answers. She stood for a long time, thinking about the past, the future, what Sam had suffered and what Brady suffered still. When would it end?

"Help him, Sam," she whispered. "Help him find his peace."

She looked around, squinting against the afternoon sun as a deep sadness rose within her. So many lives lost, wasted by this feud. All because of RosaRoja. Sudden anger gripped her, made her want to shout her frustration out loud.

It's just dirt. You're dying over dirt.

As quickly as it erupted, the anger faded. It wasn't the dead she wanted to reach, but the living. Irritated at her own foolishness, she swiped moisture from her eyes. Brady would never leave this land. RosaRoja owned him as much as he owned RosaRoja. In some way she would never fully understand, he needed all this sun and space and windy silence around him, needed it more than he would ever need her.

What was it Elena had said? *The land would never let him down.* Fathers faltered, mothers drifted away, and brothers died or moved on. But RosaRoja would be here forever. It was the one certainty in his life. How could she compete with that?

Jessica looked down at Sam's small grave. No wonder Brady clung to this land so hard. Everything good in his past lay buried in the dirt of RosaRoja. He could never leave it—not for her—not even for himself. If she wanted him and wanted to stay here with him, she would have to accept that.

Fool. A sound escaped her throat, part laugh, part cry of despair. Wanting and staying were the easy part. The hard part would be taking second place to dirt.

Foolish, foolish woman.

IT WAS LATE AFTERNOON WHEN BRADY LED HIS MEN THROUGH the arched gate. Waving the others on, he reined in beside Rikker. "You'll stay for supper?"

"I got enough light to see me home. Wanted to give this to the Englishwoman before I go." He pulled a crinkled envelope from his saddlebag. "Sheriff in Socorro sent it on." He gave Brady a sideways look. "Probably took note of those posters floating around."

Ignoring that, Brady nodded toward the letter. "From her brother?"

Rikker squinted at the writing across the front of the envelope. "From England. Looks like a woman's hand." He lifted the envelope to his nose for a sniff. "Smells flowery."

Her sister, Brady decided. Probably tracked her to Socorro through letters from her brother. Or maybe that horse's ass Ashford tried to cash in on the reward and told the sheriff in Socorro Jessica was here. "Take it on then. I'll be there directly." With a nod, he reined the bay toward the trail that led up to the mesquite tree on the hilltop.

Thoughts of Sam had plagued him all day, but in a different way than they usually did. As ill advised as his confession to Jessica might have been, it had left behind a small measure of peace. Now he could think of Sam without that sick feeling of dread. He welcomed that change, no matter the cause.

As he rode slowly up the hill, he could feel doors closing in his mind. Not slamming, as if shutting in something too terrible to face, but closing softly, as if putting whatever lay behind them gently to rest. Sam was slipping behind one of those doors. Brady could feel him drifting away, and even though it saddened him, he realized it was time to let him go.

At the fence he dismounted and ground tied the bay. Pushing open the gate, he stepped into the past.

The sun hung low, staining the stone markers with a rosy wash. Wind whispered through the mesquite branches and sent dust coiling around his boots as he walked to the corner where Sam lay.

He was surprised to see a ribbon-tied bundle of roses propped against his headstone. Bending, he picked it up and played the ribbon through his fingers. Sleek, shiny satin. Pink. He smiled, certain it was Jessica's.

The woman constantly surprised him. So pregnant she could hardly walk, yet she came all the way up here to put flowers on the grave of a boy she had never met. It was like her to do something like that. She was always worrying over other people, shedding tears for them, but rarely herself. Despite her prickly ways, the woman had a kind and giving heart.

Still smiling, Brady propped the roses back against Sam's marker. "You would have liked her, Sam. She's a pisser with freckles and red hair, just like you."

As the day drifted away on gold-tipped clouds, Brady sat beside Sam's grave, telling his little brother about the prim and fiery English-woman who had wormed her way into his heart and given him back the laughter he thought he'd lost.

JACK POKED HIS HEAD THROUGH THE KITCHEN DOORWAY. "Sheriff brought a letter for you, Jessica. He's waiting on the porch."

Elena glanced up from the potatoes she was peeling. "Perhaps he has news of your brother."

"I hope so." Jessica wiped her hands, then quickly untied her apron. That odd, anxious feeling struck her again, so powerful and unexpected, it sent the room spinning around her. She grabbed at the counter for balance, then as suddenly as it came, the dizziness faded. Disoriented and confused, she looked around. Everything seemed normal. But that feeling of something terrible looming just beyond her sight remained.

Nerves, she chided herself.

She soon decided Sheriff Rikker was the most deliberate and slow-talking individual she had ever encountered. Before they had even gotten through the niceties, she was so beside herself with impatience, she was all but tapping her toe. When he finally pulled a rumpled envelope from his vest pocket, she almost snatched it from his hand.

It was from Annie. Ignoring the sheriff, she quickly scanned the letter. Joy gave way to fear. That prescient feeling returned. Then her heart seemed to fall from her chest. "Oh, God . . . no . . ."

A terrible pain gripped her. Her vision dimmed. Her legs folded and she fell.

BRADY HEARD SHOUTS AS HE RODE BACK DOWN THE HILL. AT first he thought it was Consuelo yelling at Bullshot. The hound had a strong aversion to clean laundry, especially when it hung on a line, flapping in a stiff breeze. But it wasn't Consuelo yelling at the hound. It was Elena calling for him. He kicked the bay into a gallop.

As he rounded the porch, he saw his brothers running from the corrals toward the house and Rikker and Elena bent over something at the bottom of the steps—a woman with red hair, lying too still. He was down and running before the bay stopped. Shoving Rikker aside, he knelt beside her.

She was pale as parchment. He could see the pulse at her throat and knew she was alive but couldn't tell if she was hurt. "Get Consuelo," he snapped at Hank. "Jack, send for Doc." He turned to Rikker and Elena. "What happened?"

"She fainted," the sheriff blurted out before Elena could answer. "She was reading this letter and then said, 'Oh God,' and fainted face first down the steps. Damnedest thing I ever saw." For emphasis, he waved the crumpled letter in Brady's face.

Brady snatched it from his hand and shoved it into his shirt pocket. "Get water."

"How much? A bucket? A cup?"

Christ! "Where the hell is Consuelo?"

"*Estoy aquí*." The Mexican woman rushed down the steps, followed by Hank. When Brady wouldn't move, she shoved the sheriff out of the way and knelt at Jessica's other side. Muttering under her breath, she ran her hands over Jessica's body.

"Is she hurt?" Hank asked.

Brady sat back on his heels to give Consuelo more room. "Can't tell. There's no blood. She's breathing. I don't know. Jesus."

Consuelo flattened her palms against Jessica's belly in one place, then another. As she pressed lower down near the pelvis, Jessica moaned. Her eyes flew open.

For a moment they didn't focus. Then her gaze found Brady's and he could see the fear build. "It's him. God—" Suddenly she arched, her spine bowing off the ground. A hoarse sound escaped her throat, then she slumped back, eyes closed.

"What's wrong with her?" Brady demanded. "Do something!"

Consuelo straightened. "Nothing is broken. There is a small bump *aquí en la frente*"—she pointed to a bruise on Jessica's forehead—"*pero nada más*."

"Can I move her?"

"*Con cuidado*."

His legs wobbled so much he wondered if he'd be able to lift her. As he slid his arm under her shoulders, her eyes opened again, round and wild. "Brady," she gasped, fingers twisting in his shirt. "Help me."

That sent such a jolt through Brady, he could have lifted a yearling steer. Careful not to bang her head or feet on the walls, he carried her into the house. As soon as he laid her on the bed, Elena and Consuelo began working on the long row of buttons down the front of her dress.

He stood at the foot rail, his mind in turmoil, afraid to stay, but

more afraid to leave. He watched a wet stain spread across her skirts
and caught a terrible smell, like blood, only worse.

Jesus. What was happening to her?

Elena shoved him toward the door. "*Vete.* Go. We will call if we
need you."

He allowed her to push him into the hall, then watched the door
close in his face. He stood for a moment, not sure what to do. Then
with a curse, he whirled and headed to the porch.

Rikker was still there, talking to his brothers. They all turned when
he slammed out the door. "How is she?" Jack asked, looking as rattled
as Brady felt.

"Hell if I know." He dragged a hand over his face, trying to rid
himself of that smell, like something was dying or dead. He was familiar with the birthing process. He'd helped deliver calves and foals
and puppies and one time a fawn whose mother had been mauled by
a cougar. But this was beyond his experience. Something was wrong,
something terrible.

"Maybe she got bad news," Rikker offered.

He'd forgotten about the letter. Fishing it out of his pocket, Brady
opened it.

Dearest Sister,

*Your letter came today saying you have just landed in America! I have
been frantic with worry not knowing what had befallen you! John
was furious that you would leave us without even a good-bye. When
will you return? Or have you found George and decided to stay as you
hinted you might? You must tell John everything when he comes.*

*I am sad to write that since you left, we have fallen on Desperate
Circumstances. But with your help, dear Jessica, we may find our way
to prosperous times once again. Now that you have begun a New Life
in America, I am asking—no, begging—that you sign over the deed to
the Hall so that John can invest in a wonderful opportunity. We are in*

Dire Straits, dear Sister. Creditors hound us every day, and without the Hall to secure our debts, I fear for our future.

There is no need to come here. John is sailing next week to bring the papers to you in Socorro. You need only sign them and we will be Saved. I beseech you, dear Jessica. Help us.

Your Loving Sister,
Annie
18 May 1869
Bickersham Hall

Frowning, Brady studied the date. May. Two months ago. Crawford could be in Socorro any day now. Fury exploded. "That bastard!" He crushed the letter in his fist and threw it against the wall with such force he nearly dislocated his shoulder. "If he comes near her, I'll kill him!"

He felt the other three men staring at him. Avoiding their questioning looks, he snatched the crumpled letter from the floor and shoved it back into his pocket.

"Bad news?" Hank asked.

"Something like that." No wonder she fainted, finding out that bastard was dogging her trail. He had no doubt he could keep her safe—*if* she would let him. But since she was in no condition to run, what choice did she have? Knowing the way she felt about her sister, she would probably sign away her home without a second thought. He didn't care if she did or not, but he damned sure wouldn't allow Crawford to intimidate her into doing it. He'd kill him first. Hell, he might kill him anyway for what he had already done to her.

"Anything I can do?"

He looked up, surprised to see the sheriff still standing there, flanked by his frowning brothers. "Yeah. There is."

Without telling them about the rape or revealing more about Jessica's situation than he had to, he explained that her brother-in-law, John Crawford, was on his way from England to try to force her to sign over the deed to her home there. "He'll go to Socorro first, asking after her and her brother, George. Then he'll come here. I want to know when he's on his way."

Rikker narrowed his eyes. "Why?"

Brady forced himself to smile. "So I can bake him a cake."

Rikker didn't buy it.

"Hell, you saw her, Sheriff. She just needs warning. If she's well enough and wants to see him, then there's no problem."

"And if she doesn't want to see him?"

"Then she won't." Brady showed his teeth in a broad open smile.

Rikker didn't buy that either. "You better not start anything," he warned.

"I won't. If somehow the bastard ends up dead, it won't be by my hand. You've got my word on it."

Rikker must have found that idea hilarious; he actually cracked a half smile. "You figure he'll save you the trouble by hanging himself like Alvarez?"

"He's English. They're partial to guns."

Rikker instantly sobered. He waggled a finger. "Not a rope, bullet, knife, whip, or anything else. Your word you won't even hit him."

It rankled that the sheriff would put restrictions on him, but Brady gave his word. If he couldn't hit the bastard, he had two brothers who would gladly do it for him.

Rikker headed down the steps toward his horse. "I'll send word to the sheriff in Socorro to watch for this Crawford fellow." He tightened the cinch, then gathered the reins and swung into the saddle. "Soon as I hear back, I'll let you know."

As Rikker rode through the gate, the door into the house opened.

Elena stood in the doorway. When Brady saw the tears on her cheeks, the air left his chest.

"Is she all right?" Hank asked.

Elena nodded then held out a bundle of cloth Brady hadn't noticed before. "I need a box."

Brady stared at it, unable to move. He knew what was in Elena's hands and understood what she wanted. He just couldn't make his body respond. Then Hank started past him, and that sent him into action. "I'll do it."

Brady was shocked at how small it was. It barely spanned his open hand and probably weighed less than a three-week-old kitten. How could life account for so little? Instinctively he knew that this tiny scrap of flesh had never drawn breath, had, in fact, died long before Jessica's fall. But at one time it had held a beating heart, and because of that, it would be mourned.

"Does she know?"

Elena shook her head. "Consuelo gave her a potion to stop the birth cramps. I pray it lasts until the doctor comes."

"The other one?"

"Consuelo thinks it still lives."

He started down the steps, then stopped and turned back. "Could you tell . . . ?"

"A daughter." Fresh tears started down Elena's cheeks. "*Por Dios.*" She swayed.

But before Brady could react, Jack stepped forward to slip an arm around her shoulders. "Sit down before you fall down," he said gruffly. Gently he steered her toward the two rockers, scolding as he went. Brady was relieved to see Elena lean into him, accepting his support.

"I'll get a box." Hank clumped past him down the steps.

As it happened, the rectangular wooden box that horseshoe nails came in was a fair fit. They even found an unwarped plank for a marker. Rather than take it to Buck to be carved, Brady decided to do it himself. He wouldn't do as neat a job as Buck, but the plank was only temporary. The next time he went to Val Rosa, he would order a fine stone marker. Maybe something with angels carved on it. Jessica would like that.

An hour later, he trudged up the hill with the tiny casket in one hand, the marker in the other. Hank followed with the shovel and an armful of roses. By the time they reached the top, the sun had slipped behind the ridge and the air had started to cool. Brady pushed open the gate and walked to where Sam lay. Setting the box on the ground beside his brother's headstone, he took the shovel from Hank and began to dig.

He thought of Sam, and how hard it had been to leave him all alone in this forlorn place, without anyone he knew or loved resting close by. Then less than three months later, he was digging graves for his mother and baby sister, and Sam was no longer alone. Brady had put them to rest next to each other, so they would all be together. He wasn't sure it mattered, but he did it anyway, because that was the only comfort he could find in that terrible and bloody summer. He hoped when Jessica saw that her daughter rested next to Sam, it would bring her some comfort, too.

Hank wandered the rows, then came to stand at Brady's side. "Place is overgrown. Ought to send someone to clean it up."

Brady set the box in the hole he'd dug, then straightened and looked around.

The place did have an abandoned feel, like nobody cared and those resting here were long forgotten. It shamed him that he had let it go so bad. "I'll tend to it."

Dusk glided in on whippoorwill wings. By the time they walked silently back down the hill, the last light had faded to a distant glow, and all that remained of the day were wispy pink clouds sliding down the bruised sky like a slow wash of tears.

Fifteen

Jessica floated on a roiling black sea. She knew she was not alone. Shadowy figures moved around her, murmuring in soft worried tones while she drifted. She didn't want to waken. She sensed that beyond the blackness something terrible waited, something she didn't want to know.

Better to float in velvety blackness. Better not to know, not to feel. Perhaps she was drugged. Perhaps she was dying. She didn't know.

After a time, awareness intruded. With it came pain, rolling over her in waves that built with every heartbeat, until finally on the crest of an unending surge of crushing pain, she was thrown back into the light. With a gasp, she opened her eyes.

Elena and Consuelo hovered at her head. Dr. O'Grady stood between her bent knees. Another cramp caught her unawares, gripping her abdomen so tightly, it bowed her back. A cry tore through her throat.

Hands held her down, told her to breathe, to relax, not to push. And at last she understood.

It's too soon, too soon, her mind cried as she rose off the sweat-soaked bed with an anguished scream.

BRADY WAS AT THE WOODPILE BY THE LOAFING SHED WHEN he heard Jessica scream—a terrible fearsome sound that sent such a shock through him he almost dropped the splitting maul on his foot. His first impulse was to rush in there and demand they stop doing whatever they were doing to her. His second was to puke.

He did neither. And by the time his nerves settled, he had convinced himself her screaming was a good thing, because it proved she was still alive.

He'd spent a hellacious night. Apparently Doc didn't understand the urgency in the situation, because he didn't get his whiskey-soaked carcass there until almost dawn. Then all he did was peek in at Jessica, and announce they couldn't do anything but wait.

Wait? Hadn't they been doing that for the last twelve hours?

But when Brady explained that, and asked Doc what he intended to do to speed this thing along, he and Elena and Consuelo all ganged up on him, told him to quit yelling, and banished him from his own house. *Christ.* So for the last five hours he'd been splitting rails he didn't need, waiting on a baby that wasn't his, and worrying about a woman who could barely tolerate his touch. How pitiful was that?

She'll be fine, he told himself as he moved to where he could watch the door into the house while he split rails. This baby would be okay. Twins often came in separate sacs, so it was possible for one to be born dead and the other not. At least it worked that way with horses. And often—sometimes—the surviving foal lived. For a while anyway.

As he worked, he thought about how difficult that last birth had been on his mother, and how she'd never seemed to get her strength back. He remembered watching helplessly as she grew weaker every day, until finally, she closed her eyes and never woke up. He didn't want to go through that ever again.

But he wouldn't have to, he told himself. Jessica was stronger. She had spirit and a formidable temper. She wouldn't give up that easy.

Morning passed. Then afternoon. Other than that one awful scream hours earlier, he'd heard nothing nor had there been any word from the house. He couldn't decide if that was a good sign or not. And it disturbed him that he was so worked up about it.

It wasn't his baby and it wasn't his woman. But no matter how many times he told himself that, it didn't seem to ease the worry in his mind.

By late afternoon his shoulders were a mass of cramping muscles and he'd run out of logs to split. As he paused to wipe sweat out of his eyes, he realized he hadn't eaten all day. He thought about going to the cookhouse, then decided he didn't have any appetite anyway, so he went to the barn instead.

His brothers sat on crates near the door, oiling their tack. Busy-work. Their expectant expressions when he walked in told Brady they were as anxious for news as he was. He pulled up another crate to sit on, tipped over an empty barrel for his saddle, then reached for the oil can. It was a relief not to have to worry alone.

The smell of neat's-foot oil mingled with the scents of leather and horses and sweating men. Bullshot added his own pungent aroma when he wandered in and flopped in the straw. When Brady saw the feather in the corner of his mouth, he poked him with his toe. "You better not be chasing chickens again."

The hound blinked up at him with sad, soft eyes, then rose and went to flop beside Hank.

"You hurt his feelings," Hank said, reaching down to scratch behind one droopy ear.

"That's not all that'll be hurt if Consuelo finds him after her chickens."

Hank couldn't argue the truth of that. They oiled in silence for a while, then Brady said to Jack, "Thanks for seeing to Elena earlier."

Jack shrugged without looking up. "I did it for her, not you." When Brady made no response, he added, "She does too much. I told her she shouldn't work her hip so hard."

"Maybe she'll listen to you. She damn sure doesn't mind me."

Jack snorted. "Hell, nobody minds you. Not even that damned dog."

"They would if they had good sense. Pass that bridle."

"You wouldn't know good sense if it crawled up your butt, Big Brother." Jack sailed the bridle at Brady's head.

Brady ducked, then picked up a cinch strap and sailed it back. "If it's been up my butt, I wouldn't want to know it, Sis."

"I'm going to Fort Union," Hank said.

Brady froze, an old boot dangling in his hand. He met Jack's look of surprise, then they both turned to Hank. "What?"

Hank set his rag aside. After snapping the lid on the tin of oil, he wiped his palms down his thighs and looked up. His face was as set as Brady had ever seen. "When this thing with Sancho is over, I'm going to Fort Union." His expression made it clear he wasn't asking, he was telling.

"You joining the Army?" Jack asked.

Brady let the boot drop. "He's courting." He couldn't stop the smile from spreading across his face. "Our Hank is smitten."

"Smitten? By who?"

When Hank didn't respond, Brady answered for him. "Melanie Kinderly. She thinks our Hank is a hero come to life." He grinned at Jack. "Imagine how grand she'll think he is once we clean him up. She'll be climbing him like a cat up a pole."

"I'll be damned." Jack leaned over, slapped his oversized brother on the back with enough force to make a small frown appear on Hank's brow. "You sly bastard."

Brady's smile faded as a new thought came. "You're bringing her back here, aren't you?"

Hank shrugged. "Depends."

"On what?"

"On what she wants."

Jack snickered. "Got you by the short hairs already, does she?"

"Not everybody thinks with their cock, Jack."

"Then why think at all?"

"Why wouldn't she want to live here with us?" Brady cut in.

Jack made a derisive sound. "Take a wild guess, Big Brother."

That got Brady's ire up. "I'd expect you to cut and run, Jack. But you, Hank? Hell, I always thought—"

Jack lurched to his feet. "What's that supposed to mean—cut and run—I'm here, aren't I?"

"For how long, Jack? Until the next wind blows through?"

"Jesus, I can't do anything right by you! I'm damned if I stay, and damned if I don't."

Now Hank and Brady were up, too, and words might have expanded into a family brawl if Doc hadn't come into the barn.

"Jasus, Mary, and Joseph!"

Brady whirled, his brothers forgotten. He tried to read answers in Doc's expression, but saw only weariness and irritation. He heard his brothers move up behind him and was grateful to have them near in case Doc brought bad news. "Well?"

"Sure, and I've been calling so long I near coughed up a lung. What the divel is all this shouting about, I'm wanting to know?"

"How is she?" Hank cut in.

"Is it over?" Jack asked.

"Is she alive?" Brady demanded.

Doc scratched an itchy spot on his balding pate. "That would be fine, no, and yes. Now where's the jug?"

Brady was astounded. "You're not drinking until this is over."

A hint of desperation flashed in Doc's rheumy old eyes. "Faith, and it's going to be a another long dry night, boyo, because your Miss Laudy Daw, being English and of a grasping nature, seems disinclined to give up that babe anytime soon. Now for the love of Sweet Baby Jasus, where's the jug?"

Brady was about to relent, thinking he could use a wee dram himself, when Elena limped out onto the porch, waving her arms and yelling for Doc.

PAIN CRUSHED HER IN A GIANT FIST, SQUEEZING THE AIR FROM her lungs. It built with each cramp, drew her muscles so tight she felt taut as a bowstring and her body became a writhing bundle of screaming nerve ends. She wished she would faint, die, anything to end this terrible pressure. Then just before she splintered apart, she felt a searing pain, a hot rush between her legs, and suddenly she felt herself catapulted into numbing darkness and blessed relief.

Later—how long?—she heard the faint cry of a babe. Something moved against her side, something small and warm that fit perfectly in the crook of her arm.

She opened her eyes.

The room was almost dark. Dawn or dusk? Lamplight cast dim shadows along the walls, but there was enough light for her to see the red fuzz on the tiny head by her breast.

Victoria.

Emotion swelled in her chest. She gently kissed that downy head, felt the butterfly pulse of the fontanel against her lips, and experienced such a fierce and consuming joy, it brought tears to her eyes. *Victoria. At last.*

Dr. O'Grady moved beside the bed. She lifted her free arm to make room for the other baby, but it never came. When she saw the doctor's face, she knew why. "No."

"I'm sorry, lass."

"NO!"

The bed sagged as he sat beside her and began talking in his soft musical voice. She didn't want to hear and tried not to listen, but his words found their way into her mind anyway. Before she'd even had a chance to savor it, the joy within her died.

"He's wee but he's healthy. He'll grow fast."

He. Not she. Not Victoria. "Where is my daughter?"

The doctor shook his head, his faded eyes filled with pity she didn't want.

"Where is my daughter? I need to know where she is!"

O'Grady rose and went to the window. Pushing the blanket drape aside, he pointed toward the hill rising in sharp silhouette against the evening sky. "She's up there, lass. Brady buried her beside little Sam. And a fine job of it he did, too, with a wee wooden casket and dozens of roses and a marker he carved himself." He let the drape fall and walked back to the bed. Tucking the blanket tighter around the tiny figure by her side, he said, "It's your son who needs you now."

A son. John Crawford's son. While Victoria rested in a grave.

God, why?

But God wasn't listening or He didn't care. Strength failed her. The darkness beckoned, promised relief from the ache in her heart. Bereft, unable to look at the baby at her side, she turned her face to the wall and closed her eyes.

SHE DRIFTED FOREVER, WRAPPED IN A MANTLE OF DESPAIR that numbed her mind and sapped her will. Yet even cocooned in her misery, Victoria invaded her dreams—a laughing, beautiful, perfect child who wasn't to be. Jessica would awaken, her chest aching and her throat clogged with tears she couldn't shed, only to find that reality was much crueler than the painful yearning of her dreams.

The emptiness was unbearable.

So much easier to drift away, where hours became days, and days became forever.

But Elena gave her no peace. She was always nearby, rousing her to take water or broth or a bitter herbal brew Consuelo made for her. Jessica tried to tell her to stop, that it didn't matter, that she needed to be with Victoria. But Elena wouldn't let her go. Persistence outlasted resistance, and eventually, whether she willed it or not, Jessica's strength began to return.

"You are a mother now," Elena told her over and over. "Your son needs you."

She made a halfhearted effort. She knew what she was expected to do. But her milk was slow to come in, and she was so weak she was afraid to hold him, and when she did, it felt like a betrayal of Victoria.

So Elena tended him. She even found a wet nurse to feed him. And ultimately, Jessica wasn't needed at all. Relieved, she slept the hours away.

Time had no meaning. Isolated and alone, she drifted through hazy dreams while life went on around her. She felt disconnected from it, armored by despair and numbed by apathy, and if not for the single slender thread that bound her to the mesquite tree on that graveyard hilltop, she might have drifted away forever.

She could see it from her bed. For hours she lay staring at it, watching the colors change as the sun moved slowly across the sky. Lacy arms called her to come, but she couldn't. She hadn't the strength or the will, and as long as she didn't have to look at that tiny grave on the hill, she could pretend that it wasn't there, that it wasn't real, that Victoria still lived. It was all she had.

BRADY STAYED OUT OF IT AS LONG AS HE COULD. DOC explained that Jessica had had a rough time of it, and although her son was small, he would survive. Just a matter of time.

Yet as the days passed, it became clear that even though Jessica was making a slow physical recovery, she was falling into a rapid mental decline. He knew she was grieving. But after almost a week of listening to her son cry while she slept the days away, he realized he had to do something. He couldn't sit by and let another woman drift out of his life.

He was in his usual evening spot, sitting in his rocker, not far from her open window. He could hear almost everything that went on behind the blanket drape. He heard the baby cry when he was hungry or needed his drawers changed or when Angelina Ortega, the wet nurse,

came to feed him. He heard when they brought food and tried to coax
Jessica to eat. He heard the worried voices of Consuelo and Elena as
they moved about the room. But he never heard a word from Jessica.
He never even heard her cry.

It had been another hellacious day. His most productive bull had
suffered a snakebite, a cougar had taken five calves from the north
herd, and a landslide had filled in one of their best water holes. On
top of that came news of a slaughtered family in a charred cabin south
of Val Rosa. Not knowing if it was hostiles or Sancho, he had to prepare the ranch for either. He could handle all that. He could even
handle the fact that with Jessica laid up, he was back to Consuelo's
chili, and his stomach felt like someone was rooting around in it with
a hot iron.

What he couldn't handle was a quitter.

Behind the curtain, the baby howled for his night feeding. *Christ.*

The ache in Brady's gut moved up into his temples. Squeezing the
bridge of his nose between his thumb and forefinger, he struggled with
his temper. Was there any sound worse than that of a crying baby?
Why didn't they do something?

It's not my baby, not my woman, not my problem.

The kid hit a high note that set off tiny explosions of pain throughout Brady's skull. He started out of his rocker, then heard the wet nurse
come into the room and he settled back, relieved that at last someone
had come to tend the poor kid.

Massaging his temples with the tips of his fingers, he listened to
Angelina move about, taking time away from her own child to tend
another woman's baby. It came to him how wrong that was—wrong of
Jessica to give up her own child, and wrong of him to let her.

Damn her.

Resolved, he shot to his feet. He stomped into the house and down
the hall. Without pausing to knock, he flung open the bedroom door
so hard it bounced against the wall. Angelina looked up with wide startled eyes from the squalling half-dressed baby.

Jessica remained facing the wall.

He didn't know if she was asleep or not, and didn't care. Giving Angelina what he hoped was a reassuring nod, he waited in the doorway while she finished changing the baby's drawers. When she began loosening the tie on her blouse, he motioned for her to stop. "She'll do it." He nodded toward the door. "Wait outside."

After the door closed behind her, he picked up the baby and crossed to the bed. As he looked down at Jessica, his anger built. He wanted to shake her, demand that she come back, that she acknowledge her son. He didn't know which enraged him more—her helplessness or his. He'd tried to be patient. He'd tried to be understanding. He'd gagged down Consuelo's chili and listened to the baby crying and had kept his distance. But enough was enough. This ended now.

"Roll over."

When she didn't move, he pinned the baby against his chest with one hand, and grabbed her shoulder with the other. He pulled her onto her back.

She looked up with that same empty stare he'd seen on his mother's face ten years ago, and it sent his anger to a flash point. He thrust the crying baby toward her. "Feed your son."

She blinked and looked around. "There's a nurse—"

"No. You do it."

Awareness sparked in her eyes. "I—I can't."

"You can and you will." When she tried to pull away, he grabbed for her shoulder, missed, and got her gown instead. The thin fabric tore, exposing one swollen blue-veined breast. He watched her feeble attempts to cover herself and felt half sick. It shamed him to be doing this, but he was too angry to stop now. Shoving her hands away, he laid the baby on the bed beside her.

The baby howled, his tiny fists waving, his face red with indignation.

Jessica shrank back, but Brady trapped her head in his hands and held her fast. He brought his face close to hers. "You're his mother, damnit! Act like it."

Realizing he was scaring her, he pulled his hands away and forced himself to step back. It sickened him to see the fear back in her eyes. "Feed him," he snapped. "If I have to stand here all night, you'll at least do that for your son."

It didn't take all night, and in fact, took little more than half an hour. But by the time it was done, the baby was acting colicky, Jessica was crying, and Brady was about to puke. When it was clear Jessica had no more milk to give, he took the baby from her unresisting arms and passed him out to Angelina. After sending her to the kitchen to finish feeding him, he closed the door and went back to the bed.

Jessica lay curled toward the wall again. This time he felt no anger, just a deep sense of loss and resignation, knowing she would probably never trust him again.

"Look at me."

Slowly she rolled over. She looked ravaged, worse than after the stage crashed, worse than when she was fevered. More than anything he wanted to gather her in his arms, and tell her he would find a way to fix this and make everything right for her again.

He reached out to brush a limp curl from her face.

She jerked her head away.

Surprised by the jolt of pain her action brought him, he let his hand fall back to his side.

"You're going to do this, Jessica, because he's your son and he needs you. And because none of this is his fault, any more than it is yours."

She didn't respond, but if an expression had substance, he would be bleeding to death.

"Even if I have to come in here a dozen times a day to make sure you do. Understand?"

He waited, watched the emotions play across her face—fear, despair, fury—and he was glad, because at least now she was feeling something.

"I understand you're a bloody bastard," she finally said.

"So you've said." Then, because he was so relieved to see that spark of temper back in her eyes, and because he'd been wanting to do it ever since he'd walked through the door, he leaned down and gave her a quick kiss. Drawing back before she could bite him, he said, "Sleep. I'll see you in the morning."

SHE COULDN'T SLEEP. BRADY HAD SHATTERED THAT CARE-fully erected wall between her and her pain, and now she could find no rest, no peace.

She hated him. Despised him. How dare he do this to her.

Her anguish was immeasurable and unbearable. She had no defense against it but anger. Seething with fury, she lay staring out the window, wondering how to go on from here.

She glanced over at the cradle.

At John Crawford's son.

It might not be the baby's fault or hers, but they would both carry that curse forever, no matter what Brady said. Couldn't he understand that? Didn't he know what she was going through?

She sat up and peered over the side of the cradle.

Red fluff showed above the edge of the blanket. She heard a faint snuf-fling, as if his nose was stuffy from all his crying. He was very small.

Then why did she feel so threatened? Was it because he was male? A smaller version of the man she despised? Would the sins of the father . . .

With a cry, she slumped back, her mind in such turmoil her limbs shook.

He was just a baby. A redheaded baby who looked more like her than his brute of a father.

Her baby.

For a long time she stared up at the adobe ceiling, listening to her son breathe while tears slid down to dampen the hair at her temples.

She was a mother now. She must act like one. Her son needed her.

It was a litany she repeated over and over, until slowly the knot in her chest loosened. After a while, anger faded into numbness then weary acceptance. Finally, too exhausted to fight it any longer, she closed her eyes and slept.

She awoke to see dawn creeping across the sky. She waited until it

PIECES OF SKY 225

bathed the tombstones in golden light and backlit the mesquite tree in a fiery nimbus, then on trembling legs, she rose. Moving quietly so she wouldn't wake the baby, she pulled on her robe and stepped into her slippers, then left the room.

Her body was so sore she had to brace her palms against the walls for support as she shuffled down the hall. By the time she made it out onto the porch, she panted with exertion. Once she'd caught her breath and her eyes had adjusted to the harsh morning sunlight, she carefully made her way down the steps into the yard. The scent of roses was so overpowering it made her gorge rise. Against the stone foundation the blossoms looked like bright splashes of blood.

As she crossed the yard, the hound scrambled out from under the porch. He kept his distance, watching her slow progress with sad canine eyes, as if waiting to see what she was up to before committing himself to action. He probably sensed her dementia. Animals were good at that. After a few moments he lost interest and, with a yawn and a stretch, crawled back into the shade under the porch.

Chickens laid a trail of droppings as they moved from her path. Sharp rocks cut into the thin soles of her slippers. She should have worn her walking boots rather than these useless satin slippers. She should have taken more care. She shouldn't have fainted and fallen down the steps.

Victoria, forgive me.

Before she had traveled a hundred feet, Elena and Consuelo tracked her down. "Where are you going?" Elena called from the porch as Consuelo came down the steps toward her.

"I need to go." She waved a shaky hand toward the hill. "Up there. I need to see—"

"*Está enferma*," Consuelo cut in, taking Jessica's arm in a firm but gentle grip. "You are not well. Come. I will help you to your bed."

"No." Jessica pulled her arm free with such force, she almost lost her balance. "I must." She looked over Consuelo's shoulder at Elena watching from the porch. "Please," she beseeched her friend. "Don't stop me."

"But, *señora*—"

"Let her go, Consuelo," Elena called out.

Consuelo thinned her lips in disapproval. Then, shaking her head, she said, "*Está bien*. I will help you." She put her arm around Jessica's shoulders.

Again, Jessica pulled away. "No. Please. I must go alone."

Reluctantly Consuelo stepped aside. "*Tenga cuidado, señora*. We will watch for you."

Her progress was painfully slow. Overworked muscles ached in protest, and it took all of her concentration to keep her balance as she worked her way over the uneven ground. Less than a quarter of the way up the hill, dizziness overcame her. Leaning over, head drooping as she gripped her knees, she waited for the weakness to pass.

Rocks clattered behind her.

She looked back to see Brady riding up the hill.

Laughter rose bitterly in her throat. Her hero, riding to the rescue—or her watchdog, coming to harass and scold her. Wearily, she straightened.

Yet as she watched him ride toward her, she realized that despite that horrid scene between them last night, she needed this man. He had seen and touched what she never could. Those work-worn hands had held the child she would never know. Perhaps it was fitting that he should be there when she told Victoria good-bye.

He rode bareback, his long legs reaching below the horse's belly. Bits of hay clung to his shirt. His hair was wet, as if he'd been washing and had left in such a rush, he'd forgone his hat as well as a saddle. He didn't ride with the stiff poise of a well-seated Englishman, but with such a loose, fluid grace, it seemed he and the horse were one.

Naturally he was scowling.

As he reined in, the horse eyed her warily, nostrils flaring as it tested her scent. She lifted a hand to stroke its neck, giving as much reassurance as she took.

"What are you doing, Jessica?"

She looked up at the broad dark shape of him against the low morning sun, and felt again that unshakable connection. She was bound forever to this man. By dirt. The cruel irony of it was so piercing, it almost brought tears to her eyes. She was part of RosaRoja now, chained throughout eternity to this place and this man, by the dirt of her daughter's grave.

God was such a trickster.

Resting her head against the horse's neck, she breathed in his musky animal scent, felt his solid warmth against her brow. She didn't want to argue with Brady, or have to explain why she was doing this. She just wanted to be allowed to do what she had to do. "Please."

He hesitated, then leaned forward and held out his left hand. "Take ahold."

A moment later she sat sideways behind the horse's withers, the backs of her legs draped over Brady's thigh, her fingers gripping the horse's mane with what little strength she had left.

Powerful muscles moved against her hip as Brady nudged the horse forward. The motion tipped her backward, and when his arm closed around her waist, pulling her to his chest, she didn't resist. She needed the contact, to be held by him, to know for this time, at least, she wasn't alone.

They stopped beside the mesquite tree. He helped her down, then pushed open the gate.

Jessica moved on wooden legs, battling an unexpected and almost overwhelming urge to flee. Dread built with every halting step. Suddenly she realized she didn't want to do this, didn't want to acknowledge that under that pitifully small mound of dirt her daughter was buried. She wanted to run, and keep running, until she outdistanced this hilltop and the past and all the heartache it had brought her. Yet no matter how loudly her mind screamed against it, her legs wouldn't stop moving . . . bringing her closer . . . until she was close enough to see the roses . . . then the marker . . . then her daughter's name carved into the weathered wood. And finally the pain defeated her.

With a cry, she staggered, palms pressed over her heart, her mind reeling. A terrible howling rose inside her head. She opened her mouth to scream, but no sound came out. Then strong arms closed around her, anchoring her against a hard, solid body, as the grief finally broke free in hoarse, wrenching sobs.

ALL HIS LIFE BRADY HAD TAKEN CARE OF THINGS. WHEN Jacob went to fight the Mexicans, he took care of Ma. When Ma got sick, he took care of his brothers. While Jacob was dying, he took care of the ranch. That was his job. Most of the time he was good at it. But that morning, as Jessica cried for a baby she would never see, or touch, or know, he just stood there in gut-churning helplessness because there wasn't a damned thing else he could do.

It was the worst feeling he'd had since Sam.

She cried for a long time. When it was over and she had said her good-byes, she let him take her up on the horse in front of him again, and they rode back down the hill. He kept the horse at a slow walk, taking his time, because he knew it might be a long time before he held her again.

Right now she was drowning in pain. But come tomorrow, when she remembered what he'd done last night, she might decide she never wanted him near her again. She might even tell him that and think she meant it. But it wasn't going to be that way.

Today marked a change for both of them. They had each left a part of themselves beside the mesquite tree. In an agony of grief, Jessica had buried a part of her heart with her daughter. Brady had given up his without a fight. His feelings for Jessica were so strong now, he could no longer deny them. He didn't want to deny them.

He tightened his arm around her, felt the delicate ridge of her shoulder blades against his chest, and a sense of rightness moved through him. He wanted this woman. He wanted her pain, her laughter, her body, and her heart. He wanted her with him forever. And he would do damn near anything to make that happen.

Dropping his face to the top of her head, he pressed his lips to her silky hair.

You're mine.

Sixteen

AFTER HER ORDEAL AT THE CEMETERY, JESSICA WAS SO EX-
hausted she slept until early afternoon, awakening to the sound of her
son's hungry cry and the sight of Brady looming in the doorway.

"About time," he said, moving aside as the wet nurse—Angelina,
wasn't it?—left after changing the baby's napkin. "I was about to let
Bullshot have at you." He picked up the squalling infant, wincing as
the hungry howls rose in pitch. "Has your temper, I see." Holding him
in outstretched arms as he might a thrashing piglet, he carried him toward the bed. "You want to do this lying down or sitting up?" he asked
as matter-of-factly as if he inquired about sugar for her tea.

"Sitting."

Holding the baby against his chest with a hand that dwarfed the
tiny body, he slid his other arm beneath her shoulders to help her sit
up. Once she settled against the headboard, he lowered the baby into
her arms, then stood back, studying her. If he noticed she still wore the
torn gown from last night and her trip up the hill earlier that morning,

he said nothing, although Jessica could see it held an inordinate amount of his interest. "Do you plan on watching?"

He looked up from his perusal of her chest and had the audacity to smile. "I don't mind."

"I certainly do."

Thankfully he didn't argue, and dropped into the chair beside the window. After a moment, he rose again, slid the drape to one side, and opened the window as wide as it would go. "This room needs airing." He gave her a look. "In fact, you could use—"

"Hush." But to her utter disgust, she realized he was right. How long had it been since she'd bathed? It was revolting that she had sunk so low. Needing to change the subject, she said in a peeved tone, "This is improper, your staying in here while I feed him."

"It bothers you that much?"

The question gave her pause. She considered how she would feel if he left, compared to how she felt now, with his male vitality so dominant it overrode all the dark memories trapped within the room. She was surprised to realize that not only did it not bother her, but she actually wanted him to stay. Another rule trampled by circumstance. "You may stay." Tipping her head back against the headboard, she closed her eyes and gave herself over to the unfamiliar and indescribable sensation of having a baby nurse at her breast.

A baby. Her baby. No one need ever know John Crawford was his father.

She must have dozed off. When next she awoke, the baby was back in his cradle, Brady was gone, and Consuelo was pouring a kettle of steaming water into the copper hip tub that had been moved from the upstairs water closet after the Kinderlys left.

Brady returned for the evening feeding, and despite the impropriety of having him present while she nursed her baby, she was glad to see him. Perhaps she was lonely or simply insane, but when he showed up in her doorway wearing a big grin and a form-fitting shirt that showed off his impressive physique and matched his astounding eyes, she couldn't help but grin back.

"You're looking better." He stepped into the room. "Smell better, too."

"I was not that bad." Trying to maintain at least a semblance of propriety, she pulled the edge of the blanket over her son's head as he nursed.

"Maybe not bad enough for Bullshot to roll on you, but getting there."

She refrained from snorting. "This from a man ever in need of a shave and a trim."

"I may be scruffy, but I'm clean." He said it as if cleanliness were a rare and commendable thing, which around here, it might very well be. "I bathe all the time."

"Where?" She couldn't believe she was actually asking about his personal habits. Nor could she imagine him fitting into the small tub she had just used. Just picturing it brought a smile to her lips and a flush to her brow.

"Lots of places." He walked over to stand beside the bed. His eyes moved over her, then he turned and went to stand at the window. "Mostly the creek if it's warm enough. Or there's an oversized tub behind the cookhouse. But it's got tick dip in it now."

She didn't ask if the dip was for the livestock or the cowboys. "You bathe outdoors?" It struck her anew how much she had changed that she could even ask such a question.

"Sure. The water's cool and clean as long as you stay upstream of the cattle. There's even a shady swimming hole. Elena goes there sometimes. Or I can take you if you'd prefer." His grin told her which he would prefer and why. *Cheeky.*

He circled back toward the bed again. "I won't let you hide out, you know."

They'd had this conversation before. "I am not hiding out."

"Because I watched it happen once before, and I won't watch it again. Fair warning."

Was he referring to her avoidance of strangers? Or his mother's death? Before she could ask, he went back to the window. He seemed distracted, edgy. She wondered if he felt constrained in small spaces. Whenever he came into the room, he seemed drawn to the window. Perhaps that was why he seemed to prefer the porch to the courtyard, and why he spent more time in his rocker than at his desk. A man his size needed space around him, more room to stretch than most. Yet in Brady's case, it seemed as much a mental need as a physical one. Another piece to the puzzle.

The baby finished nursing and drifted to sleep. Jessica studied him, enjoying the milky smell of him, the warmth, the connection of this tiny body resting against hers. Elena was right. He was a beautiful baby.

"Is he done?"

She glanced up to find Brady studying her. "For now."

He nodded. But instead of taking him from her arms as he had last night, he went to the door and called for Angelina. After the young woman settled the baby in his cradle, Brady asked her to stay. Then before Jessica knew what he was about, he came back to the bed, scooped her up in his arms, blankets and all, and headed toward the door.

"What are you doing?" she choked out, unaccustomed to being carried. But then she had never met a man who could carry her, or who would have even dared such a thing. Other than Hank and that no-necked blacksmith in Bickersham Village, she had never met anyone of Brady's size or strength. She wasn't sure she liked it.

But she wasn't sure she disliked it either. "I am capable of walking, you know."

He grinned. "I know, but this is more fun." He shifted his grip to angle her through the doorway onto the porch. "You've lost weight."

"I did just have a baby." *Two babies.* "But thank you for noticing."

He laughed, sending a tingling vibration from his body into hers. "Hell, I notice everything about you, woman."

She didn't know how to respond to that.

He lowered her and her blankets into her rocker, then positioned his beside it and sank down with a deep sigh. "Now isn't this better?"

She was too busy trying to cover herself with the blanket to answer, and by the time she was satisfied modesty was maintained, he was reaching for her hand. "I've missed our evenings out here." He pressed a kiss against her knuckles. "I've missed you."

"As well you should," she teased, trying to hide the pleasure his words brought.

They rocked in comfortable silence, watching the shadows lengthen as the sun slipped lower in the western sky. She had missed this, too, she realized. She had missed him. Looking down at the fingers gripping hers, she felt a gentle ache move across her heart. This hand had touched the daughter she never would. A sad, but comforting thought.

After a while, needing to clear the air, she said, "I'm sorry. I haven't handled all this very well." She made an offhand gesture with her free hand, then let it fall back into her blanketed lap. "I was distraught."

He didn't speak, but she felt that hum of intensity charging the air between them.

"If you hadn't intervened, I . . . well . . . I suppose I owe you another debt of gratitude."

"Hell."

She glanced over.

"It's not your gratitude I want." He stopped rocking, forcing her to stop as well. He leaned closer until his shoulder brushed hers and his big body blocked the low sun. "You know that, don't you?" His lips brushed hers.

"No—I . . ." Words failed her as he kissed a slow, hot trail across her jaw and up her cheek.

His voice was a whispery rush in her ear. "What I want is you under me and open to me, your hair spread around us like liquid fire and your long, coltish legs holding me tight. That's what I want."

As the words sank in, she pulled back with a gasp. "What an outrageous thing to say."

He straightened. "You think it's too soon?"

"How could you even suggest such a thing?"

"You're right. We should wait until you're healed." He resumed rocking. "When do you think that'll be?"

If she hadn't been so shocked, she would have bounded from the rocker. Or called him to accounts. Or blocked the images he had planted in her mind.

But before she could regain the power of speech, he said, "Tomorrow we'll bring little what's-his-name out here with us. By the way, what is his name?"

She gaped at him, still so rattled she couldn't form words.

"You have named him, haven't you?"

She didn't know how to respond even if she could. She was ashamed to admit she hadn't named her son. She was ashamed that she couldn't get those pictures out of her mind. She was ashamed to be sitting in public in her nightclothes while Brady Wilkins talked about doing . . . that . . . with her. Didn't he know just the thought of it sent her into mindless panic?

"Hell, it's been almost a week, Jessica."

She drew in a ragged breath and tried to think. "Adrian," she blurted. "Adrian Benjamin Thornton." As soon as she said it, she knew the name had been in her mind all along.

"Adrian? Isn't that a girl's name?"

"It was my father's name." She should leave. She should run as fast as she could from this man.

"Was he a girl? Never mind." He scratched at his whiskered chin. It sounded like sandpaper on wood. "Benjamin is good. You could name him Benjamin Franklin Thornton."

Relieved to have a new focus for her rampant imagination, Jessica said, "What is this family's insistence on naming children after dead American statesmen? Especially when you don't even use the names you pick."

He gave her a questioning look.

"*Patrick* Henry Wilkins? *Andrew* Jackson Wilkins? And whom are you named after? Some obscure so-called patriot who threw perfectly good tea into Boston Harbor?"

"Grandpa Brady," he said proudly. "A black Irishman with a bent toward mischief until he got religion. Poor bastard was struck down by lightning when he was standing in the river baptizing sinners."

"Well, that explains a great deal."

He gave her that grin. "It does, doesn't it? So you see how important it is that the boy has a name to live up to, like I did. And Benjamin Franklin Thornton would be a fine name."

"He has a fine name. Adrian Benjamin Thornton." Simply saying it aloud gave her son substance. No longer was he a shadow in the back of her mind. He was her son.

"If you don't mind, I'll call him Benjamin."

"His name is Adrian."

"Ben, then. Allow him that, at least. The kid's manhood is at stake."

"And an overrated thing *that* is," Jessica said dryly.

They rocked in silence. Jessica watched the wind drive a spiral of dust across the hilltop and whip the branches of the tree into a dancing frenzy. She thought of Victoria resting under that tree throughout the years to come, and she wondered at all the living who had passed by it, and all the dead who would spend eternity beneath it.

"It's bigger than most, isn't it?"

His gaze flew to hers. "What is?"

She motioned toward the hilltop. "The other mesquite trees I've seen are much smaller. What makes this one so large?"

His mustache twitched. "Water," he said. "Jacob was convinced its roots had found an underground river. I think it's more than that."

"Such as?"

"The Indians call it a 'Spirit Tree.' Because of its size and age, they think it has magical powers. Even now we occasionally find small offerings and charms left by the trunk."

"Do you think it has magical powers?"

He thought for a moment, then shrugged. "I think it has grit. It's survived drought and cold and fire. It's outlasted the Spaniards, the Mexicans, the Indians, and someday it'll outlast us, too. I take comfort in that. I like knowing that whatever mischief we humans get ourselves into, that tree will still be here, watching over those who rest beneath it. It endures. I admire that."

Jessica studied the tree. As Brady's words settled in her mind, they brought with them a feeling of peace. Acceptance. The grief would always be there, but it helped knowing that the mesquite tree would be there to shelter Victoria for all the years ahead.

"Rikker sent word."

It took a moment for the words to make sense. "About George?"

"No."

And suddenly she knew why he had seemed distracted, and what he had avoided telling her. She stiffened in the chair, bracing herself for the words she had dreaded to hear since the moment she had opened Annie's letter. "Crawford."

His grip tightened on her hand. "I don't want you worrying. Just tell me what you want me to do and I'll take care of it."

Fear rippled through her. But she couldn't give in to weakness now. She had a son to protect.

"My offer still holds."

Kill him? She looked over, saw the resolve in his eyes, and almost gave in. Then she reminded herself they were talking about her sister's husband and Adrian's father. As vile as Crawford was, she didn't want his death on her conscience. "How long do I have?"

"Two days, maybe less." He reached out, trailed the fingertips of his free hand down the side of her face, calming her with his touch and his strength. "I won't let him hurt you, Jessica. You know that, don't you?"

She laid her hand over his, anchoring his palm against her cheek. "I know."

A spark ignited behind his eyes that sent an answering heat through her body. "Good." His teeth showed in a smile that was both triumphant and deadly in intent, then his hand slipped from beneath hers to fall back to his side. "What do you want me to do?"

She thought for a moment. There was only one way to stop Crawford and keep those she loved safe. "Can you get a solicitor to the ranch?"

"If you mean a lawyer, I can have one here by tomorrow afternoon."

"Excellent." She smiled, feeling more in control than she had in days. "You get him here and I shall do the rest."

THE LAWYER CAME AT PRECISELY ONE O'CLOCK THE FOLLOW-ing afternoon, and brought with him his stenographer assistant and a satchel bulging with forms. Brady introduced him as Phineas Higgins. His assistant, who was also his son, was named Horace. Both wore round, wire-rimmed spectacles, but while the elder had the stooped shoulders of a man who had spent most of his life hunched over a desk, the younger would have passed for a stonemason if not for the empty sleeve on his right side. Jessica was moved to pity until she saw the sharply intelligent glint in his kind hazel eyes. She smiled, deciding they would do.

Brady graciously allowed them use of his office, and by the time the forms had been drawn up, checked, and witnessed, it was late afternoon. Jessica instructed them to send copies to her solicitor in England, gave them a letter to post to Annie explaining what she had done, then waved them through the gate. Exhausted, she sank into the rocker, hoping she had done everything she could to protect her family from John Crawford. If she failed and something happened to her, it would be up to Brady. If he agreed.

That night, for the first time since Adrian was born, she took dinner with the brothers and Elena in the kitchen. She had expected it to be somewhat awkward in view of her crisis, but everyone seemed genuinely glad she was recovering, and although solicitous of her health, none made comment about her ordeal.

She was relieved. She was deeply ashamed of her earlier behavior toward her son. She also didn't want to discuss the daughter she had lost. Victoria was her private pain, and she knew that time, not well-meant words of sympathy, was what she needed now.

Deciding her plan might be better received on full stomachs, she waited until the brothers had taken the edge off their voracious appetites and were settling into their second—or in Hank's case, third—helpings before she spoke. "I have something to discuss with you, if I might. It concerns Adrian."

Jack looked up. "Who?"

"She means Ben," Brady answered, reaching for another tortilla.

"Adrian," she insisted, giving him a look. "And the man on his way here."

This time four heads came up. Elena smiled encouragingly, but the glances passing between the three brothers told Jessica discussions had already commenced. And without her.

Understandable, but provoking nonetheless. She didn't consider herself helpless and was somewhat irritated that they did, although in view of her recent behavior, she could see why they might. However, she was stronger now and able to take back the reins of control, which she fully intended to do. And she would begin with the truth, no matter how distasteful.

"The man coming here tomorrow has papers he wishes me to sign. His name is John Crawford. He is my sister's husband and he . . . he is also the father of my son."

Hank and Jack reacted with predictable surprise. Elena smiled encouragingly, and Brady's scowl deepened. Taking a deep breath, she pressed on.

"The papers are the deed to my family home in England. Once before he tried to get me to sign over the property. When I refused, he punished me in the most degrading way possible, and promised he would continue to do so, unless I gave him the deed."

Jack frowned. "What does that mean, exactly?"

"Christ, Jack."

"It means he forced me."

Silence.

Hank glowered at his plate.

Jack rounded on Brady. "What are you going to do?"

"It is not up to him," she cut in.

When his brothers started to argue, Brady held up a hand to forestall them. "I gave my word to Rikker. And her." It was an effort to stay out of it, but he knew she wouldn't welcome his interference. This was her time, her moment. She was rising out of the ashes on the wings of her own power, and it was an amazing thing to see.

But he'd be there to catch her just in case she fell.

"If there is any bloodletting to be done," Jessica said over Hank and Jack's furious objections, "I shall do it. And I assure you if he touches me again, I will gladly carve him like a Christmas goose." She smiled, liking the idea. By their expressions, they liked it, too.

It was laughable, really. After years of having to fight her battles alone, now she had more protectors than she knew what to do with. Dear, sweet men. She wanted to hug them all.

"If I do decide to do away with him, you may each have a go at him. Will that satisfy?"

While his brothers nodded, looking delighted at the prospect, Brady loosened his fists and pushed his plate away before he threw it against the wall. Every time he thought about what that bastard had done to Jessica, it sent his mind in raging spirals. Knowing what she had suffered, watching her struggle against her fears and finally overcome them, filled him with such a surge of emotion it was all he could do to stay in his seat.

And beneath the rage, what he felt most was pride.

"What is it? A castle or something?" Jack grinned at Hank. "Must be, if he's coming all this way to get it."

"It is but a small manor house and some acreage," Jessica said.

"How much acreage?" Hank asked.

"Three hundred and twenty."

"Hardly seems worth the trip."

"Apparently John Crawford would disagree." She masked her aggravation. It was always about size with this overlarge family. But in a land where everything was so new, it was no doubt difficult to understand a three-hundred-year history of family and tradition. "He needs it to pay off his creditors, either by securing loans against it, or mining the coal beneath it."

Hank looked skeptical. "How much coal can there be under a half section of land?"

"A great deal, since it lies in the middle of the richest vein in Northumberland. With productive mines all around us, it would be economical as well as convenient to mine our land, too. There's even a branch railway nearby. The mining consortium has been after us for years."

"Why not sell?" Hank persisted. "Then he'd have no reason to come after you."

"It's not mine to sell. I simply hold it for my oldest daughter, and my daughter's oldest daughter, and so on." Seeing their confusion, she explained. "Bickersham Hall has been passed down through the elder daughters of my mother's line ever since it was granted as a dower property in the sixteenth century. I will not be forced by a despicable coward like John Crawford to break a three-hundred-year tradition. I will never sell."

Brady felt that surge of pride again. It pleased him the woman understood the value of land and how important it was to build something that would last for generations. It was a concept his brothers lost sight of from time to time.

"What happens if there's no daughter?" Jack asked.

"Then it would be Adrian's to hold in trust for his daughter."

"And if Ben died before he had children?" Brady asked.

"If my line dies out then, it would go to my sister, Annie."

"Crawford's wife."

"Yes."

Jessica could see by their expressions when full understanding dawned. Jack looked furious again, Elena anxious, Hank scowled behind his beard, and Brady seemed to be grinding his teeth.

"You see now why I ran." She sent Brady a pleading look, willing him to understand and not think her a coward. "He would have killed me to get the deed. Then who would have protected Annie and her children? As long as I'm alive and I refuse to sign, they're safe."

Forget your sister. What about you? Brady doubted the wisdom of letting her handle this. She was so busy protecting everybody else, she didn't see the danger to herself.

Hank looked shocked. "He would kill his own family?"

"I don't know. I underestimated him before and paid the price. I will not do so again."

Brady propped an elbow on the table and idly tugged at the corner of his mustache. Maybe he should kill the bastard after all. Maybe give him a rattler to play with. Take him for a long walk and forget to bring him back. Or let him ride Widowmaker. That would be a treat.

Jessica watched him, sensing that pent-up restlessness in him, that need for action. But instead of jumping in and assuming control as he was accustomed to doing, he left the reins in her hands. She appreciated the effort that took.

"So what do you want us to do?" Hank asked.

"The papers have been drawn and witnessed, and are now locked in the bank. Additional copies have been sent to my solicitor in England. With your help, I hope to convince Crawford to give up and leave without the deed."

"What papers?" Hank asked.

"My Last Will and Testament, for one. It names Adrian my heir and provides for the transference of Bickersham Hall to him should I die. I have also set up a trust that would ensure his safety and support until his majority."

Hank and Jack nodded. Brady remained impassive, although she saw his eyes had taken on a considering look that didn't bode well. He had stopped tugging on his mustache, and now his forearm lay on the table in front of him, his blunt-tipped fingers drumming softly on the tabletop. "Explain this trust."

Heat inched up her neck. She gripped her knees so tightly she could feel the sharp edge of fingernails through her skirt and two petticoats.

How many times had this man already come to her rescue? Whenever she had faltered, he had been there, quietly offering his strength to help her back onto her feet. Could she impose on him one more time?

"As I said, it names Adrian trustee of the Hall until he has a daughter." She hiked her chin, determined not to weaken under those watchful eyes. "It also names a guardian for him."

"And who is this guardian?"

"You."

No one spoke. Jessica held his gaze, letting him see her need, hoping it would convince him to do this one last thing for her and for her son. "If you consent, of course."

Before Brady could answer, Jack's palm slapped the table with a crack as loud as a gunshot. "Hell, you ought to just marry the sonofabitch."

"W-What?"

"Marry Brady."

Shocked silence. Elena and Hank stared at Jack. Brady stared at Jessica. But still, he didn't speak. A telling silence.

"Well, why not?" Jack looked around the table. "She needs a husband, the kid needs a father, and he damn sure needs a wife. What say, Hank? Elena?" He laughed, clearly enjoying himself. "Maybe we should throw in some trinkets to sweeten the deal."

"*Cállate*, Jackson," Elena scolded, unsuccessfully hiding a smile.

Brady tried to keep his temper in check while he planned all the ways he would make Jack pay. He could see Jessica was upset, but the little bastard had backed him into a corner. Now no matter what he said, she would probably take it wrong or think Jack had pushed him into it.

Shocked and a bit hurt by Brady's silence—not that she had any intention of marrying him or anyone else, but still, if he didn't want her, why had he said those outrageous things last night?—Jessica adopted what she hoped was an expression of amused tolerance. She raised a cautionary hand. "There is no need to martyr your brother on the sacrificial altar, Jack. This is not about my safety. It's about Adrian and his future should I die. I have named Brady guardian because I know he would never allow anything to befall my son." She waited to see if he would refuse her, wondering what she would do if he did.

"I'd be proud to watch over Ben," he finally said.

My woman. My son. In his mind Brady raised a fist in triumph.

Jessica sank back, so relieved she almost forgot that she had had to force him into it. "Adrian," she corrected with a gracious nod.

Brady just smiled.

THERE WERE TWO WAYS TO CALM AN UPSET WOMAN, BUT Brady doubted Jessica would allow him to do either. So instead of going out onto the porch after supper as he usually did, he grabbed Jack by the scruff of his neck and steered him down the hall to his office. He used his brother's head to open the door, shoved him through, then slammed the door shut behind them.

"You little sonofabitch!"

Jack grimaced and rubbed his forehead. "You bent my hat."

"I'll bend your ass around a stump and call the dogs if you ever do that again!"

Jack squinted at him as though trying to focus. "What's that mean, exactly?"

"It means I'm mad, you stupid bastard."

"No. That thing about the stump. Why would the dogs—"

"Shut up." Brady stomped over to the desk. Yanking open the bottom drawer, he grabbed his special bottle of Hannah Goodman's Red-Rye Whiskey, reputed to be the finest brew to come out of Mormon country and guaranteed to turn an ugly woman pretty, or a confirmed bachelor into a polygamist with a single sip. He took two swallows straight from the bottle. Plopping down in his chair, he propped his feet on the corner of his desk and waited for his lips to go numb. *Christ.*

"What about me?" Jack asked, eyeing the bottle.

"Go to hell."

"Then where's the jug?"

"Doc stole it." With a curse, Brady opened the drawer again, pulled out a dusty bottle of Forty Rod, and tossed it to his brother. "Suck on this."

Jack made a face. "This stuff tastes like cow piss."

"Better'n you deserve."

"It'll make my eyes bleed."

"Then give it back."

Jack took a sip and made a gagging noise. "Jesus. It's worse than her coffee."

"Shut up about her coffee."

Pulling one of the rope-strung chairs from a corner, Jack sat and propped his heels on the other side of the desk. "You seem touchy, Big Brother. I wonder why?"

Brady toyed with the idea of shooting him, but decided that would probably wake the kid. He thought about dragging him to the barn, where he could beat the sass out of him in privacy, but discarded that idea, too. Maybe tomorrow. After Crawford left, he'd be wanting to hit something, and God knows Jack deserved it. "You shouldn't have said what you did."

Jack took a sip then swiped at his watering eyes. "Why not?" he wheezed. "It's plain you have warm feelings for her. I was just trying to soften her up."

Warm feelings? Brady almost laughed. His feelings were so warm, his balls felt blistered. But now, thanks to Jack, it might be weeks—months—forever—before he got her primed again. "Just stay out of it."

Jack shrugged. "If that's what you want."

"It's what I want." Brady held out his hand. "Give me the bottle and get out."

"Although . . ." Jack tipped the chair back on two legs and studied the ceiling. "She did seem taken with the idea."

Brady's hand sagged onto the desktop. "She did?"

"Not openly, of course. But if you understood women like I do, you'd know the signs." He took a swig, coughed, then grinned. "I think it's a good idea. I think you should marry her."

Brady studied his bottle, wondering how the conversation had drifted so far. "Yeah. Well. I intend to." And he sure as hell didn't need advice from his little brother. Jack had the morals of a mining camp faro dealer and his taste in women proved it. Jessica was a different breed altogether.

"When?"

"When what?"

"When are you going to marry her? Assuming she'll have you."

"When this thing with Sancho is over."

Jack laughed. "That could be forever. Your tongue is hanging out as it is."

"That's not my tongue."

Which only made Jack laugh harder. "Just do it. Before she leaves you standing in the dust with your cock in your hand."

"Hell, I'd need two hands for that."

"I'm just saying you better make your move before it's too late."

"Oh? How's this, then?" Brady drove a foot hard against Jack's propped boots and sent him toppling backward. His brother and the chair hit the floor with a rewarding thud that made the glass doors of the bookcases rattle.

He peered around the side of the desk to see if Jack was hurt and was disappointed to see he wasn't. As he settled back, a baby's indignant cry echoed through the hall. "Now look what you've done."

"Me?" Jack untangled himself from the chair and struggled to his feet. "You're the one who pushed me over." He winced, this time rubbing the back of his head. "I think I'm getting a headache."

"Serves you right."

His woman. His son. Brady sure liked the sound of that.

Seventeen

JESSICA AWOKE AT DAWN, EXHAUSTED FROM NIGHTMARISH dreams of John Crawford.

Throughout the morning she stayed busy, battling the anxiety that built with every hour. When she wasn't pacing the confines of her room or tending Adrian, she sewed, taking in dress seams she had let out two months ago and finishing the samplers for the ranch women who had donated so many lovely things for her babies.

She whipped her needle in short, furious strokes, wishing it were his face she was stabbing. It had been over six months since she had last seen her brother-in-law. Did he think she was still the weak, frightened woman he had overpowered before? Didn't he realize she would never let him do that to her again? Just the thought of it made her want to vomit— the smell of him—the whiskey and sweat—the feel of his hands—

I can't do this! Panting with fear, she lurched to her feet. Her eyes swept the room, looking for escape. Then her gaze fell on Adrian, and the need for flight slowly died. She sank back into the chair, cupped her head in trembling hands, and waited for the panic to subside. When it did, she picked up her sewing, tore out the ragged seam, and began again. But inside, the rage simmered.

Morning dragged into afternoon. Moving Adrian's cradle near the window so she would hear him if he woke, she paced the porch, marking time by the slow arc of the sun across the cloudless sky. What if something had happened? What if Crawford never came, and she spent the rest of her life in this terrible limbo of wondering, and waiting, and looking fearfully into the face of every man she saw?

She couldn't bear it. She would die.

Bullshot wandered out from under the house and sat in the dirt, scratching and watching her pace. After a while the sun chased him up into the shaded porch. He flopped onto his belly, his head on his paws, those doleful eyes tracking her steps.

"You think I'm pathetic," she said to him as she started another circuit. "All this walking but going nowhere."

He cocked his head, belly-crawled forward a few inches, and stopped. When she said nothing more, he sighed and dropped his head back onto his paws.

When she wearied of pacing, she sank into the rocker. Shadows lengthened. The hound inched toward her with hopeful canine insistence, until finally he leaned against her skirts, his wide head a heavy weight on her knee. "If you drool on me, I'll spank you," she warned, stroking one long velvety ear.

"Leave her alone, Jack," a familiar voice called through the open door into the office.

Jessica bit back a smile. "I was talking to your dog," she called back.

A moment later, Brady strolled onto the porch. Jessica watched him come toward her and felt that low flutter where the babies used to be. The man had a way of moving that was music to her eyes.

"Is Bullshot bothering you?"

She forced herself to look away. "No, he's fine." She hadn't seen Brady since last night, when Jack made that outlandish suggestion. She wondered if it had embarrassed him as much as it had her. She wondered why his silence had hurt so much. Hurt still.

From the corner of her eye she watched him stop beside her chair. His legs seemed to go on forever. They didn't, of course, and she knew if she turned her head the slightest bit, she would see exactly where they stopped. She looked down at his surprisingly large boots instead.

"He crossed the boundary line an hour ago."

Her gaze flew to his.

He must have seen her terror, because he hunkered by the rocker so their heads were at the same level. Taking her clenched hand in his, he gently forced open her fingers and laced them through his. "It's not too late to change your mind."

God help her, she wanted to. She wanted to dump it all into Brady's capable hands so she could pretend it had never happened, that she was safe and whole, and would never have to look into that hated face again.

But she wasn't safe. Nor was she whole. And she never would be, unless she did look into that face one last time. That, or live in fear forever. "I haven't changed my mind."

"Good." He released her hand and started to rise.

She caught his arm and brought him back to her side. "But I don't want him to know about Adrian. It doesn't matter who fathered him. Adrian is my son, not his. Crawford never need know. It might be safer for Adrian if he didn't."

"All right."

She realized she still gripped his arm and pulled her hand away. But those eyes continued to hold her captive. Ancient eyes, like those of an old man who had seen more of life than he wanted to, or a young man who had seen enough to have few illusions left. They were the saddest and most beautiful eyes she had ever seen.

Without thinking, she reached out, wishing she could soothe those lines of worry on his weathered face. "Do you ever shave?" she asked, trailing a fingertip along the masculine perfection of his prickly jaw.

"I shaved yesterday."

"With what? A rusty knife?" She could hear the scrape of his beard against her nails, see silver hairs in his sideburns. She wanted to touch the springy curls, brush the fall of hair from his brow, test the softness of the glossy waves hanging past his collar. The incongruity of silky curls against that powerful neck made her smile. "You need tending."

"Any time, any place."

The way he said it, the way his eyes seemed to pull her in, sent her thoughts in flight. Smiling at that fancy, she let her hand drop back into her lap. "I know you're tired of hearing this, but once again, thank you. I wouldn't be able to do this alone."

"You're stronger than you think."

"Am I?" She gave a shaky laugh. "I have my doubts."

"You shouldn't. What other woman would try to geld a man with an umbrella?"

She frowned, confused. Then she pressed a hand to her mouth as the scene at the stage stop flashed through her mind. She tried not to smile, but couldn't help it. "I thought I hit your face."

He chuckled, an unfamiliar but welcome sound that brought a quiver of joy to her heart. "I figured it was worth it when you waved that lacy doo-dad and offered to tend my injury. I thought . . . well, finally . . . a woman who knows how to apologize. But you just wanted to tend my pretty face." He said it like he didn't know his face could drive a vicar's wife to sin—or a twenty-six-year-old spinster to ruin.

A giggle escaped her, then another. She, who hadn't giggled in over a dozen years. It felt good. "I thought you were attacking me, that you were a desperado."

"I thought you were the finest thing I'd ever seen." His gaze swept her face, came to rest on her mouth. "I still do."

Laughter faded under a rush of heat. "You do know how to turn a girl's head."

"I'm trying," he murmured, reaching up to pull her face down to his.

Oh, Brady, she thought as his lips moved against hers. *If you're thinking to distract me, you're doing a marvelous job.*

* * *

CONSUELO RUSHED INTO THE KITCHEN. "*¡SEÑORA!* HE comes!"

A jolt of fear almost buckled Jessica's knees. Then Elena touched her arm and reason returned. She swept into motion, whipping off her apron as she spoke. "Elena, please take Adrian upstairs to the farthest room. I don't want Crawford to hear him if he cries. Consuelo, would you please find Angelina in case he wakes for his feeding. Where's Brady?"

"On the porch."

She took a deep breath, released it, took another. She wiped her damp palms down her skirts. *You can do this*, she told herself as she left the room.

Brady stepped forward to take her hand as she came onto the porch. Behind him, Hank and Jack leaned casually against the posts at the top of the steps, watching a carriage coming down the road, escorted by two ranch hands.

"Looks like he's alone." Jack laughed. "Stupid bastard."

Brady led her to the top of the steps. "Feeling mean?" he asked, giving her hand a gentle squeeze before releasing it.

"Scared."

"Want me to get your umbrella?"

She tried to smile, but the muscles in her face felt frozen. Glancing around, she saw a dozen or more ranch hands drift into the yard. "What are they doing here?" If fear overcame her, she didn't want to humiliate herself in front of all these men.

"Protection. In case you get out of hand."

The carriage cleared the iron gate and turned toward the house.

Her legs began to shake.

The hound scrambled out from under the house and set up a racket until Brady told one of the men to lock him in the barn.

Scarcely able to draw breath, Jessica watched the carriage approach. Even at a distance, she recognized the arrogant tilt of Crawford's head, the familiar posture of a small man trying to look taller. She pressed her palms against her rolling stomach. *If he touches me, I'll die.*

Brady stood behind her right shoulder, not near enough to make contact, but so close she could feel the tickle of his breath against the hair on the top of her head. "Mmm. You smell good. What is that?"

"R-roast beef. Onions." *Oh God oh God.*

The carriage pulled to a stop in the yard.

"Don't leave me."

She didn't realize she had spoken aloud until Brady whispered close to her ear, "I won't. Now breathe."

She tried, but her chest felt so tight and her throat—

Brady's hand slid up her spine. At his touch, the constriction eased. For a moment, she leaned back against him, drawing in his strength as she gulped in air. The dizziness faded. She found her balance and straightened. His hand fell away.

Crawford climbed down from the carriage. He made a show of brushing dust from his trousers and jacket, then looked up at her with a smile that didn't reach his eyes. "Jessica, my dear." He walked toward the steps. "I have found you at last."

Her heartbeat roared in her head.

He looked smaller than she remembered, narrower through the shoulders. Had he always been of such insignificant stature? She studied him, terror giving way to shock and confusion, seeing things about him she had never noticed before.

His hands were almost womanish. He was portly, his bottom-heavy form perched like a giant egg atop legs no sturdier than her own. He dressed like a dandy and moved with that same prissy saunter she had seen in Stanley Ashford.

How had she ever allowed this weasely little man to overpower her?

Because she thought he was just trying to scare her and would eventually listen to reason. Because she thought their familial relationship would protect her. Because once she realized what was happening, it was too late, and the silk ties were around her wrists.

Rage engulfed her. She thought of all that this little maggot of a man had taken from her, all that she had suffered and still suffered because of him, and she wanted to scream her outrage. She watched him stop at the bottom of the steps and willed him to come closer so she could hit him, kick him, claw that smug look from his face.

"Dear Jessica." His eyes flicked over her. He bared his teeth in a parody of a smile. "You are looking well, I must say. This pest hole of a country must agree with you."

"The bruises are gone, if that's what you mean."

His smile faded. "May we talk privately?"

"No."

"I had hoped we—"

"What do you want?"

Fury sparked in his pale gray eyes before he masked it behind an expression of mild regret. "You received Annie's letter? You know why I have come?"

"I know your wastrel ways have put her and the children in jeopardy, so you have come begging to me like the craven dog that you are."

Anger flashed, was again quickly veiled. "Now, Jessica." He put a foot on the bottom step.

Immediately Hank and Jack came off the posts. The circle of cowboys in the yard tightened.

Blinking in surprise, Crawford glanced from the brothers to the living fence of hard-faced men crowding his back. "What is this?" He turned back to Jessica and, in the silky whisper of her nightmares, said, "Are you afraid of me, Jessica?"

Acid rose in her throat. Was he so convinced of her cowardice that he thought just the threat in his voice would bend her to his will? Had she made it that easy for him?

"Afraid of you?" She pressed a shaking hand to her throat, unsure whether to weep or run shrieking down the steps. "I saw your face in every man I met, felt your cruelty in every touch, every glance. But I was wrong." She gave a strangled laugh. "Look at you. You're nothing. An insignificant popinjay of a man. A joke. How could I ever be afraid of you?"

Crawford's face turned an alarming shade of red. For a moment his mouth worked as if he chewed on his own tongue, then words spewed out of him like bile. "Do not use that tone with me, you slut! I will not stand for it!"

Brady was around her and down two steps before she stopped him with a hand on his shoulder. "You promised Rikker," she reminded him. "And me."

She watched him struggle with it, saw it in his clenched fists, felt it in the tautness of the muscles beneath her hand.

But Crawford was too stupid to see the danger. He gave a harsh laugh and waved a hand at the men surrounding him. "Do your brave defenders know what they are protecting? Do they know you fornicated with your sister's husband? Or have you spread your legs for them, too?"

This time a team of oxen couldn't have held Brady back.

Too late, Crawford saw his peril.

Brady caught him by the seat of his pants and the back of his jacket, and yanked the much smaller man off the ground and over his head. For an instant he stood, magnificent in his frustration and fury, Atlas undecided. Then with a curse, he heaved Crawford into the rose bed.

Cheered by hoots and laughter from the men in the yard, he turned and came back up the steps, teeth flashing in a smile that would make the Devil sweat. "Rikker didn't say not to throw him," he told his grinning brothers as he once more took his place at Jessica's side.

Her hero. How she loved him for it.

Fighting a smile, she sent an arch look over her shoulder. "I said I would handle it."

"Sorry," he said without even the pretense of remorse. Then he leaned down and against her ear added, "I think I wrenched my shoulder. Maybe you could rub it for me later."

She didn't want to laugh, sensing she was too close to the edge of hysteria. But with Brady standing guard at her shoulder and John Crawford rolling in thorns at her feet, how could she not?

To the vast entertainment of the onlookers, it took quite a while for Crawford to extricate himself. When he finally stood before her, bleeding from a dozen scratches, his clothing torn and mussed, his face contorted in a rictus of rage, she had to remind herself that despite his comical appearance, this man was capable of great evil. She knew not to underestimate him. She also knew that he was a coward and a coward always responded to a threat. Especially if that threat was real and substantial and frightening. Like Brady.

"Heed this, Crawford," she said once he had his breathing under control. "You will never get the Hall. Ever. And as long as you live, I will see that it never belongs to Annie either."

Crawford dabbed at his bloodied cheek with a handkerchief. "You can't do that."

"I can and I have." She smiled, reveling in the rush of power that swept through her. "The documents have been filed. If you doubt it, check with my agent in Posten Cross."

"You would willingly impoverish your sister?"

"I have written to Annie and explained my decision. I have told her that she and her children are welcome to come here to me."

"Bugger that, you stupid woman! If you know what's good for you . . ." His voice trailed off as the men around him drew closer. He said nothing more, but fury glittered in his darting eyes.

She almost laughed out loud. "You dare threaten me? In front of all these men? How foolish are you?" She paused, rather hoping he would suffer an apoplectic fit and bring this farce to an end. When he didn't, she was forced to continue. "This is not England. And these"—she motioned to the glowering brothers standing guard—"are definitely not Englishmen. They know what you did. And the only reason you're still breathing is because I have asked them to let you live. For Annie's sake, not yours."

Suddenly the fury was back, pressing against her throat. In a voice so savage she scarcely recognized it as her own, she said, "So listen well, John Crawford. If anything—*anything*—should befall me or anyone in my family, you will answer to these men. And they answer"—she glanced over her shoulder at the avenging angel with Satan's smile—"to him. Do I make myself clear?"

"You won't get away with this, you bloody bitch!"

"I already have." She slashed her hand in furious dismissal. "Go! Leave before I allow these inventive gentlemen to have their fun. I am done with you." She turned toward the door.

"Whore!" Crawford yelled after her. "I will find a way to stop—"

With a fiendish grin, Brady swept past her and down the steps.

Without waiting to see more, Jessica walked quickly into the house. She was almost running by the time she reached her bedroom. Dashing through the door, she slammed it shut behind her, then sagged onto the foot of the bed, her strength finally giving out.

It's over.

Shaking violently, she pressed her hands to her face as all the anguish and fear and shame she had held inside for months exploded from her chest in choking sobs.

It's over.

She heard the door swing open, and looked up to see Brady in the doorway.

"Is he gone?" Before he could answer, she rushed to the window and threw the drape aside. Through a blur of tears she saw the carriage bouncing out the gate in a cloud of dust. Her knees gave out and she sank onto the broad recessed windowsill, laughing and crying.

It's over It's over It's over.

A shadow loomed over her, then she felt Brady's hand patting her shoulder in that confused and endearing way men had when they want to help but are unsure how. "He's gone, Jessica. He'll never hurt you again. I swear it."

She nodded and wiped at her face, struggling to stem the stream of tears rising from the bottomless well in her chest. "I kn-know."

He eased down beside her, crowding her skirts and taking up most of the space on the sill. She smelled dust, leather, his own masculine scent, and she drew it in like a drowning woman starved for air.

"There's no reason for you to be upset."

She hiccupped. "I—I'm not upset."

"Oh. Well. You seem upset."

"I'm n-not." She gave a choking laugh and tipped her forehead against his shoulder, needing the contact, wishing she could get closer still and burrow under his skin where she would be safe and protected and part of him forever. "Th-this is the ha-happiest day of my life."

"You're happy?"

She lifted her head and gave him a shaky smile, wishing he could understand. "It's over. I'm free." Laughter bubbled in her throat, and suddenly she wanted to sing and shout and dance a jig across the wooden floor. "I have my life back. Isn't that grand?"

To Brady, what was grand was seeing her happiness and hearing that seldom-heard laugh. This giddiness was a side of her he had never seen, and he was so struck by it, for a moment he couldn't draw a breath. Just watching her awakened his own joy and brought a sting to his eyes.

Christ. She was turning him into a blubbering fool. Forcing sentimentality aside, he grabbed a handful of her skirt and held it out. "Here," he said gruffly. "Wipe your nose."

She pushed his hand away. "I will not wipe my nose on my clothing. That's disgusting."

"A runny nose is pretty disgusting, too."

"You big dolt." She gave his arm a gentle punch, then rose and went to the dresser. Pulling a hanky from the top drawer, she dabbed at her face.

Brady watched her reflection in the mirror as she repinned tumbled curls, his gaze drifting from her chestnut mane, down her raised arms, to the lush swell of upthrust breasts. He pictured her watching him in the mirror as she took her hair down for him, imagined himself moving up behind her, reaching around to slide his hands over those soft feminine curves.

He wanted her so badly, he was choking on it.

She sent him an impish smile over her shoulder. "How was I?"

"What?"

"Do you think I scared him?" She turned back to the mirror. "I rather think I did."

Brady would have blushed if all of his blood hadn't been rushing elsewhere. Leaning forward, he rested his forearms on his knees, hoping to disguise the effect she had on him. With a poor attempt at a laugh, he said, "You were fearsomely brave. A dragon. After you left, three of my men had to change their unions."

She made a face at the mirror. "Easy to be brave with you standing behind me."

"It's never easy to be brave."

The seriousness of his tone caught her attention. She turned and looked at him, those whiskey brown eyes both unsure and hopeful, as if she wanted to believe, but wasn't sure if she should.

He let his expression show her the truth. "I'm proud of you, Jessica."

Her chin wobbled. Blinking hard, she raised a hand to cover it. He was relieved when she found her smile again. "I'm proud, too." Then she laughed and twirled, arms thrown out, her teeth showing in a wide, openmouthed smile. "I did it! I ran him off forever!"

Brady watched her, emotion clogging his throat, thankful that he had a part in bringing her such joy. He would bring her anything—do anything—to see that smile and hear that laughter every day for the rest of his life.

Jesus, I love this woman.

The twirling stopped. "I must get Adrian." She rushed toward the door, stopped, whirled, and rushed back toward him. Before he knew her intent, she grabbed his face in both hands and pressed her lips against his. "Thank you," she said and kissed him again. Then before he could gather his senses and grab hold of her, she tore out the door, a whirlwind in calico, taking with her all the air and joy from the room.

Dazed, Brady blinked at the empty doorway and waited for his heartbeat to return to normal.

Dinner was a celebration. Brady asked Buck and Iantha to join them, and soon everyone was talking at once and serving dishes were flying around the table like horses at a racetrack. Choking on laughter, Jessica regaled the newcomers with a recounting of her confrontation with Crawford and his dive into the rose bed.

Brady enjoyed watching her and seeing that glow of happiness bring out the freckles across her cheeks. He wondered if she wore freckles everywhere, or only where the sun touched her skin, and decided he'd have to check. Soon. The thought made him grin.

He looked around the table at these people who were so much a part of his life. His family. His woman. He glanced at the corner where Ben slept. His son. This was his purpose. To protect these people and watch over the ranch. And now, with Jessica and Ben in his family, his life would be complete.

But not yet. Not while Sancho was out there gunning for him. Not while she was still recovering from childbirth and celebrating her victory over Crawford. He'd give her time, let her heal in body and spirit, before he asked her to yoke herself to him forever. Meanwhile, he would end this thing with Sancho so they could both start anew.

A couple of weeks. A month at most. Then it would all be over—or just beginning. Either way, everything would change.

Eighteen

JESSICA FLOATED THROUGH THE DAYS IN A EUPHORIC DAZE. All of her senses seemed sharper, as if a veil of gloom had been lifted from her life, and every morning she awoke invigorated.

It helped that Adrian's feeding schedule eased from every three hours to almost five. He grew so fast, each day brought new discoveries, new advances. In her purely objective opinion, he was without doubt the handsomest and cleverest boy in the entire world.

Iantha showed her an ingenious way of draping a cloth sling across her shoulder and around her waist so she could carry Adrian against her body while keeping her hands free. No longer confined to the bedroom, she took it upon herself to clear some of the clutter from the hallways and organize the chaos of the armory–dining room. Within a week, she felt recovered enough to relieve Iantha and Consuelo of most of the cooking chores, allowing them more time with their own families. Every day she felt stronger, and every day was a joy. She wished it could go on forever, but knew she couldn't rely on charity forever. Soon she would have to leave. But until Dr. O'Grady pronounced her recovered enough to travel, she would grasp what happiness she could.

One afternoon, a month after the birthing and almost three weeks after she had booted Crawford down the road, she settled Adrian on a blanket in a shady corner of the courtyard and began separating and transplanting chives.

It was another cloudless day. The high adobe walls of the courtyard shielded her from the lowering sun, but they also blocked the breeze. Perspiration dampened her hair and made the fabric of her dress cling to her back. Her gloves were so tattered, her fingertips poked through, so she tossed them onto the bench and went to work with the hoe. It felt good to work the earth again, to do something useful. She liked being needed.

She had almost finished, when the gate opened and Brady looked in. "There you are."

She set the hoe aside as he walked toward her, Bullshot panting at his heels.

He had been very busy lately, moving herds to fresh grass, clearing old watering places, leading night patrols in hopes of crossing paths with Sancho. Over the last week, she had scarcely seen him except for the few times he made it back in time for dinner.

It worried her, the way he drove himself. She understood the tasks he had before him, and recognized the enormity of the responsibilities that rested on his able shoulders. Nonetheless, she was concerned. He looked tired. He might even have lost weight. In addition to that, she missed him—the banter, the teasing, that heart-stuttering smile. And now, as she watched him cross the courtyard, she realized how especially much she missed his kisses, too.

Perhaps she was a wanton, after all. At least where Brady Wilkins was concerned.

"Been looking for you," he said, coming to a stop beside her.

The hound bounded forward, almost knocking her down with his slobbery greeting. Holding him off with one hand, she shaded her eyes with the other and squinted up at Brady. "Apparently not very hard. I've been here all afternoon."

"Don't be sassy." He hunkered beside Adrian and waggled his tiny toe. "He's starting to look like an actual person."

"He is an actual person." Finally managing to push the hound away, she wiped her slimy hands on her apron. "You big drooler."

"Only around you. Oh, you mean Bullshot." He winked—actually winked—at her. "And speaking of droolers." He made a face at Adrian. "This one needs fresh drawers." He glanced over, his gaze tracing a slow, sweet trail from her head to the scuffed slippers showing beneath the hem of her skirt. "You look a little ripe yourself."

Jessica almost snorted. He was so dusty his mustache looked more brown than black, his shirt was rimed with dried sweat, and he smelled worse than his dog. She was about to bring that to his attention when he pulled a packet from his back pocket.

"Bought these in Val Rosa." He shoved Bullshot away from Adrian, and handed her the package. "Thought you might like something other than roses."

She opened the bundle to find several smaller packets inside. Flower seeds. Marigold, morning glory, snapdragon, and aster. She was so surprised, she didn't know what to say.

"Iantha said it's a little late, but if you plant them now, you'll have flowers in the fall."

Jessica looked up at him. Did he expect her to be here then? Did she want to be here then? Confusion sent heat rushing up her neck. "Thank you," she said, avoiding his gaze. "I shall plant them straightaway."

"Later. I'm hungry. Anything left to eat?"

She tucked the packets into her apron pocket. "I can probably put together something."

"Good. We'll take it to the swimming hole. Bring Ben. We can take a dip to clean up, then have a picnic supper. What do you say?"

"I don't swim. Nor do I bathe outdoors."

"You'll like it." He steered her toward the house. "Pack a picnic basket. Bring clean clothes and a blanket. I'll wait here with Ben."

"And you'll change Adrian's napkin while I do all that?"

"Better yet, I'll rustle up some grub. You get yourself and Ben ready."

Even though Jessica had no intention of swimming—she had no bathing costume, after all—she thought she might want to wade if the water was clean, so she brought dry clothing, a bar of castile soap, and a supply of drying cloths, as well as blankets, extra napkins, a fresh sleeping sack for Adrian, the stuffed bunny Iantha had made for him, and his nightcap. She had just finished stuffing it all into her portmanteau when Brady arrived at the bedroom door with a leather pouch thrown over his shoulder.

She nodded toward the bag she'd packed. "If you'll carry that, I'll get Adrian."

"Hell, woman, we're just going to the creek."

"It never hurts to be prepared."

"For what? A siege?"

"Do you want us to go with you, or not?"

He picked up the bag.

FROM HIS PERCH ON THE RIDGE, SANCHO WATCHED THE RANcho. He had been so long without sleep, his eyes felt raw. He should not have to do all this watching and waiting by himself. Paco should have been here. And those men at the cantina should have come with him instead of laughing at him. Now they were laughing with Paco in hell, and he was up here all alone.

Pendejos.

Ducking back into the shade of the overhang, he squatted against the rocky wall and crossed his arms atop his knees. How long had he been here? Two days? Three? Long enough to learn well the routine of the rancho. He knew when the patrols left and when they returned. He knew there were always guards at the house, that riders never went out alone, that Elena, that *puta*, had moved into the house. Probably selling her favors to any vaquero with the coin to pay. Just like their whore of a mother.

He spit into the dirt. *"¡Pinche puta!"*

Fury pounded through him for a moment, then seeped away, leaving the scent of roses drifting like a soft mist through his mind. He closed his eyes and let his head drop down onto his crossed arms.

He was so weary. Always she was there, whispering in his ear, crying, crying. Why could she not leave him alone and let him sleep?

"Madre, no me molestes."

He began to hum, trying to block her from his thoughts.

Why had she run from him? Even at the end, when he was trying to save her, she ran from him. Why? He was not a monster. Did she not know that? Did she not understand it was his duty as her son to keep her safe from Jacob Wilkins?

The wind rose, whining through the overhang like a scolding voice.

"¡Déjame en paz! Leave me alone! *¡Vete!"*

The sound of his voice bouncing off the overhang startled him. He jerked his head up, heart racing. He heard a dog bark—distant, but still near enough to break the hold of the past.

Crawling to the edge, he stretched on his stomach and looked down.

A man and woman walked past the corrals toward the creek. A dog raced ahead of them. The woman had hair as red as rust and walked without a limp, so he knew she was not Elena. The man was tall. Sancho chewed at his mustache, wondering which brother he was. From a distance they all looked the same. If he could see his face, he would know. How could he not recognize those eyes that had haunted his nightmares for twenty years?

No es importante.

He crawled back into the shadows. Soon he would have those cold blue eyes on a string around his neck. He would take his tongue next. Then he would move slowly down with a cut here and a slice there, being careful to keep Wilkins alive and aware of all that was happening to him. After he cut off his cojones and sliced through his hamstrings, he would move back up and start on the fingers, one by one, joint by joint. He wanted it to take a long time. He wanted Brady Wilkins to die screaming in agony.

First Elena, then Wilkins. The thought of it made his cock rise.

Sancho rolled onto his back and rubbed a hand over his crotch, picturing Elena in his mind. He wondered if before he killed her, he should use her like the whore she had become. Would she scream and fight? Would she beg him to let her live?

An idea came to him that made him smile. Why wait? He could take her now. He knew in the evenings the younger brothers often joined the vaqueros in the bunkhouse, where they drank and gambled. If the man with the woman was Brady Wilkins, Elena would be alone at the house. He could kill her right under their noses. Or he could bring her back to the cave, and use her until he tired of her.

Sancho rubbed harder as pictures formed in his mind.

His sister, crying and twisting beneath him, her mouth open in mindless terror.

Yes. He would like that. His eyes drifted closed. He would like doing that again and again. Perhaps tonight.

"WHAT A LOVELY SPOT."

Jessica smiled in delight at the clear pool of water ringed by large tumbled stones and leafy shrubs, separated from the faster, wider creek by a broad bedrock shelf. Tall cottonwoods crowded the bank, shading the pool from the afternoon heat, while shafts of sunlight filtered through the leaves to cast diamond sparkles on the rippling water. There was even another, more secluded pool, set apart from the larger one by a huge boulder decorated with glittering bits of quartz and crude carvings. "What's this?" she asked, walking closer to study the markings.

"A message rock." Brady began unpacking the portmanteau. "This was a natural crossing before a spring flood cut a better one downstream. Pilgrims crossing here often left signs for those who followed." He pulled out the second blanket, muttered something, and continued digging. "Some of the markings go way back. There's even one dated

1538. Jack figures it was left by a soldier with Coronado, but since the Rio Grande is southwest of here, he must have been lost." He pulled out Adrian's stuffed bunny. "You're determined to make him into a girl, aren't you?" With a look of disgust, he tossed the toy aside. "I'll have Iantha make him a horse or something. Don't you have any soap in here?"

"I do, but I doubt you'd like it." She walked up the bank toward the trees, looking for a flat grassy place to spread the blankets. "Not manly enough."

If he caught her jibe, he gave no sign, although he did stop pawing through the bag.

She found a soft shady spot and spread a small blanket for Adrian. His last feeding was an hour before they left, so hopefully he would sleep for a while. Once he was settled, she spread out a larger blanket and reached for the food bag Brady had packed, which immediately brought the hound to her side. Shooing him away, she asked Brady if he wanted to eat first or swim.

"Too hungry to wait," he called over his shoulder as walked to the water's edge. Squatting on his heels, he splashed water over his face and neck. He made quite a to-do of it, snorting and blowing and flinging water like a child at his bath.

She found it vastly amusing.

Bullshot saw it as a call to play. With a bark of delight, he launched himself.

A moment later Brady lay sprawled facedown in the water, while the hound splashed and frolicked around him, his tail wagging so vigorously water flew in all directions, creating misty rainbows in the streaks of sunlight.

Jessica was so astonished, she laughed out loud.

Cursing roundly, Brady struggled to his feet, wiping water from his eyes with one hand and fighting Bullshot off with the other. By the time he got the hound under control and found his footing, Jessica was hooting with laughter.

"How's the fishing?" she called, then doubled over again. He looked ridiculous, scowling through the wet hair plastered to his face, bits of moss clinging to his scruffy beard, and his trousers so waterlogged they drooped on his lanky form.

She probably shouldn't have told him that, though. And once she had, his expression should have alerted her. But she could scarcely see through the tears of laughter, and didn't register that sinister smirk until he already had the hound by the scruff of the neck and primed for attack.

"Get her," he ordered, and shoved the hound in her direction.

She put up an energetic defense, but was no match for Bullshot's exuberant affection. By the time Brady slogged out of the water and pulled the sodden beast off, she was soaked, covered in dog hair and slobber, and stank of wet dog.

"You beast," she railed, slinging a streamer of drool off her arm.

Brady gave the hound a reassuring pat. "She doesn't mean it."

"I was talking to you, you dolt. Look at me. I'm soaking wet."

"Not so funny now, is it?"

Fool that she was, she tried to send him back into the water by planting both hands flat on his chest and shoving as hard as she could.

Other than the diabolical grin spreading across his face, he didn't move. "You shouldn't have done that." And the next instant he had her slung over his shoulder like a sack of grain, and was heading back into the water.

She didn't go easily or quietly, but was too winded from her bout with Bullshot, and still laughing too hard, to be effective. "Brady, please!" she wailed, pounding on his broad back.

He stopped, water lapping at his thighs. "Please what?"

"Please, put me down. I beg you."

"Well, if you're going to beg . . ." And dipping his shoulder, he let her drop.

Brady doubted it was deep enough to drown her, despite the racket she put up, but remembering she said she couldn't swim, he stayed close in case she got into trouble. When she finally rose out of the water, spitting and flailing, he couldn't help but notice how her wet dress clung so sweetly to those curves he'd been thinking about so often of late.

Apparently she noticed him noticing. "Stop staring," she gasped, tugging and jerking on the fabric, but accomplishing little. "How could you do such a thing!"

"Do what?" Jack was right. She did have a nice pair, all perky and puckered and pushing against the thin cloth so that he could almost see—

"Stop that!"

He jerked his eyes away. "Stop what?"

She clasped an arm over her chest. "You're the most depraved man I ever met!"

He laughed and peeled off his wet shirt. "Then you need to spend more time around Jack."

"Why bother? You're just like him. What are you doing?"

"There's a huge difference between me and Jack." Wadding the shirt into a ball, he tossed it onto the bank, then sent her a suggestive leer. "His feet aren't nearly as big."

She would have been outraged had she not already been in a state of openmouthed shock to be confronted with Brady Wilkins's unclothed torso. That quick peek at the stage stop should have prepared her. It was no wonder he carried her around so easily. The man was an Adonis . . . all corded muscles and glistening black hair that trailed down his chest to point straight at . . . his belt buckle . . . the very buckle he was loosening right before her eyes.

With a strangled gasp, she whirled, tangled her legs in a floating billow of skirts, and almost lost her footing again. "What are you doing?" she sputtered.

"Going for a swim," he said, grunting and splashing behind her.

"Not here you're not! Don't you dare remove any more of your clothing!"

"Uh-oh." She heard the slap of wet cloth on rocks. "Too late."

Scandalized, she charged for the shore, slipped, went down, and came up gasping to find him grinning at her, bobbing in water that thankfully covered him to his shoulders.

"Where are you going?" he asked, showing most of his teeth and both dimples in a winsome grin, which might have been more effective had it not been directed at her breasts. "You're already wet. Might as well stay for a swim."

"Have you no decency whatsoever? You—you're naked!"

"Been peeking, have you?"

"Certainly not! Nor will I cavort about like a licentious lightskirt with a naked man!"

"Licentious lightskirt. You must be rattled if you're bringing out the fancy words." The grin became an outright laugh. "Damn, I love the way you talk."

She turned for the shore again.

Still laughing, he caught her skirt. "Don't go. Use the other pool. That way you'll have privacy, and I can wash without you ogling me the whole time."

"I was not ogling you!"

"It sure felt like an ogle."

"It was probably a fish."

That leer again. "A really big fish."

Eventually he let her go, but only after she allowed him to talk her into using the other pool, which she had already decided to do anyway. It required trudging about in wet shoes and clingy clothes, gathering soap, dry clothing, and toweling, then picking her way over the rocks to the other pool, all under his amused gaze.

Lascivious man.

But it was worth it. To be able to wash her hair and rinse away the dirt of the garden, while submerging her entire body in cool clear water, was heavenly—even though for propriety's sake, she kept on her underthings and one petticoat. She enjoyed it so much she might have stayed in for the rest of the afternoon had she not known Brady Wilkins lurked nearby.

By the time she dried and dressed, she could hear Adrian waking for his late-afternoon feeding and her own stomach rumbled with hunger. As she worked her way back to where she had left the blankets and food bag, she realized how changed her life had become. Allowing scandalous liberties, bathing in public wearing nothing but her unmentionables, swimming with a naked man. Heavens, she hadn't worn a hat or corset in months. It was unbelievable.

And unbelievably liberating.

She almost laughed out loud at the pure joy of it—then abruptly froze when she stepped into the shady glade and saw Brady—fully dressed, thank goodness—sprawled on his stomach, asleep, with Bullshot twitching in dreams on one side, and Adrian practicing infant calisthenics on the other. She didn't know why the sight so captivated her, or why that familiar yearning struck her with such force her chest ached. But she was certain that the image of the three of them, sharing a blanket by the river's edge on a lazy summer's day, would remain etched in her mind and her heart for all the years to come.

It was so beautiful, so perfect.

She drank it in, memorizing all the small details so she would never forget. The way Brady's absurdly long eyelashes made a dark crescent on his sun-browned cheek. The sheen of damp hair tumbling over his brow. The strength of the big hand that lay cupped so protectively around Adrian's tiny head.

A sense of belonging gripped her, a feeling of connection even stronger than she had felt before, and so poignant it brought tears to her eyes. She wished this moment could last forever. She wished she were unafraid. She wished she had the courage to reach out and run her hands over that long solid body.

And suddenly she knew. She felt the rightness of it the instant the thought blossomed in her mind, unbidden and fully formed.

I love this man.

The realization flowed through her, filling her, making her feel whole.

She loved this man. This outrageous, courageous, beautiful man. He brought her happiness she had never known.

He also frightened her. The idea of him—of this place and this life that was so much a part of who he was—was daunting. Was this where she truly belonged? Here in this harsh and beautiful land, bound to a man who might never need her as much as she needed him? Could she be satisfied with only half his heart?

The answer cut cleanly through the doubt in her mind.

Yes. This was what she wanted. Loving him would be enough. She would make it be enough, because the idea of spending a life without him was unbearable. She laughed softly, giddy with joy. She felt like singing, weeping, soaring through the air.

Until Adrian's hungry cry brought her soundly back to earth.

Swiping tears away, she went to retrieve her son. Moving quietly so she wouldn't wake Brady, she sat with Adrian against a boulder several yards away. After she settled him at her breast, she leaned back against the stone and closed her eyes, wrapping herself in the perfection of the moment—the warm sun and cooling breeze, the music of rustling leaves, and trickling water, and gentle masculine snores. She cherished the gift of it because she knew that even in the richest life, such perfect moments didn't come often.

She must have slept because when next she opened her eyes, Adrian was asleep and Brady was awake.

He hadn't moved and still lay sprawled on his stomach with his head turned toward her. But his gaze was locked on her exposed breast with an intensity that sent tingles of awareness dancing along her nerves.

She didn't move or cover herself, frozen by the intimacy of his gaze. It was as if everything around them had gone utterly still and only the two of them existed, held captive by that unseen and undeniable bond that pulsed between them. It shocked her, intrigued her, made the blood in her veins run hot and thick.

His gaze moved slowly up to meet hers, and of all the emotions she saw reflected in those aqua eyes, the strongest could be summed up in a single word. Hunger.

"Marry me, Jessica."

Her breath caught, her mind so filled with love for this man, she couldn't find words. It would be so easy to surrender to the pull of those eyes. He could protect her and shelter her and be her shield against all the ugliness that threatened. If she said yes, she could surrender all her doubts and fears to him, hide her weakness behind his strength.

And lose herself forever.

So easy. She loved him so much.

Yet, she could not.

And in that instant of hesitation, she realized that loving Brady and marrying him were two entirely different things, and neither could be bought without pain.

Suddenly embarrassed, she lifted trembling fingers and buttoned her dress. She felt him watching, and wondered what he was thinking. But when she looked up, his thoughts were hidden behind that expressionless mask.

Without taking his eyes from hers, he rolled onto his side. Bending his arm at the elbow, he propped his closed fist beneath his cheek. "You're not answering."

"I'm thinking. And wondering."

"About what?"

She wasn't sure how to answer that. She wanted this man. She craved what he offered. But as comfortable a place as it might be, she wasn't sure she wanted to live in Brady's shadow forever. So she retreated to safer ground. "If Jack finally goaded you into it." She said it with a smile, hoping to ease the undercurrents weighting the air between them.

He didn't smile back. "Jack had nothing to do with it. In fact, he made it harder. If I'd said anything the other night, what would you have thought?"

"That Jack had goaded you into it."

"Exactly."

"But by saying nothing at all, you made me think you had no interest."

He smiled crookedly. "Then you're a spoke short. I've been interested from the first."

"Even after I tried to geld you?" she said, trying to tease the tension away.

"Well, once the pain stopped." He sat up and opened the leather food pouch. "You got my attention, I'll give you that."

"Ah, so it worked."

He looked over at her, that shuttered look back in his eyes. "You're still dodging. Why?"

She reached down to brush a fly from Adrian's cheek. "I'm concerned. We're so different. I worry that we don't suit." *Or that you will never love me as much as I love you. Or that I will lose myself in you, and forget who I am.* He was such a dominant, dominating man.

He gave her a sidewise look that told her he wasn't buying it. "You have doubts?"

She shrugged. "Some, perhaps."

"About me?" Before she could answer, he added, "I know I'm a bit rough, but I can change. I'll even shave more often and try to quit cussing, if that's what you want."

He sounded nervous and that surprised her. She didn't think anything could make Brady Wilkins nervous. "I don't want you to change, Brady. Ever. Except perhaps for the cursing."

"Then what do you want?"

"Time. When I met you, I was a frightened, twenty-six-year-old pregnant spinster hiding behind her Rules of Deportment and overblown hats. Since then I almost died on the desert. I birthed two children and buried one. I've been run to ground and have risen up fighting." She lifted her free hand in a helpless gesture. "I've changed. I scarcely know who I am anymore. I need time to find out."

He studied her for a long while, as if seeking a deeper meaning behind her words.

She wondered if Brady ever had doubts. He radiated so much confidence it probably never occurred to him to question who he was or what he should do.

"I can't change what happened in the past, Jessica," he finally said.

"But I can promise you a better future. When you're thinking, think about that." He turned back to the pouch. "How hungry are you?"

Apparently he suffered no lingering disappointments, she thought, watching him paw through the food pouch. How convenient to have everything so simple, and all one's thinking set up in neat little compartments. How comfortable to have no doubts. But then, his pragmatic self-assurance was one of the things she admired most about this complicated and confounding man.

After carrying her sleeping son back to his shady resting place, Jessica returned to sit on the blanket beside Brady. "You haven't eaten?" she asked, taking the pouch from his hands.

"I was waiting for you."

Both Brady and his hound perked up as soon as she began pulling food from the bag. Smoked ham, roast beef, a tin of peaches, an entire loaf of bread, two chicken legs, a completely mashed half a rhubarb pie, and one rather soft apple. A feast indeed.

As they ate, the earlier tension eased into a comfortable silence. Letting herself relax, Jessica put her worries aside as she watched Brady try to keep the hound under control by locking the dog's head between his knees and doling out tidbits and dire threats in alternating intervals.

"You need to discipline that dog," she said, more amused than irritated.

He dangled a piece of ham before Bullshot's nose. "He's just a pup."

"He's gray at the muzzle. As are you, I might add."

That brought his head around. "You saying I'm old?"

"Seasoned, perhaps."

"I'm just reaching my prime. I got plenty of go left in me. Want to see?" And before she knew what was happening, he had her on her back, one heavy thigh thrown over her legs.

She stiffened, shocked by the suddenness of his assault, by the weight of his big body pressing down on hers.

"Relax. I won't bite." He nibbled at her earlobe. "Well, maybe a little." Leaning up on one elbow, he looked down to watch his hand move over her body, sliding from her neck, blatantly over her breast, and on to her hip.

Fear scurried through her mind. She tried not to think of other hands touching her, a different body holding her down. "W-What are you doing?"

He lifted his head and pinned her with those compelling eyes. "Trying to show you."

This time he watched her face as his hand retraced its path from her hip, back up to cup her breast. "We may not suit in some things," he said, his fingers tracing a gentle circle that sent her mind bouncing between fear and desire. "But in this we do." His head came down, his mouth seeking hers.

Sound receded. Sight narrowed. For a moment, time hung suspended. All she could hear was her own frenetic pulsebeat and all she could see was him—so big he blocked the sun, so heavy he drove the air from her lungs. She reminded herself that it was Brady, that she was safe and he wouldn't hurt her. But other memories sent fear skittering along her nerves. She put a hand on top of his, whether to stop him or encourage him, she wasn't sure.

Terror built.

It felt like drowning. Dying. Being tied and smothered.

Twisting her head to the side, she struggled to draw a full breath—couldn't—and panic exploded. "No!" She bucked against him, heels digging into the blanket. "Stop! Get off!"

And suddenly the weight was gone.

She lurched upright, gasping, rubbing frantically at her wrists as she battled to drag air into her aching lungs.

"What the hell . . . ?"

She caught movement, saw his hand coming toward her, and before she could stop herself, she jerked back. "Just—just give me a m-minute."

His hand dropped away. Abruptly, he stood and walked to a cottonwood at the edge of the glade. He kept his back to her, his wide shoulders rising and falling with his own labored breathing as he adjusted his clothing. She knew what he was doing and why, and it shamed her that she had brought them both to this point. How could she let this happen?

Curse you to hell, John Crawford!

Squeezing her eyes shut, she tried to shut her mind to that hateful presence. Why wasn't she strong enough to keep him out of her head? She touched her arms, half expecting to feel the bands still encircling her wrists. But he had known silk would leave no permanent marks.

"I'm sorry," she said hoarsely.

Brady made a harsh sound, almost, but not quite a laugh. Bracing one hand on the tree trunk, he leaned over and spit, as if needing to rid himself of the taste of her.

"You're so heavy," she said in a faltering voice. "I couldn't breathe. All I could think about was when he—"

"Don't!" He whirled, his eyes terrible in their fury, his mouth a slash of clenched teeth beneath his dark mustache. "Don't you ever confuse me with him!"

"I'm not! I couldn't. But every time I close my eyes—"

"Then open them! See *me*, not him." He stalked toward her, hurt and anger vibrating with every step. "I've tried every way I know, Jessica, to show you that of all the people in your life, I'm the one you can trust. I'm the one who'll protect you. Me!" He slammed his fist so hard against his chest, she could hear the hollow thump of it from three feet away. "For once look past your fear. I'm here. I've always been here."

Shame crushed her. She never meant to hurt him. But she didn't know how to stop the fear, how to make him understand. "I know. I want to, Brady. I try to control it, but it's always there." She pushed the heels of her hands against her temples, trying to stop the whirlwind in her mind. "I don't know how to stop being afraid."

"Find a way. Conquer it, or it conquers you."

"I'm trying, Brady."

"Try harder!"

She pressed her lips tightly together, desperate to keep the anguish from bursting free in hysteria. Her emotions were in such disarray, she couldn't find the words she so desperately wanted to say, didn't know how to make him understand. Mutely, she looked up at him, unshed tears thick in her throat. Why couldn't she open her mind to him as easily as she had opened her heart? Why couldn't she love him like she wanted to? "Try to understand, Brady. Please."

Some of the tension left him. He closed his eyes. For a moment his expression was that of a man battling a frustration so baffling and profound, he couldn't find words to express it. Then he exhaled and opened his eyes. The anger was gone, replaced by weary resignation. "I do understand, Jessica. I just don't know what to do about it."

She could feel him drifting away, and that aroused a new kind of panic. "Just give me a bit more time. I'll get past this, Brady. I promise."

He opened his mouth as if to say more, then closed it. He knelt beside her and, with savage efficiency, began repacking the portmanteau. "We better go. Mosquitoes will be out soon." After tossing the food scraps into the brush, he sat back on his heels and looked around. "Where's Bullshot?"

Battling tears and heartache, she picked up Adrian. "He was here a moment ago."

From the direction of the house came the hound's deep bark.

"Perhaps he's on the trail of something," she offered lamely, saddened that they had retreated into such inane conversation.

"Chickens."

He stuffed Adrian's blanket into the portmanteau and stood, the luggage in one hand, the leather food bag in the other. Both hands full. She wondered if he did that intentionally, so he wouldn't have to touch her. The thought hurt more than she could have imagined.

They walked in silence up the grassy trail, and with every step she felt the distance between them grow. After carrying the portmanteau to her room, he left to tend his chores. Or so he said.

She went numbly about her own tasks of putting Adrian to bed, unpacking the portmanteau, braiding her wet hair, and changing out of her wet shoes. Then because she was too restless to sit, she went to the courtyard to gather the gloves and bonnet she had left earlier.

The quiet solitude of the garden fitted her mood. Sinking onto one of the stone benches, she let the stillness of the evening soothe her battered spirit. How could she fix this? What was wrong with her that she would allow fear to overshadow trust, even love?

A sound caught her attention—a soft whimper.

Glancing around, she saw movement in the shadows along the back wall. She rose and moved toward it, poised to flee if it was one of those Gila monster lizards, or some feral animal that had found its way past the courtyard gate.

It was Bullshot.

Even in the fading light, she could see the bloody wound on his side. Murmuring softly, she reached out, then snatched her hand back when he snarled, eyes wild in pain. Realizing she needed help, she rushed across the courtyard.

She was almost to the gate when she heard a crash then a woman's cry coming from one of the rooms that opened onto the covered walkway skirting the courtyard. Elena's room. Every instinct told her to run, that something terrible was happening in that room.

Instead, she threw back her head and screamed for Brady as loudly as she could. Then she grabbed the gardening hoe she had left propped beside the gate and raced toward Elena's door.

The room was dim, lit by a single lamp on the dresser, but there was enough light to see the hunched form on top of Elena and the terror on her face as she fought him. Jessica ran toward the bed, hoe raised. She brought it down across his back with such force the dry wood splintered and the shaft broke in two.

With a guttural cry, he swung out and knocked the broken hoe from her grip.

She raced after it.

He reached it first and kicked it away, then kicked at her as she bolted for the door.

She went down hard, saw him raise his leg, and rolled to the side as his boot slammed to the floor beside her head. Grabbing the broken handle, she swung blindly as she struggled to get up.

A glancing blow sent her down again. He came toward her, snarling and cursing. She scrambled back, the handle in her hand, waiting for him to lift his foot to kick her again. When he did, she drove the jagged end of the splintered hoe into his other leg.

With a cry, he staggered back, clawing at the stick impaled in his thigh.

"Elena, run!" she screamed. Wildly scanning the room, she saw the other woman huddled in the corner by the bed, her face streaked with blood. "Run!"

Shrieking in Spanish, the man started toward Elena, then froze when voices rose outside. As he turned toward the door, Jessica saw his face—the scraggly beard, the crazed look in those dark almond-shaped eyes that were so like Elena's—and realized it was her brother, Sancho.

Elena cowered as he turned toward her. But instead of renewing his attack, he grabbed the lamp from the dresser and threw it against the door.

The lamp shattered, sending arcs of liquid fire shooting throughout the room. Flames exploded, engulfing the wood, the wall. As Sancho lunged for the window, the bedding caught fire, then the curtains. Elena began to scream.

Jessica crawled toward her, saw Elena's gown was on fire, and tore it free. Grabbing the injured woman around the waist, she dragged her toward the door. Flames blocked their way. Coughing, she crawled toward the window.

Heat built. She couldn't breathe. The smoke was already so thick she could scarcely see. Elena went limp in her arms.

Then suddenly the door exploded inward, and men rushed into the room. Hands grabbed at her. "Take Elena," she rasped, shoving her friend forward. "She's hurt."

Then her vision dimmed as arms lifted her from the floor.

Nineteen

A MOMENT LATER SHE FOUND HERSELF STRETCHED ON THE ground in the courtyard, staring up into a smoky starlit sky and Brady's scowling face.

"Damn you, woman! Are you hurt?"

She might have taken offense if his voice hadn't been shaking and his face hadn't looked so pale beneath the sooty smudges. He still cared. She hadn't ruined everything after all. She tried to reassure him, but the effort to speak sent her into a fit of coughing. Propping up her head, he thrust a cup of water into her face and commanded her to drink.

She tried, but his hand trembled so much, most of the water spilled down her chin. When she finished, he lowered her back down rather than help her sit up, which was for the best, since even the smallest movement made her wooly-headed.

"How can you be so goddamned stupid?"

"I thought you were going to stop cursing," she managed in a raspy voice, then frowned when she saw the redness on the back of his hand. "Are you hurt?"

"You could have gotten killed!"

"I knew you would come. It was Sancho. He was hurting Elena. When I saw him on top of her, I . . . did he . . . is she hurt?"

"He hit her, that's all. Bruised and a few blisters, but she's okay."

How can a woman ever be okay after an assault like that?

He must have anticipated her other concerns because he quickly supplied answers to her unspoken questions. "The fire's out, Hank's working on Bullshot, and Angelina's with Ben."

"Sancho?"

That look came over his face, the one that had made Oran Phelps sweat and John Crawford scurry like a crab across hot rocks. "He left through the window. We were more worried about getting you and Elena out than chasing after him."

"I stabbed him." She shuddered, remembering the sound of the stick going into his flesh. "In the leg. He was bleeding."

"You're safe now."

She pushed herself upright, wincing at the sharp pull of bruised muscles. He helped her to the garden bench, then once she was settled, he began to pace, his hands working at his sides. "Jesus, how could I have let this happen? He was in the house, for chrissakes! He could have killed her." He whirled, his eyes frantic and furious. "Or you. From now on, don't leave the house without at least two men with you. Don't even come into the courtyard or—"

"Brady, stop! Don't do this to yourself. This was not your fault."

He lifted his hands in agitation. "I'm in charge. How can it not be my fault?"

"Please. Sit. You make me dizzy with all your pacing."

Reluctantly, he sat. Bracing his elbows on his thighs, he clasped his hands tightly between his knees.

She studied him for a moment. As she did, she realized something that had eluded her, the most important piece to the puzzle of who he was and why he made the choices he did. He was afraid. Afraid of failing, of being found unworthy, of opening his heart to forgiveness and love. He had already lost so much, it terrified him to think that it might be his mistake, his weakness, that would cause further loss.

"Things happen, Brady," she said quietly. "Evil men disrupt our lives. People we love die. Stagecoaches crash and we survive, while others do not. You cannot anticipate everything."

"I know that."

"Then why are you so eager to take the blame when anything bad does happen?"

He looked over at her. "What're you talking about?"

"What happened tonight. Elena's hip. Sam's death."

His mouth flattened into a thin, grim line.

She pushed on, determined to say it all. "You're not expected to be everywhere, Brady. Or think of everything, or foresee every danger or pitfall. It's impossible. Especially when a madman like Sancho Ramirez is involved."

"It's my job," he muttered, staring at his clenched hands.

"Then I fear you're doomed to failure, because even you cannot control everything."

"I don't try to control everything. Just the important things."

"Don't you? What about Sam? Why haven't you told your brothers what happened?"

He frowned over at her. "What's Sam got to do with this?"

"You're not responsible for what happened tonight, Brady, any more than you're responsible for what happened to him. Or Elena. Or your parents, or any one of the other dozen lives lost to this feud."

She wanted to reach out and gently wipe that haunted look from his face. But she sensed he wouldn't welcome even that small comfort. Brady hoarded his pain like gold, as if the sharing of it would diminish him somehow.

"Tell your brothers. Relieve yourself of that burden, at least."

"To what end?" he said in an exasperated tone. "What would telling them accomplish? And why are we even talking about this?"

It might lessen your guilt, she thought. *It might open the door to for-*

giveness. To love. To me. "The truth is what it is, Brady. Hiding it won't change it, and often brings more pain than ease."

"And you know this how?" he lashed out in challenge. "By telling your sister what her husband did? By telling Crawford about his son?"

She stiffened, her defenses coming up. "I'm trying to protect Adrian."

"And I'm trying to protect my brothers."

The fight went out of her. He was right. She was right. They were both wrong. "Point taken," she said as she stiffly pushed herself to her feet. She started toward the house, then hesitated. Looking down at his bent head, she said, "But do you ever question it, Brady? Who is it we're really protecting—them, or ourselves?"

SANCHO CROUCHED UNDER THE OVERHANG, FEEDING THE tiny fire with sticks and dry grass. He was so furious his hands shook. Who was she, that *puta* who had kept him from taking what was his? How dare she raise her hand against him.

He glanced down at the bloody kerchief tied above his knee, and his fury built until it was a white-hot fire burning through his mind. He would kill her. Peel the skin from her body. Stake her in the sun for the ants and scorpions to enjoy.

With a shaking hand, he pulled the knife from his boot and cut away the fabric to expose the wound she had given him. Jagged and seeping, it showed splinters and bits of cloth embedded in the torn flesh. He poked at it with his finger and shuddered with pain. Cursing through his teeth, he forced himself to clean the wound. When he had finished, he slid the blade of the knife into the coals then reached into his saddlebag for the bottle of tequila.

As he drank, he thought about the woman with the red hair. Did she belong to Wilkins? His whore? She must be. He smiled, thinking how he would use her in front of Wilkins. Before he finished with her, she would lick his feet and beg him to end her pain.

He took several more swallows, then braced himself and poured the last of the whiskey into the wound. A cry tore through his throat. He hunched over, gasping and nauseated. After the shaking stopped, he wrapped a rag around the grip of the knife and pulled it from the coals.

"*Madre de Dios, ayúdame.*" Teeth clenched, he pressed the glowing blade against the torn flesh. An instant of searing pain, a sizzling sound, then he tumbled into darkness.

When he opened his eyes, the fire barely glowed and the stars shone high overhead. The pain in his leg was so terrible he could not move, could not think. Shaking and sweating, he stared up into the sky, breathing in that familiar sweet smell of charred meat. It reminded him of Maria.

Whispering her name, he closed his eyes and surrendered to the pain.

"He was in our house, for chrissakes!"

Brady rubbed the heels of his palms against eyes still stinging from smoke. He was so drained he felt like he was swimming through mud. "I know, Jack."

"If he came once and got away with it, he'll come again," Hank said, his normally mild expression hardening into an aspect as harsh and forbidding as any Jacob had presented.

"I know." The image of Jessica huddled over Elena in that fiery hellhole was branded into Brady's mind forever. After that fiasco at the river, it was like losing her all over again. He sighed bitterly. The two most important women in his life and he couldn't even protect them.

"So what are we going to do?" Jack demanded.

Brady rose and went to the open door onto the porch. He sensed change all around him—in this room, out there, within himself—and for the first time in a long time, he felt doubt. Maybe Jessica was right. Maybe if he stopped holding on so tight, everything would start to make sense again. But for that to happen, he would have to start with the truth and he wasn't ready for that.

He went back to his desk. Pulling the bottle of whiskey from the drawer, he took a sip then passed it to Hank. After the bottle made two circuits, he recorked it and dropped it back into the drawer. "Besides the ranch, what does Sancho want? Me. I propose we give him exactly that."

Jack snorted. "Pin a bow in your hair and stake you out for him to find? Helluva plan."

Brady pulled a map from the drawer and spread it open across the desk. "I say we move the Reservation herd to Vintin Canyon." He pointed to a spot south of Blue Mesa. "It's boxed in, broad enough to feed that many cattle for a week, has good water and sheer sides. Easy to guard if he tries to run a stampede."

Hank looked doubtful. "Easy for him to hide, too."

"But it's not the herd he wants. It's me. We know he watches the compound. So I make a show of coming and going to check on the herd. When he sees me ride out, he won't be able to resist. When he comes after me, we'll be ready."

"Unless he guns you down from a distance," Hank argued.

"A bullet wouldn't be any fun. He prefers knives, remember, and he'll want to work me over for a long time. I'll stay in the open, so if he does shoot, he'll be too far away to be accurate. If he doesn't, and he takes the bait, he'll have to leave cover to get me. Then we'll have him."

Hank frowned. "We'll be spread thin, guarding the house and herd both."

"Why are you so sure he wants you bad enough to take the bait anyway?" Jack asked.

Brady hesitated, knowing what he said next could change everything. He could still dance around it, or he could tell them the truth and let them make of it what they would. "Because he tried once before." Now that he'd opened that door, a feeling of dizziness swept over him. Sinking back in his chair, he gripped the armrests and tried to keep his voice steady. "He and Paco saw me ride out. They planned to ambush me when I came back. Instead they got Sam."

"Alvarez told you that?"

"And Sam."

Jack looked at Hank, then at Brady. "I thought Sam was already dead when you found him."

"Not quite." Jessica's words echoed in his head. Why had he been withholding the truth? To shield them, or himself? The thought sickened him.

To distance himself from it, he rose and walked to the porch doorway, turning his back on his brothers' questioning eyes. He looked out at the lofty peaks cradling the valley and wished he could magically transport himself beyond those ridges to some clean and distant place, where everything was new and untainted and he could begin again.

But he couldn't. He'd started this. Now he had to finish it. Turning, he faced his brothers. "I need you to understand. Sam was in a lot of pain. He was dying."

Hank studied him, his sharp gaze cutting through all of Brady's defenses. "Brady," he said, hesitantly. "What are you telling us? What did you do?"

"What I could. What he asked me to do." He watched Hank piece together what hadn't been said, and when the shock of realization came over his brother's face, Brady turned away rather than look into those wounded eyes.

But Jack, never subtle, made him spell it out. "What does that mean, exactly?"

Staring out into the valley, Brady said, "It means I helped him the best way I knew."

Silence. Then hesitantly, "You . . . killed him?"

He forced himself to turn so his brothers could see the truth in his eyes.

Jack lurched out of the chair. "Christ, Brady! He was our brother!"

He watched the fury build in Jack's face. He understood it, and in some odd way almost welcomed it. "That's why I did it. Why I'd do it again." He braced himself, expecting Jack to come at him, wishing he would.

But Jack's rage and confusion were so great, all he could do was stand there, staring at him, his fists opening and closing at his sides. "But Sam . . . Jesus, Brady . . . how could you?"

Brady's own despair coursed through him, made his voice sound harsh and desperate. "I could because he was in agony. Because he begged me. Because it was the only peace I could give him." *Or myself.*

But Jack would never understand that, would never be able to look past his own pain to see why Brady had to do what he did. "If it's any consolation, Jack, I'll burn in hell for it."

"You're damn right you will, you bastard!" Jack started forward.

Hank pulled him back, his expression bleak, his eyes filled with an ancient sadness that added its own weight to the burden Brady bore. "There was no other way?"

Brady shook his head.

"He wanted this?"

"He begged me. I didn't know what else to do."

"You're sure?"

"I'm sure. Don't ask for details."

Whirling, Jack stomped from the office.

"He'll get over it," Hank said after the door slammed behind him.

"I doubt it."

Jack would never understand. Brady accepted that, but it hurt to know that because of his part in the death of one brother, today he had lost another. Feeling drained but unaccountably less empty than he had in a long time, he sagged into the chair at his desk.

Avoiding his brother's gaze, he took his time refolding the map. By the time he'd returned it to the drawer, that feeling of awkwardness had passed. He moved on to a safer subject.

"Jessica said she stabbed Sancho in the leg. He may have left a blood trail. Have a couple of men look for it in the morning."

"If he's hurt, it might buy us time to move the herd."

"How's Bullshot?"

"He won't be running for a while, but he'll make it. We were lucky."

Brady stared at the blisters rising on the backs of his hands and realized again how close he'd come to losing Jessica and Elena. "Yeah. Lucky."

Hank started toward the door, then stopped. He swung back, his face grim and resolved. "I'll say this, then we're done here."

Brady pressed his palms against the desktop, wondering if he was about to lose this brother, too.

"I don't know how you did it, Brady. I don't think I could have. But I'm glad he wasn't alone, and I'm glad he didn't have to suffer more than he already had."

Brady nodded, unable to speak, staring mutely at his splayed hands.

After Hank left, Brady felt that swell of emotion blocking his throat again. Abruptly he rose and went onto the porch. Bracing his hands on the railing, he stared out at the valley stretching before him, and felt for the first time a subtle easing of that gnawing ache inside him that never seemed to go away.

JESSICA FELT A SENSE OF DREAD EXPECTATION SETTLE OVER RosaRoja, as if every living thing paused, breath caught, senses alert . . . waiting. Voices seemed muted, laughter stifled, even the everyday sounds of cattle and horses and chickens seemed subdued. With the brothers absent much of the time, the house felt so empty the least sound seemed to echo through the adobe halls. She never thought to admit it but she even missed Bullshot's annoying bark.

But she missed Brady most of all.

One week. Two. She spent her days tending to Elena and Adrian and struggling with the endless task of bringing order to the house and garden. Her nights she spent battling confusion and despair. Should she leave? Or stay?

She came to no decisions.

She rarely saw Brady, and when she did, it was as if they had never shared those magical evenings on the porch or an afternoon picnic in the shade by the creek. He was politely distant, his thoughts hidden behind that expressionless mask. And each time she saw that guarded look, it tore away another piece of her heart.

She didn't know what to do, how to be. She just knew she couldn't go on this way. Yet she hadn't the strength to walk away. Odd, that. She, the one so easily driven to flight, had forgotten how to run.

Elena, like Bullshot, recovered slowly. Her bruises faded to a ghastly greenish-yellow, and the cut on her brow and her blisters had healed well. Her fear of her brother would take longer to leave her, if ever. Ironically, talking Elena through her fears helped Jessica begin to face her own.

Late one afternoon, Doc came by with news from the doctor in San Francisco. The surgeon, Dr. Sheedy, wrote that he might be able to do something for Elena's hip, but required further information before asking her to make the long trip to his hospital.

Following Sheedy's instructions and with Jessica's help, Doc examined Elena's hip, taking measurements, checking mobility, probing, pulling, twisting, and gouging. By the time the examination ended, Elena trembled with exhaustion and pain, but seemed as determined as ever to see the ordeal through, no matter what.

Jessica admired her courage. If Elena was willing to suffer the pain and uncertainty of surgery to achieve wholeness, surely she could find the strength to heal her own wounds.

Before he left, Doc pronounced Jessica recovered and Adrian "a foine lad, blessed with the look of the Irish in his wee thatch of red hair." She didn't tell him the color came from Scottish ancestors, not Irish; she was just thankful it wasn't the lackluster blond of his father.

Having been declared fit for travel, she still didn't know what to do, and that inability to decide kept her tossing at night. Unknowingly, Elena offered her a reprieve. Not aware of Brady's proposal or that horrid scene at the river, she thought Jessica's reluctance to leave was because of her missing brother. She suggested that if Dr. Sheedy decided to proceed with the surgery, and if Jessica still hadn't found her brother, they could go to San Francisco together.

Jessica gratefully agreed, relieved to have another reason to delay a decision.

If Brady wondered why she made no plans to leave now that she was well, he made no comment. In fact, he hardly spoke to her all, which only deepened Jessica's distress.

With Jack not knowing about the surgery, and Brady not knowing about the possibility of her going to San Francisco, Jessica felt trapped in a tangled web of secrets and half-truths. She hated it. But she still couldn't make a decision.

How could she walk away from Brady and her daughter?

Yet how could she accept Brady's proposal when the thought of the marriage bed sent fear thundering through her veins?

So she waited. And fretted. And watched Brady drift farther and farther away.

That sense of anxious anticipation grew stronger as the days marched relentlessly toward that inescapable moment when everything would change and Sancho would be stopped and the feud would end. It seemed they were all poised and waiting, not sure what to expect but knowing the future raced toward them, immutable and unstoppable, the culmination of events put in motion two decades ago.

Only Brady seemed unwilling to sit back and let the future unfold. Typical of his headstrong nature, he charged full force to meet it. Elena told her about his plan to set himself up as bait to lure Sancho out into the open. The idea terrified Jessica, sent her bolting upright in the night, gasping from nightmarish visions of Brady in danger, in pain, writhing in flames.

Her first awareness of the rift between Jack and Brady came one evening almost three weeks after the fire. She had just put Adrian to bed for the evening and had gone onto the porch, seeking respite from the heat. The rockers still sat side by side in the shadows, lonely reminders of better times. Foolishly hoping to recapture that sense of contentment, she sank into the one that so perfectly fit every contour and curve of her body. Closing her eyes, she tipped her head against the high back and rocked slowly, letting her mind drift through bittersweet memories.

"You can't keep at him, Jack. This has gone on long enough."

Startled from her reverie, she opened her eyes to see Hank and Jack coming up the steps at the other end of the porch.

"He was wrong, Hank. You know he was wrong."

Hank grabbed Jack's arm and swung him around so they faced each other. "We weren't there, Jack. How do we know what we would have done?"

"I damn sure wouldn't have killed him."

"You'd have let him suffer?"

"Jesus, Hank. He was our brother."

With those words, she understood what they argued about, and it unleashed a wave of fury that sent her out of the rocker and charging toward them. "Are you talking about your little brother?" she asked in a voice vibrating with anger.

They turned toward her, surprise on their faces.

She stalked forward, speaking as she went, heels hitting hard on the plank floor. "The brother whose every breath was torture, whose poor body was so flayed even the slighted breeze made him scream in agony?" She stopped before Jack, hiked her chin in challenge. "Are you talking about Sam?"

His surprise became confusion, then outraged disbelief. "He told you about Sam? He keeps it from us for ten years, but tells you?"

"Perhaps he knew I wouldn't judge him."

"How can I not judge him? He killed our brother!"

"At the cost of his own soul!" Feeling her temper slipping, she took a deep breath and tried for a calmer voice. "What would you have had him do, Jack?"

He looked away, his jaw working. "He could have found a better way."

"Better for whom? Sam, or himself? Because I assure you, if he had been less merciful toward his brother, Brady wouldn't be suffering so today."

"Brady suffering?" Jack laughed bitterly. "The only thing Brady suffers over is this ranch. We're just here to strengthen his hold on it."

She slapped him. "You selfish fool! He does it for you!"

Eyes round with astonishment, Jack gaped at her, one hand against his face.

But once unleashed, her fury couldn't be checked. "Brady has given everything for his family. Are you so blinded by your petty resentments you can't see that? Would you prefer that he dump it all onto your shoulders? Would that ease your envy?" She jabbed a finger into his chest. "If you think to step into your brother's shoes, Jack, you had best grow up!"

Jack's eyes seemed to catch fire. But before he could speak, Hank reached between them and pushed her pointing finger aside. "He didn't mean it that way," he said in a placating tone that did little to cool Jessica's ire. "Did you, Jack?"

Jack glared at her for a moment. Then muttering under his breath, he looked away. "I want no part of this goddamned ranch. I never have and never will."

"You have made that abundantly clear."

"Thank God somebody sees that."

She sighed, her own anger fading. In so many ways, Jack was an innocent. Irrepressible and openhearted, he viewed life in the simple, clearly defined terms of a man who has never had to look too deeply into the darkness of his own heart. It saddened her to see some of that innocence stripped away, but it saddened her more that it prevented him from seeing the terrible choices his brother had had to make.

"Imagine yourself in Sam's place, Jack," she said in a calmer tone. "Imagine what he suffered. Then ask yourself who in all the world would have the courage and strength to give you release from such pain. Answer that before you judge your brother."

She watched him wrestle with it, and knew that acceptance would come slowly, and forgiveness perhaps not at all. But at least now he might see Brady's side of it.

Jack dragged a hand through his sandy hair in a gesture so like that of his big brother, it tugged at her heart. "How could he do it, Jessica? That's what I don't understand."

"How could he not?" Lifting a hand, she laid her palm against the cheek that still bore the mark of her fingers. "He loved him, Jack. As he loves you and Hank. Right or wrong, give him that, at least. He doesn't deserve your hate."

Looking into those Wedgewood blue eyes, she caught a glimpse of the boy Jack had been, as well as the man he struggled to become. The juxtaposition of the two made her smile. Letting her hand fall back to her side, she tried for a lighter note. "If you think it troublesome being his little brother, think how difficult it must be to be him. He's much harder on himself."

"Younger brother," he corrected. "And he deserves to be harder on himself. He makes more mistakes." He rubbed a hand against his jaw. "Brady said you had a temper. I guess I should thank you for not using your fist. Or your umbrella."

"You're not nearly as aggravating."

"Christ, I hope not." He sighed heavily, looking less angry than resigned. "I don't hate him, Jessica. I never hated him. I just don't understand him."

She shrugged. "He's a complicated man. But a good one. And fiercely protective of those he loves."

"He's not the only one." He rubbed his jaw again. A sly grin deepened the web of squint lines fanning out from the corners of eyes. "Marry him. Please. Maybe he'll quit riding me if he can ride—"

"Shut up, Jack." Hank shoved him toward the door.

"I'm just saying the man could use a—"

The second shove sent him staggering into the hall. Laughter floated back as Jack continued on toward the kitchen.

Hank loomed over her, color inching up his neck. "Sorry about that."

"About what?" she asked, hoping her own blush wasn't as apparent as his.

He studied her, his sharp brown eyes missing nothing. She imagined she saw approval reflected there, even friendship. Hard to tell under all that hair.

"Thanks," he said.

"For not using my umbrella?" She wondered if she'd ever seen Hank smile.

"For trying to talk sense into him. Sometimes Jack's temper gets away from him."

"Fortunately mine doesn't."

"Of course not."

"Don't patronize me."

"I wouldn't."

"You are."

"I'll stop." He studied his overlarge feet for a moment then looked up, his face expressionless but his brown eyes twinkling. "You needn't be afraid of him."

"Of Jack? Don't be ridiculous."

"Of Brady. He might seem a bit gruff but he's—"

"A puff pastry. Soft as warm pudding. I know." She waved a hand in dismissal of such an absurd notion. "Other than when I, um, accidentally struck him with my parasol, I have never been afraid of Brady." Not really.

"Good." He grinned.

It rocked her back on her heels. Even half hidden by the beard, it was astonishing. Beatific. Brady without the devilry, Jack without the lechery. It was, simply put, the most beautiful smile she had ever seen. *Oh my.* On behalf of the fragile hearts of women everywhere, Jessica offered silent thanks for the concealing beard, for without it, dear Hank would leave a trail of heartache in his wake. Mercy, what beautiful children these brothers would sire.

"Then marry him," he said, wrenching her out of her daze. "He needs someone who'll go at him with an umbrella from time to time." And before she could regain her senses, he ducked his head and stepped inside.

Bemused, she stared after him. *Marry him.* As if she hadn't said the same thing to herself countless times over the last three weeks. As if it were that simple.

Shaking her head, she turned back to the rocker. As she did, her eye caught movement. Glancing over, she saw Brady in the shadowed opening of the barn, watching her.

How long had he been there? How much had he heard?

She couldn't read his expression, couldn't tell by the set of his body what he was thinking. But she could feel his intent in the almost tangible change in the air . . . as if his arms closed around her . . . as if his thoughts seeped into her mind.

She stared back, unable to move, unwilling to break the hold of those eyes.

Her heart began to thrum. Her blood slowed, thickened in her veins.

Then he turned and disappeared into the shadows of the barn, leaving her alone with her doubts once more.

BRADY COULDN'T BELIEVE WHAT HE'D JUST WITNESSED. JESsica, defending him, taking on Jack. For him. How could she push him away one day, then jump to his defense the next? It didn't make sense. She didn't make sense. She was driving him insane.

Muttering and cursing, he paced the darkened barn.

Ever since that scene at the river three weeks ago he had avoided her, giving her the time she said she needed, trying not to mess up things worse than he already had. Every day he stayed busy from dawn to dusk, trying not to think about her. Every night he fell into bed so exhausted his mind could hardly form a thought. And every morning he awoke, aching from sweaty dreams of firm-bodied women with long red hair who shrank from his touch.

And now she was defending him?

What the hell did that mean?

From a shadowed stall, he watched her settle in the rocker. He thought about going over there and sitting down beside her and taking her hand in his. But he knew if he did and she rejected him again, it would damn near kill him.

No. He'd wait. As long as it took, he'd wait for her to make the next move. And if she didn't, well . . . he'd wait some more. *Sonofabitch.* He wished he had it in him to beat a woman.

Twenty

"HE WANTS ME TO COME!" ELENA RUSHED INTO THE KITCHEN waving a crumpled telegram. "He thinks he can help me."

Jessica looked up from a mountain of potato peelings. Consuelo turned from the pot of beef stew she stirred on the stove. The brothers had ridden in a while ago and they anticipated a full table at dinner. It had been over a week since they had all shared a meal together and Jessica missed their boisterous company, the rumble of their voices, the way they filled the room with their male energy.

She also missed seeing Brady at the other end of the long table, and that subtle but undeniable thread of tension that danced along her nerves whenever he was near.

Elena sank into a chair at the kitchen table, wisps of black hair fluttering around her flushed face. "He writes that because the surgery is untried, he will not make me pay. That is good, yes?"

"Indeed." Jessica smiled, delighted for her friend despite the unease building in her mind.

Elena's expressive eyes brightened with sudden moisture. "It is truly going to happen. I did not think . . ." Her voice faltered. Then she laughed and pushed herself to her feet. "I must tell Brady. Do you know if he is here?"

"The three of them went to the river to wash. Will you tell Jack as well?"

"Brady will tell him after I leave. Have you decided what you will do?"

Jessica shrugged, still mired in the uncertainty that had plagued her since that day at the creek. "When does the doctor want you to come?"

"Soon. He wishes me to leave the first of the month if that is possible."

Two weeks. Jessica sank into a chair at the table.

Elena went to the door, then paused. "Have you told Brady you might go with me?"

Feeling as if time were rushing away from her, Jessica clenched her hands tightly in her lap as if by sheer will she could hold it in check. "No." *Two weeks.*

"Then I will say nothing." Elena left.

Jessica looked up to find Consuelo studying her, her dark eyes troubled, her expression sad.

Suddenly too restless to sit, she rose from her chair. She hesitated, driven to move but no destination in mind. Then she realized where she wanted to go. After telling Consuelo not to wait dinner and asking if she would listen for Adrian, she slipped out the door and headed up the hill.

It was another lovely evening, and she marveled at each poignant detail, fearing her time to enjoy it might be drawing to an end. Everything was so beautiful—the glowing sunset, the heady scent of roses, the bright splashes of color from the myriad tiny blooms that had burst out after a short afternoon rainstorm several days ago. How had she ever thought this country a barren wasteland?

The mesquite tree whispered in welcome as she stepped through the iron gate. She looked around in surprise, noting that someone had scythed the weeds and straightened the tilted tombstones. There was even a small stone bench in the corner beside the Wilkins family graves. But the most shocking change of all was the new stone marker on Victoria's grave.

She moved closer, trying to read the inscription through a sudden blur of tears.

VICTORIA THORNTON.
BELOVED DAUGHTER OF JESSICA ABIGAIL REBECCA.
SHE SOARS WITH ANGELS.

Beside the date were two carved winged cherubs.

Her legs gave way and she sank onto the bench, so moved she couldn't keep the tears at bay.

He did this. For her. For Victoria. Dropping her head into her hands, she wept, her heart so filled with joy and love and grief it seemed to fill the hollow of her chest.

How can I leave this place . . . this tiny grave? How can I leave a man who would do this?

Later, after that painful rush of emotion had passed and the sun had faded to a distant glow behind jagged peaks, she heard the creak of the gate. She looked up to see Brady walking toward her. It sent a shock of awareness through her, awakening that heady breathless feeling that always sent her thoughts into flight. Tears rose again. But for a wholly different reason.

He stopped on the other side of the tiny grave and studied her, his hands thrust into the front pockets of his trousers, his eyes shadowed by the fall of damp, wind-tousled hair. If he noticed she'd been crying, he said nothing. "You shouldn't be alone this far from the house."

She let her gaze drift over him, felt again that low clenching within her own body. She recognized it now as desire. But she knew that somewhere within it, like a snake coiled in the grass, was fear. Would the two always be entwined in her mind?

Pushing that disturbing image aside, she nodded toward the head-stone. "You did this?"

His eyes slid away. "I guess I should have checked with you first."

"No. It's beautiful, Brady. Perfect. It means more than I can say."

He nodded and rocked on his heels. "We missed you at supper."

She gathered herself to rise. "I suppose I should get back. Adrian—"

"Consuelo's got him," he cut in. "Parading him through the cabins like a blue ribbon calf."

"Oh. Well." She sat back, idly smoothing her skirts as a silence weighted by too many unspoken words hung in the air between them. From somewhere down the hill came the solitary call of a whippoor-will. It awakened such an answering loneliness within her heart, for a moment it hurt to breathe.

She studied him from beneath her lashes. Did he feel it, too, that emptiness where laughter used to be? Did it bother him that they had moved so far apart they seemed unable to even talk to each other?

He stared down the valley, his eyes fixed on some distant point be-yond her vision. What did he see, to bring such a haunted look to his face?

"Have you ever thought of leaving?" she asked on impulse.

"Leave? RosaRoja?"

"It's only dirt."

"Dirt bought with Wilkins blood. But yeah. I've thought of leaving. Many times."

"Yet you don't."

He gave an odd, harsh laugh. "I don't know how." Lifting one broad hand, he gestured toward the valley and the peaks rising behind it. "This is all I know. All I am." He let his hand fall back to his side. "Me and the ranch, we're two parts of a whole, one part fitting the other."

And the circle is complete. She felt a stab of sadness, realizing people would always come second in his heart. "How fortunate you are to have everything you want."

"Do I?" He tilted his head, as if that might make it easier to see her face in the fading light. "Do I have everything I want?"

She stared back, held captive by the intensity of his beautiful eyes.

Then a horse nickered, breaking the bond. He turned, posture tense. She watched him scan the barn, the house, the outbuildings. Apparently seeing nothing to cause alarm, his body relaxed.

Always on guard, never at peace. *But who guards you, Brady?*

"Did you talk to Elena?" she asked after a lengthy silence.

He nodded, his attention focused on the cottonwoods by the creek.

"Isn't it wonderful news?"

"It is. Although I'm not sure I like her traveling all that way on her own."

"Perhaps I'll go with her." She regretted the words as soon as she heard them. Why had she said such a thing when she hadn't even made the decision?

He went utterly still. Slowly his head turned toward her. "To San Francisco?"

She shrugged and wiped her palms on her skirt, fearful of what she might have set in motion with her foolish prattle. "It's a big city. I thought there might be a market for my hats there. Enough to support Adrian and myself."

"I see." The clipped tone told her he was angry.

Which spurred her to greater folly. "But then I thought . . . how can I leave this place? My daughter is buried here. I have friends here, people I . . . care about. I can't leave." *Ninny.* Even to her own ear, it sound like gibberish. When would she learn to shut her mouth?

A pause. "So you're staying?"

"Yes—no. I'm not sure." She realized she gripped her hands so tightly her nails had left crescent-shaped marks in her skin. "After what happened, I wasn't sure if I should."

"Do you want to stay?"

She forced herself to look at him. He was frowning—not surprising insomuch as she was babbling like a witless fool. "Do you want me to stay? I mean, after I, well—I wasn't sure if—"

"Christ!"

She blinked in surprise as he clasped hands to his temples and almost shouted, "You're killing me!" He stalked away, whirled, covered the distance back in two long strides, and before Jessica realized his intent, he grabbed her by the shoulders, yanked her off the bench, and kissed her.

It was unlike any kiss he'd given her before. No gentle coaxing this time, but an assault on her senses—a demand—so filled with need, it overrode reason and even fear.

The female within her responded. She leaned into him, desperate to breathe him in, to feel his big body against hers, to surrender to the power of his touch.

He pulled back, breathing hard through clenched teeth. "How can you walk away from that?" he demanded harshly, his fingers biting into her shoulders.

Before she could answer, he thrust her away. "Damnit, Jessica." Dragging his hands through his hair, he stalked a tight circle. "I can't do this anymore." He slowed to a stop. Hands falling to his hips, he stared up at the fading sky as if asking for patience, help, deliverance.

From her?

"Jessica, I can't spend the rest of my life holding hands on the porch," he said, his voice sounding harsher than he intended. "I can't be around you and not want more." Even now, the need to touch her was like a fire inside him. Why was she making such a simple thing so complicated?

Say something! he wanted to shout.

But she just stared at him, one hand pressed to her mouth.

Her silence defeated him. He didn't know what else to do, what she wanted from him. He'd shown her in every way he knew that she could trust him. If that wasn't enough, words wouldn't help. He sighed, too weary to fight it anymore. "It's getting dark. We'd best head back while we can see where we're stepping."

She nodded, still so rattled she couldn't marshal her thoughts. She had no idea what had just happened or what it meant. But she felt a terrible emptiness spreading inside.

Without speaking, Brady swung open the gate for her, closed it behind them, then fell into step beside her as they started down the hill. Wind rushed up the slope, billowing her skirts and peppering them with fine grit. As it swept over the hilltop, the long mesquite pods made a noise like rattling bones—a terrible, lonely sound that echoed the hollow feeling within her heart. In desperation she reached for Brady's hand.

He glanced over at her, then quickly away. But when she threaded her fingers through his, his hand closed around hers in a tight grip—too tight. She didn't mind. He was her anchor, her salvation, her hope.

This is the way it's supposed to be. This is what I want.

And at that moment, like stones once tossed into the air finally falling back to earth, all her scattered thoughts and conflicted emotions tumbled into place, and everything made sense at last.

She didn't need someone to save her, or shield her, or make all her problems go away. She just needed someone to love her. If she had that, she could do the rest. She just had to make sure he loved her, and that she had the courage to love him back.

And with sudden and sharp clarity, Jessica knew what she had to do.

As soon as they reached the house, Brady collected his rifle and left to make his rounds, needing to put distance between himself and Jessica. She had him twisting in the wind and he didn't like it or know what to do about it. He ought to just throw her down and be done with it. The idea had some appeal but not much merit. *Hell.*

He had already posted guards; Rufus in the barn loft, Putnam by the creek, Langley patrolling the cabins, and Sandoval keeping an eye on the bunkhouse and cookhouse. He was convinced Sancho would make his move soon or not at all.

Unless he was dead.

Jessica might have nicked an artery when she stabbed him, or infection might have pulled him down. They had found no blood trail after the fire, but they could have missed it.

Or Sancho could be waiting for an unguarded moment. He didn't seem interested in taking the bait Brady had put out there, namely himself, so he might be planning to come to the house again. Brady wanted to be ready if he did.

As he crossed the yard, he glanced up to see Rufus sitting on a crate just inside the opening into the loft. "How's it going, Ru?" he called out.

"Like a church on Monday, Boss."

"Is Hank around?"

"He and Jack went to the north pasture to check on a new foal."

Brady nodded and swung open the barn door. A shadow hurled out of the darkness and would have knocked him off his feet if he hadn't been expecting it.

"Down!" he ordered, trying to hold Bullshot off without hurting him or getting either of them tangled in the tie rope. Once he had the animal somewhat under control, he checked the wide bandage around the dog's ribs. It showed no seepage, so Brady left it alone. Other than a lingering stiffness on the left side, the hound seemed to be healing well.

Brady scratched a floppy ear. "What'd you chew up today?" He glanced around, relieved to note nothing new in the assortment of half-gnawed items strewn across the floor. They had already lost a saddle blanket, a breast collar, a slicker, and an old bridle to the dog's irritation at being tied up in the barn for so long. "You want out, don't you, fella?"

The dog whined and pressed against his leg.

"Why not?" He untied the rope, preferring to have the hound's sharp nose sniffing around the compound than cooped up in the barn. "You can make my rounds with me." Before the words were out, the hound bounded through the door, nose to the ground.

Brady checked on Sandoval, then swung through the cabins. All was quiet. He enjoyed a slice of Iantha's sweet tater pie with Buck, then headed down to the creek.

It was his favorite time of day—enough of a breeze to keep the mosquitoes away, the sky a fiery wash fading behind the mountains, and all around him the scents and sounds of RosaRoja. But tonight, mostly what he noticed was the stillness, like before a lightning storm or a norther blew in, as if the whole world held its breath, waiting. It signaled change of an undisclosed nature, and that always made him nervous.

He found Putnam leaning against the message rock and Bullshot hunting frogs in the reeds by the edge of the creek.

"Almost shot your hound," Putnam said. "Thought he was a puma the way he tore out of the brush."

Brady looked in disgust at the dog snuffling and floundering in the water. "I was hoping to use his nose tonight, but he's probably snorted up so much water he couldn't even smell Red if he snuck up and kicked him in the butt."

Putnam laughed. "I don't know. Red's pretty ripe. The boys are threatening to toss him on the manure pile to sweeten him up."

Brady watched cattle moving to water on the opposite bank. They seemed calm, but how smart was a cow? "Things pretty quiet?"

"Quiet enough to hear a mouse fart."

Brady nodded. Slapping his leg to get the hound's attention, he said good night and headed back toward the house. Bullshot charged ahead, limping a little more from his exertions but still game. Brady tossed a stick. The hound snatched it from the ground, then stopped dead. His head lowered. The stick fell from his mouth as a low growl rumbled in his throat.

Brady ducked behind a cottonwood, rifle up. He scanned the trail ahead, saw nothing. The hill. Nothing. Thirty yards behind him, Putnam idly tossed rocks into the creek. He glanced back at the hound. Bullshot stood motionless, ears cocked toward the hill, a ridge of hair quivering along his neck and shoulders.

Brady squinted into the fading light. The mesquite tree stood silhouetted against the muted sky, its drooping branches the only things moving in the gentle breeze. He slowed his breathing and listened. Cows, crickets, a bobwhite. Quiet evening sounds, except for Bullshot's low growl.

Then near the base of the hill something moved.

Brady flattened against the tree trunk, following it with the rifle. Bullshot inched forward, his head tracking the same arc.

From down the valley came a yodeling howl. At the base of the hill, an answering bark.

A coyote. *Christ.*

Brady let out the breath he'd been holding and lowered the rifle. After a moment, he stepped back onto the trail, slapping his leg to call Bullshot.

The hound came reluctantly, his hackles still up, his head swiveling toward the hill every third stride. Ten yards farther and he was nosing the weeds again. "You're worthless," Brady said.

The hound looked up with a grin, then stuck his prized nose into a mouse hole.

Still uneasy, Brady angled toward the corrals. The horses rested quietly, heads drooping, ears relaxed. He went on to the barn. "Hey, Ru."

Footsteps thudded, then a face peered down from the loft opening. "Yessir?"

"You hear anything?" Brady asked.

"Nothing but you two. Why?"

"Bullshot's acting strange."

"He's a strange dog."

"Check the hill. Anything odd?"

Ru looked up, then back at Brady. "Nothing. What's going on?"

Brady watched the hound dig in the straw pile for mice. "Nothing, I guess. But if you hear anything, call out or fire a round. Something feels off."

"Yessir."

Retrieving the tie rope from the barn, Brady tied Bullshot to the hitching post beside the door. "Sorry, boy," he told the pouting hound. "I need every hand I can muster tonight." With a final pat on the drooping head, he crossed to the porch steps.

At the door, he paused for a final look around.

Ru lounged on the crate in the loft opening. Laughter drifted from the bunkhouse. The horses rested peacefully, and his well-trained watchdog busily gnawed on his rope. Still, that itchy feeling persisted. Maybe he was still strung tight because of Jessica. Or overtired. Or just impatient for Sancho to make his move.

Maybe.

With a sigh, he pushed open the door. What he needed was a drink.

JESSICA STARED IN PANIC AT HER REFLECTION IN THE CHEVAL mirror. Her hair was almost dry from her bath, her robe was buttoned all the way up to her chin, and the face staring back at her had the expression of a felon facing the chopping block.

How could she do this?

How could she go on if she didn't?

With trembling fingers, she unbuttoned the top button on her satin robe. Then two more. She tested a smile. The reflection grimaced back. Pulling two long curls over her shoulders, she spread them out so they covered her breasts.

She practiced smiling, achieving better results each time. Then she heard footsteps moving past her door, followed by the muted thud of the office door closing.

He was back.

It was time.

She felt like laughing, crying, casting up her accounts—as nervous as a fainthearted debutante at her first ball, or a virgin headed for sacrifice. Alas, she was too old for one, and too used for the other.

On trembling legs, she moved silently down the hall, and out onto the porch.

*   *   *

BRADY TIPPED THE NEAR-EMPTY WHISKEY BOTTLE INTO HIS
tin cup and cursed Doc for drinking him dry. Again. Could this day
get any worse? Sancho lurking out there somewhere, Jack talking about
Australia again, Hank itching to get to Fort Union, Elena packing for
San Francisco, and Jessica . . . hell, he had no idea what she was doing.
Christ.

He tossed back the last sip, then slapped the cup onto the desktop.

How had it all gone so wrong? It had started out straightforward
enough—protect the family, protect RosaRoja, build something he and
his brothers could take pride in, then find a strong healthy woman and
breed sons to hold it. Simple. But now everything was turning to crap
in his hands and he didn't know how to stop it. What was it all for if
there was nobody left but him?

In a sudden burst of frustration, he threw the cup out the porch
doorway. An instant later he fired the bottle after it.

To hell with all of them.

JESSICA JUMPED BACK AS A TIN CUP BOUNCED OFF THE PORCH
railing. Before it hit the floor, a whiskey bottle sailed by, tumbling end
over end into the rose bed. She glanced at the office doorway then back
at the cup slowly spinning to a stop at her feet. In a temper, was he?
Perversely, she found that more amusing than frightening.

When she deemed there would be no more missiles, she picked up
the cup. She smiled. Hopefully, if she didn't lose courage and bolt for
cover, and if he wasn't in one of those uncommunicative moods that
made talking to him such a chore, she might find a way to put the dear
man in a better mood.

She pressed a hand to her fluttering stomach, took a bracing breath,
then walked into the office.

Brady was staring morosely down at the desk between his propped
elbows, the heels of his hands pressed against his throbbing temples,

when he caught movement from the corner of his eye. He jerked his head up.

Jessica stood in the doorway, the tin cup swinging from one long, graceful finger. "Cleaning out your office, are you?"

He blinked, wondering if he could possibly be drunk on just two sips of whiskey. Her hair was down and she wore a satiny pink robe, and little pink slippers, and not a whole helluva lot else.

Drunk or dreaming.

"Not feeling talkative?" she prodded.

He sat back, watching her move toward him, captivated by the way lamplight played over the shiny cloth like a slow fall of water, highlighting every curve, every dimple and pucker.

What would he do if this woman walked out of his life?

"I left the bottle in the roses."

He saw the slight tremble in her fingers as she carefully set the cup on the edge of the desk, and wondered if it was because of him. He resolved to keep his mouth shut, to do nothing to scare her off. Swiveling the chair, he watched her move around the desk to peruse the bookcases along the back wall, leaving in her wake a gentle drift of flowery soap and woman.

Her hair hung in silky disarray down her long slim back. Thick chestnut curls swayed with every movement, brushing against gently rounded hips, drawing his eyes to that pear-shaped bottom he'd admired down at the creek. He imagined moving up behind her, sliding the robe off her shoulders, kissing every coppery freckle on that sleek, smooth skin.

His mouth went dry.

Clasping his hands in his lap to hide the effect of his own randy thoughts, he cast about for something to say, something that might intrigue or amuse her, and maybe entice her to take a seat and stay awhile.

"What do you want, Jessica?" he said instead, like a bumbling thirteen-year-old.

She turned. She no longer smiled but wore an expression close to desperation. Even in the lamplight, he could see her color was high, her eyes bright and wide. With fear?

"You."

He blinked, confused, not sure he'd heard right.

His silence seemed to egg her on. "What happened at the creek was . . . unfortunate. I thought perhaps—if you—if you and I—perhaps we might try again."

"Like a test?" he asked guardedly, still not sure what she was up to.

"Not precisely."

"What then? We have a go at it, and if we can get through it without you clawing my face off, then everything's fine? If not, we'll know it's a mistake?" It sounded funnier in his head than it did spoken aloud.

She didn't seem to find it amusing either. "I can see this was a bad idea." She swung toward the hall doorway.

"Wait," he said, bringing her to a stop. "What changed your mind?"

Slowly she turned, her body still poised for flight.

"Why aren't you afraid of me anymore?" he asked.

An odd look crossed her face. "I was never afraid of you, Brady. How could you think such a thing?"

He couldn't even respond to that. Had she forgotten what happened at the creek? "You were afraid of something. If not me, then what?"

"Of being smothered. You were on top of me. I couldn't breathe."

He frowned, even more confused. Other than one knee over her thighs, he hadn't been on top of her. Knowing he probably outweighed her by at least a hundred pounds, he'd been careful not to put his full weight on her. How had he smothered her?

Something didn't add up. He studied her, watched her rub her wrists like she did at the creek, as if spiders were crawling along her arm. "What did he do to you, Jessica? Did he tie you?" In light of his own aversion to confinement, he couldn't image many things worse than being tied and helpless.

As if realizing her hands had betrayed her, she quickly clasped them together, her fingers laced so tight, her knuckles lost color. "Why are we discussing this?"

"He did, didn't he?"

"Fine. Yes. He tied me then climbed on top of me and raped me. Satisfied?"

Silence. She stared down at her pink slippers. He stared at her, while pictures formed in his head—terrible, awful pictures that sent fury pounding through his veins. He wished Crawford was still here so he could beat him until bones shattered under his hands, then revive him and do it again.

"Why are you doing this, Brady? Why do we have to talk about this now?"

When she lifted her head, her eyes glistened in the lamplight, filled with that never-forgotten terror he had stupidly forced her to relive again. It shamed him. He looked away, tried to bring his anger under control. "You're right. I'm sorry. We won't talk about it again." He didn't think he could bear to hear more anyway. He took a deep breath, then held out his hand. "Come here." He put on a smile to reassure her.

Hesitantly—reluctantly—she came toward him until she was close enough that he could reach out and take her hand. From there it was just a tug to get her onto his lap. After the stiffness left her shoulders and she allowed herself to lean against him, he kissed her temple and said, "Now, where were we? Oh, yeah. You were propositioning me."

"I was not propositioning you."

"Seducing, then."

She sat up. "If you're going to be difficult . . ."

"Difficult?" He had to laugh. "Hell, I'm so easy it's embarrassing." He pulled her back down. "Okay. I'm seduced. Now what?"

She didn't respond.

But his cock did, opportunistic bastard that he was. There were only a few things sweeter to a man than having a woman's soft bottom nestled in his lap, and Brady planned to enjoy them all before this night ended. "So what's the plan?"

"I have no plan."

"No? Well, maybe I can come up with one." He had several in mind,

in fact. He started by nuzzling her neck. She seemed to like that, so he
kept at it, improvising as he went until his heart thundered in his ears
and the back of his neck started to sweat. "It's stuffy in here," he said,
finally coming up for air. "Don't you want to take off that hot robe?"

"No."

"You feel hot."

"I feel fine."

"I wouldn't want you to get overheated."

"Can we please not talk anymore and just . . . do . . . whatever?"

Music to a man's ear. Without giving her a chance to change her
mind, he leaned forward to blow out the lamp, then gathered her in his
arms and stood.

Suddenly the enormity of what was about to happen unnerved him.
She had placed all her fear and trust and hope in his hands. A wrong
move would be ruinous. It was enough to shrivel a man's resolve.

He looked down at her, trying to read in her face what she was
feeling.

She stared back, so pale her eyes looked like two drops of dark rye
whiskey in a bowl of strawberry-tinted cream.

"You sure this is what you want?" he asked, wondering what he
would do if she changed her mind.

"It's what I want." To prove it, she slid her arms around his neck.

Thank you, Jesus.

Trying not to run, Brady carried her out the door and down the
hall.

Twenty-one

"BE CAREFUL NOT TO WAKE ADRIAN," JESSICA WARNED AS Brady lifted a foot to kick open the door to his-her-their bedroom.

He let his foot drop. "Ben's in there?"

"Where else would he be?" She tilted her head back to look at him. "What's wrong?"

"I don't want him watching us."

"He's asleep."

"What if he wakes up?"

"He's a baby."

"Still."

"You dolt. He's in the corner behind a screen."

"That's different." But he was careful not to make too much noise. Luckily she'd left a lamp burning. After he lowered her onto the bed, he gave her a quick kiss then straightened. "I just hope you don't wake him with all your carrying on." He unbuttoned his shirt.

"I do not carry on," she said, staring—not unhappily, he thought—at his chest.

"You will." As he tossed the shirt aside, he noticed she hadn't started on her robe. "Need help with those buttons?" he asked, loosening his belt buckle.

"Um, no."

Reminding himself that in all the ways that mattered Jessica was still an innocent, he turned his back as he finished stripping. Behind him he heard furtive rustlings and muttering, and by the time he slid under the sheet, her robe hung over the foot rail and she had the sheet, blanket, and counterpane pulled to her chin.

Rolling onto his side, he propped his head on the heel of his hand, careful to keep some distance between them, but still close enough to see her clearly in the dim light. She had never looked more beautiful to him, her face pale and anxious, but her eyes full of trust and her chestnut hair spilling across the pillows like liquid fire.

"Aren't you going to put out the lamp?" she asked in a tinny voice.

He shook his head, almost overwhelmed by the feelings she roused in him. It would be difficult to hold himself back, but he knew this would go better if he let her set the pace. "I want to see you," he said, smoothing a curl across the pillow with his fingertip. "I want you to see me and know it's me and not him."

"Oh." She gave him a martyr's brave smile.

He almost laughed aloud. She had no idea how grand this was going to be. "I won't force you to do anything, Jessica." As he spoke, he wound the silky curl around his index finger. It was so fine it caught on the roughness of his skin. "But I need you to tell me what you like and what you don't. Will you do that?"

She nodded, as solemn as a pallbearer at her own funeral.

"Good." Careful to keep his body from touching hers, he leaned over, brushed a kiss across the tight seam of her mouth, then worked his way down her jaw to the hollow of her throat. He could feel the little puffs of her quickened breathing against his hair and sensed that, beneath the fear, she was a passionate woman. In fact, he planned on it.

"You can thrash around all you want." He pressed his lips against that butterfly pulsebeat in her throat then lifted his head and grinned. "But keep the 'hallelujahs' to a minimum so we don't wake Ben. I'll do the same."

"You're making a joke, right?"

He just smiled and slid his hand under the covers.

Moving slowly, gentling her as he might a frightened colt, he ran his open hand from her throat, over her breast, and down to her hip. He felt a slight dampness on his fingertips and realized it was milk leaking from her breasts. It felt alien and mysterious and so profoundly feminine, it aroused within him an almost desperate need to shelter and protect this fragile woman. His woman.

Smiling down at her, he stroked her again. By the third pass, she quivered beneath his touch. "Do you like that?" he asked softly, watching her reactions play across her expressive face.

"Ah—no—yes."

"And this?"

"Oh." Her eyes closed.

He could feel her heart pounding beneath his palm and wondered if it was from fear or desire. "Think about me, not him." He kept his movements gentle and slow. "Think about this. And what's happening now . . . in this room . . . just you and me." She arched against his hand like a cat.

"Say my name."

"B-Brady."

He ran his tongue over the seam of her lips. "Again."

"Brady." With a sigh, Jessica surrendered to sensation, her body coming alive under his touch, her mind soothed by his voice. It was remarkable and frightening and wonderful. For such a powerful man, he had the gentlest hands she'd ever known.

Time slowed. Fear receded. When he finally pulled the covers away, cool air danced across her heated flesh, making her shiver. She watched his eyes move over her body and shivered again. But not from the cold.

"Freckles. I knew it." He kissed a path from her breast up her neck and across her jaw, stopping when he reached her ear. "You know how to ride a horse?" he whispered.

Somehow she managed to nod.

His lips tugged on her earlobe. "Astride?"

"No."

"Time to learn."

He rolled onto his back, taking her with him until she lay on top of his body. Startled, she stiffened her arms against his shoulders, trying to put some space between them. But he gently pulled her down until her breasts flattened against his chest and her cheek rested above his heart. He covered them with the sheet then just held her, his hands moving in lazy circles on her back.

The feel of flesh against flesh—especially *there*—was shocking—as was the fact that his chin rested against her temple yet her toes scarcely reached to his ankles. If something went wrong, she would be powerless against him. A wiser woman would stop now.

Instead, she let herself relax, enjoying the tickle of masculine hair against her breasts and legs, and the solid feel of his strong body against hers without the weight of it pressing her down. Lulled by his warmth and the steady thrum of his heartbeat beneath her ear, she let her mind drift.

This isn't so bad. I can do this.

"Touch me," he whispered against her hair.

Tentatively she stroked a hand across his chest, heard his sharp intake of breath as muscles jerked beneath her palm. She watched her fingers thread through crisp dark hair and marveled at the textures, the scents, the strength of the body so different from her own.

His hands stroked down her back and over her bottom, slipping lower to clasp the back of her thighs. "Sit up," he said, pulling her knees forward on either side of his hips.

She did, bracing her palms on his chest, and the sheet slid down her back, leaving her open and exposed. Heat rushed up her neck. But she made no move to cover herself.

Watching her through heavy-lidded eyes, he moved against her in a most shocking and intimate way. "Do you like that?"

She let her head drop forward and closed her eyes, unable to speak, trapped between desire and fear, yet unwilling to tell him to stop.

"Then you're really going to like this." His hand skimmed up her thigh.

Coaxing her to open to him, he taught her the power and passion within her own body, arousing her to a need that left no room for fear. He made her mind soar, her body burn. And when he finally slipped inside her, he wouldn't let her hide beneath the fall of her hair, but reached up to cup her face in both his hands. "Look at me."

She opened her eyes.

"Say my name."

"Brady."

Brady. I love you.

Locking his gaze on hers, he began to move within her, awakening her body to an ancient rhythm that matched his own. "Say it again."

She did. Over and over. Imprinting him on her mind as well as her body, until the past faded away and fear became a distant memory and there was nothing left between them but the joy they brought each other.

It was like dying and being reborn.

THEY LAY SIDE BY SIDE STARING UP AT THE CEILING, SHOULders touching, fingers entwined between their sweating bodies. The sounds of their breathing filled the silent room.

"That's unbelievable," she said in a fluttery voice.

Brady agreed. He hadn't felt this way since . . . well . . . forever. Loving Jessica was magical, better than he ever dreamed. His heart still pounded like something was trying to kick its way out of his chest. "I'm gratified you think so." He tried to sound modest, but it was difficult. She had set a daunting task before him, but he'd managed pretty damn well, even if he said so himself.

"No. I mean it's unbelievable that we're not covered in spider bites. Look at those cobwebs up there."

Cobwebs? She's thinking about cobwebs? He turned his head to remonstrate with her and found her grinning at him. "Sassy woman." Rolling onto his side, he tickled her until her heels drummed the mattress and her stifled laughter gave way to pleas to stop. He kissed her soundly, then rolled onto his back again, knowing if he didn't take his hands off her, he'd be at her again like a randy adolescent. Maybe later. "Now you'll marry me."

When she didn't answer, he turned his head to look at her.

She was stretched on her side, studying him. Her cheek rested on her clasped hands in the pose of a child at sleep. But she wasn't asleep. Nor was she smiling. And even though she was so close he could feel the soft exhalations of her breath on his shoulder, the look in her eyes told him she had drifted beyond his reach.

He frowned. What happened? What had changed? Like smoke rising from the last ember in a dying fire, doubt unfurled in his chest. She couldn't refuse him. After what they'd just shared, he'd hogtie her before he'd ever let her get away. "You *will* marry me."

"Perhaps."

Perhaps? What the hell did that mean? Doubt became confusion and then, because uncertainty was intolerable to him, it flared into a spike of anger. This was a test. Now that she had him where she wanted him, she'd whip out a list of conditions before she sealed the deal.

A part of him almost crowed with laughter that she would try to manipulate him. Another more vulnerable part shriveled in trepidation. He couldn't go through another rejection like the one at the creek. It would kill him. But to let her go without even trying to convince her to stay, would kill him even more. "I suppose you want me to quit cussing."

"Well . . . a true gentleman never uses foul language in front of a lady." The smile tugging at her lips gave him hope.

"Even when she tries to geld him with an umbrella?"

"Even then."

"What else?" he asked, matching her teasing tone.

She pursed those slightly swollen, lightly chaffed lips in thought. "A gentleman always eats with his mouth closed."

"Then how does he get the food in?"

"With a fork and in very small bites." She patted his chest. "It's not that difficult. We'll practice together."

"Ah. So you don't know how to do it either."

Smiling, she idly plucked at the hair on his chest. He wondered if she was even aware of doing it. He sure as hell was.

"And a gentleman always rises when a lady enters or departs the room."

"I do rise when you enter the room. That's why I don't stand up."

"Wicked." She gave him a playful slap on his sternum. "Let's see . . . after a gentleman has his way with a lady, he should *always* express his gratitude and admiration."

"If she's just let him have his way with her, would she still be a lady?"

A shadow moved behind her eyes. "One would hope."

Ah. There it was. The reason behind her hesitation and what he should have realized from the first. This wasn't about him or what he lacked. It was about what she needed that he hadn't yet given her. He almost laughed in his relief. *Women. Hell.* They complicated the simplest things.

Rolling over, he took her face in his hands and gave her a long, hot, thorough kiss that should have been all the reassurance she needed. But when he finally lifted his head to take a breath, he saw that it wasn't. "Jesus, woman. You're killing me." Unable to bear seeing his own doubt and uncertainty mirrored in those whiskey eyes, he tipped his forehead against hers and closed his eyes. "I asked you to marry me, Jessica. What more do you need?"

The words. Jessica felt like weeping. *Say you love me, even if it's a lie.* She knew RosaRoja would always come first with him, but she had to know she was at least important to him before she gave her heart into his keeping. "Do you love me, Brady?"

He lifted his head to stare at her. "Hell, yes. Christ, yes. You need to ask?"

"I need the words." And never more than at this moment from this man.

A sad look crossed his face. "You still doubt me? Haven't my actions shown you how I feel?"

How could she answer that? In the broadest terms the actions were the same—whether it was the magic she had just felt with Brady or the horror of John Crawford's attack—intercourse was intercourse. It was love that made it magical, and without that connection, it was simply another kind of betrayal. A woman didn't need to be raped to feel used.

"No one has been more steadfast than you, Brady. No one has protected me so well. I have no doubt you care about me, but I need to know where I fit into your life."

Stunned, Brady leaned up on one elbow so he could see her face clearly in the lamplight. It was as if another door into her mind had opened to him, revealing why she had kept that distance between them. She had been let down so many times by men she should have been able to trust, she didn't believe it wouldn't happen with him as well. Somehow he had to break through that barrier. Now, more than any other time in his life, he had to find the words—the right words—to tell her how he felt and how much he needed her in his life.

His woman. His son. He couldn't—wouldn't—allow it to be any other way.

"Then know this, Jessica," he said, hoping, despite his fumbling words, she would see the truth in his eyes and hear it in his voice. "You're here." He spread his palm over his heart. "Inside me. Part of me forever. If I raise my hand against you, I hurt myself. If I disrespect you, I bring shame on myself. Whether you stay with me or not, that will never change. But if you stay . . ."

The idea of her not staying made his throat seize, and for a moment he couldn't go on. He inhaled, exhaled, and tried again. "But if you stay, Jessica, I'll never abandon you. Or lie to you. Or put anyone above you. And no matter what, I'll never stop loving you. Every day, all day, for all the days I have left. That's how you fit into my life."

He watched tears well up and slide down her cheeks into the hair at her temples. It made his own eyes sting. "But if you cry, I'll drop you like a bad habit."

"Will you?"

"I will." He kissed one cheek, then the other, gently licking the salt of her tears from her skin. "I swear it."

"Oh, Brady." Leaning up, she pressed her lips to his, then moved her mouth along his jaw. "I love you, too," she whispered into his ear.

BRADY AWOKE WITH A START. HE COULDN'T HAVE SLEPT LONG because the lamp still burned and the wick wasn't smoking. Jessica lay tucked against his side, her breath warm against his neck, one hand on his chest, one long leg draped across his thighs.

An indescribable feeling came over him, a mix of so many emotions he couldn't separate one from the other—and they all centered on this woman beside him.

He lifted his head to study her, letting his gaze drift over high cheekbones, her freckled nose, that perfect little ear. As always, her beauty stunned him—like at dinner when he glanced up and saw her smiling from the other end of the table, or when he watched her move across the yard, or when he saw the look on her face when she held Ben. Sometimes just the sight of her made him abandon reason.

The unwelcome thought arose that this must have been what his father had felt about Maria. If so, it was no wonder Jacob had collapsed in hopeless despair when he realized he couldn't have her. Jessica had that same power over him. Like a blind foal on a short lead, Brady knew he would stumble along wherever he was led—as long as she was on the other end of the rope.

A terrifying thought. Pitiful.

Jack would pop a button laughing at him.

Even so, pitiful had never felt so good. Smiling, unable to keep his hands off her, he lifted a stray curl from her cheek and brought it to his face. It smelled of roses and lemons, and in the lamplight it was the exact color of his mother's honey and apricot jam. The thought of it made his stomach rumble.

Her eyes opened. She gave him a sleepy smile and stretched like a well-fed cat.

Watching her, Brady realized he would do anything, risk anything, to wake up to this sight every day of his life. "You're so beautiful." Her hair was as soft as the belly of a new foal, her skin like warm satin under his palm. "So fine and delicate."

She finished stretching and settled back against his side. "I was never delicate."

"When I first saw you, you reminded me of one of those china music box dancers."

"Indeed? Was that before or after I tried to geld you?"

He gave her a scolding look. "I'm trying to be romantic here."

"Are you?" She batted burnished copper lashes. "Then pray continue."

"I judged you easy on the eyes, hard on the cojones, and much too beautiful to touch."

She smiled wickedly. "Apparently you've gotten over it. The touching part anyway."

"You shouldn't mock a fellow when he's courting."

"This is courting?"

"It is." A man could lose himself in those wide whiskey eyes. Forget everything—give anything—for a single touch. It was a need, a compulsion, he was powerless against.

Like father, like son. Right then, he couldn't decide if that was a good thing, or not. Nor did he care. Especially with her rubbing against him like that. "Where were we? Oh, yeah. I was giving you a riding lesson."

Where the first time had been slow and sweet, this time was a romp of twisted sheets and hushed laughter and sweaty bodies twining together—and even better because she was as eager for it as he was, and came to him without holding anything back. The woman was a wonderment and a delight, and Brady thanked God for putting her in his path.

When Ben woke them for his late-night feeding, Brady rose and brought him to Jessica. He climbed in beside her, pulling her back against his chest so he could hold them both while Ben nursed. It aroused such a deep emotion within him, for a moment Brady felt unraveled and off-balance, and almost desperate with fear that this wasn't real, that it was all an illusion and he'd wake up and find himself trapped in the life he'd once thought so complete.

After Ben had finished and Jessica had changed his drawers, they played with him for a while. Everything about him fascinated Brady, from the tiny toes to the downy red fuzz on his head to the way his little hand took ahold of his finger and his heart. A fleeting thought of the man who'd fathered the baby intruded, but Brady pushed it away. Ben was his son, not Crawford's, and he wouldn't think of it any other way.

When Ben's eyes started to droop, Jessica rose and returned him to his crib.

Brady watched her move about the room. Even though she wore her robe, just picturing all the curves and hollows it hid sent blood humming through his body.

It embarrassed him to be so out of control. And when she bent over the cradle to sing Ben to sleep, and he found himself staring at her soft, round bottom with all manner of raunchy ideas bouncing through his head, Brady realized he had to put some distance between them or he'd be on her again like a drooling fifteen-year-old.

He sat up and reached for his trousers. "You hungry?"

She turned. Her gaze slid down to his lap then quickly away. Color inched up her neck even as a siren's smile tugged at the corners of her wide mouth. Slowly she moved toward him, her nearly unbuttoned robe showing tantalizing glimpses of those long legs with every step. She stopped at his knees, let her gaze drop, then move up to meet his. "He certainly seems to be."

Sweet Jesus. Never—not once—in a single one of his sweaty dreams about Her Ladyship had he ever thought they would have a conversation about his privates. Grinning, he let his trousers drop to the floor and he pulled her closer. "Do you post?"

"Letters?" she asked innocently.

"On horseback."

"Sidesaddle?"

"I was thinking astride, but we can try that later if you'd like." And lifting her astraddle his lap, he proceeded to give her a second and even more enjoyable lesson in the finer points of Western-style horsemanship.

"Now are you hungry?" he asked later, once his heart had slowed and he was able to think again.

She pulled her robe closed. "I do believe I am."

He set her onto the bed beside him and, while he still had some control left, did up the more crucial of her buttons. "Anything left from supper?"

Knowing the brothers, Jessica doubted it. "There may be some ham in the larder." She watched the play of muscles across his shoulders as he bent to retrieve his trousers from the floor. On impulse she reached out to stroke the long hard-muscled plane of his back. She couldn't help herself. She was a creature she no longer recognized, driven by urges and emotions beyond her experience. He was her obsession, the blood pumping through her body, the marrow in her bones. With his magical touch he had driven out the fear and awakened within her a need and a passion she had never known was there.

She was changed forever.

Perhaps she would regret it tomorrow. But for now, she reveled in him—in the salty taste of his skin, the husky whisper of his voice, the feel of his body, like heated marble, beneath her stroking palm. He was utterly beautiful to her.

He grinned over his shoulder at her. "At least let me eat something to get my strength back."

Had she spoken her thoughts aloud? She should have been mortified. Instead, she laughed and lightly scored his back with her nails, leaving faint red lines on the smooth sun-browned skin. "Dolt."

He stood. "Don't go anywhere," he said as he padded barefoot across the room. "I've got plans for you." At the door, he turned and gave her a satyr's grin. "Ever play leapfrog?"

"You're depraved."

"Exactly." Laughing softly, he slipped into the hall.

Jessica fell back across the bed and watched lamplight dance across the ceiling. Was it real? Was the fear truly gone? Had this night truly happened?

Her body said it had. She ached in unusual places, had whisker scrapes in other unusual places, and felt as wrung out as a charwoman's washrag. But she also felt like a woman well and truly loved. And no matter what tomorrow might bring, she would never regret that.

As Brady came into the kitchen from the larder, his arms full of assorted edibles, he heard an odd noise, like cracking wood, coming from the direction of the barn. His first thought was that his brothers had ridden in, then that Bullshot had chewed through the hitching post. But even as he dumped his plunder onto the table, he discounted both notions. He'd heard no horses, and when last he looked, Bullshot was working on the rope, not the post.

That itchy, anxious feeling returned full force.

He quickly blew out the lamp and moved to the window.

Dim moonlight highlighted the angular shapes of the barn and corrals. Even though everything was in shades of gray, he could make out the larger details. The barn doors were closed, as he'd left them. The loft opening was a dark hole, but he couldn't see Rufus in the shadows. Below it he could make out the water trough and hitching post—no

Bullshot—and on the ground near the doors, what looked like a busted crate. The crate Ru had been sitting on. Had it fallen and that was the sound Brady had heard?

Maybe.

Maybe not.

Moving quickly down the hall to the office, he grabbed the Winchester, made sure it was loaded, then went back to the kitchen. He peered out the window but saw nothing amiss. The night was silent as a tomb.

He crossed to the hall.

At the door onto the porch he paused to chamber a round into the rifle, then slowly lifted the heavy iron door latch. He slipped outside. For a moment he hung in the shadows, letting his eyes fully adjust to the darkness while he scanned the yard and barn. No movement. The cabins and bunkhouse were dark. Not even a cricket chirped. On bare feet, he moved down the steps and across the yard.

The object by the doors was a busted crate. Ru had probably dozed off, slipped from the crate, and in the process, accidentally kicked it out the loft opening.

Maybe.

Maybe not.

He moved toward the barn. The doors were closed but not bolted. Yet he remembered sliding the wooden crossbar into place after getting Bullshot's tie rope. He knew better than to leave the barn open at night, especially in grizzly and cougar country. Something was wrong and his gut told him what.

Sancho.

Finally.

A sense of exhilaration swept through him. Then he thought of Jessica and Ben and Sam and all the others he had fought so hard to protect, and that sudden burst of energy settled into a cold and desperate resolve. He would end this now, and if both he and Sancho died in the process, then at least those left behind would be free of this damn feud.

But he had no intention of dying. Not tonight. And not by Sancho's hand.

He considered his options. There weren't many. He debated going to the cabins for more men. But if Ru was hurt and Brady went for help, that would leave the house unprotected—with Jessica and Ben and Elena inside. And if he went back for them, that would leave a hurt or dying man in the barn with Sancho.

He was on his own, and he had to make his move now before Sancho got into the house or set another fire. He took a deep breath, let it out. Flattening against the wall of the barn, he crept forward, rifle cocked and ready.

Movement behind him.

He whirled. But before he could find a target, something slammed into the side of his head.

He staggered, felt the rifle slip from his hands, then his legs gave way.

Twenty-two

JESSICA TOOK ADVANTAGE OF BRADY'S ABSENCE TO DO A QUICK wash and don a fresh gown, then she brushed the tangles from her hair and tied it back with a ribbon. The air had cooled as it did in the middle of the night, so she put on a heavier robe and made sure Adrian was well covered. Then she sat on the edge of the bed and waited for Brady.

Her intended. The man she was going to marry. Her lover.

She pressed her fingertips against her lips to keep from laughing aloud. Who would have thought such a thing possible? Certainly not she. Four months ago she had been in desperate flight, pregnant and alone with an uncertain future—a future that almost ended under the hot desert sky. Yesterday she had been so burdened with fear she had almost condemned herself to a lifetime of loneliness. Now she was to be married to a strong, decent man with battered hands and a craggy face that hid a kind and loving heart. How unpredictable and wondrous life could be.

Not that the fear was gone forever. She knew a small part of it would always remain, but no longer would she allow it to rule her. It was manageable now, easily tucked into a back corner of her mind where it would gradually fade into another unpleasant memory best left alone. Brady had done that for her. He had freed her. For that gift she would love him forever.

For that and other things as well.

She flopped back onto the bed as memories rushed over her. *Hallelujah, indeed.*

She realized she must have dozed off when something sent her lurching upright, her heart pounding. Groggy and disoriented, she glanced around. Brady hadn't returned. Adrian slept peacefully in his crib. Then what? She went to the door, but saw no one in the hall and no light in the direction of the kitchen. Curious, she stepped into her slippers and left the room.

The kitchen was empty. Although the lamp was unlit, there was enough moonlight coming through the window for her to see the food scattered in disarray across the tabletop. But no Brady.

Uneasy, she went back into the hall. Seeing the door onto the porch ajar, she went outside. He wasn't there either. She was becoming concerned when she noticed the faint yellow glow of lamplight shining through a crack in the barn door. He must be checking on Bullshot. The poor dog had developed the most annoying habit of howling his displeasure at being penned up and Brady must have gone to quiet him. Not that he could. The man was incapable of disciplining the rambunctious hound and was doubtless bribing him instead.

Smiling, she went down the steps and across the yard. As she approached the doors, she saw something on the ground beside a broken crate. Alarmed, she stopped and scanned it from a safe distance. Because of its long shape, she thought at first it was a snake, then she saw the glint of moonlight off metal and realized it was Brady's rifle. She studied it in confusion, knowing he would never toss it onto the ground nor be so careless as to leave it out in the night air. Careful lest it was loaded, she picked it up.

She was no stranger to long guns. Papa had taught her and George to use his scattergun and had even allowed her to accompany them on a few grouse hunts. But she had no experience with repeating rifles. Even so, she could see that the hammer was back, which meant it was cocked and ready to fire. Had he been preparing to shoot but was interrupted before he could? Shoot at what?

Voices rose in the barn. She recognized Brady's low rumble even if she couldn't make out the words. The other was heavily accented, angry. She stiffened, suddenly alert. Rifle in hand, she eased forward to peer through the gap in the unlatched doors.

Her heart lurched in her chest.

Brady was lashed to the center pole, his wrists bound by a rope hanging from the overhead beam. Blood was everywhere—oozing from a cut on his temple, streaking down his arms from his lacerated wrists, running in red rivulets from two long cuts below his collarbones. It soaked the waistband of his trousers and stained the straw at his feet.

For a stunned moment she couldn't move or think. Then she saw Sancho and the bloody knife in his hand. When he stepped toward Brady, she flew into motion. "Stop!" she cried, yanking open the door.

Sancho whirled.

"Put it down!" she ordered, aiming the wobbling rifle barrel at his chest. "Now!"

"Shoot! Do it!"

Startled, she looked at Brady, scarcely recognizing his voice. His eyes were wild with terror. She knew that look, that fear. Trapped. Tied. Helpless.

From the corner of her eye, she saw Sancho rush toward her.

She jumped back, heard motion behind her, and squeezed the trigger just as Bullshot hurtled through the door, crashing against her hip and knocking her off balance. Noise exploded in her head. The recoil sent her staggering backward. Bullshot lunged for Sancho.

The barn erupted in chaos—snarls, shouts, screaming. Panting with terror, she struggled to pull the hammer back. Her fingers felt numb. It took her two tries before it snapped into the cocked position. She raised the rifle just as Sancho landed a vicious kick that sent the hound slamming against a stall door. With a yelp of pain, the dog crumpled into the straw.

Sancho swung toward her.

She squeezed the trigger.

The hammer clicked down, but the rifle didn't fire.

"Work the lever!" Brady shouted.

Desperately, she thumbed the hammer back. Squeezed again. Click.

Sancho kept coming.

Blood roared through her head. Her hands shook so badly her fingers wouldn't work as she tried to cock the hammer a third time.

"Work the lever! Work the lever!"

What lever?

Then it was too late.

Sancho yanked the rifle from her hands and drove his fist against the side of her head.

Pain blinded her. She slammed to the ground, ears ringing. She heard Brady yelling as Ramirez kicked her in the side, driving the air from her lungs. Then he jerked her to her feet and locked his arm around her throat, cutting off her air. She bucked, raking at him with her nails, as blackness crowded the edges of her vision. Growling like a beast, he dragged her toward the stalls, lifted the smoking lantern from a hook, then dragged her toward Brady.

Gasping for air, Jessica clung to the arm around her throat. Surely someone had heard the gunshot. Surely someone would come. *God send them now.*

"This is your whore, yes?" Sancho snarled.

"Let her go." Brady's voice was hoarse with fear. Jessica scarcely recognized him through the blood. So much blood. "Do whatever you want to me, but let her go."

Sancho gave a laugh that made her mind reel with terror. "I will enjoy using her like your father used my mother." Her gorge rose as he licked the side of her face, his breath hot and rank against her skin. "I like white meat."

Her knees threatened to buckle.

Shouting and cursing, Brady fought the ropes so hard the overhead beam groaned. "Jessica, fight! Don't give up!"

She tried, but every time she moved, he squeezed his arm tighter around her throat.

Sancho lifted the lantern high. "If you get out of this barn alive, *pendejo*, you know where to find me and what is left of your *puta*. If not . . ."

He slung the lantern in a high arc toward the front doors. It hit with a crash of shattered glass. Flames whooshed to life, quickly fed by the straw on the floor. Within a heartbeat, hell opened at their feet.

Over the roar of flames, Sancho taunted, "If not, know that I have your woman, *pinche cabrón*. Think about what I will be doing to her while you burn." Grabbing her breast with his free hand, he gave it a brutal squeeze.

She tried to twist away but his hold was too tight.

Brady bucked, blood running down his arms.

Laughing, Sancho dragged her toward the back of the barn.

In mindless terror, she fought him, kicking and clawing, but growing weaker by the moment. She felt herself falling, fading. Dimly she heard Brady shouting, and with the last of her strength, she twisted to look back at him.

Her eyes locked on to his. And for a single instant, everything stopped—as if there were no time or space, no sound, or pain, or fear. She watched his lips move, struggled to hear the words over the thundering in her head.

"Stay alive! I'll come for you! Stay alive!"

Then smoke billowed up, blinding her. The last thing she saw as Sancho dragged her through the door was the loft catching fire.

THE ROPES FELL AWAY AND BRADY WAS FREE.

He floated. Sound receded. The air cooled and pinpricks of light danced overhead. *I'm dying*, he thought just before he slammed to earth.

"Breathe!" a voice shouted in his face.

Numbness exploded in choking terror. Hands pawed at him as his body convulsed, fighting for air. Slowly the spasms eased enough that he could draw breath into his burning lungs. He opened his eyes.

Buck's face bobbed above him in a pool of starlight. "Leave off, Red. He comin' to." He patted Brady's shoulder, his faded eyes filled with concern. "Easy, boy. You be jist fine."

"Jessica." Brady bolted up then fell back, coughing. "He's got Jessica."

"We gittin' the horses now."

"Ru . . . ?"

Red shook his head. "Bastard slit his throat. We found the hound, though. Busted bad. Iantha's tending him."

Dead, dying. *Jessica.*

He struggled to sit up, then rolled onto his hands and knees as nausea bubbled in his throat. He hung there, head sagging, while Buck told him he'd sent for his brothers and set men working the fire, but it looked like the barn was a goner for sure.

Brady barely heard him. Groaning with the effort, he worked a knee under his body then pushed. Pain burned across his chest where he'd been cut. He slumped back, half sick. "Boots," he told Red. Each word burned in his raw throat. "Jacket. The Colt."

He tried again and this time made it onto his feet. He staggered for balance, found it, and breathed deep to clear his head. "My horse." When Buck tried to argue, Brady cut him off. "Stay. Mind the fire. I'll get her."

Beams buckled as the barn roof fell in. Flames shot a hundred feet into the air and sparks danced through the night sky like a million fireflies.

Somewhere out there Jessica waited. He had to go. He had to find her.

"Consuelo said to put this on." Red held out a jar of salve.

Brady scooped a gob, smeared it over the cuts on his chest and wrists, then reached for his boots. Pain shot across his shoulders, up his neck, and suddenly everything tilted.

Red shoved him back upright and held him there until Brady got his boots on. Then he handed him a shirt. By the time Brady fumbled through the buttons, the cuts had reopened and the shirt stuck to him. He pulled on the jacket then reached for the gunbelt and Colt.

"You sure you're up for this?" Red asked.

Brady ground his teeth as he worked at the buckle. His hands wouldn't work. His eyes wouldn't work. Everything jumped around so bad he couldn't get the holes lined up. He took a breath and tried again. Finally it hooked. He stood shivering, his mind spinning.

"Maybe you should wait for your brothers."

He blinked at Red, wondering why there were two of him, why his head hurt so bad, why he was still so dizzy he could hardly balance. Touching his head where Sancho hit him, he felt a hard, sticky knot the size of a quail egg.

Buck led a skittish bay past the burning barn. It took Brady three tries to get his foot in the stirrup and pull himself into the saddle. "He took her to the cave." He reined the nervous horse toward the moon-tipped silhouette of Blue Mesa. "Send my brothers there."

"Estamos cerca."

Jessica scarcely heard him over the ringing in her ears, her mind so sluggish she had to look at everything twice before it made sense. She was surprised to see they had left the rolling flats of the valley behind and now rode into a shadowed canyon. Trees loomed darkly ahead, crowded against sheer walls that rose hundreds of feet into the starlit sky.

The horse slowed to splash its way across a rocky creek bed. As it scrambled up the other side, the upward angle threw her back against the man riding behind her. With a shudder, she jerked upright, clutching the horse's sweaty mane in nerveless fingers.

She tried to pull her scattered thoughts together, but the pain in her temple was so intense every plodding step the horse took felt like a hammer blow inside her head. Sancho had hit her. She remembered he wanted her to get on the horse but she'd fought him because—

Oh God, Brady . . .

She clamped her eyes shut as images flooded her mind. Was he still in there? Burning? Dying? Dead? Slumping over the horse's withers, she retched but nothing came out.

Stay alive—I'll come for you.

Clinging to that hope, she pushed herself upright and tried to bring her fear under control.

The horse moved silently across a thick carpet of pine needles as they climbed deeper into the canyon. Trees closed overhead, shutting out the faint glow of the moon. The scent of pine mingled with the stench of smoke and sweat and blood that came from the man behind her.

Why had he taken her? If it was just to kill her, why hadn't he already done it? If not . . . if he intended to force her . . . God, she couldn't endure that again.

The trail grew steeper. She leaned forward, brushing her forehead against the horse's neck rather than let her back touch the man behind her. And still they climbed. The horse labored, its sides pumping. Its neck grew foamy with sweat.

How could Brady find them? How would he know where Sancho had taken her?

"Estamos aquí." They stopped.

She looked around as Sancho dismounted. They were in a small clearing ringed by tall trees and boulders. A steep slope rose on one side. From the other came the gurgle of a stream. The air smelled of old camp smoke and garbage and urine.

Sancho yanked her from the saddle. When her legs started to buckle, he jerked her upright.

"Don't touch me," she ground out, pushing at his hand.

He let her go and turned to strip the weary horse. While he was distracted, she looked back the way they'd come, wondering if she could find her way in the dark. She had seen the bloodstained tear in his trousers where she had stabbed him when he had attacked Elena. He probably couldn't go far or run as fast as she. If she could get a head start and maybe hide until—

His hand clamped over her arm. "*Vámonos*," he snarled and started up the slope, pulling her after him.

There was no path, just a dusty track of rocks and brush that seemed to go on forever, heading nowhere. Twice she fell. He didn't slow, but dragged her after him until she struggled back upright. She lost her slippers. Sharp rocks lacerated the soles of her feet. Blood trickled from a cut on her shin and her scraped knees burned with every step.

When they reached the top, she was panting with pain and terror, her feet on fire and her shoulder throbbing from being yanked along. Lifting her head, she saw huge boulders framing a yawning blackness. She knew then that he had taken her to his cave hideout.

Hope sparked in her mind. Brady would know that. He would find her. If he was still alive.

Sancho pushed her ahead of him into the opening. She stumbled, blinded by the dark. Terror clutched at her throat as she gulped in musty air that carried a sickly sweet smell, like the memory of decay.

A match flared. A moment later, he walked toward her with a smoking lantern in his hand. Grabbing her arm again, he pulled her toward the back. As they moved deeper, a heaviness closed around her, awakening that fear of confinement, of being tied and smothered. She clenched her teeth to keep from screaming, knowing if she started, she wouldn't be able to stop.

They came to an opening in the back wall. He ducked inside and yanked her after him. She didn't know to bend and struck her head on the rocky ceiling. She stumbled, but he jerked her along, muttering in Spanish under his breath. Water dripped onto her back as she followed him at a crouch. The rocky floor felt slimy under her bare feet. A sharp turn, a few more yards, then the tunnel opened into another, taller cavern. He set the lantern on a rocky shelf then shoved her toward the back corner.

She tripped on her robe and fell to her knees. Too exhausted to rise, she crawled over to the rocky wall and slumped against it, watching as he paced the small cavern.

He limped. She was right; the wound she gave him still bothered him. She wished it had festered and killed him. She wished she had stabbed him in the heart instead.

Lamplight cast wavering shadows along the walls. Shivering as the cold seeped from the rocks into her body, she pulled the tattered robe tightly around her and watched him pace back and forth, muttering, his voice whispering off the rocks, rustling across her nerves like spiders on the march. He seemed to be struggling with himself, with some decision. The way he glanced at her every few steps told her it had to do with her.

Her teeth began to chatter, whether from the cold or fear, she didn't know. The only thing that kept her sane was the knowledge that Brady would come. He said he would and he always kept his promises.

Be alive . . . please be alive to come for me.

She tried to picture Adrian's face, his perfect little hands. Instead she saw flames, Brady twisting in the ropes—and her despair was so intense it sucked all hope from her mind.

Weeping, she dropped her head onto her crossed arms. *God let him be alive.*

The muttering and pacing stopped.

She looked up.

Sancho crouched against the far wall, watching her with the feral intensity of a predator watching its prey. He rocked back and forth, his long hair swinging in front of his face. Through the matted tangles she saw the glitter of eyes so black they seemed without pupils, without depth or mercy. The eyes of insanity.

Her heart drummed frantically against the walls of her chest. She tried to calm it, reaching out with her mind for hope, a prayer, a plan, anything to keep her from splintering to pieces.

Stay alive—I'll come for you.

He stopped rocking. His gaze moved over her. She watched his tongue flick out to wet his lips, and a whimper of terror swelled in her throat. A new tension moved through the air. She felt it, and like a caged beast turning from the prod even though there was no place to run, she crawled blindly along the wall toward a shadowed corner.

Then suddenly he was on her, his hands around her neck. "Whore!" he shrieked, lifting her up and pinning her to the wall.

She clawed at his eyes. He jerked back. She kicked, trying to hit his injured leg. He kneed her in the hip. She thrashed and flailed in helpless terror, a high-pitched cry tearing from her throat.

"*Ellos están muertos.* Dead! All but you, Maria. Why?" Still gripping her throat, he slammed her again and again against the wall. "How many times do I kill you before you die?"

"I-I'm not M-Maria," she whimpered, ears ringing, the pain in her head so intense she could hardly speak. "I'm Je-Jessica."

Something moved behind his eyes—a shadow there then gone, replaced by a look of such unbridled fury she thought he would end it then, tighten his grip on her throat until it was over.

Then as suddenly as it came, the fury left him. His grip loosened. As Jessica gulped in air, his gaze drifted over her face. He smiled, a slow, crafty smile that showed gaps in his broken teeth. "His whore . . . now mine."

That look. Oh God oh God.

With his free hand he yanked open her robe. "Do you spread your legs for him, *puta*? Does he touch you like this?" Grabbing her breast, he twisted until she cried out. He moved his hand to her crotch and thrust at her with his fingers. "Does he put his fingers into you?"

Sobbing with terror, she tried to push him away, close her legs against his prying hand.

"Do you like it rough, *puta*?" He ground his pelvis against hers.

"D-Don't—no—please God . . ." The rank smell of him filled her nostrils, sent bile surging in her throat. His breath was a hot blast against her face as he fumbled to open his trousers. She felt him press his body against her and something in her mind shattered. Everything went silent and still. She felt herself slipping away, drifting beyond the pain and terror.

She wanted to give in to it. She wanted to fall into nothingness. She wanted to die.

Fight. Stay alive—I'll come for you.

Like a hand pulling her from drowning waters, Brady's voice called her back. Gasping and choking, she fought her way out of the darkness. With a scream of outrage, she launched herself at Sancho, clawing at his face, his eyes, yanking at his hair.

Caught off-balance, he stumbled back, hands up to ward her off.

She drove her knee into his groin.

He doubled over.

Screaming and cursing, she kicked again and again, her bare foot ineffective until it landed against his injured leg.

He buckled and fell backward.

She raced across the cave, frantically searching for a weapon—a rock, a stick—anything to use against him. She saw the lantern and snatched it from the shelf. She heard him move up behind her and whirled, swinging the lantern as hard as she could.

A crack—then a shower of kerosene and glass as the lamp exploded against the side of his face. Flames engulfed his head. He screamed, batting at his face, his hair, his shirt. Then suddenly he was a human torch lurching blindly, arms flailing, his inhuman shrieks ricocheting off the rocky walls.

In mindless horror, she scrambled into the tunnel.

BRADY HEARD SCREAMS AS HE CHARGED UP THE ROCKY SLOPE. He had heard agony like that only one other time in his life—the day Sam died. Hearing those blood-chilling wails now and knowing Jessica was in there sent such a wave of terror through him he almost lost his footing. Heart pounding, he raced through the arched entrance just as something sailed out of the darkness and slammed into him.

He stumbled back, raising an arm to knock it aside, then froze when he recognized the voice and the body pressed against his. "Jessica?" he choked out, his arms locking around her, so weak with relief his legs threatened to give way.

She clung to him, shaking and crying. "Y-You're a-alive, you're alive." Her arms were so tight around his neck he could hardly breathe.

The shrieking from the back of the cave stopped.

Trying desperately to stay focused, he pulled back and trapped her face in his trembling hands to keep her still. "Are you hurt? Did he hurt you?"

She shook her head, her teeth chattering so hard she could hardly speak. "I th-thought you were d-dead—I thought he—"

"Shhh . . . it's over." He kissed her, kissed her again, then again, wanting to pull her inside him so he could keep her with him and safe forever. "I'm here. It's over." With shaking fingers he wiped red smears from her face, hoping it was his blood, not hers. "You're safe now."

She saw his bloody fingers and recoiled. "You're bleeding! Your cuts."

From the darkness came a noise—part whimper, part cry—a sound no human should make.

Jessica threw herself against him. "He's still alive! How can he still be alive?"

Thrusting her behind him, Brady scanned the darkness at the back of the cave. He caught a whiff of something rank and sickeningly familiar, but saw no movement. "Where is he?"

"I h-hit him with the lantern and—and he started burning and—"

Voices behind them, then Hank and Jack ran through the entrance, panting, guns drawn.

Quickly Brady told them what happened and that Sancho was still alive in the back of the cave. "Hank, stay with Jessica. You wouldn't fit in the tunnel. Jack, come with me." Spotting a lantern by the entrance, he lit it and headed toward the back of the cave, Jack trailing behind.

"What's that smell?" Jack asked as they ducked into the tunnel opening.

"Sancho."

"Jesus, did she burn him?"

The stink grew stronger the deeper they went, almost making Brady gag. Wishing he had a kerchief to pull over his mouth and nose, he crawled through the tunnel into the inner cavern. As soon as he had headroom, he straightened and held the lantern high. It was a grisly sight.

"Damn," Jack muttered, his voice muffled behind his hand. He looked around, then nodded toward the broken lantern. "She must have hit him with that."

Thank God this time she fought.

"Fried him good, didn't she?"

"She was fighting for her life, Jack."

"I'm not complaining. Saves us a bullet."

Holding his shirttail over his nose and mouth, Brady bent over Sancho's twisted, smoking body to see if he was still alive.

He was. Barely. His face looked melted. His lips were gone, his teeth showing in a ghoulish grimace. His seeping eyes were open but Brady couldn't tell if they saw anything. He was breathing but appeared to be unconscious.

Suddenly all the fury that had eaten away at him for twenty years uncoiled in Brady's mind. He reached for his pistol. "I've got you now, you sonofabitch." Drawing the Colt, he thumbed the hammer back and pointed the barrel at Sancho's head.

But he couldn't pull the trigger.

His hand started to shake. Gritting his teeth, he squeezed the pistol grip so hard his swollen knuckles turned white. Still, he couldn't pull the trigger. It was as if he had turned to stone, his mind shouting orders but his body unable to move.

Sancho made a garbled sound, his scorched body jerking with spasms.

Slowly the rage faded, leaving a sour taste in Brady's mouth and an ache behind his eyes. This was what he wanted, he reminded himself. A long, agonizing death was what Sancho deserved. Shutting his mind to the tortured breathing, he eased the hammer down and reholstered the pistol.

"You're not going to shoot him?" Jack asked.

"Let him suffer." For Sam. For Jessica and Ru and all the others. He turned to his brother. "You and Hank take Jessica to the ranch. Sancho set the barn on fire. It could spread to the house."

"What about you? You're bleeding like a stuck pig."

"Send someone for Doc. He can tend to me when I get back."

"You're staying?"

Suddenly Brady felt so weary he was light-headed. Every muscle ached. The cuts on his chest throbbed and his throat still burned from all the smoke he'd inhaled. Moving to the other side of the cave, he slumped down against the wall where the air was less rank. Mindful of his lacerated wrists and swollen hands, he rested his folded arms on his upraised knees and leaned back. "I'll wait. This shouldn't take long." After twenty years and more death and destruction than he wanted to contemplate, it was fitting he and Sancho should spend these last hours together.

Jack left.

Silence, except for the rasp of Sancho's breathing. Brady watched his struggle and thought of all the people this smoldering ruin of a man had hurt. And for what? A piece of land?

It sickened him.

Maybe Jessica was right. Maybe he should walk away. Start over somewhere else.

As soon as that thought popped into his mind, all the reasons it would never work shouted it down. And the one that kept resounding in his head the loudest was the one hardest to overlook: Without the ranch, who was he? What would he do if he started over? How would he live the years he had left? A man needed something to hold on to. Something bigger than himself. If he couldn't build something lasting and worthwhile, what was all the struggle for?

"Was it worth it, Sancho?" he asked wearily.

Sancho had no answer.

Brady didn't either. He just wanted it over.

Time passed, measured by the slow dimming of the lamp and the gradual stiffening in Brady's battered body. He tried to rest but couldn't, plagued by a steady march of memories. He realized that with Sancho dead, he would never know who killed Maria and Don Ramon. In his mind he saw his father's slack face, his haunted eyes begging for understanding, and it came to him that he no longer cared about his father's guilt. His own lack of forgiveness troubled him more. It shamed him that he had let his father die without giving him that at least.

So many wasted years, so many mistakes. There had to have been a better way.

Wearily he dropped his head into his crossed arms, wishing he could start over, do things different. But what? This was what he was, what his life was all about—struggling to dig out an existence in a land that didn't want to be conquered, fighting for just one more day, one more chance, hoping tomorrow would be better. If he walked away from the ranch, he'd be walking away from himself.

Sancho's breathing changed.

Brady looked up to see the dying man twitch, his seared muscles jerking and flexing. His moans echoed along the walls. "*Ayú . . . da . . . me . . .*"

Moving stiffly, Brady rose and crossed the cave. He stared down at the charred face, watched those blind eyes move toward him. Sancho said something but Brady couldn't make it out. Trying not to breathe, he leaned closer.

"H-hel . . . ne," Sancho rasped, with only his blistered tongue to form the words. *Help me.*

Brady straightened, repelled by the stink, the moans, the utter agony reflected in those sightless eyes. Walking to the far wall, he rested his palm against the cool sandstone and tried to shut his mind to the sound of that raspy voice. He didn't want to feel sympathy for this pitiful wreck of a man. Vengeance was in his hands. He didn't want to weaken.

"Shoot . . . ne . . ."

Brady squeezed his eyes shut as the past pressed against him, demanding its due. Vengeance or mercy? He wasn't sure what he was supposed to do anymore . . . what any of it meant or why it all rested on him now. He was so sick of the hate and killing, he felt like he was drowning in blood.

He wanted it over. He needed it to be over. Now.

"*Dios* . . ."

With grim determination, Brady drew the Colt and walked toward Sancho. Lifting the pistol, he cocked it and aimed at Sancho's head. He took a deep breath. Silence thundered through his head. Too much silence. He lowered the gun.

Bending over Sancho, he searched for movement, some sign that he still lived. Nothing.

He straightened and slipped the gun back into the holster.

For a minute he stood there, unable to walk away, waiting for something—some sense of satisfaction, of triumph. But he felt nothing beyond a soul-deep weariness. The feud that had consumed him for most of his life was finally over. The enemy he had battled for two decades lay dead at his feet. He'd won. Shouldn't he feel something more than this empty relief?

When no answers came, he picked up the lantern and left the cave.

He decided to leave Sancho where he was. At first he had thought to give the body to the sheriff, like he'd done with Alvarez. But at some point during those long hours while he waited for Sancho to die, Brady realized that, for better or worse, this broken man was as much a part of RosaRoja as he was. In his own twisted way, Sancho loved this land, too. Maybe it was weakness, or maybe he didn't care anymore, but Brady decided to let him stay. He'd get some black powder or a few sticks of dynamite from one of the mines nearby, and seal Sancho in his cave forever. But for now, he stacked rocks in the tunnel opening to keep scavengers out and let it go at that.

It was long past dawn when he finally trudged down the slope to where his horse waited.

As he rode toward home, a spark of hope ignited in his weary mind, and with every step away from the cave it grew. Maybe without the feud hanging over his head, things would be different. Maybe he could build something worthwhile, find a better way to spend the years he had left. With Jessica beside him, anything was possible. She had a way of making him feel like he could do it all.

Riding down into the home valley, he noticed a pall of smoke hanging in the still air, turning the sun a deep orange in the morning sky. Despite the thickening smoke, he could still see the glow of the fire long before he reached the compound. And when he finally got close enough to see the extent of the destruction, he reined in, staring in shock.

The barn and paddocks were lost. The house was a sheet of crackling flames. Most of the outbuildings had been reduced to tangled piles of glowing timbers. The only things standing were a few of the more remote cabins and the loafing shed. It looked like the fires of hell.

He stared in disbelief, unable to get his mind around what his eyes were seeing. Gone. Everything. The losses were immeasurable, not just because Ru had died or because of all the structures that were lost. It was the loss of years—decades of backbreaking work—years he didn't have anymore. He was thirty-three. Not in his lifetime could he make RosaRoja into even a shadow of what it once was.

Gone. All of it.

A sudden tightness gripped his chest. He couldn't breathe, couldn't think. Slumping over the saddle horn, he struggled to pull air into his aching lungs as his mind grappled with the terrible reality that faced him. He saw nothing ahead but endless toil and years of struggle.

Could he even survive a future like that? Probably.

Could Jessica? Probably not. And he couldn't even ask her to try. *Sweet Jesus.*

A terrible emptiness spread within him. He saw everything clearly now, all his failures, his sins—Sam, Jacob, Paco, and Sancho—all the bloodshed, the forgiveness withheld—all the mistakes he'd made as he'd blindly forged ahead on a path he'd never questioned.

This was his accounting, his payback for all the sins of the past.

He was doomed and damned.

But he wouldn't bring Jessica down with him.

Suddenly dizzy, he gripped the pommel with both hands, fighting for balance as he realized the full extent of the debt he had to pay. More than the destruction of the ranch, more than the end of the dream, it was the loss of Jessica that would bring him to his knees.

With an anguished cry, Brady lifted his face to the bloodred sky.

His day of reckoning had come.

Twenty-three

JACK MET HIM AS BRADY RODE UP. "IT'S OVER?"

"It's over." Brady reined in, even though what he wanted to do was ride on, find Jessica, try to salvage something from the ruin of his life. But he'd carried the weight of responsibility too long to shrug it off now. His brothers, all these people who were a part of RosaRoja, depended on him. This was their home, too, and their futures going up in smoke same as his.

Jack pulled off his hat and mopped his brow, leaving sooty smears across his face. "It's bad, Brady. But unless the wind kicks up again, I think the worst is over."

Brady studied the collection of furniture, clothing, and kitchen items piled in the yard. Beyond it, men leaned wearily on rakes and hoes and pitchforks, while others slapped at escaping sparks with wet rags and burlap sacks. "Anyone hurt?"

"Blisters here and there. A couple of the horses may have to be put down. Hank's working on them now. It could be worse, I guess."

Brady thought of Ru and Jessica and wondered how.

Jack settled the hat back on his head. "We salvaged what food we could from the house and larder and moved it to the loafing shed. Elena and the other women are there now, helping Sandoval put together some grub for the men."

"Jessica and Ben?"

"Bedded down at Buck's." Stepping back so that Brady could move on, Jack added, "Iantha left clean clothes for you on the porch."

Brady nodded and reined his horse toward the small cabin where Buck and Iantha lived. Despite how badly he wanted to reassure himself that Jessica was safe, a part of him didn't want to see her. Now that he knew he had to cut her out of his life, he didn't think he could stand the pain of being around her. When he thought about loving her last night and how it had felt to have her wrapped around him, her breathy voice whispering his name in his ear, that feeling of loss rose up so strong it almost choked him.

How could he convince her to walk away from this nightmare?

How would he go on when she did?

Moving with painful soreness, he dismounted and tied the bay to a post by the cabin's front porch. He stripped beside the trough. After rinsing off as much of the dried blood as he could, and reopening the cuts in the process, he pulled on clean trousers from the pile Iantha had left on the porch, grabbed his clean shirt and bloody clothes, and went inside.

The house was quiet. He was both relieved and disappointed to see no sign of Jessica or Ben. But Doc was there, slouched at the kitchen table with Buck's whiskey jug. His eyes widened when he saw the bloody cuts. "Saint's preserve us, lad. What did the bastard use? A pig sticker?"

"Something like that." Brady dabbed at the blood with his dirty shirt, then gave up and tossed it aside. Slumping into the chair across from Doc, he motioned to the jug. "Pass it over."

Doc did, then reached for his medicine satchel. "Take a healthy dose," he advised. "You'll be needing it, I'm thinking."

Despite all the blood, the cuts weren't as deep as they looked and required less than a couple of dozen stitches. The cuts on his wrists would be fine with Consuelo's slippery elm salve, and the rawness in his throat should pass in a day or two unless it developed into a prolonged cough, which might indicate more damage to the lungs than Doc suspected. Although the headaches might linger awhile, the head wound was minor, and Doc said that despite all the bruising, he didn't think anything was broken or cracked. All in all, Brady was lucky.

He didn't feel lucky.

After Doc left, Brady pulled on the clean shirt and reached for the jug again. He took a deep swallow. Then another. It didn't help. No new insights softened the bleakness of reality. Nothing changed what had happened or what it meant, and as the sun crawled across the smoky sky, he gave up trying.

Dropping his head onto his crossed arms, he closed his eyes and surrendered to the numbness of sleep.

IN THE SPARE BEDROOM DOWN THE HALL, JESSICA AWOKE with a lurch that brought her up on her elbows, heart pounding. Then she saw Adrian sleeping in his cradle by the dresser and relief sent her sagging back against the pillows. She resisted the impulse to rush over and pick him up, to reassure herself yet again that he was safe and unharmed. From the moment she had seen the house aflame until the moment Iantha had put him in her arms, Jessica had been almost paralyzed with fear. But it was over.

Adrian was safe, she was safe, Brady was safe.

Pushing back the quilt, she sat up. The room reeked of smoke. Hazy sunlight behind the lace curtain told her that it was well into the day, and even though she had lain down only a few hours ago, worry over Brady wouldn't allow her to remain in bed.

Moving quietly so she didn't wake Adrian, she washed and dressed as quickly as her bruised muscles would allow. She looked down at her bandaged feet and thought of Brady and his poor feet after hiking for help, and realized how far they had come since then. And yet, despite all the pain and heartache, they had found each other. And survived. What a gift that was.

Smiling, she rummaged through the pile of clothing stacked beside the bureau. Thankfully most of her personal belongings had been pulled from the house before the bedroom wing caught fire, so she had something clean to wear, even if it smelled of smoke. After plaiting her hair in a long thick braid, she tiptoed out, gently shut the door, and moved down the hall to the kitchen.

In the doorway she stopped, struck by the sight of Brady slumped at the table, his dark head resting on his folded arms.

He snored. The sound of it was so commonplace, so endearing, it brought tears to her eyes. For a long time she stood watching the rise and fall of his broad shoulders, the twitch of his big hands, the dark sweep of eyelashes against his sun-browned cheek. A few hours ago she had thought him dead, lost to her forever. Now he was snoring at the kitchen table. Alive.

"Thank you, God," she whispered, grateful tears running in hot streaks down her cheeks.

His head jerked up, eyes wide and searching. When he saw her in the doorway, he sat back and rubbed a palm across his face. He gave her a sleepy smile that quickly faded when he saw her tears. "What's wrong? Is Ben all right?"

"He's fine."

"Then why are you crying?"

"I'm happy." She wiped tears from her cheeks and gave him a wobbly smile. "I thought you were dead. I thought I was dead. We're not." More tears threatened, but she blinked them away. "That makes me happy and sometimes I cry when I'm happy."

"Well, don't. You know I don't like it." He held out his hand. "Come here."

She raised a brow. But despite the highhanded attitude and clipped words, there was something in his expression that compelled her, a vulnerability she had never seen in him before. He seemed so resigned, so weary.

"I just want to hold you, Jessica."

She moved toward him. As soon as she came within reach, he slid his arms around her waist and pulled her closer until his cheek lay over her heart. The gesture was intimate and possessive.

"Jessica," he said.

Just that. Nothing more.

But there was such emotion in the way he said it, it almost made her cry again.

Emboldened, she ran her fingers through the dark curls at the back of his neck and was rewarded by a slight lessening of the tension across his heavy shoulders. Closing her eyes, she surrendered to the scent of him, the warmth, the rightness of having his arms around her. It felt so good to be held again, to touch and be touched by this man. The joyful wonder of it was almost more than she could bear.

She felt a shudder go through him as she began to gently stroke the hard planes of his back, learning again the dip of his spine, the sharp ridges of his shoulder blades, the knotted muscles in between. A sense of possession moved through her, that feeling of connection she'd never known with anyone but him. She embraced it, craved it, needed it as much as she needed the next breath. Pressing her lips against the crown of his head, she said, "I love you, Brady."

His grip tightened. But he didn't speak.

She waited, confused by his silence. Growing alarmed but trying not to show it, she pulled away. "So, it's over then? The feud?" She tried to keep her voice light despite the tightness in her throat. Something was different. She stepped back.

His arms fell to his lap. "It's over. In all the ways that matter."

Horrid images of Sancho lurching and screaming chased her to the cookstove. She fussed with a blackened coffeepot, checked the coals, wiped her hands on a towel hanging from a peg. "I didn't mean to burn him," she blurted out. "He came at me and the lantern was all I could find. I didn't intend for him to die that way. But I'm not sorry he's dead."

"You shouldn't be."

She sensed him watching as she moved inanely around the room, touching this, straightening that, in futile attempts to mask the confusion in her mind. If not Sancho, then what? Something had changed. He was as distant as he had ever been, as if last night had never happened. She turned to face him. "Then what's wrong, Brady?"

He sighed wearily. "Sit down. We need to talk."

The way he said it reawakened all the doubts she thought she'd put behind her. Something had happened. He'd changed his mind. He didn't want to marry her anymore. She tried to cover her anguish with a smile, but all she could think was *Why?* Why had she believed him— why had he changed—why was it so hard for her to be loved? Her pride in tatters, she glanced at the door, caught between the urge to flee and the need to stay.

"Please, Jessica."

On wooden legs she walked to the table and sat. She had suffered betrayal before—Papa, George, Crawford—what man in her life had not hurt her or walked away from her? She had survived that. She would survive this, too. Hiking up her chin, she looked him in the eye.

"It won't work, Jessica. I can't see any way around it. It just won't work."

She noticed his voice sounded strained, and was glad he found this wretched conversation as difficult as she. "What won't work?" She needed to hear him say it.

"This. Us."

She thought she had prepared herself but she was wrong. Her body seemed to shrink into itself. Her throat felt so tight she could scarcely breathe. "I see," she finally managed. "It was all a lie then."

"No. Never. I—"

"You bloody bastard." Somehow she found the strength to stand. But before she could move away, his hand closed over her wrist.

"Wait. Let me explain—"

"It's not necessary."

"Yeah, it is."

"I don't want to hear it."

"Damnit, sit!"

She glared down at him, using anger to mask the hurt.

He glared back. Then he sighed and released her arm. "Damnit, sit . . . please."

She sat. But only because her legs felt too weak to hold her. Clutching her trembling hands in her lap, she struggled to adopt an expression of bored interest. Apparently some pathetic part of her needed to hear what he had to say. She hoped she had the courage to stay and listen.

She waited, watched him struggle over the words, and realized again she wasn't the only one suffering.

"My mother was a strong, capable woman," he said. "She had to be to raise four sons alone while my father was off fighting in the war. But once we came out here, the heart went out of her."

"My condolences." She rose.

"I'm not finished."

She sat back down.

He took a moment to regain his thoughts, then continued. "For years I told myself it was because she probably guessed Jacob had feelings for Maria. I realize now it was more than that. Life is hard out here, Jessica. More so for a woman."

What tripe. "And it is your intent to save me from hardship? How gallant." She would have laughed out loud if she hadn't been on the verge of striking him. "However, it is not necessary. I can save myself." *And you taught me.*

He seemed not to notice her acid tone. "I watched it suck the spirit out of my mother. I won't watch it happen to you. I won't let it happen to you."

"You won't *let* it?" A rush of fury propelled her from the chair. "Who gives you the right to decide what I can and cannot endure?" Before he could answer, she rushed on, her voice rising with every word. "Dear God, Brady, is anyone ever enough for you? Pure enough? Loyal enough? Strong enough? Your father, Jack, me. Are we all doomed to fall short in your eyes?"

"That's not what I meant."

"Isn't it?" Too agitated to stand still, she paced, gesturing wildly, her voice dripping disdain. "Already you've judged me and found me lacking. Without even giving me a chance, you cast me aside because *you* have decided I lack the fortitude to withstand a bit of adversity. You arrogant bastard!"

"If you'll just listen—"

"To what?" She stopped before him. "More fumbling excuses? Do you truly imagine a few setbacks would send me into a decline? I am not some hothouse tea rose, you dolt! And furthermore"—leaning down, she poked her finger square in his chest with enough force to send him halfway out of his chair—"despite the fact that I must continually remind you to curb your disreputable language and oafish behavior, I am bloody well *not* your bloody mother either!"

He gaped at her with that stupid look men get when confronted with their own idiocy.

So aggravated she could scarcely look at him, she drew herself up, planted her fists on her hips, and glared down at him. "If you no longer want me, say so. But do not *dare* think to convince me, or yourself, that you are doing it for my own good!" Whirling, she started for the door.

He caught her wrist. "That's not what I meant, Jessica!"

She tried to pull free.

He held her fast. "You call them setbacks, but have you looked outside lately?" He released her arm and waved toward the window. "I don't have a home anymore. Or a barn. Hell, I don't even have a damn outhouse."

Of course she'd noticed. She'd also noticed the blood spot blossoming on his shirtfront—exactly where he had been cut, exactly where she had poked him. Guilt and horror warred within her, but she managed to quell both. He deserved it. Besides, it wasn't spreading all that quickly. "So. Rebuild."

"Look at me."

She jerked her gaze from his chest. "You're bleeding."

"It's okay."

"I should check."

"It's okay." His look forbade her to fuss.

Fine, then. The dolt could bleed to death for all she cared.

"It would take years to rebuild," he went on in a taut voice. "Decades. I don't know if I have the fortitude to survive a future like that. But I damn sure know it would kill you."

"Rubbish. I'm English. We invented fortitude." She realized she was twisting her hands and forced herself to stop. *Please, God, don't let him do this. Don't let me lose him now.* "I'm stronger than I look."

He had the audacity to smile. "I know."

"Then stop being such a twit."

"Jessica . . ." His smile faded. He sighed and raked a hand through his hair in that familiar gesture of weary frustration. It almost broke her heart.

Love me, Brady. That is all I want from you. I need nothing else.

Reaching out, he captured both her hands in his and pulled her to stand between his gaped knees. "You know I want you. I'll never stop wanting you. But . . ."

She stared down at him, dread swelling in her chest. There was a terrible grimness to his drawn face that made him seem older than he was. Where was the ardent, teasing man who had loved her so gently last night? Who was this weary stranger staring back at her through bleak and defeated eyes?

Don't do this to me, Brady. To us.

"It's not you that's lacking, Jessica. It's me." Reaching up, he touched her face, trailing his fingertips across her jaw, her cheek, her brow. She watched his eyes track every movement as if imprinting her face in his mind. "I won't come to you empty-handed, Jessica. You and Ben deserve better." His hand slid beneath the braid at her nape.

She opened her mouth to protest, but before she could, he pulled her face toward his.

It was a gentle, tender kiss, without the heat and hungry demand she'd grown to expect from him, but so achingly sweet it made her tremble. A good-bye kiss.

"I love you, Jessica," he whispered against her lips. "I always will." He pulled back. His hands dropped to his thighs. "But you can't stay. There's nothing here for you."

An unseen fist seemed to grip her heart. "There's you."

"It's not enough."

"It is for me. We can leave. Go somewhere else."

He didn't speak or look away. Yet with every heartbeat she felt the distance between them grow. It panicked her, sent words tumbling out in a rush. "We could go with Elena to San Francisco. Start over. We don't have to live here."

"Jessica, don't."

She didn't realize she was crying until she tasted the salt of her own tears. Angrily she swiped them away. "Don't what? Cry? Argue with you?" It felt like something was ripping apart inside. "You told me to fight for us. Now you say give up. I can't do that, Brady. I won't."

Those aqua eyes moved over her face, her hair. "I love you, Jessica. Never forget that."

She wanted to strike him, shake him, scream at him until he listened. "Then believe in me, Brady. I can do this. We can do this. I know we can." She clutched at his arms as if she could hold him fast to her side and keep him from drifting away. "Together we can do anything. We can work this out."

The look Brady gave her opened up a hole in her heart. "I wish we could, Jessica. I wish that more than anything I've ever wished in my life. But winter is three months away and I have over two dozen people to feed and shelter. How can I do that and worry about you and Ben, too?"

The irony of it all was too much. It was macabre. Absurd. A twist of fate she had never expected. Laughter bubbled in her chest, but before it burst from her throat, it had changed to tears.

God had tricked her again.

Twenty-four

ADRIAN COOED ON A BLANKET IN THE SHADE OF A JUNIPER behind Buck and Iantha's cabin while Jessica toiled over a washtub, up to her elbows in sooty water. She was exhausted. For two days she had worked dawn to dusk. For two nights she had battled tears and heartache as she lay in sleepless misery in the tiny room she shared with Elena and Adrian.

She didn't know how she could go on. She didn't know how she couldn't.

She didn't know why loving someone should hurt so much.

Adrian's coos escalated into a babble, and she turned to see Brady standing over her son. Joy thundered through her.

Except for distant glimpses, she hadn't seen him since their argument the morning after the fire. He looked worse than she felt. Sooty, haggard, so drawn with weariness and worry he seemed to have aged ten years. She wondered what he ate, where he slept, if he thought of her at all.

She doubted he had the time.

It was a monumental undertaking, the task before him. Although it was late August and they had three months before winter came full force, when one begins the task of constructing housing for several families and almost two dozen ranch hands with scarcely a stick of wood or a nail in hand, three months wasn't a long time. And Brady would never shirk his duty to greedy RosaRoja. It was only people he was able to set aside.

Even so, she would give anything for a touch or a smile.

Weakened by longing, she studied him, committing to memory the sight of him smiling down at her son. How could she live beyond his touch? Beyond that heart-wrenching smile?

He must have sensed her watching him. He gave her a quick look, then hunkered beside Adrian. "He's growing fast," he said, offering a finger to her son.

With a look of fierce concentration, Adrian tugged it toward his mouth.

Jessica cleared her throat. "They do that." She wiped her damp palms on her work apron and forced herself to walk slowly toward them, when what she wanted to do was to run, throw herself into his arms, and never let him go.

"Strong, too." Smiling, Brady engaged in a gentle tug-of-war until Adrian conceded with a howl. "Still has your temper, I see."

"And yet, inexplicably, it's only apparent in your presence."

He might have smiled at her quip, but with his head down, she wasn't sure.

Rising as she approached, he pulled a yellow envelope from his back pocket and held it out. "This came a couple of days ago. The telegraph office was waiting for someone from the ranch to come into town."

A sense of dread gripped her as she took the envelope from his hand. The last time she had received a missive was the day Victoria died. She remembered that odd prescient feeling she had felt when the sheriff handed her Annie's letter. She felt it again now. With trembling fingers, she tore open the envelope.

"It's from Annie." Quickly, she skimmed the abbreviated message. "Oh, my God . . ." For a moment she couldn't speak, couldn't draw air into her lungs. "He's dead. John Crawford is dead." An odd sound escaped her throat. It sounded like laughter. She couldn't seem to stifle it. "He was killed. In Boston, of all places. A tavern brawl."

Her mind couldn't seem to grasp it. Dead. Gone forever.

She gave the letter to Brady. "Creditors are after the Hall. Annie wants me to come home."

Brady read it, then handed it back. "How could creditors be after the Hall? You didn't mortgage it, did you?"

"Crawford must have forged my name to secure loans." Shaking her head, she folded the paper and slipped it into her apron pocket. "Poor Annie. Widowed with two children, and now this." She looked up at him. "What should I do?"

"What you have to, I guess."

His air of indifference infuriated her. Didn't he understand what this meant? "You mean leave? Go back to England?" She couldn't leave now, not with things so unsettled between her and Brady. Or didn't that matter to him anymore?

"If that's what you need to do," he said noncommittally.

"Is that what you want me to do?"

"What I want doesn't matter anymore, Jessica. I told you that two days ago." And without a backward glance, he turned and walked away.

THAT NIGHT, AFTER IANTHA AND BUCK WENT TO BED AND Adrian finished his night feeding, Jessica told Elena about her feelings for Brady.

Elena didn't seem surprised. Laughing in delight, she gave Jessica a hug, telling her how happy she was to have a sister.

"Before you get too carried away, read this." She gave her Annie's letter.

Elena's smile faded as she read it.

"I don't want to leave," Jessica blurted out. "I can't." The thought of walking away from that tiny grave up on the hill, from Brady and all these people she had grown to love, was intolerable. She simply couldn't do it.

Elena pulled a lace-edged handkerchief from the drawer of the night table and pressed it into Jessica's hand. "Then stay."

Jessica blotted her tears. "But it's my sister." She waved the hanky in agitation. "If she loses the Hall, what will become of her and the children?"

"*Pobrecita.* Such terrible choices." Tears of sympathy glistened in her dark eyes as Elena patted Jessica's hand. "You and Brady are so alike. He also feels the pull of duty. He will understand."

Jessica rose and went to the window. Even after two days, tendrils of smoke coiled above the pile of charred timbers that had once been the house. "I don't want him to understand, Elena. I just want him to love me." It sounded infantile and pitiful, but she couldn't help it. She felt like a child who'd been given a treasured gift only to have it snatched away before it was fully within her grasp.

"He does love you. It is there for all to see."

Was it? But did he love her enough? For just this one time in her life, Jessica wanted to be first, to be loved more than money, or land, or duty. Was that too much to wish for?

God. She was beyond pathetic.

Turning, she walked back to the bed. "If I asked him to leave with me, do you think he would?" she asked, grasping at anything to keep her hopes alive.

"Perhaps. But is that truly what you want?" At Jessica's questioning look, Elena explained. "A woman defines herself by the people she loves. She calls herself wife, mother, sister, daughter. But a man defines himself by what he does. Brady is a *ranchero.* He knows nothing else. If he goes with you to England, what is he to become then?"

"A proper gentleman?" She sighed and sank down beside Elena. "I know it sounds selfish and prideful, but I just want him to choose me."

"And deny the greater part of himself? He would not be the man you love then, would he?" She brushed a curl from Jessica's shoulder. "Go. Do what you must for your sister, then come back to him. By then he will have restored his home and his pride."

Jessica almost snorted. "His pride? What does his pride have to do with this?"

"*Es todo.* Today he is a rancher with no ranch house, a *ganadero* whose herds are scattered to the wind. No matter how much he loved you, his pride would never allow him to come to you with so little to offer."

Jessica let her expression reveal how ridiculous she thought that was.

"*Sí. Es loco.*" Elena spread her hands in a helpless gesture. "But he is only a man, yes?"

New tears filled Jessica's eyes. "How shall I manage without you, dear friend?" Reaching out, she wrapped Elena in a fierce hug. "You have become the sister of my heart."

"*Sí,*" Elena whispered, hugging her back. "*Hermana de mi corazón.*"

THE NEXT MORNING BRADY WAS NOWHERE TO BE FOUND, so Jessica explained to Jack that she had to leave and asked him to make arrangements to get her and Adrian to the Overland Stagecoach Office in Val Rosa.

Jack seemed genuinely distressed, which touched her. It was also the first in a series of difficult and heartbreaking good-byes. Not even leaving England had been so hard. By evening she was packed.

And still no Brady.

Weary but too distraught to sleep, she pulled on her robe. Leaving Elena and Adrian sleeping, she walked to where the house had once stood.

Only the porch was recognizable, the sturdy pine posts and beams rising defiantly from the ashes. Seeing the two blackened rockers in the rubble brought up the pain she had fought so hard to keep inside. How could she leave this place? This man? Her daughter?

Coils of smoke and ash danced in the gentle breeze. The scorched posts wept slow amber tears. But no answers came.

As Brady rode from the creek after his wash, his mind was so preoccupied with the thought of Jessica and Ben leaving the next day, he didn't realize she was there until the horse lifted its head and snorted. He reined in and watched her.

She stood where the porch used to be, her face lifted to the night sky. Moonlight highlighted her features, gilding her satiny robe in a hazy aura of white. He saw glistening silver streaks on her cheeks and knew she was crying. It weakened him. He had avoided her all day, thinking that would be easier for both of them. But watching her now, he realized no amount of time or distance would ever lessen the pain of this parting.

The saddle creaked as he dismounted. Letting the reins drop, he crossed toward her.

At his approach, her head swung toward him. "I've never seen so many shooting stars."

He stopped beside her. "Saint Lawrence's fiery tears. Happens this time every year."

"It's magnificent. A gift."

He studied her, battling the urge to wipe the tears from her cheeks, to pull her against him so her soft warmth would fill the empty ache in his arms. "What are you doing out here?"

"Remembering." She looked back up into the sky. "And listening."

"For what?"

"The last-time bell." A small, wistful smile moved across her mouth. "Endings should never come unannounced."

He waited for her to explain.

Instead, she told him a story about her childhood and an ancient, drooping oak tree that she and her brother, George, had played in one summer.

"We imagined ourselves pirates and knights and highwaymen bent on mischief. It was a lovely summer. Because we were children, we thought those lazy days would go on forever. But winter came, and by the next spring Papa was dead, I was busy tending Annie and Mum, and George had suddenly become the man of the house. We had outgrown childish games."

She picked up a handful of pebbles and began idly tossing them into the ruined rose bed.

"That summer, lightning struck the tree, splitting it in two. I remember standing at the window by Mum's sickbed, watching the workers cut it into logs. It took forever. Then one day it was simply gone, as if it had never been. Not even a stump showed in the tall grass."

She opened her hand and let the last of the pebbles drop back to the ground. "It was quite sad, really. I remember feeling betrayed. Cheated. If only I had known I would never climb those limbs again. If only I had thought to savor those last moments of that last summer. But I didn't."

She dusted her hands, then watched a falling star shoot across the sky. "So to remind myself to treasure all the last moments before they're lost forever, I invented the last-time bell."

Brady tried to remember the last time he had heard Sam laugh or felt his mother's hand brush the hair from his brow. He couldn't. And he determined that this moment, standing here beside Jessica in the moonlight, with the smell of burnt wood and dead dreams swirling all around them, would be a memory he would never lose. "Are you hearing it now?"

"Now I'm remembering. The stars. The sunsets. Our evenings on the porch." She turned toward him, letting him see the sheen of tears on her cheeks. "You."

Brady didn't move, his face a dark shadow beneath the brim of his hat. Jessica watched his fists clench at his sides and sensed he was bracing himself. Against her? How sad if that were so. "Was it real, Brady? Did it mean so little that you could so easily throw it away?"

"It meant everything. It always will."

"You said you would never abandon me and yet—"

"I'm not abandoning you, Jessica," he cut in, his voice harsh and low. "I'm letting you go. There's a difference. And don't think it's not the hardest thing I've ever done."

The brittle shell of her anguish cracked, leaving her open and exposed. "Show me."

She watched his chest move as he breathed deep. "I'm trying to do the right thing here, Jessica. I can't—"

"Please." She opened her arms to him. "One last time."

"Jesus, woman . . ." And the next instant he was pulling her against him with such force her ribs ached. "You're killing me."

Jessica clung to him with a desperation that robbed her of thought. Weeping with joy and need and a love so desperate it made her tremble, she ran her hands over him, pressed her face against his neck, dug her fingers into his back. If she could have climbed inside his chest, she would have. He was her lifeline, her salvation, everything she would ever need to sustain her for all of her life. "I love you, Brady."

With a harsh sound, Brady swept her up into his arms and carried her to his horse. He lifted her into the saddle then swung up behind her. Locking her between his arms, he kicked the horse into a lope, away from the ruined buildings and out into the open valley.

Jessica leaned back against him. Lifting her face to the sage-scented wind, she felt time and the past fall behind, until there was nothing but endless open sky, and the drumming of the horse's hooves, and the feel of Brady's arms holding her safe.

They rode to a treeless knoll rising out of the valley floor. All around them tall tufts of buffalo grass rippled in the wind like waves on the sea. It was magical, like being on a tiny island awash in moonlight, with nothing between them and the heavens but the wind and stars.

The half moon perched atop the ridges as Brady lifted her down. In silence he cleared a space of rocks and pebbles, then untied the bedroll lashed behind the saddle. He spread it on the ground, then turned and held out his hand.

She walked toward him. There was a sweet solemnity as they joined hands under that vast, star-streaked sky, a sense of timelessness and rightness, as if they stood alone and together before a heavenly host preparing to make their vows. In Jessica's heart she was already married. There could be no other for her than Brady. No matter what happened after this night, even if she never saw him again, there would always only be Brady.

As he slowly undressed her, Brady didn't consider the right or wrong of what he was doing. He was in the grips of something beyond his control, beyond his strength to resist. There was just the two of them. No past, no future. Only this time, this moment.

Wanting to give them both a memory that would last through the lonely years ahead, he took his time, gave her everything he could, everything he had. And as she moved above him, her hair a soft, dark cloud streaked by moonlight, her beautiful body silhouetted against an endless spray of stars, he realized never again would anything be as good as loving Jessica, while her tears dripped onto his chest, and the wind whispered around them, and meteors shot in fiery arcs across the indigo sky.

"I'LL WRITE TO YOU. WILL YOU WRITE BACK?"

They had ridden in an hour earlier and now sat on Iantha's porch steps, watching dawn trim the morning sky with golden ribbons and gauzy purple clouds.

When he hesitated, she gave him a prod. "You do know how to write, don't you?"

His mustache lifted at one corner. "And count. All the way to twenty."

She didn't laugh, afraid it would come out a sob. She was trying so hard to be strong, but with each passing minute, she bled a little more. Lacing her fingers around her knees, she looked at the stark framework of the new barn. "How long to rebuild?"

"All of it? Years. Decades. Maybe forever."

She couldn't bear that, living on dwindling hope for so long. She would wither and die. "Ask me to stay and I will."

He looked over at her, but said nothing.

Hope died, leaving a hole in her chest where her heart should have been. A distant part of her was amazed she survived the pain of it.

The sun cleared the ridges. A wash of golden light spilled down the east-facing slopes, then raced across the valley floor. When it highlighted the mesquite tree on the hilltop, Brady gathered himself to rise.

That terrible desperation gripped her again, and before she could stop herself, she flung herself toward him, her arms reaching around his neck. "I love you," she whispered against his bristly cheek. "I will always love you."

He held her hard against him for a brief moment, then gently pushed her away. He rose.

She thrust a hand into the pocket of her robe and withdrew the piece of paper she had put there the evening before. She pressed it into his hand. "This is my direction. Come to me. I'll wait a year, no more." Who was she fooling? She would wait a lifetime for this man.

He stared down at the paper, then with shaking hands, carefully folded it and slipped it into his shirt pocket. He stood for a moment, staring down at the ground. When he lifted his head, she saw that the vibrant light she so loved was gone from his beautiful eyes.

"You were the best thing that ever came into my life, Jessica. Never forget that." Then he turned and walked away.

An hour later, after a tearful good-bye to the women, she and Adrian left for England.

Twenty-five

NOTHING LASTS FOREVER, NOT EVEN MISERY.

Or so Brady told himself at least once a day those first weeks after Jessica and Ben left. There were no good days, only bad days and worse days, followed by nights so long and lonely he damn near paced a groove in Iantha's front porch—until Buck got tired of hearing him tromp around and built him a new rocker. But that only made it harder, because all Brady could think about while he rocked were those evenings on the porch with Jessica.

Bad days or worse. After a while they all blended together. Somehow he managed because that's what he did. He managed. He got by. He persevered. It wasn't much of a life, but for those first six months, that was how it was.

Even so, progress was made.

Because of the fire, they were able to wrangle an extra week out of the Army so they could round up the scattered herd for their bid on the Reservation contract. That brought enough money to weather in the tack shed, bunkhouse, cookhouse, and several cabins before the first snow.

Elena delayed her trip to San Francisco, hoping the rail line through El Paso or Oklahoma might be completed soon. Doc worried that her hip wouldn't tolerate a long trip in a bouncing stagecoach. But she was determined that come spring she'd go, whether the lines were laid or not. She still hadn't told Jack.

In October, Hank spruced up and headed to Fort Union. Two weeks later he returned, empty-handed and untalkative. Brady asked him what happened. All Hank said was, "She married someone else." Brady waited for him to say more. He knew his brother had no tolerance for weak-minded women, and Melanie Kinderly was surely that, the way she let her mother run roughshod over her. But Hank didn't elaborate and Brady didn't push it. He had his own problems; he didn't need to insinuate himself into Hank's. But it saddened him that Hank was even quieter than usual and had started growing the beard again.

Weeks became months. Jack continued to talk up Australia and all the things there that could kill you, not including climate or humans. An impressive list. He also spent more time around the compound—especially around Elena. He didn't seem in a hurry to take off, which was a relief to Brady. Even with winter closing in, there would be plenty of work finishing the inside of the new buildings.

Plenty of misery. too. Soon after recovering from Sancho's beating, Bullshot had a run-in with a rattler. He didn't make it and Brady missed him sorely. He wasn't sure when he'd get another dog.

Bad days and worse days. Brady moved through them in a constant state of exhaustion, because that was his only armor against memories he couldn't face. If he stayed weary enough, he didn't think—and if he didn't think, he didn't remember. Except at night when he awoke aching from dreams of Jessica.

But things change. Sometimes they get better, sometimes worse, sometimes both at the same time. November sixteenth was both the high and the low point of that fall. That was the day Jessica's first letter came.

She'd made progress, too. After hard legal battles, the liens against her home were lifted, although the debt remained and had to be repaid. Toward that end and with great reluctance, she began negotiations with the mining consortium.

The rift with her sister was harder to mend. That she had arrived with Ben in tow was a shock. To reveal who had fathered him was an even bigger shock. It drove a wedge between the sisters. He admired Jessica for not trying to hide the truth.

I fear she blames me for leading her husband into indiscretion. She maintains the fantasy that John Crawford was a good man easily led astray. She even excuses his forgeries as a desperate attempt to provide for his family after I refused to sign over the deed. I understand she is frightened and alone. Hopefully, soon she will open herself to the truth and we can move past this coil of deception and distrust John Crawford has wrapped us in.

Brady admired her capacity for forgiveness, too. He might be able to carry a heavier load, but Jessica was far stronger than he would ever be.

Her letter indicated she battled loneliness as well. He regretted that. He had hoped time and distance would help her accept the way things had to be.

But a part of him was gratified she still cared.

I miss all of you so much. I have not seen a star in weeks, and when there is a sunset, it seems bland and colorless compared to those over RosaRoja. I fear I no longer fit here. Now that I must once again bow to the rules of propriety and decorum, I realize how utterly ridiculous my pamphlets truly were. Have I finally opened my eyes? Or have I changed that much? I do not know. I hunger for news. I hunger for you.

Your Jessica

He didn't sleep for three days after that letter, but at least he knew she was safe.

Winter was a howling sonofabitch that came too early and stayed too late. After each norther dumped its load of snow, Brady spent days patrolling the drifts, digging out what cattle he could find. There had been worse winters with higher losses, but this year they were on such a thin edge he was determined to save every cow he could.

An early thaw revealed at least a hundred dead. Then a late blizzard sent temperatures plummeting again. Desperation made him stupid, and he rode out when he shouldn't have. If Hank and Jack hadn't found him before the drifts filled in the ravine where he and his horse had fallen, he'd be there still, frozen stiff as a poker, waiting for spring. As it was, he was laid up for weeks with a bad knee and, for a month after, limped with a cane like a crippled old man.

Jack got a lot of enjoyment out of that.

February brought another letter from Jessica, which surprised him, since he hadn't answered her first one. Nothing had changed the direction of his life, and he had no hope that anything would, so what could he say? He knew Elena wrote regularly. Any news he had would be the same.

But this second letter troubled him. A lot.

Apparently negotiations with the consortium had gone well. The debts had been paid and they were now mining Jessica's land. Or rather, they were tunneling from the adjacent property to hers. She wouldn't allow them to touch the surface, so the coal had to be carted through the tunnel to the mine entrance next door, then loaded on rail cars and hauled out from there.

Cagey of her. He admired that, too.

She also wrote that a mining engineer named Percival Frederick Bothingham III had been so helpful in the negotiations, she had hired him to oversee the mine.

Helpful. What the hell did that mean? How helpful? And what kind of weak-sister name was Percival Frederick Bothingham *the Third*, for chrissakes?

Brady didn't answer that letter either.

He told himself life would look better come spring. As long as he didn't think about Jessica and Ben he was all right. Like an amputee teaching himself to get by without a limb, he struggled to re-train his thoughts away from memories that festered like an unhealed wound in his mind. But the phantom pain of it never seemed to fade. He wearied of it.

Spring brought with it a blanket of wildflowers and a renewal of spirit. As Brady watched RosaRoja flourish with new life, he realized if he was ever to build a livable future he had to make some hard decisions. And he had to learn to let go.

He started with Elena.

"You still want to go to San Francisco?" he asked her one evening when he returned from Val Rosa to find her sitting in his new rocker on Buck's porch.

She set her sewing aside and smiled up at him. "*Sí.*"

"The spur line to the Transcontinental won't be laid until next year. You'd have to travel by stagecoach to Raton, and that'd be hard on your hip."

She shrugged. "I will manage."

He studied her a moment, Jessica's bell ringing in his mind. What if something went wrong with her surgery? What if she never came back? She looked so fragile in the evening light, so full of trust and hope. Another delicate music box dancer, easily broken in the wrong hands.

He sighed, hoping he was doing the right thing.

"There's a family leaving for San Francisco. Church people. Young, three kids. They would welcome your company." He held out an envelope and a leather pouch. "Here's a voucher and enough money to get you there. I'll wire more once you arrive."

She stared at him.

"You still want to go, don't you?"

"*Sí.*" She nodded, her eyes brimming despite the wide smile spreading over her face. "*Otra vez,* you come to my rescue. How do I ever repay you, *querido*?"

"By packing," he said gruffly. "The stage leaves next week."

It was tricky because of the secrecy involved. Elena insisted he not tell Jack until after she was gone. He guessed she wasn't sure if Jack cared enough to go with her, and wasn't ready to find out. Brady wasn't sure either. Even though Jack could be guileless as a kid, he was hard to read sometimes. So Brady sent him to check the water holes in the north range, then took Elena to catch the stage.

Another hard good-bye. Another woman gone from his life. He'd miss her.

THAT EVENING, HE WAS STANDING IN THE SHELL OF THE OLD house, wondering why he should rebuild it if there was no one but him to live in it, when Jack rode up.

"Red said you needed me?" he said as he dismounted.

Brady pointed up at the few remaining timbers. "I was thinking two-foot beams across here. Something sturdy, like the porch."

Jack made a sound of exasperation. "You brought me all the way from Quartz Creek to talk about beams?" Sighing, he pulled off his hat to scratch the top of his head then put it back on. "Although, I admit I'll be glad to have a room of my own again. Red smells worse than the ass end of a dead pole cat."

Brady studied his brother, trying not to see him as the kid he once was, but as the man he had become. Despite their differences, Jack had always been there when he was needed. Brady appreciated that. And although he would miss the little sonofabitch—the laughter, the antics, that open-eyed innocence he envied—it was time Jack moved on. Brady knew what it meant to lose a dream to duty and he was determined that didn't happen to Jack, too.

Unless staying was what Jack wanted, of course. Brady wasn't trying to control anything, just offer choices. There was a difference.

"So when do we start?" Jack asked.

"We don't. I'll start next week. You'll go to Australia."

So maybe he was a little controlling, but he did it for Jack's own good.

Jack blinked at him, clearly confused. And not nearly as grateful as he should be. In fact, his entire reaction was wrong. Brady watched his brother pick up a shard of broken crockery, make a show of studying it, then toss it aside.

"Maybe I've changed my mind," Jack said.

Brady looked at him.

"Maybe I've decided to stay."

"Because of Elena."

Jack shrugged. "Maybe." Then his seeming indifference gave way to a sheepish grin. "The truth is, Big Brother, I'm smitten with the woman. The conniving wench has me wrapped around her finger." He looked as pleased about that as a kid with new boots.

Brady stared up at the charred beams and rocked on his heels. "You're giving up Australia for Elena?"

"Hell, yes. I'll give up anything, do anything, so long as she'll have me."

Brady bit back a smile. When the men in this family fell, they fell hard. At least Jack seemed to have better luck at it than him.

"Is that okay?" Jack dug the toe of his boot into the ashes. "I mean, I know you and Elena have been, well . . . is that okay by you?"

Brady sent him a sidewise look. "Would it matter if it wasn't?"

"No."

"Then it's okay." Controlling might be bad but it sure felt good.

For a while, they stood in a companionable silence, enjoying a respite from the crowded bunkhouse and the endless chores RosaRoja demanded. Brady tried not to look too far ahead or dwell on how quiet the place would be with everyone gone. He'd made his choices. He just had to find a way to live with them.

Jack punched him in the arm. "So when you going after Jessica?"

Brady resisted the urge to punch him back. "We've had this conversation."

"I thought you had feelings for her."

"I did. I do."

Jack threw his hands up. "I don't understand, Brady. Explain it to me. Explain how you can give up a woman like Jessica for this."

The way he said "this" told Brady that whatever hold RosaRoja had on him, it didn't stretch as far as Jack. That saddened him yet relieved him at the same time. A man had to follow his own dream, not someone else's, and RosaRoja had never been Jack's dream. There were times when Brady wondered if it had ever been his either. Then he would wake up to the smell of sage and greasewood and cattle—when dewdrops flashed like tiny diamonds on a thousand cactus spines, and the air was so crisp he could make out every dip and spike on ridges ten miles away—and he would know this was his dream after all. This was where he belonged.

He tried to explain that to his brother. "You say it like I have a choice, Jack. I don't. For most of my life every thought, every move, every decision, has centered around RosaRoja. I don't know anymore where it ends and I begin. I don't know how to walk away."

Jack studied him intently, his gaze so unwavering, it made Brady uneasy. Jack might be a pinhead sometimes, but he could also be damned perceptive. "But do you love it, Brady? Do you need it more than anything else in your life?"

Brady looked away, embarrassed by the question. "Love" was not a word he felt comfortable with. In fact, the only time he ever remembered using it was with Jessica. Did he love RosaRoja? At one time, he would have said yes. But lately what he felt was more like duty, obligation. "I don't know, Jack."

"Maybe Jessica can help you figure it out. Go after her. The ranch will be here when you get back." Hooking an arm around Brady's shoulders, he steered him out of the rubble of the house toward the creek. "And don't dillydally. England's a long way and you're not getting any younger."

Brady scratched his chin. "Seems a lot of trouble to go to for a woman."

Jack waved a hand. "I don't see any others riding hell-bent through the gate, do you? Jessica may be your last shot. So unless you're willing to start writing love letters to that gotch-eared heifer in the back paddock, you better go after her."

"You think so?" Sometimes teasing Jack was too easy.

"I do. Luckily I don't have your knack for running off women. But since you're my brother, I'll be glad to give you pointers on keeping them."

Brady thought about Elena boarding the stage in Val Rosa and tried not to smirk. He would enjoy getting back some of his own. "I can't believe you're giving up chasing women."

"Hell, I'm not giving up chasing women. I'm giving up chasing *other* women. For this woman I'd dance a jig on the courthouse steps, wearing nothing but my wooly chaps and a red bandana." Jack stared off in thought. "Although I did that once for the judge's wife and it wasn't nearly as rewarding as I hoped. Probably the cold."

There was a picture to make a man shudder. "No more whoring around?"

Jack laughed. "I prefer to think of it as practicing, honing my skills, so I can show the love of my life all the wondrous things I've learned just to please her." He gave Brady a sly wink. "There's nothing more generous than a satisfied woman."

Brady was starting to get uncomfortable. Elena was like a sister, after all. He stopped and faced his brother. "Just so you know, Jack. If you hurt her, I'll bullwhip you."

Jack's grin faded. "Just so *you* know, Brady. If I hurt her, shoot me."

Brady nodded. They continued to the creek. When Jack bent to pick up a skimmer, Brady planted a foot on his butt and shoved him face-first into the water.

Jack came up sputtering. "What the hell did you do that for?"

"For that time you kicked my cane out from under me. And for calling me old. And because it was fun. Besides, I thought you might want to clean up before you go."

"Go where?"

"San Francisco."

Jack slogged onto the bank, dripping water and streamers of mossy reeds. Lowering himself onto a boulder, he tugged off his water-filled boots. "Why the hell would I go to San Francisco? I told you I'm staying here with Elena."

"Elena's not here."

Jack's head snapped up. "Where is she?"

"On her way to San Francisco. There's a doctor there who might be able to fix her hip. She asked me not to tell you until after she left, but I said—"

"You sonofabitch!" Jack jumped up and started stomping the ground, trying to jam his wet foot back into his wet boot. "And you let her go? Alone? Christ! When did she leave?"

"She's not alone. She's with a missionary family. They'll watch out for her."

"Shit—sonofabitch—get on, you bastard!"

Brady watched in amazement as Jack, the fearless, unflappable brother who never took anything seriously and thought the world was created solely for his amusement, got himself so worked up he was hopping in circles. And all because of a woman. It was a wonderment.

Jack got his second boot on and started toward his horse. "How long has she been gone?" he shouted, charging up the slope.

"About four hours," Brady shouted back.

Jack stumbled to a stop. Brady watched his shoulders sag in relief and wondered if there was a more gratifying sight than Andrew Jackson Wilkins at a loss for words. Probably not.

Jack's silence didn't last long. "You're a bastard."

"I know." Grinning, Brady walked toward him.

As they headed up the path, it struck Brady that he might not see Jack for a long time, years maybe, and suddenly his head seemed filled with all the words he'd never said. For the last decade he'd been more of a parent to Jack than a brother. And even though they didn't always see eye to eye, it was hard to let him go.

When they reached the remains of the house, Brady waved him on. "I'll see to your horse. Tell Hank you're leaving. And get some clean clothes. You smell like a wet goat."

A half hour later Jack returned and stuffed clean clothes into his saddlebag.

"You have money?" Brady asked.

"Some. Enough."

Brady pulled a pouch from his pocket. "Here's more. And a voucher."

Jack stared at the items Brady held out, then met Brady's amused smirk. "Pretty sure of yourself, aren't you?" he said, adding them to his saddlebag.

"Pretty sure of you. If you cut north, you can catch them at the Bridge Creek stopover. I'll send one of the boys to get the horse later."

Jack nodded. He gathered the reins then turned to Brady.

And suddenly there was nothing more to say.

For a moment they looked at each other, years of memories stretching between them. Finally Brady held out his hand. "Watch your back and take care of Elena."

Jack took his hand in a strong grip. "You're not going to cry, are you?"

Brady cuffed him on the side of the head. "Get going. I got things to do."

"Like going after Jessica?"

"Maybe. I'll think on it." Not that thinking would change anything.

Jack stepped into the stirrup.

Brady battled a sudden impulse to pull him back, make him stay where he could keep him safe. Instead, he rested a hand on the horse's neck and looked up at his brother. He forced a smile. "You turned out all right, Jack. I'm proud of you."

The grin spreading over Jack's face told Brady he should have said it sooner.

"Thanks, Ma." With a tip of his hat, Jack rode away.

Brady watched until he disappeared over the far ridge, then walked back toward the cabins. As he trudged up Buck's steps, he wondered when he'd started feeling so old.

ROUNDUP CAME AND WENT. DESPITE WINTER LOSSES, THEY had a good crop of calves, and Brady began to feel mildly optimistic. The fall Reservation bid was due in two months, and if they did as well as he hoped, they might be able to start curing logs for the house.

It had been a hard year. Seeing his family dwindle had taken its toll on him, and that feeling of aloneness cut more keenly than it ever had before. He saw himself fifteen years down the road, standing before a restored RosaRoja and reveling in his accomplishment, only to look around and find himself standing there alone. It disturbed him, made him question things he'd never questioned before.

"How long you going to mope around?" Hank asked at supper one evening in July.

It was a Saturday night. Most of the men were either chasing women in Val Rosa or playing cards in the bunkhouse. He and Hank were alone in the makeshift tack shed that also served as their sleeping quarters, enjoying some of Iantha's leftovers and their first sit-down meal in a week.

"I'm not moping. I'm thinking. There's a difference."

Hank studied him, his cheeks bunching as he chewed. "So what are you *thinking* of doing?"

"About what?"

"Jessica."

Brady blinked at him, wondering at the question. They never discussed Jessica. In fact, with Hank being about as talkative as a trout, they hardly spoke at all. Which suited Brady fine. He didn't have much to say either.

"If you don't want her, I'll take her," Hank offered, reaching for the butter crock.

Brady put down his fork and sat back. "I thought you swore off women."

"For her I'll make an exception."

Brady forced a laugh. "She wouldn't have you." At least he hoped not. But he hadn't seen a woman yet who didn't react when his brother tamed the hair and turned on the charm.

Hank glanced over, that slow smile moving across his face, the one

that turned women into simpering simpletons throughout the territory. "You think not?"

Brady picked up his fork and stabbed a beet. "You'd have to shave."

Hank shrugged. "A small sacrifice, considering. Any potatoes
left?"

"No. And why are we talking about Jessica?"

"A woman like her is too good to waste. Pass the collards then."

Brady shoved the bowl toward him. "She's not wasted. She's just
gone back to where she belongs." He knew Hank wasn't truly interested in Jessica that way and suspected he was trying to bait him into
doing something foolish. Well, he wouldn't bite. He'd made his decision. End of conversation.

"You think I should go after her, is that it?" he heard himself say.

His brother gave him that silent stare that always made Brady
uneasy.

"And do what, Hank? Bring her back here? To this?" Brady waved
an arm at the unfinished walls, the rough-cut floor, the saddles piled in
the corner. "She deserves better."

"You done with the beans?"

TWO DAYS LATER, THEY SAT IN THE CORNER OF THE LOAFING
shed, where they'd set up a temporary office—Brady with his boots
propped on a keg of nails as he thumbed through a cattleman's catalog
and Hank hunched over the plank desk, reviewing the latest tally.

Brady hadn't slept well lately. Worries were piling up and he felt
like time was running against him. And thanks to Hank, he'd been
thinking of Jessica and Ben too much, fretting over things he couldn't
do anything about.

"Maybe the Army needs fresh beef until the bids this fall," Hank
said after a while. "We can spare a few yearlings."

"How many?" Brady asked, turning the page.

"Thirty-seven. Maybe forty. Might bring in enough to finish the
bunkhouse."

Brady didn't question Hank's assessment. His brother had a born knack for figures and could store the most astounding facts under that bushy dome of his.

"'Course you'd have to ride to the Army post," Hank added doubtfully. "I know how reluctant you are to leave the ranch."

"I'm not reluctant. I just don't have a reason." When his brother didn't respond, Brady lowered the catalog to his lap. "This is about Jessica again, isn't it?"

"Did I say anything about Jessica?" Hank pulled a hardware pamphlet from the stack on the end of the table and began leafing through it.

"You think I should go to England, don't you?"

"What do you think of these hinges?" Tagging an illustration with his finger, Hank held up the page for Brady to see.

"Maybe learn to drink tea from a fancy china cup? Ride around on one of those silly pancake saddles? That's a fine idea."

Hank studied the drawing. "They'll last longer than leather and be a damn sight cheaper than the ones the smithy makes."

Brady looked out the double doors at Iantha digging in the new vegetable garden. They'd already harvested peas and beets and collards, and the corn and potatoes were coming along well. But would it be enough? Would anything ever be enough?

"I can't go to England," he said. "I'm needed here."

"I'll order three sets," Hank decided. "One for here and two for the loft."

Brady picked up the catalog again. "Don't forget the pump house."

"Four, then."

IT WAS EARLY AUGUST. THE AIR WAS SO HOT AND THICK WITH dust the sunset was a riotous wash of color across the western sky. Summer sunsets were a wonderment to Brady—that last fiery battle before the day died—so violent to the eye, yet so silent to the ear.

This evening the biting flies were out in full force as he watched Hank work his magic on a headstrong, dish-faced gelding that wasn't taking kindly to being sacked out. But if anyone could manner a dodgy horse, Hank could. He had a knack with animals, too. After an hour both Hank and the roan dripped sweat but they seemed to have reached a point of mutual respect and cooperation.

"I think he'll do," Hank said, leading the horse over to where Brady leaned against the fence, arms folded across the top rail.

"His eyes are different colors," Brady noted.

"They both work."

"Seems indecisive. Hard to trust an animal that can't make up its mind."

Hank gave him a look but said nothing.

Brady watched his brother rub the horse with a burlap sack, moving it slowly over the animal's face and ears, along its belly then up and down its legs. The roan allowed it without protest. Satisfied, Hank slipped off the bridle and gave the weary horse a final pat.

"I bet they don't have sunsets like this in England," Brady said.

Hank didn't respond.

"Not that it matters. I'll never go to England."

"He's got a nice slope to his pasterns," Hank observed, watching the horse wander across the paddock looking for a place to roll. "Should be a smooth trotter."

"Why should I? Nothing's changed. I'm still poor as dirt. She would do better with that tea-sipper Percival Bothingham *the Third*."

The horse flopped to the ground. Churning up dust and flies, it rolled from side to side, legs thrashing.

"But you're still thinking I should go after her, aren't you?"

The horse regained its feet. After shaking like a wet dog, it backed toward a fence post.

"Nice withers, too," Hank said. "Should keep the saddle from sliding. Especially if you ride English-style."

"Which I don't."

Unbuckling his *chaparreras*, Hank tossed them over the fence rail.

Brady watched the horse rock side to side, rubbing its butt on the rough wood. "Maybe I should go after her."

Hank rested his elbow on the top rail and looked at him.

"Yeah. I could go after her and bring her back. And if she won't come . . . then . . . well . . ."

Brady wondered why his brother showed no reaction to this momentous decision. Didn't he realize Brady might never come back?

Having attended its itchy places, the roan wandered over to stand expectantly by his new best friend, hoping for another rubdown, no doubt.

"Unless you think I shouldn't."

Hank shook his head. "What I think is you're dumber than a bucket of rocks. That's what I think." Muttering, he turned and walked away.

The roan snorted, either in protest to Hank's leaving, or in agreement with his assessment.

"Well. Okay, then." Brady nodded to the horse. "Talked me into it."

The horse wandered away, tail swishing at flies.

Brady watched an eagle float past on invisible currents, chasing its earthbound shadow across the rocky ground. The day was so still, he could hear the whisper of wind across the glossy feathers. Did they have eagles in England, he wondered. Or mountains? Or desert storms that could light up the night sky?

A feeling of panic gripped him. He felt like a man perched on the edge of a cliff, a fifty-foot drop in front of him and a twelve-foot grizzly at his back.

Then he thought of Jessica—and how beautiful she looked in the moonlight, and how perfectly she fit in his arms—and everything settled. Doubt faded. Chaos dimmed. And in its place, spreading through his mind like rain over parched earth, was the most profound sense of completion he'd ever known.

It felt good. And right. And how it was supposed to be.

Feeling as if the weight of the world had slipped from his shoulders, he looked east, past the foothills and the mountains to the endless stretches of sky that lay between them.

"Hold on, Jessica. I'm on my way."

* * *

THINGS CHANGE.

Sometimes it happened slowly over a span of years, in increments so small the changes went unnoticed until one day you looked in a mirror and saw a stranger wearing your face and you wondered when the hell you got to be so old.

Or sometimes it came like a light at the end of a long tunnel of doubt and confusion, growing brighter and stronger with every step . . . like his decision to go after Jessica.

Or sometimes it happened so suddenly it left a man staggering blindly for balance. That's how it was on that August morning when Brady and Hank took the dynamiter up to seal Sancho's cave. It was Brady's last task before he left for England, his way of shutting the door on the past so he could get on with the future.

It was a beautiful day with cotton ball clouds building behind the peaks and a gentle breeze out of the west that smelled like rain. The kind of day he would miss in England. While the dynamiter laid his charges, Brady waited with Hank at the foot of the slope, his mind weighted down by memories. He didn't want to look back anymore. It was time to bury those memories with Sancho and look ahead to a new beginning with Jessica and Ben.

"All clear?" the dynamiter called from his perch halfway up the slope.

"All clear," Hank shouted back.

The dynamiter struck the match to the fuse, then a puff of smoke raced up the rocky slope and disappeared into the cave. They waited. From deep inside the mountain came a muffled boom, followed by a rumbling sound that grew louder until it erupted in a thunderous belch of dust and rubble as the entrance collapsed.

Silence, except for the clatter of pebbles and rocks bouncing down the slope.

Then Brady felt the ground shiver beneath his feet. On the slope, more rocks tumbled free. Then more. And suddenly, in a hellish roar of

cascading boulders and trees and brush, half the hillside and a shrieking dynamiter came barreling down the slope toward them.

They barely escaped with their lives. Once the dust settled and
Brady found his footing again, he saw that Hank had a bloody gash on
his forehead and the dynamiter, apparently a man new to his job, shook
so badly he kept falling over. Or maybe his leg was broken. Brady was
so mad he didn't care.

"What the hell was that?" he shouted, still reeling from a dozen
cuts and bruises and maybe even a cracked rib.

"Christamighty . . ." From his sprawled position, the dynamiter
gaped up at what was left of the slope.

"You could have gotten us killed, you stupid bastard! Where are
the horses? Somebody get the horses. Hank, quit bleeding." Belatedly,
Brady realized neither the dynamiter nor Hank paid him any heed as
they stared past him at where the cave used to be. He turned.

Air rushed from his lungs. His mouth fell open.

"Is that what I think it is?" Hank choked out.

"It is," the dynamiter said in an awed voice. "Unless I miss my guess,
that's one helluva vein of silver ore."

Sonofabitch. Brady's legs folded and he plopped down onto a toppled
boulder. After a moment of stunned silence, he dropped his head into
his hands and began to laugh.

Redeemed at last. Praise the Lord.

WITHIN THE WEEK HE HAD THE HOUSE PLANS DRAWN AND
supplies ordered. Then he renamed the ranch Wilkins Cattle & Mining, had Phineas Higgins set up a mining company, and hired an engineer to run it. By the end of the month, construction had begun on the
stamp mill and concentrator, mining machinery was on the way, and
he had a railway engineer surveying for a short haul line to carry the
ore from the mine to the proposed branch off the Transcontinental.
Finally, when he was satisfied everything was headed in the right direc-

tion and there was nothing more he could do, Brady dumped it all into Hank's capable hands, told him *adiós*, and left for England.

If he was lucky and didn't drown at sea or end up on the wrong island, he might make it to Posten Cross before his year deadline was up.

Twenty-six

Bickersham Hall, Northumberland, England

JESSICA STARED AT THE LETTER IN HER HAND, WONDERING WHY she had bothered to write it. He probably wouldn't receive it until after his year was up, and by then her plans would be in motion.

Putting the letter aside, she crossed the library to stand at the window overlooking the side garden. A soft mist curled through the trees. Roses bowed like ladies-in-waiting, their blossoms weighted down by the morning rain. Somewhere a lark sang, oblivious to the turmoil in her heart.

She turned away. As she did, she caught her reflection in the mirror between the windows, and was arrested anew by how much she had changed over the last year.

Months of rosewater and borax compresses had bleached the freckles from her face. Regular rinses with powdered blue vitriol solution had gradually taken the brassiness from her hair. Exhausting walks, a lack of appetite, and a return to the restriction of a corset had trimmed her new-mother curves. But nothing seemed to alter that lackluster stare in her eyes.

Annie said she was prettier than she had ever been. Percy said she looked mysteriously aloof. Jessica knew it was simply too much heartache and too many sleepless nights.

Well, no more. She was tired of waiting for happiness to come to her. She would find it on her own. If she had learned anything from the ordeal on the desert, it was to snatch all the joy she could in this life and waste no time on regrets.

He had made his decision. Now she had made hers.

Resolved, she crossed to the bell pull and gave it a hard yank, then went back to the desk. She was sealing the letter in a mailing pouch when Dougal pushed open the door, yawning as he scratched the wiry, gray hair at his sideburns. "Aye, lass?"

"Has the post come today?"

"Ye woke me to ask about the mail?"

"You are in service, Dougal. You should be attending your duties, not sleeping."

The old man reared back, the watery blue eyes round with indignation. "I'm no' a servant, lass. I'm here because yer da asked me to look after the tew of you. As a guardian. No' a servant."

Realizing she shouldn't be taking out her ire on Dougal, much less engaging in a battle she would never win, Jessica gracefully ceded. "You are correct, Dougal. I apologize." Smiling sweetly, she held out the letter. "On your way back to your nap, if it's not too much bother, would you please put this on the foyer table?"

"Aye." With a show of weary reluctance, he took the letter. "And I'll check on the post. But only this one time, lass, nae more." He turned toward the door.

Bracing herself, Jessica added, "And also send someone for Percy Bothingham."

He stopped, let out a great huff of breath, then swung back. "Ye've decided."

Jessica nodded.

"Then I'm for leaving, lass. I'll no' stay and take orders from the likes o' him."

"I understand." Jessica bit back a smile. She dearly loved this cantankerous old man. He had been more of a father to her than Papa ever was. "And where will you go, if I may inquire?"

Dougal scratched the stubble on his chin. "I've a mind tae see a buffalo, lass."

Blinking back tears, she walked over and put her arms around him. "Then you shall," she whispered against his bristly neck. "And I will happily pay your passage."

"As well ye should."

Brady arrived in England on an overcast morning in late October, desperate for dirt beneath his boots, a bed that didn't move, and anything to eat that wasn't salt pork.

He hired a hansom cab—which was English for a two-wheeled covered carriage—and after a quick stop at the Bank of England to exchange the silver in his saddlebags for British currency, he went to the hotel recommended by the ship's captain, which luckily, was far enough across town the stink from the River Thames was barely noticeable.

Even so, by the time he arrived at his lodgings, he had a headache from all the noise and chaos and crowds that seemed a part of every big city he'd ever been to, which—counting London—was one too many. On the good side, although the weather was dismal and foggy, it wasn't raining.

The Stilton Hotel was a grand place with shiny marble floors, potted plants as big as trees, and chandeliers that would outweigh a yearling calf. He was careful not to walk under one as he made his way to the front desk with his luggage, which consisted of his saddlebags and saddle—he wasn't about to ride around on one of those pancake things. He noted the odd looks cast his way. Probably the Stetson. Or maybe the gunbelt. None of the people staring at him wore either.

It reminded him again that if he was to become the kind of man

Jessica expected him to be, he might have to make some changes—in appearance anyway.

At the front desk, which was guarded by an elderly fellow who wore the pinched expression of a man who had just caught a whiff of something foul, Brady set the saddle and saddlebags on the marble floor and asked for the biggest bed they had.

The old man's eyes raked over him. Then he smiled in a way that didn't involve many facial muscles and said as carefully as if he were addressing a moron, "That would be in the Chamberlain Suite, sir. Our grandest." He paused to give Brady a sharp look. "And also our most expensive."

"I'll take it." Brady slapped a wad of bank notes atop the counter. "Cash."

A magic word, it seemed. The fellow instantly became Brady's dear friend, offering all kinds of services—which he called "amenities"—including that of a barber, a tailor, a valet, and a maid, which was mentioned in an undertone and accompanied by a waggle of white eyebrows.

Brady declined the valet and maid, asking that the barber, the tailor, and several plates of food be sent to his suite. Then he picked up his gear and climbed the wide, curving, gilt and marble staircase to begin his transformation from hardscrabble rancher to high-toned Englishman.

It was harder than he thought. The barber wanted to shave his mustache, which Brady wouldn't allow, and since Brady had never been fitted for a custom suit, he found the tailor's groping and measuring a bit unsettling. In addition to a pointy-collared, tight-necked shirt, he was expected to wear something called a "cravat," which looked like a fluffy bow tie. Luckily, since there was no time to have proper shoes made, he was allowed to keep his boots.

He settled with the barber and paid the tailor double to have the suit and shirt finished by morning, then ate the food sent up—which wasn't the supper he expected, but something called "high tea"—tasty, but not that filling—then he went back down to the lobby. More stares, but with his fresh shave and haircut, people didn't scramble out of his way quite as fast as before.

After the innkeeper gave him directions to the nearest livestock yard of good reputation—which he called a "horse mart"—Brady threw the saddle over his shoulder and left the hotel.

The mist had thickened to almost rain, the kind that was near useless and less wet than aggravating. But it was still enough to clear the coal soot from the air and people from the streets. After being cooped up aboard ship for so long, Brady enjoyed the walk.

He hadn't seen much of England, but of all that he had seen, the English Thoroughbred horse was the best. Tall and lanky, with wide intelligent eyes and an earnest desire to cover ground, it was everything he could want in a mount. If he ever returned to the ranch, which he probably wouldn't, he'd bring with him some breeding stock and try crossing a Thoroughbred with a mustang. Could be interesting. He smiled, wondering what he'd call it. A Thoroughtang? A Musthorough?

The head groom at the horse mart, a bow-legged little Scotsman with an accent Brady could hardly decipher, was very helpful and forthcoming, especially when he learned he would be paid outright, rather than on credit. He also knew his horseflesh.

After looking over several fine mounts, Brady picked out a leggy bay with three white stockings, a proud headset, and friendly eyes. He was about to give the animal a try, when the Scotsman saw the saddle Brady intended to use.

"Ye'll break his back, puir thing."

Which didn't say much for the horse. But unwilling to argue about it, Brady dropped the saddle, grabbed a handful of mane at the horse's withers, and vaulted onto the gelding's back.

The horse was responsive and willing, with an even temperament and a long, smooth stride. By the time Brady had put him through the paces, he knew he'd found a match, and the hostler was grinning. "Ye've the hands of a piper and the balance of a Cossack, lad. One of them Wild West cowboys, I'll warrant."

Reining in beside the Scotsman, Brady flipped his right leg over the horse's neck and slid to the ground. He gave the gelding a pat on the neck. "How much?"

They settled on a price. Then Brady asked the Scotsman for a list of the best-known and most respected stud farms in England. If he was going to give up ranching, he might as well try his hand at horse breeding. Assuming he stayed in England. Which Jessica would probably expect. After the hostler gave him a list of three breeders, and grudging permission to use his own tack on his own newly purchased horse, Brady left the saddle and asked to have the animal ready at dawn.

Back at the hotel, he ate again—this time it was called dinner—then asked the innkeeper for general directions to Posten Cross. Feeling pretty satisfied with all he'd accomplished during his first day in England, he stretched out for his first decent night's sleep since he embarked in New Orleans.

He figured it would take him three, maybe four, days to reach Jessica.

Five days later, he climbed the steps to the Sheep's Head Inn in Posten Cross, so tired he was staggering. He had ridden through half of England, suffered the worst food he'd ever put in his mouth, and slept on beds that were at best a foot too narrow and two feet too short, but he was finally here. His plan was a bath, a nap, enough food to restore his stamina, then Jessica.

Dropping his saddlebags beside the door, he approached the skinny, thin-necked innkeeper studying him through narrowed eyes from behind the plank counter. "I need a room and a stall. One night. Maybe more."

The man's nostrils quivered.

"And a bath," Brady added.

Pressing his lips in a disapproving line, the innkeeper studied the registry book. "And which will you be taking, sir? The stall or the room?"

Brady looked at him.

The condescending smirk became a fawning simper. "The room. Of course. I shall have the bath sent up straightaway." Slapping a key onto the counter, he directed Brady to their "loveliest top-floor room with magnificent views of the Cheviot Hills," then hastily stepped back, as if he expected Brady to reach over the counter and do something unmannerly or even violent, which was pretty perceptive, Brady thought.

After asking directions to Bickersham Hall, he left his new tailor-made suit and shirt to have the wrinkles taken out—he wasn't sure how, nor did he care—ordered a meal to be ready at four o'clock, then went upstairs to his tiny loft room, washed as best he could in his tiny copper tub, then collapsed onto his tiny, lumpy bed, where he slept three hours straight without rolling over.

He awoke to a knock on the door and a growling stomach.

"Your suit, sir," the fawning innkeeper said. "And if I may say so, a very handsome one, indeed." After hanging it in the empty wardrobe and reminding Brady that his meal awaited him in the taproom, he backed out of the room, bobbing and bowing with every step.

Brady dressed. It took him three tries to get the fluffy bowtie right, and although it looked a bit mangled by the time he finished, he decided it would have to do. He checked himself in the mirror on the back of the door. Then, regretfully, he discarded the Stetson and gunbelt and checked again. Better. In fact, he looked so English, Jessica might not even recognize him. His brothers sure as hell wouldn't.

Down in the taproom, he downed three plates of tasteless food and two shots of the best sipping whiskey he'd ever enjoyed, then climbed back in the saddle and headed to Bickersham Hall and Jessica. By his calculations, he'd arrive in time for tea and three days short of his deadline.

"You seem restless."

Jessica turned from her study of the wide pebbled drive beyond the front terrace and gave her sister a strained smile. "Do I?"

"You've paced before that window every day for weeks." Annie eyed her over the tatting she sewed along the edge of the bridal veil. "Do you expect someone?"

Jessica laughed. "Someone other than the seventy-five guests arriving this evening?"

"You know precisely who I mean. You expect *him*, don't you?"

Not anymore. Not after months of watching and waiting without even a single word to let her know he was alive and well and still remembered her. "Not at all," she said with false brightness as she moved to sit beside Annie on the newly upholstered damask settee.

She glanced around at other new pieces, expensive drapes and imported rugs, crystal decanters, the refurbished marble work on the fireplace. So many changes since she and Adrian arrived nearly a year ago to find the Hall shabby and worn, the grounds unkempt, her sister prostrate with grief and worry. Now they were solvent. More than solvent. Thanks to the coal beneath her land and Percy's able management of it, they could have anything they wanted.

Well, almost anything. What she truly wanted was beyond price.

And she was weary of waiting for it—and him. She couldn't live on hope forever.

"Perhaps the preparations for the ball have put you out of sorts," Annie suggested.

"Don't be a goose." Seeing the worry in her sister's soft hazel eyes, Jessica donned her cheeriest smile. "I'm excited. Truly I am. I can scarcely wait." This was the first time in years Bickersham Hall had hosted such a gala, and Jessica was determined it be everything her sister had dreamed. She owed her that.

It had been an awkward homecoming with Adrian to explain and creditors circling them like scavengers. She didn't know how they would have managed without Percy Bothingham's help. He had been a godsend. In more ways than she could count. "Is all in readiness?"

Annie nodded. "The orchestra has arrived, the flowers are in their vases, Cook seems to have everything under control, and Dougal is guarding the champagne."

"Dougal?" Jessica gave a wry smile. "I hope there will be enough left for the engagement toast. Are the guns safely locked away?"

"Those that still work." Annie let the veil fall into her lap. "Oh, Jessica. I cannot believe you're truly leaving in less than a fortnight. I shall miss you terribly."

"And I shall miss you." She gave her sister a quick hug, glad they had found their way past the pain and distrust that was John Crawford's legacy. They were thriving. The children were thriving. Things couldn't be better.

And yet . . .

Jessica studied her sister, hearing the last-time bell echoing through her mind and wondering what changes another separation might bring.

Even though she still saw her baby sister in the shy smile and tousled auburn hair, they were both grown women now with children of their own. It was time they moved beyond what was, toward what could be. But it still hurt to think of a future without her little sister near. "Am I doing the right thing, Annie?" she blurted out.

"Now who's the goose?" Annie set aside the tatting and rose. "You said this is what you wanted. Have you changed your mind?"

"No. Of course not."

"You don't have to go through with this. Percy can—"

"Yes—No. I'm sure." Resolved, Jessica sent one last glance at the empty road, then turned to her sister with a smile. "Hurry along, Miss Priss. Or we'll both be late for the ball."

ALL DURING THE LONG TRIP FROM HOME, BRADY HAD pictured Jessica in the sprawling log and stone house he'd designed with her in mind—sitting in her new rocker on the wraparound porch, stirring a pot of something other than chili on the combination stove he was having shipped from Philadelphia, smiling up at him from their oversized bed.

But those images turned to dust when he rode up the long pebbled drive to Bickersham Hall.

Pillared gate, shaded lawns, a huge stone manor house with tall mullioned windows, massive arched entry, side porticos, and wide stone terraces. It wasn't a house, it was a mansion, and one that had been in her family for hundreds of years. How could he expect her to leave that?

Fancy carriages lined the drive. Uniformed servants moved past the windows, holding trays laden with food and tall goblets. Music never heard in a Western saloon wafted onto the terrace as dark-suited men and bejeweled women waltzed gracefully past.

That wasn't *cabrito* they were serving. And this wasn't a fandango. And he didn't belong here any more than a calf at a christening.

But Jessica did.

A hopeless feeling swept through him. And at that moment, as he sat on his horse staring at Jessica's ancestral home, he understood in a way he never had before how truly different he and Jessica were. It wasn't a matter of money or possessions but a difference in perception and expectation.

She looked at land and thought flowers. He looked at land and thought cattle. She was liveried servants and ivy-covered stone. He was hard-living cowboys and rough-hewn timbers. Champagne and Forty Rod. The two didn't mix.

But there was still something . . . something he couldn't name or define . . . that drew them together, despite all those differences that threatened to pull them apart.

He left the Thoroughbred munching flowers in a big stone urn by the drive, and, with both anticipation and dread, mounted the worn stone steps.

The door flew open before he reached it. A wild-eyed old man stepped out, glaring up at him from beneath white wooly eyebrows. "What do ye want?" His boozy breath almost singed Brady's mustache.

When Brady didn't answer, the old man poked him in the chest with the octagonal barrel of an ancient flintlock dueling pistol. "State yer business. And if I dinna like yer answer, laddie, I'll be having yer wee bollocks for breakfast."

Brady looked down at the pistol and was relieved to see the flint was missing. "Jessica," he said, gently pushing the barrel aside with his index finger.

The barrel swung back. The old man's gaze narrowed. "Is that yer horse eating the shrubbery?"

Brady nodded.

"She'll no' like it."

"It's a he."

"What?"

"The horse. It's a he."

"I can see that, ye great bluidy fool. What do ye want?"

Feeling a headache build, Brady squeezed the bridge of his nose between his thumb and forefinger. How was he ever going to live in this mist-shrouded land surrounded by odd-talking Scotsmen and tippy-toeing Englishmen? And where the hell was the sun? Lowering his hand, he nudged the pistol aside again. "I've come to see Jessica Thornton. Is she here?"

"O'course she is. It's the engagement ball, ye daft foreigner. Be gone wie ye."

Engagement ball?

The old man turned toward the door.

Brady yanked him back with enough force to lift the Scotsman off his feet and send the pistol spinning across the flagstones. "Whose engagement ball?"

He must have shouted it, judging by the old man's flinch. "The lassie's."

Brady felt like he'd been hit. *The lassie? Jessica? Engaged?* "Who's she marrying? Bothingham?"

"A-Aye."

"That sonofabitch!" Thrusting the old man away, he looked around for something to hit. Couldn't she even wait a year?

"It's you!"

He turned back to see the old man regarding him with stunned disbelief.

"Aboot time ye got yer bluidy arse over here!" The Scotsman rushed over and began pounding his back. "It's me, Dougal. Dougal McRae. Of the Killiecrankie McRaes, no' the Inverness." He gave a belly laugh, which turned into a choking fit that felled insects within ten feet of his vaporous breath. "Come in, laddie," he said, wiping tears from his red-rimmed eyes. "Ye're just in time for the toast to a long and happy marriage." Then he was off again, choking and hacking and laughing.

Afraid he might puke, Brady turned and walked down the steps toward his horse.

"Lass," Dougal called loudly as Jessica swept through the entry toward the kitchen. "There's a man out front needs a word. Seems upset."

Lovely. Cook having conniptions over some missing champagne, Sir Henry propositioning the footmen, Adrian throwing frogs on the Ellerton twins—where did a fifteen-month-old get frogs?—and now an irate tradesman. "Can't it wait?"

"Best not. The puir lad's come a long way."

She sighed. "Very well." She crossed to the front door, speaking over her shoulder as she went. "Take the frog away from Adrian and put it back where it belongs."

"What frog?"

"The one you gave him. And return the champagne to Cook."

Ignoring Dougal's mutterings, she opened the door and stepped onto the terrace.

A man stood at the bottom of the steps talking to his horse. A tall man with dark hair and mustache and shoulders so wide they looked padded.

Her breath caught. She took a hesitant step forward then another, until she was close enough to grasp the stone balustrade for support. "Brady . . . ?"

He turned. Eyes the color of a hot summer sky swept over her.

"Oh, God . . ." Her heart stuttered in her chest. Air rushed from her lungs. She swayed as her legs lost strength. Why now? After all her plans were in motion, why did he come now?

Brady saw her teetering and took the stairs in two strides. As he steadied her on her feet, she clutched at him, eyes wide and round in her ashen face, her mouth open and closing as she tried to speak. "Are you real? Is it really you?"

His gaze moved hungrily over her. She wore a gauzy green dress that showed off the curves that had kept him awake for a year. Her skin was paler without the freckles, her hair had lost the golden streaks left by last year's sun, and she looked more like a china doll than the flesh-and-blood woman who had left him a year ago. But he remembered that flowery scent and the way she fit so perfectly in his arms. "It's me."

She pressed a trembling hand against his cheek. "You're here? Truly?"

Her touch made his skin feel tight and his knees weak. How had he managed a year without this woman? "I'm here. Truly." Blinking hard, he smiled.

Tears flooded her eyes. "I—I can't believe you came." She stared up at him a moment longer, then gently pulled out of his grip and wiped at her eyes. "I had given up . . . I didn't expect . . ." She busied herself brushing at her skirts, patting her hair, checking the jewelry dangling from her earlobes. "You never wrote."

When she finally quit fussing, he said, "You're not marrying Bothingham."

She looked up at him, a small frown forming between her auburn brows.

That sinking, hopeless feeling gripped him again. Where was the lively, headstrong Jessica he remembered? This woman was a stranger to him. She looked nearly the same and sounded the same, but the fire was gone. Even her riotous curls had been tamed, and those whiskey-colored eyes had lost their luster and just looked . . . brown.

"Who said I was marrying Bothingham?"

"Your doorman. About the time he pulled a gun on me."

"Dougal." She made a dismissive gesture with one shaky hand.

"He's Scottish. He pulls a gun on everyone." Her eyes darted to the faces grinning at them through the windows. "We're making spectacles of ourselves."

"I don't care."

"I do." She started fussing with her skirts again. "It's unseemly."

And just like that, Her Ladyship was back—the starchy tone, the pinched expression, the rigid posture. It sickened him. He'd come too late. He'd lost her. Turning, he started down the steps. "Good-bye, Jessica."

"W-What? Where are you going?" When he didn't answer, she moved to the top of the stairs. "You're right, I'm not marrying Percy," she called in a rush.

He stopped.

"Annie is."

When he looked back, she burst into tears. "Why didn't you write, Brady? I waited and waited, but you didn't even send a single letter and I thought . . . I thought . . ."

This was the Jessica he remembered, the emotional, babbling, vulnerable woman who needed him almost as much as he needed her. He bounded back up the steps. Grabbing her hand, he pulled her away from prying eyes, down the stairs, and around the house to the privacy of the torch-lit side gardens.

Not too late. Still his. Relief roared in his head, sent such a charge of energy through his body it was all he could do not to break into a run.

The path ended at a gurgling stream, banked by leafy shrubs and long-limbed oaks that formed a drooping canopy overhead. For once it wasn't raining, but the air was thick with fog rising from the damp ground. Flowers blooming beside the path gave off a scent unfamiliar to him, and somewhere, in a call he didn't recognize, a bird fussed at their intrusion. Breathing hard, he turned to Jessica .

With mist swirling around her feet like spun sugar clouds and torchlight shimmering off her jewels and tears, she looked like something from his dreams. He wanted to hold her, to assure himself she was real, but uncertainty held him back. The year had changed her.

She was no longer his Jessica. Nor was she wholly Her Ladyship . . . but something in between. More assured. Older. Sadder. And if possible, more beautiful. Releasing her hand, he stepped back and said the only thing he could think of—the only thing that mattered. "I love you, Jessica."

She drew in a deep, shuddering breath and slowly let it out. She wiped a hand over her wet cheek then lifted her head and studied him. "Why have you come now, after all this time?"

Not the response he'd hope for. But he pushed gamely ahead. He knew she was angry, and allowed that she had a right to be. And if he was required to do a bit of groveling to win her back, he'd gladly do it. "I realized there were worse things than losing the ranch."

"Like what?"

"Losing you."

Anger flashed. "You didn't *lose* me, Brady. You threw me away."

Groveling *and* begging. "I thought I was doing the right thing, Jessica. I was wrong."

"It took you a year to figure that out?" She started crying again, which only added fuel to her anger. "Now look what you've done. I never cry. Yet around you I become a watering pot."

Brady had noticed that. He wasn't sure how it was his fault but he knew better than to argue.

Conjuring a lacy handkerchief from somewhere, she blotted the tears from her cheeks. Once she had herself in hand, she hiked her chin in that familiar defiant gesture that always brought a catch to his heart. "Are your intentions to stay or take me back?"

"Either. Whatever you want." Which he suddenly realized was the absolute unequivocal truth. Echoing Jack's sentiment—Brady knew he would do anything, live anywhere, be whatever Jessica wanted, as long as she would have him.

She blinked puffy eyes. "What about RosaRoja?"

"Hank can take care of it."

Jessica's heart faltered, then accelerated to a frantic wing beat against her ribs. "You're giving up the ranch? For me?"

He spread his hands. "I'm here, aren't I?"

Her mouth went slack. Then joy surged through her. *He chose me. Over RosaRoja.* She felt like singing, laughing, dancing a jig through the mist. *I won.*

Brady watched her, a confused but hopeful smile on his face. He looked so dashing in his fine suit, so properly English—except for the boots and the ever-present stubble and that wrinkled cravat. So . . . un-Brady. If she didn't know the heart of the man standing before her, she wouldn't have known how great the sacrifice he had come here to make.

For her.

She almost burst into tears again.

Brady. In England. Where there was too little sky and too many fences. Doing what? Sitting on the terrace sipping tea while he visited with the vicar? Making a list of all the words he would have to cross from his vocabulary?

It would destroy him.

Which was why her trunks were packed and the tickets bought, and in two weeks she and Adrian, escorted by Dougal, were to begin the long journey back to where they belonged. Back to him. What if they had crossed en route? The irony of it almost made her laugh out loud.

She dabbed at her running nose. "I doubt you'd be happy here." Nor would she, watching him try to become something he wasn't. She loved him for what he was, not what she could make of him. Although in that suit he was utterly charming. Maybe she could convince him to keep it.

"I'd be happy wherever you are, Jessica. You're my lodestone. My true north. Without you, I'm lost. Don't you know that?"

She felt another tear roll down her cheek. With a shaky laugh, she brushed it away, but more came. The man knew how to charm her, he surely did.

"I'm sorry I hurt you, Jessica. It won't happen again. I swear it."

I'm sorry. Two simple words. But coming from this man, they made her heart whole.

"You're crying again."

"Happy tears."

She felt his hand brush along her cheek. "Does that mean you forgive me?"

Lifting her head, she smiled at the man before her—this magnificent, arrogant, utterly exasperating man who had traveled thousands of miles to arrive unannounced on her doorstep, expecting her to simply jump into his arms as if he had not completely ignored her for almost a year.

She adored him beyond reason.

She would forgive him anything.

Before she could tell him that, words rushed from his mouth. "I'm rich now, Jessica. I can give you anything you want. We struck silver and—"

"I don't care." Pressing her palm against his solid chest, she felt the hard, fast beat of his heart. Just having him within reach calmed her . . . sustained her.

His voice grew strained, almost desperate. "I'm building a new house—a big house, with lots of windows and wide porches and a cookstove sent all the way from—"

"I don't care." She lifted her hand to trail fingertips over his bristly jaw. It didn't matter where they lived. Annie could watch over Bickersham Hall until a daughter was born. And if she and Brady never had a daughter, then so be it. Annie's daughter, Rebecca, could have it. All that was truly important was that she and Brady were together, wherever that might be.

Air exploded from his chest. "Then what do you want, Jessica? Just tell me."

She smiled, despite the tears she couldn't seem to stem. "You." Reaching higher, she grabbed his earlobe and gently tugged his face down so she could press her lips to his. "I want you, you big dolt," she whispered, kissing him again. "You're all I've ever wanted."

Tension seeped out of him in a long shaky breath. "You've got me."

She felt the tremble in his arms as they closed around her, pulling her so tightly against his body her toes barely touched the ground. It was the most wonderful feeling in the world. "And now that you do," he said, resting his forehead against hers, "what are you going to do with me?"

She tilted her face to nip his bottom lip. "I suppose I'll have to marry you and take you home. It would be the proper thing, after all, insomuch as you've already had your way with me."

He stilled. Then he slowly lifted his head. In the glow of the torchlight, his eyes seemed to burn with blue flames. "Whose home?" he asked in that husky voice. "Mine? Or yours?"

"Ours, you sweet, silly man." At his look of relief, she laughed, joy overflowing her heart. "Something sturdy," she said, slipping her arms around his neck. "With windows all around—"

"And rockers on the porch," he added.

"And a lovely view of the mesquite tree."

HERE'S A PREVIEW OF THE NEXT BOOK
IN THE BLOOD ROSE TRILOGY BY KAKI WARNER . . .

OPEN COUNTRY

COMING SOON FROM BERKLEY SENSATION!

Prologue

Savannah, Georgia, October 1871

"MOLLY? WHAT ARE YOU DOING HERE? HOW DID YOU GET in?"

So much for a warm welcome, Molly McFarland thought as she set down her valise and turned to meet her sister's husband as he came down the staircase of his elegant Savannah home. "The door was open."

"Damn those kids." Reaching past her, he shut the door so forcefully the panes in the window beside it rattled. Standing back, he glared at her. "Why are you here?"

"The doctor sent for me." Molly unpinned her hat and hung it on a hook beside the door, then turned to her brother-in-law with what she hoped was a pleasant expression. In truth, she despised Daniel Fletcher, especially after the callus way he had treated the family—most particularly, his two stepchildren—after her father's death a month ago. "How is she?"

Fletcher made a dismissive motion. He seemed distracted and on edge. Not his usual, fastidious self with that unshaven beard and soiled shirt. "Fine, fine. There was no need for you to come all the way from Atlanta."

"The doctor seemed to think there was. Lung fever is quite serious." Hearing the snappish tone in her voice, she reined in her temper. "I'm not here to interfere with the doctor, Daniel. I've come as her sister, not a nurse. If there's anything I can do to—"

"There isn't," he cut in harshly. "You're not needed."

Molly looked steadily at him, refusing to back down, wondering as she had so many times, why her older sister had taken such an unpleasant man as her second husband. Grief over her first husband's death had been part of it, no doubt. And fear of raising a six-year-old daughter and eight-year-old son on her own had added to it.

"May I see her?" she asked.

Being the weak, bullying man he was, Fletcher looked away first, his gaze as shifty as that of a guilty child. "Oh, all right. Stay if you must." He turned and went down the hall to his office, slamming the door hard behind him.

Molly wondered how he could bear to go into that room. She had only had the courage to venture through that door once. The walls had been cleaned by then, the reek of gunpowder and blood masked by the cloying scent of funeral flowers and smoke from Daniel's cigar. But Papa's ghost had lingered. She could feel him still.

"Did you come to save Mama?"

Molly looked up to see her nephew, Charlie, sitting on the top step of the stairs. He looked lost and small and too knowing for his eight years. He'd already lost his father and grandfather. Was he to lose his mother now, too? "I've come to try," she answered.

"It doesn't matter. He'll get her anyway."

Molly frowned in confusion. "Who will get her?"

"The monster. He'll get us, too." Jumping to his feet, Charlie darted away, his footfalls ending with the thud of an upstairs door.

Frowning, Molly started up the stairs. As she rose above the parlor, she looked down through the open door to see it was a shambles, rugs thrown back, drawers half open, books scattered about the cluttered floor. Apparently, Fletcher hadn't seen fit to hire a cleaning girl during Nellie's illness. Typical.

Outside the master bedroom, she paused for a moment to prepare herself, then knocked. When there was no response, she gently pushed open the door.

The room beyond was still and dark, the curtains pulled tight over the tall windows. The air was rank with the smell of soiled bedding, illness and despair. Except for labored breathing, it was silent.

How long had her sister been left unattended? When had she last had her bedding changed, her face washed or her hair brushed? Had Fletcher simply left her in the dark to suffer alone? "Nellie?" she called.

"Molly . . . is that . . . you?" The voice was a weak rasp, followed by a bout of coughing that seemed to rip through her sister's throat.

Rushing across the room, Molly bent beside the bed, her years of medical training at her father's side overcoming her disgust with Fletcher and her terror for her sister. "Yes, I'm here," she said in the calm, soothing voice Papa had taught her.

Nellie looked ghastly, a mere shadow of the lovely woman she had once been. Her skin seemed stretched over her bones and was an unhealthy gray except for bright spots of color high on her cheeks. Her lovely green eyes shone feverishly bright and her welcoming smile looked more like a grimace.

Recognizing encroaching death when she saw it, Molly sank weakly onto the edge of the mattress. *Dear God*, she cried in silent desperation, *don't take Nellie from me, too.* "Oh, Nellie," she choked out as tears flooded her eyes. "Why didn't you send for me?"

"Daniel . . . wouldn't . . . let me."

To cover her shock, Molly brushed a lock of lank auburn hair from her sister's hot forehead. "Well, I'm here now, dearest. And I won't leave you."

"You must . . ." Reaching out, Nellie grasped Molly's shoulder and pulled her closer. Her breath stank of the infection in her lungs. Her eyes glittered in her gaunt face—but with feverish desperation, not madness.

"Take my . . . babies," she gasped. "Before it's . . . too late."

Molly struggled to understand. "Take them where?"

"Away . . ."

"From Daniel?"

"He's up to . . . something. Something . . . bad. Bombs. A new . . . war." Her voice was so weak Molly had to lean close to hear. Every word was a wheezing struggle. "Thinks children . . . took papers. Threatened . . . hit . . . them." A coughing fit gripped her and Nellie writhed, eyes scrunched tight as she struggled to drag air into her flooded lungs. Once the spasm passed, she opened her eyes and Molly saw that desperation had given way to grim determination. "Promise me . . . take them . . . away before . . . too late."

"But, Nellie—"

"Must . . . hide them . . . keep safe." Nellie was panting now, her eyes frantic. "Now. Tonight."

"I c-can't just leave you."

"Must." Tears coursed down Nellie's temples to soak into the filthy bedding. "Keep babies . . . safe. Promise me . . . sister."

Molly blinked back her own tears. "I promise."

A WEEK LATER, IN A DARKENED ROOM TWO HUNDRED MILES west of Savannah, Daniel Fletcher peered nervously through the shadows at the man seated in a wheeled chair behind the wide cherry wood desk.

It irritated him that Rustin didn't have the lamps lit. Even if the old man didn't need light, the rest of them did. He looked around, sensing other people in the room. Probably the artillery expert, maybe the professor.

"Well?" Rustin demanded in his papery voice. "Have you found it?"

"Not yet," Fletcher answered, hoping his voice didn't betray his growing alarm. Why hadn't any of the others spoken? And why hadn't Rustin offered him a chair? He felt like a fool standing here in the dark talking to a disembodied voice.

He had never liked Rustin. Even though the old man was the glue that held them all together, Fletcher thought it hypocritical that after stealing all that gold from the Confederate coffers, Rustin would use it to foment another rebellion a decade later. But this wasn't about breathing new life into the wounded South. It was about money. "I've literally torn the place apart," Fletcher said nervously. "If my wife hid it somewhere before she died, it's gone now."

"Who else could have taken it?"

"No one was in the house but me, my wife and her children. Occasionally the doctor came by, and near the end, Nellie's sister came, but the book had disappeared long before that."

"Could Matthew McFarlane have taken it? He must have known something if he came all the way from Atlanta to confront you about it."

Fletcher felt that quiver of guilt move through his stomach. *Poor, stupid Matthew.* His wife's father had always had an overblown sense of integrity. "He had heard rumors. That's all. He knew nothing about the book when he—when I questioned him."

It was a moment before Rustin spoke again. "How old are your children?"

"Stepchildren. Eight and six, I believe."

"Have you questioned them?"

Battling the urge to wipe his clammy palms on his coat, Fletcher glanced around, wondering again why the others hadn't spoken. This was beginning to feel like an inquisition. Turning back to Rustin, he said stiffly, "The children are no longer at the house." *And good riddance.* Always underfoot, poking into things they shouldn't. He was glad to be shut of them.

"Where are they?"

"I-I'm not sure."

Finally a voice erupted from a darkened corner. The Professor's. "Christ, man! They could have taken it and might even now be showing it to the authorities!"

Fletcher could hear whispering in the shadows, a furtive, hushed sound, like rats skittering behind walls.

"They wouldn't have left on their own," Rustin said. "Who is with them?"

"Their aunt, my wife's sister. Molly McFarlane."

"Why did she take them from your care?"

That dry, choking feeling returned to Fletcher's throat. He coughed to clear it. "I d-don't know."

Anger swirled in the closed room like coils of greasy smoke.

"She must have taken it," a voice accused.

Fletcher shook his head. "How could she have even known about it?"

"Maybe your wife told her."

"You imbecile!" Rustin cut in with such an explosion of vehemence Fletcher flinched. "You idiot!" Leaning forward in his chair and into a pale slant of light penetrating the edge of the drawn drape, Rustin spread his bloated hands on the desktop. His milky eyes seemed to stare into Fletcher, although Fletcher knew that was impossible. "You go find them, you bumbling fool! You find that woman and those children and get that book back! Now!"

"Y-Yes. All right." Fletcher edged toward the exit. As he swung open the door to the blinding brightness of the hallway, Rustin's voice drifted out behind him.

"Send for Hennessey. Just in case."

One

East of El Paso, Texas, November 1871

"That old man looks like a bear, doesn't he, Aunt Molly?"

Blinking out of her reverie, Molly glanced at her niece, Penny, then up to see that the bearded man seated at the front of the passenger car was staring at her again.

Pursing her lips, she shifted her gaze to the shoulders of the woman seated in front of her. Men didn't usually study her so intently—healthy men, anyway—and it made her acutely uncomfortable. But Penny was right. He did look a bit like a bear with his great size and all that dark hair, although it could only be from a six-year old's perspective that he be considered old.

"He isn't scary like the other one," Penny added, sending a shy grin in the man's direction.

"What other one?"

"The ugly one. He was watching us, too."

Watching us? Frowning, Molly looked around. "When? Here, on the train?"

"By the kitty in the window. 'Member the kitty in the window?" Penny bounced her heels against the front of the bench seat and smiled. "I like kitties."

Molly vaguely recalled a tabby dozing in the display window of a general store in . . . where was that? Omaha? But she hadn't noticed anyone watching them. "Is that the only time you've seen him?"

"He was in the red town, too. He waved at me but I didn't wave back."

Someone waved at her? Why?

Reaching up, Penny twisted a curl around her finger as she often did when she was anxious. "I didn't like him. He looked like a candle."

"A candle?"

"His face was all melted. He was scary."

Melted? Was he old? Did he have a burn scar? Molly thought of all the faces she'd seen in the last weeks, but none stuck out. She had tried to be vigilant in case Fletcher had come after them, but what if he had sent trackers instead? The thought was so unsettling it was a moment before Molly could draw in a full breath.

"I had a kitty once but he went dead." Penny peered up through her flyaway blond hair. "Can I have another one, Aunt Molly? I promise I won't sneeze."

"Perhaps. We'll see."

What if someone had followed them this far? What if he was on the train even now? Nervously Molly glanced at the other passengers then froze when she found the bearded man staring at her again. Suspicion blossomed in her mind.

Several times that morning she had looked up to find his assessing gaze on her. At first, she had thought nothing of it. They sat facing each other, after all. Since the man was apparently too large to fit comfortably into the narrow forward facing passenger seats, he had taken the bench at the front of the car. It was natural that their gazes might cross occasionally. But after years of being invisible and for the last three weeks trying desperately to attract as little notice as possible, Molly found it disconcerting to be the object of such interest, idle though it might be. Could he be a tracker sent by Fletcher?

The man looked away, but Molly continued to study him.

He wore a thick shearling jacket so she couldn't see if he wore a gun. But those work-worn hands hinted that he earned his living doing more than just waving a pistol about. And his face, despite the low hat and concealing beard, didn't seem particularly threatening, although that dark stare was a bit unnerving.

Turning her attention to the window, she tried to remember what she knew about him. She had first seen him that morning when the train had stopped in Sierra Blanca to fill the tender with water, and she and the children had gotten out to stretch their legs. He had been supervising the loading of some sort of machinery onto a flat car. The men assisting seemed to know him, as did the conductor, who had stopped to chat with him when he'd passed through the car a while ago. That meant the bearded man had reason to be here other than to track her and the children. It was simply coincidence that they were on the same train. That, and nothing more.

Letting out a breath of relief, she glanced at the children. On her left, wearing his usual scowl and chewing his thumbnail, Charlie stared morosely out at the west Texas landscape bouncing by. On her right, Penny dozed, her thumb stuck in her mouth. It was a habit she had resumed of late and indicated she battled the same troubling fears that Charlie did. That they all did.

Hopefully, soon it would be over and they would be starting a new life in California. She would find employment—either as an assistant to one of her father's medical colleagues, or in a clinic or hospital—and then they could cease this erratic flight. If she only knew what it was they were running from and why, maybe she could find a better way to protect them. But Nellie had been so weak and distraught the night Molly had spirited the children away from Savannah, Molly hadn't questioned her. Now she wished she had.

Feeling the weight of exhaustion pulling her down, Molly tipped her head back against the seat and closed her eyes. How long had they been traveling? Almost three weeks?

The children had hardly spoken at first. Confused and terrified, they hadn't understood why they had to leave in such a hurry or why they'd had to leave their mother behind. Penny still didn't understand, but Charlie did. He had lost so much in his eight years it made him fearful of what might be taken from him next. Because of it, he trusted no one. Not even her.

Opening her eyes, Molly's gaze fell on her nephew. She had no experience with children. She didn't know what Penny and Charlie wanted or needed or expected, and her inadequacy terrified her. But she loved them with all her heart and hoped to find a way to reach them and gain their trust. They were all that was left of her family now, and probably the only children she would ever have, and she was all that stood between them and Fletcher and whatever threat he posed. She was resolved to protect them at any cost.

Moved by concern for her troubled nephew, Molly reached over to stroke the fall of auburn hair from Charlie's furrowed brow.

He jerked away.

Molly let her hand fall back to her lap. "Charlie," she said, and waited for him to look at her. When he did, she saw fear in his eyes, and more anger than any child should ever carry. "Why are you so angry?"

He stared silently at the back of the bench in front of him, his lips pressed in a tight, thin line.

"I know you're upset about your mother."

His head whipped toward her. "Why didn't you save her? You're supposed to be a nurse. You should have made her better."

"I tried, Charlie. I wanted to help her. More than anything in the world."

He glared at her for a moment more, then the fight seemed to drain out of him. "It doesn't matter," he said and turned toward the window. "The monster would have gotten her anyway."

The monster again. Molly sighed. How often over the last weeks had she awakened to her nephew's screaming nightmares? "There is no monster, Charlie," she told him as she had so many times. "It's just a bad dream."

Charlie continued to stare out the window, a wall of silence between them.

With a sense of defeat, Molly looked down to see that her hands had curled into tight fists. With effort, she opened them, forcing her fingers to straighten one by one until they lay flat against her thighs. At least she had control over her fingers, she thought wryly, even though everything else in her life seemed to be spinning out of control.

A distant voice shouted. Footsteps pounded overhead as someone raced across the roof of the passenger car toward the rear. A moment later, metal squealed on metal so loudly the children covered their ears. The car lurched as the brakes took hold. Charlie careened against her shoulder. Penny almost tumbled off the seat before Molly caught her.

A woman screamed. Men's voices rose in alarm. The screech of metal grew deafening and acrid smoke began to seep through the rear doors from beneath the back platform where the brakes were.

"What's happening?" Charlie cried, clinging to the armrests as the car began to shudder and buck.

"I don't know," Molly shouted over Penny's wails. "Hold on!"

Another lurch threw Penny to the floor. As Molly reached for her, a falling valise slammed into her shoulder. Then suddenly the car was rocking so hard bodies were flying every which way.

"Penny!" she shouted, terrified the child would be trampled or smothered.

Then big hands scooped the terrified child from the tangle of passengers. A flash of brown eyes as the bearded man thrust her into Molly's arms, then he stepped over thrashing bodies and charged into the smoke billowing at the back landing.

Windows broke. Valises flew from the overhead racks. Then in a thunderous crack, something tore loose from the undercarriage.

Feet braced, her arms wrapped tightly around the wailing children, Molly looked back out the cracked window to see the last three cars of the train topple off the tracks in a thunderous roar of splintering wood.

Immediately their car shot forward, rammed into the car in front of it, then shuddered to a stop.

Amid shrieks and screams from terrified passengers milling about in the smoke, Molly managed to keep a hold on the children and get them out of the car. By then, men had beaten back the flames where the brakes had caught fire beneath the rear platform, and other men were pawing through the wreckage of the baggage car, looking for survivors. Once she made certain the children were unharmed, Molly settled them at a safe distance from the wreckage then went back to help where she could.

Most of the injuries were relatively minor—bruises, scrapes, a few broken bones and cuts from flying glass. But three men were missing and it took an hour for the men digging through the rubble to find them. Both the conductor and a brakeman were dead. The third man was barely alive. The bearded man.

After loading him and the rest of the passengers into the less damaged of the two passengers cars, the train continued on, finally limping into El Paso several hours later.

Luckily, word of the catastrophe had already reached town and a railroad representative named Harkness, the local physician, Dr. Murray, and several townspeople led by a Reverend Beckworth and his wife, Effie, were waiting at the depot to meet them. While the Beckworths herded the battered passengers to their nearby church, and the undertaker carted off the dead men, Dr. Murray had the injured man carried directly to his infirmary on Front Street.

"Not that I can do him any good," Molly overheard him say to the nervous railroad representative. "Poor bastard will probably be dead by nightfall."

"Christ." Harkness wiped a handkerchief over his sweating brow as he studied a column of figures in a small tablet. "This will cost the railroad a goddamn fortune. Two already dead, and another on the way. That's three hundred each in death payments to their families.

And I haven't even added up what we'll have to settle on the injured. Christ."

After assuring the Beckworths he would come to the church as soon as he finished at the infirmary, Dr. Murray hurried down the street, leaving Harkness muttering and scratching numbers into his book.

Again, Molly helped where she could. As she stitched and bandaged, Harkness's words kept circling in her mind. Three hundred. Not much for a life, but enough for a new start. A widow could live a long time on three hundred dollars.

As soon as the doctor came into the church, she settled the children in the rectory under Effie Beckworth's watchful eye, and hurried to the infirmary.

An idea had come to her—a despicable idea—but she was desperate. And if she had to do something despicable to keep the children safe, she gladly would.

Unless she was too late and the bearded man was already dead.

After slipping through the side door into Dr. Murray's infirmary, she paused in the shadowed hallway, listening. Outside the chaos continued—dogs barking, men shouting, the clang of the fire bell. But inside, all was quiet. She started down the hall, checking doors as she went.

The doctor's living quarters were on one side of the house while the infirmary rooms opened along a long hall heading toward the back. Praying Dr. Murray would remain at the church a while longer, Molly moved silently toward the medical rooms in the rear.

The familiar odors of unguents and balms and chemical solutions wafted over her, pulling her backward in time. For a moment she thought she heard Papa's voice reassuring a patient then realized it was a groan coming from one of the two rooms at the end of the hall. The door on the right was closed. The one on the left stood open.

She peered inside.

It was deserted and dark, the single window shaded by a thin curtain. A desk faced the door. Two chairs stood before it, their slatted backs at rigid attention as if braced for bad news. Against one wall, stood an examination table partially hidden by a privacy screen; against the other, an overflowing bookcase.

Not the room she sought.

She moved to the door across the hall. As she neared, she heard a rhythmic "shushing" sound, which she recognized as labored breathing.

She cracked open the door.

Afternoon sunshine reflected off the glass-fronted cabinet on the east wall, the shelves of which held medical paraphernalia and varying sizes of brown medicine bottles with glass stoppers and white labels. In the corner beside it, stood a straight chair next to a spindly wooden stand with a chipped washbowl on top and a basket of soiled towels below. Perpendicular to the back wall and separated by a small cabinet with a lamp, were two cots.

One was empty.

In the other lay the man the doctor said was dying—the man who could save her and the children. The bearded man. Her heart pounding so hard she could hear the rush of arterial blood past her ears, Molly approached his bed.

Dr. Murray had done a halfway job of tending the obvious injuries. Bandaged and wrapped, but no stitching, and the patient still wore his trousers and boots. Leaning over the bed, Molly quickly assessed his condition.

He appeared to be unconscious. Beneath the beard, his face was swollen and bruised. A bloody bandage, held in place by wide gauze strips, covered the left side of his head. A deep laceration, she guessed. Or possibly a concussion, if not a fracture of the skull. Gauze strips also swathed his bare chest, tufts of dark hair poking through the stretched cloth. His shallow breathing indicated a rib injury, but the absence of a pink froth on his lips told her his lungs hadn't been punctured. More bandages covered his left forearm. Judging by the distorted shape and the amount of blood that had soaked through the wrappings, he probably had a compound fracture. The hand below it was swollen and discolored. She saw no wedding band or evidence he had worn one recently.

Good. It would only complicate matters if he had a wife somewhere.

The thought shamed her. She pushed it aside, and trying to ignore the smell of blood and sweat and chemical compounds, she bent over him, needing to look into the face of the man she was about to deceive in the vilest way.

Seeing him up close, she realized that without all the hair he might have been handsome, although it was difficult to be certain with all the swelling and bruising. Dark brows, a wide, stern mouth, a strong nose marred by a small lump of scar tissue along the bridge that indicated a long-healed break. His eyes were closed beneath dark lashes spiky with dried blood, but she remembered they were brown.

She felt a shiver of unease. She didn't know if he was aware of her or not . . . if he was staring back at her through those slitted eyes or not. The thought made her heartbeat quicken.

Taking a step back, she let her gaze drift down the long length of his body.

He was bigger than she had thought—dwarfing the cot, his booted feet extending well beyond the low foot rail. The boots were well made, with rounded toes and sloped heels. A horseman's boots. Over denim trousers, he wore a tooled leather belt with a silver buckle. On his right hip, facing forward, hung an empty holster with back-to-back Rs burned into it like a brand.

Right-handed. Also good. If he lost his left arm, he could still function.

The absurdity of that caught her unaware and a sound escaped her throat. Almost a laugh, but not quite. The sound of hysteria. She pressed fingertips to her lips to stifle it. The doctor said he was dying. What would it matter if he left this world with one arm, or two?

But what if he survives?

The thought bounced through her mind, spinning out other thoughts like stones cast from beneath a racing wheel.

What if he woke up and realized what she'd done? He was a powerful man, strong enough to have lived this long despite his injuries. What if—

No, don't think it!

Furious that she had let her emotions get away from her, Molly pressed a hand against her churning stomach and struggled to bring the panic under control. He was dying. He probably wouldn't last the night. He would never know.

He. He who?

What had the conductor called him? Wilkes? Weller? She had to know. She couldn't do this without at least knowing the poor man's name—who he was, how he lived, where he was going.

With his heavy shoulders and muscular arms, he had the look of a man more accustomed to the plow than a horse. But those weren't a farmer's boots and a farmer rarely wore a gun on his belt. Maybe he was just another anonymous cowboy. She hoped so. She hoped he was a loner with no home, no family, no one to come around asking questions.

Was he kind? Was he loved? Would he be mourned?

Sickened by the thought of what she was about to do to this inno-cent man—the same man who had saved Penny from being trampled on the train—Molly swallowed hard against the sudden thickness in her throat. Gently she brushed a lock of blood-crusted hair from his bandaged forehead. He didn't appear much older than she. Early thir-ties. Too young to die.

Another absurd thought. She had seen enough death to know the young died as easily as the old and fairness had nothing to do with it. Perhaps she'd lost the capacity for grief. She didn't know. She didn't care. All that was important was that she get enough money to keep her and the children moving west.

Money this man's death would provide.

She rested her palm against his bare shoulder, needing to feel his skin against her own, as if that might ease the guilt that clawed like a beast in her stomach.

He fought hard. She felt it in the tremors of his sturdy body, saw it in the strain of muscles in his neck as he struggled to inhale against the restrictive bandages. His quick, gasping breaths seemed loud in the small room and hearing them made her throat ache in sympathy.

Feeling an unaccountable sadness at the waste of another life, she bent down to whisper into his ear. "Forgive me. There's no other way."

"What are you doing in here?" said a voice from the other side of the room.

Startled, she jerked upright.

Dr. Murray scowled at her from the doorway as he dried his hands on a piece of toweling. Gaunt and middle-aged, he wore a black leather patch over his right eye and had less hair on his head than on his chin, which was mostly gray stubble. He looked irritated. "What do you want?" he demanded, the words slightly slurred, as if he'd been drinking spirits or had just awakened from a deep sleep.

"Do you know . . ." She made a vague gesture toward the patient. "I couldn't tell . . . he's so . . . there's so much swelling. Do you know his name?"

The doctor tossed the cloth into the basket of soiled towels beneath the washstand then with careful deliberation rolled down his sleeves as he walked toward her. His wrists were slim, his hands narrow and long-fingered with short, trimmed nails. An artist's hands, but cleaner. "Harkness called him Wilkins," he said, stopping beside her. "Hank. Or maybe Henry. I don't remember."

She was relieved Dr. Murray didn't smell of whiskey, but was concerned about his slow movements and slurred speech. Was he ill?

"I remember you from the church," he said, studying her. "You helped."

Molly nodded.

Frowning, he looked around. "Don't you have kids? I don't want any kids running through here, messing with my things."

"They're with Effie—Reverend Beckworth's wife—at the church."

He made a dismissive gesture. "Go back to them. I don't need help here." Leaning over the patient, he pushed up one lid then the other.

Molly noted the dark brown pupil of the patient's left eye was marginally larger than that of the right. Was he bleeding in his brain?

"Is it true?" she asked. "He's dying?"

The doctor nodded, a single dip of his head as though he had little energy to waste on extravagant motion. Pulling a stethoscope from his apron pocket, he fitted the earpieces into his ears and held the diaphragm against the patient's chest. "If the head wound doesn't kill him, gangrene in his arm probably will." Motioning her to silence, he tilted his head and listened. After a moment, he removed the earpieces and returned the stethoscope to his pocket.

"You're sure of it?" Molly persisted.

With a huff of impatience, he swung toward her, moving his entire body a quarter circle so he could glare at her with his one eye. It was a sad eye, more gray than blue, with a downward slant that hinted at more than mere weariness. "The man was almost crushed. He shouldn't even be alive. Goddamned railroads." Suddenly his eyes narrowed in speculation. "What's it to you? Who are you?"

Molly hesitated, knowing the lie she was about to tell would damn her forever.

Could she do it? Should she? Would it even be legal?

Doubt swirled through her mind. Her stomach knotted and acid burned hot in her throat. She took a step back, then thought of the children and stopped.

She had no choice. She had to have that money.

God forgive me, she prayed silently. Then hiking her chin, she looked Murray in the eye. "I'm Molly McFarlane," she said. "Henry and I were to be married."